CONSTANCE

by Lawrence Durrell

CONSTANCE

or
Solitary Practices

A novel by

LAWRENCE
DURRELL

faber and faber

First published in 1982
by Faber and Faber Limited
3 Queen Square London WC1N 3AU
Printed in Great Britain by
Redwood Burn Ltd Trowbridge Wiltshire
All rights reserved

British Library Cataloguing in Publication Data

Durrell, Lawrence
Constance, or, Solitary practices
I. Title
823'.912 [F]   PR6007.U76
ISBN 0-571-11757-0

for Anaïs, Henry, Joey

Pour Faire Face au Prince des Ténèbres
qui a un royaume formé de cinq éléments
le Père de la Grandeur évoque la Mère de
la Vie qui, à son tour, évoque l'Homme
Primordial qui a cinq fils: l'Air, le Vent,
la Lumière, l'Eau et le Feu.

Cahiers d'Etudes Cathares,
Narbonne

AUTHOR'S NOTE

This book is a fiction and not a history, but it is based on in-numerable conversations and a residence of fifteen years in Provence; though here and there I may have taken a liberty with the chronology of an ignoble period, the sum of the matter has a high degree of impressionistic accuracy as a por-trait of the French Midi during the late war. I have also studied serious historians like Kenward but owe more to French sources like the books of M. Aimé Vielzeuf of Nîmes.

I originally intended to carry two texts in the appendix – that of the Protocols of Zion, and that of Peter the Great's Testament. The former, however, is so prolix and cumber-some, as well as being available elsewhere in critical editions, that I abandoned the idea; but the Testament of Peter is such a singular document and so apposite to the times as well as to this book that I decided to leave it in.

In conclusion I would like to acknowledge with gratitude the lynx-eyed surveillance of my text by Mrs Helen Dore which saved me from many errors.

LAWRENCE DURRELL

Contents

ONE

In Avignon

IN THE BEGINNING THE TWO TALL GATE-TOWERS OF MEDIEVAL
Avignon, the Gog and Magog of its civic life, were called
Quiquenparle and *Quiquengrogne*. Through them the citizens
of this minor Rome passed by day and night, just as memories
or questions or sensations might pass through the brain of
some sleeping Pope. The clappers of the great belfries defied
the foul fiend with their rumbling clamour. The shivering
vibrations fanned out below them, thinning the blood to deafness for those in the street. It was quite a different matter when
the tocsin sounded – it made a gradually increasing roar such
as a forest fire might do, or else sounded like the vicious hum
of warlike bees in a heating bottle. He had lived so long with
them as history that now, half-starved as he was, the very war
sirens seemed to resemble them. After the tremendous beating
he had endured – to the point of unconsciousness – he had been
thrown into a damp cell in the fortress and attached to the wall
with such science that he could not completely lie down, for
they had hobbled his neck to a ring in the wall, as well as
pinioning his elbows. Quatrefages had now reached a stage of
blessed amnesia when all his various aches and pains had
merged into one great overwhelming distress which elicited
its own anaesthesia. He had subsided in ruins on the floor, and
leaned his head against the wall; but the rope was just short,
by intention. The pressure on his carotid, in a paradoxical sort
of way, kept him from going out altogether. He heard the soft
rumbling of military vehicles as they mounted the cobbled
slope and rolled down into the garrison square; the rubber
wheels slithered and the engines roared in and out of gear.
For him it was as if a long line of knights were riding away by

torchlight upon some heroic Templar adventure; the garble of horses' hooves upon the cobbled drawbridge bade them goodbye. A sort of vision, born of his fatigue and pain, allowed him to delve into the real subject-matter of his life – for it was he who was documenting the Templar heresy and hoping to run down clues as to the whereabouts of the possibly mythical treasure. Now he had fallen into the hands of the new Inquisition, though the priests of the day wore field-grey and bore swastikas as badges and amulets. With them death had come of age. So this was to be the outcome of his long search – to be tortured to reveal secrets he did not possess! When he laughed in a desperate hysteria they had smacked him across the mouth, knocking his teeth into his throat. But all this came much later. . . .

As for Constance and Sam, they were not alone, for the whole world seemed to be saying goodbye; yet the present was still a small limbo of absolute content, of peace, among the vines. The high tide of a Provençal summer would soon be narrowing down towards a champion harvest which must certainly rot, for by now the harvesters had almost all been called to arms, leaving only the women and children and the old to confront these other armies of peaceful vines. There they stood, the plants, in all their sturdiness, staring up into a sky of blue glass, with all their plumage of dense leaf and dusty fruit spread out as if in an embrace.

The lovers were very inexperienced as yet, neither knew what a war was, nor how to behave towards it. This created an uncertainty which was made more agonising by the fact that their love-making had only just begun; they had wasted more than a month of adolescent skirmishing before coming to terms with each other. Their vertiginous embraces could not disguise the stark gaps in their physical knowledge of the love-act. And now, on top of it all, to be overtaken by the unwanted war which might be forced upon them by a mad German house-painter: no, it was impossible to believe in this war!

But Sam's uniform had arrived – it was as if the war had advanced another stealthy pace towards them. It needed alter-ing, the uniform, and the cap was a trifle too large. Sam felt both glory and foolishness as he tried it on before the mirror on the balcony floor of the old house. She said nothing as she lay humbly naked on the gold and blue coverlet, cupping her chin in her hands. He looked so sad and abashed and so very handsome – a naked man in a military tunic and cap without badge as yet! Sam gazed and gazed at himself, feeling that he had undergone a personality change. "What a pantomime!" he said at last, and turning, embraced her impulsively with a wave of desperate sadness. She felt the buttons cold upon her breast as he pressed himself upon her with the ardour of his uncertainty. In the prevailing world-madness they had decided to do something quite mad themselves – to get married! What folly! Both said it, truly both felt it. But they were anxious to get closer to each other before parting, perhaps forever. Mean-while the damned uniform had been the cause of the first quarrel among the four boys during that marvellous summer.

It was soon over; it occurred while they were playing pontoon by moonlight on the rose-trellised verandah where day-long the lizards dozed or skirmished on the crumbling walls. It had been largely Blanford's fault; he had started it by being pompous and high-minded on the subject of conscien-tious objection and had added fuel to the irritation this had caused by sneering at men in uniform who had surrendered their identity to the "herd-mind". It was the fashionable talk of the day in literary circles. The moon was so bright that they did not really need the old and shaky paraffin lantern which stood by them on the table. "Cut it now, Aubrey," cried Hilary, and his sister Constance sharply echoed him, "Yes, Aubrey, please." But she could not forbear (for Sam had looked really wonderful in his new uniform) to add her own barb to the conversation: "Just because Livia has been making you suffer so much, keeping you on a string all summer!" Blanford paled to the ears as the shaft went home. He had really had a miserable time with Constance's sister who had provoked in him a self-destructive calf-love which she only half-assuaged while at the same time manifesting an almost equal partiality for his young friend the consul, Felix Chatto, who now sat furiously staring at his hand and saying, "Your bank, I think!"

Livia had made fools of them both. No, it was not by mere caprice, that is what made her so fascinating – it was simply that there seemed to be no continuity between successive impulses, she jumped the points and did not bother to reflect upon any hurt she might be causing. She was either heartless, or else her heart had never been touched. It was vexatious to think of her in these terms, but there were no others. Both Aubrey and Felix were hovering about the point of making definitive declarations when she suddenly took herself off as she had always done in the past, leaving as an address a Paris café and a second one in Munich. Poor Blanford had even gone so far as to get her a ring – she had allowed it to get to this point. No wonder he was behaving in such an acid way, conscious of his own miscalculation but also of the huge weight of the love Livia had provoked in him. And then on top of this the cursed war!

It gave Constance a sudden pang as she watched them from the upper window of her room, their rosy, youthful features full of trust and inexperience, so unfledged and so uncertain. Her brother Hilary sat in his usual way, one leg over the other with his cards held lightly in his brown fingers. How handsome he was, with his blond hair and his fine sharp features and blue eyes! His bearing expressed a sort of aristocratic dis-

4

dain which contrasted with the simplicity and warmth of Sam's address. Blanford and Felix were less striking – one might have divined that they were just down from Oxford and were bookish young men. But Hilary looked like a musician, sure of himself and fully completed as to his opinions and attitudes. At times he even gave the impression of being a somewhat supercilious young man, almost over-sophisticated and over-bred. He lacked his sister's gorgeousness and her warmth. His coldness masked him, where she remained always vulnerable. She felt sorry now for having stung Blanford and tried to make amends as best she could, while Sam, from the depths of his intoxication (after all, he was *loved*), allowed his magnanimity to overflow in expressions of friendship which were, for all that, quite sincere and full of concern for his friend. Earlier that evening they had all been down to the weir for a cold swim and Sam had said, "Constance is always asking me how you can let yourself be made miserable by Livia whose behaviour never varies, and is quite predictable." Blanford groaned, for he knew what was coming: another dose of the intoxicating Viennese lore which Constance was stuffing down their throats from breakfast to bedtime – all the Freud she was acquiring in the course of her studies in Geneva. "Livia is a woman at war with the man in herself, consequently a castratrice," said Sam; it was extremely funny, his expression as he uttered the words. He himself understood nothing of these sentiments, he had learned them by heart from his beloved, who had a tendency to be rather bossy in intellectual matters. "Constance can go to hell with her theory of infantile sexuality and all that stuff," said Aubrey manfully.

Actually the whole theory fascinated and repelled him, and he had eyed with distaste the clutch of pamphlets in German which she carried about all through the summer. "Freud!" He knew that one falls in love, oh yes, for quite other reasons. Livia had discovered one of his notebooks and, without asking permission, had riffled through it. She was lying on the bed and as he came in she looked up, like a lizard, like a snake, as if she were really seeing him for the first time. "I *see*," she said at last, drawing a surprised breath. "You are a *poet*." It was an unforgettable moment: she went on staring at him, staring right through him as if by some optical trick, right into his future. It was as if she had suddenly invented him anew, invented his career and the whole future shape of his inner life by the magic of such a phrase. One cannot help loving someone who divines one so clearly, throws one's whole obscure destiny into clear focus. What could she have been reading among his sporadic scribbles? Just squirts of thought which one day might become poetry or prose or both. "My death goes back a long way to a time when women were coy or arch, or both, or neither, or simply MUD – the outstretched legs of mud into which I dribble my profuse and living blood, my promise of need, while my harp, whose sinews echoed all time, rebounded on the silence where it found it." She did not have to add that it was beautiful, her eye said it for her. He felt found out, both elated and terrified.

Hilary dealt them another hand and became snappy and priggish about Blanford's decision to retire to Egypt with the Prince. "It will look like running away," he said, and Blanford snapped back, "But I am, that is precisely what I *am* doing. I feel no moral obligation to take sides in this ridiculous Wagnerian holocaust." Constance reproached her brother at once, saying, "O, let's not spoil this marvellous summer we've had. . . ." and instantly the images of Provence, of Avignon, and the sweet limestones of the surrounding hills rose in their memory with a sort of lustful repletion. What an experience it had been – the whole Mediterranean world opened before them as if on a scroll.

"I'm sorry," said Hilary and Blanford echoed, "So am I." They had been living in the vast, echoing, ugly old house for weeks now, in close friendship and affection. These small bickerings left a bad taste. Tu Duc – that was the name of the place. Constance had inherited it. The name rang in their minds like a drumbeat, signifying everything they had encountered and enjoyed during this long, unhurried stay above a village which was only a stone's throw from Avignon of romantic renown. City of the Popes!

Later that night some of these regrets surged up among the dreams of Constance, but not too powerfully to spoil the moonlight on the window-sill, the smell of honeysuckle and the deep gloating warmth of the male body beside her. It was marvellous to spend the whole night with a man, to feel the drum of his chest rising and falling under her fingers while he slept. Their love-making was becoming increasingly expert with practice. At times it seemed that they were on a toboggan travelling at ever-increasing speed down a dizzily whorled snowrun. A toboggan often out of control. "Sam, for goodness sake: I am terrified you will make me pregnant." She had not foreseen this love affair and, though an emancipated young woman with the whole of science at her fingertips, she had left what she called, rather irreverently, her "tool kit" back in Geneva. Nor could Sam help himself. "I can't help it," he gasped, and steered her more and more forcefully towards the slow dense crisis which at last overwhelmed them. They were panting, exhausted, as after a race. Sam, who specialised in quotations from limericks to which he could never put a beginning or an end, quoted from one now: "So he filled her with spunk, and then did a bunk, that stealthy old man of Bulgaria."

That was awake, but it was when he lay asleep that she could spend ages watching him, head on elbow, full of the mystery of his lazy gladiator's body which seemed to store heat like a vacuum flask. She loved to feel the soft tulip of his sex lying against her side, in repose now in his deep sleep, but so quick to wake at her summons – at a wave of a wand almost, and it woke the sleeping cobra of their youthful desires. Her blood ran cold when she recalled that for more than a month he had not spoken to her, had stayed cold and distant as a star when she was simply dying to become the target for his affections. She had pretended, like a fool, to be having a love affair with an older man, a psychiatrist, and the result of this foolish piece of boasting had been to chill Sam to the backbone; how long it had taken to rectify this silly error! As a matter of fact she had last year slept with a doctor, but that was curiosity, and she had no mind to repeat it, so insipid had it turned out to be. But now Sam! In him she had succumbed to the least intelligent, the most simple-minded man you could imagine. But she was ferociously in love now, she felt like a wild cat; she had decided that she would endow him with all he needed of marvellous brain and sensibility and insight – all these treasures she had reserved for him. He would realise through her all that she divined in him now, hidden under his callowness and shyness, under his fitful reserves; she would pierce through his crust of flippancy, the friendly footlings of his idols, like old Wodehouse, and strike sparks off his inmost soul! How he would have trembled, poor boy, if she had put all these sentiments into words. It was bad enough as it was, his feeling of total inadequacy! But such a programme would have put him into a real panic.

In the middle of the night he woke her, and turning her face to him asked in a husky whisper, "Tell me, darling, do you think me a coward for offering my services?" It was obvious that Blanford's thoughtless talk had wounded him. Nor was he satisfied with the passionate, simple complicity of her embrace, though an agony of sympathy was echoed by it. "Answer," he said doggedly, as one might demand something in writing. "Of course you are not! In spite of that stupid vote in the Union – typically Oxonian! Of course you are not!" she said hotly again, hugging him to her until she was all but out of breath.

8

"It's quite right that England doesn't mean anything to Aubrey – why should it? But I should be hard put to explain why it means anything to me."

He closed his eyes upon the word and saw a sort of jumbled composite picture of grey buildings, low hills, and wrinkled rivers, and backing them all the romantic image of the golden Kentish Weald in harvest-time, raised like a golden buckler to heaven. He was reminded, too, of a brief and awkward love affair with a girl who was picking hops. He had been lent one of those funny little oast-houses by the parents of a friend, ostensibly to study. The affair was awkward and pitiful, though the hop-picker was brave and beautiful and as blonde as Constance. But what a trial their ignorance turned out to be, for she feared pregnancy, and he feared some venereal affliction about which he knew hardly anything! In the lavatory of a nearby pub there stood what looked at first sight to be an automatic fruit-drop or cigarette machine; but it was full of French letters. The legend said, "Place two shillings in slot and tug handle of the Dispenser sharply!" What a wonderful word – "Dispenser"; what a miserable wreck of an affair; what a beautiful girl worthy of someone more experienced and more at ease; what a fool he had been not to show more skill and kindness! But in spite of everything the shining Weald was there, in his inner consciousness, raising its blazing corn to heaven under a deafening sunshine! In a sense, too, weald for weald, Constance had become part of this picture, had merged with it. (All these matters would sort themselves out once the war was over – if ever it decided to break!) At lunch he had said, "How I wish the damn war would break!" which Blanford had echoed with, "How I wish I could wish!"

Now they lay in each other's arms, burnished dark gold by the sun, and asleep, oblivious to scurrying of mice in the old house, or the remote snore of one of their friends from an upper attic. It is strange, too, that they did not feel more helpless – but then they were full of the delusive elation which love brings. Thoughts scurrying in the attics of the brain, the feet of mice among the dying apples, the presence of ghostly women whose voices were brought by the wind, conversing, complaining, keening. The house was like an old schooner, creaking and groaning with every shift of wind. And yet in their dreams sadness came, sadness overtook them as they thought of separations and bereavements and death – yes, even death was there sometimes; and the tears of distress at their goodbyes trickled down the sirens of booming liners, saying farewell. What a confusing business! In dreams they felt the pains which waking they cared not to show.

Lord Galen's bizarre mansion up the hill was also being snugged down for the winter, and his last dinner parties became more improvised and more perfunctory; his trip to Germany and his financial gaffe with the Nazis had thrown him into a deep depression. But he was glad to see the youthful band from Tu Duc – he had taken a great fancy to Constance and regarded Sam as a highly eligible young man despite his lack of fortune. The Prince was also often there at the hospitable table of Lord Galen, and it was indeed during one of these dinners that he had proposed outright to take Blanford on the strength as Private Secretary, and to sail with him for Egypt within a week or so. Originally it was in this context that the word "conscience" had cropped up; it represented a key consideration, after all, but it somehow stung the Prince like a gadfly. "Conscience?" he exclaimed sharply. "No one comes to Egypt to struggle with his conscience!" He gazed keenly round the table under frowning eyebrows. "Egypt is a *happy* country," he went on, "and when you think that, in terms of gross inequality of wealth, criminal misgovernment and civic profligacy it takes the highest place of any nation in the world, one wonders how this can be. The poor are so poor that they have already starved and died and come out the other side, roaring with laughter. The rich are negligent and callous to an unimaginable degree. Yet what is the result? A *happy* people! Indeed the people, wherever you go, throw up their clothes and show you their private parts, roaring with laughter as they do so. It puts everyone in a very good humour." Lord Galen looked somewhat unnerved. "Good heavens!" he exclaimed feebly, "What effrontery!" It sounded enchanting to Blanford. "What does one do in reply?" he asked amid the laughter, but the Prince was not saying. "One responds with good humour," he said evasively.

Max, the violet negro, who was Galen's chauffeur and general factotum, spent a part of every morning now draping white dust-covers over the furniture; he had started on the upper floors and had worked downwards, to leave the inhabited rooms free for living in. But it was like a swimming-pool slowly emptying itself, and at the last occasion there remained only the grand salon and the dining-room free. A piled mass of waiting dust-covers was stacked in the hall. Galen sighed. It was very sad to have the summer cut short like this, and not even to be *sure* that the whole spectre of war might not melt away into some last-minute treaty of peace. What would they do then? Could they just resume the old life as if nothing had taken place? No, something profound in the heart of things seemed to have suffered a sea-change. The beating of the German drum had presaged something – some new orientation. But the future was still so dark and ambiguous and full of portent. ("Making love to her," thought Sam, "is like doing a double jack-knife with a sword swallower.") Blanford rolled breadcrumbs and reflected. There was another, a more private reason why he loved Livia – but it would have sounded fatuous to relate it. She had left him the new Huxley, his favourite writer, with the first essay on the nature of Zen Buddhism in it, the very first mention of Suzuki, which had opened like a shaft of light in the depths of his skull. It had set him dreaming once more of faraway peoples educated in harmlessness, in places like Lhasa, by the reading of golden sutras engrossed in golden ink. . . . This, like the discovery of his avocation as a poet, was also her gift to him, a gift no other woman would ever match. Who could understand such a thing?

Yet the failure of communication between them as sexual and affective animals had been nothing less than calamitous; at times it so enraged him that he could have picked her up and shaken her like a rat, shaken some sense into her – or out of her! And where was she now? He could only guess, though it very much depended on whether she had the money to stay in such a place, even though it was only middling-expensive: the Fanechon. Up in the bustling raffish and dirty Boulevard Montmartre with its *couscous* joints and tinny Arabic cinemas. She loved this small, select hotel because the side-door of the lounge opened directly into the Musée Grevin, and, slipping out of it, she would spend quite a large part of her time wandering among the waxworks, and tracing the path of French history (or the bloodier part) through its tableaux, her face taking on a new beauty from the soft abstraction into which these shadowy scenes threw her. The agony of Marie Antoinette, the death of Marat (the authentic bath was the one on view!) and the sweet limpidity of expression with which Jeanne d'Arc walked to the stake – hours passed and she was still there, sunk in thought before these waxen reinactions of a vanished yet still living past. The fête on the Grand Canal, too, with its thrilling blue night sky and shining waterscapes, or the evening, the momentous soirée at Malmaison with the entire cast of a Stendhal novel as guests! The modern exhibits hardly stirred her interest at all. But in the suffocating little hall of the distorting mirrors she lingered a good while, trying out different postures and studying the distortions with attention, never with amusement. Then she might buy some chewing gum and slip into a cinema to dream about the length of

Descartes' waxen nose or the sly expression on the face of
Fouquier. Blanford thought of her with a dull ache now and
said to himself, "Poor girl, she has a past like a paw full of
thorns."

It would have to be Egypt, then. "In Egypt," he assured
Felix Chatto, "the girls have independent suspension, it is the
latest thing." It was the latest fad on the new cars like the Morris
which Chatto shared with Lord Galen's clerk, Quatrefages,
and in which he promised to take Constance back to Geneva
and her studies – for come what may these at least must be ter-
minated in due and correct fashion. Sam insisted on it. Later,
when he returned from the wars with the appropriate bullet-
hole in the breast-pocket bible he would be carrying, she
would be there waiting for him, with the whole weight of
science heavy upon her shoulders! "Then you will realise how
stupid I am and decide to leave," she cried out in protest.
Actually these studies were helping her to understand the
nature of her love for Sam. An only child, his mother had
overwhelmed him with her love but, wisely, never encumbered
his own powers, his need to fly. She had detached herself from
him at the correct moment. She had, in the new lingo Constance
was learning, broken the transfer at the fruitful moment to set
him free. No *Sons and Lovers* would ever be written about *him*,
she reflected. He had bathed in the mother flow, his flesh was
sated and at peace – hence the sexual magnetism which those
lazy brown limbs held for her. He had a skin of velvet because
he had once been correctly, sensually loved as she, in some
miraculous fashion, had also been. They were made for each
other, their sensibilities mixed like dyes! "O! Stop *gloating*!"
she told her reflection in the old pier-glass – she had become
solicitous for her beauty and now made up carefully each
morning and evening, lest he look elsewhere! When, however,
she asked Aubrey whether her beloved did not look like
Donatello's David, he had irritated her by replying in that

negligent, weary, Oxonian manner, "Everyone sees himself or herself as somebody quite different. Hence the confusion because everyone is acting a part. He sees you as Iseult, whereas you are really Catherine of Russia. You see him as David, but I see only the eternal British schoolboy in love, elated because he is undressing his mother." She was furious. "Damn you!" she said and went on doggedly making up while he tried to shave in one corner of the great mirror with equal doggedness.

The royal steam-yacht sent by Farouk signalled its arrival at Marseille, prepared to carry the Prince to Alexandria. Blanford called on him at his hotel in Avignon in order to find out what plans he had made for the journey and found the little man hastily wrapping up his treasures and distributing them about the numerous cabin trunks with their brilliant filigree-worked Turkish designs in leafy gold – he must have inherited them from some Khedival ancestor. At the door stood the outsize remover's van which housed the larger effects of the Prince – his chairs and folding tables (he gave numerous bridge parties); a couple of palm trees in tubs; opulent vases and gold plate and the two peregrine falcons. He showed Blanford round all these items with evident pleasure. But he did not propose to get on the move for a day or two. Asked if there were any special clothes which might be *de rigueur* for the new post he said in an offhand way, "The Princess will kit you out. Just come with one *tenue de ville* and a tie so I can introduce you respectably. Later on you'll need some shark-skin dinner jackets, I suppose. But I know where to get them cheap for you in Alex. Here, look at this." He produced a large scarlet velvet-covered hat-box, the kind a conjuror might carry about, or an actor. It was a sort of oriental wig-box, in fact, but inside it there was a shrunken human head, a male head, coated heavily in resin but with the eyes open. Blanford was startled. "Good Lord!" he said, and the Prince chuckled appreciatively at his reaction. "It's the head of a Templar; it comes from the Commanderie in Cyprus – I had it traced when I bought it in the Cairo Souk. The Museum wanted it, but I thought it would make such a nice present for Lord Galen that I brought it to offer and please him. . . ." He paused on a note of dismay. "But, you know, he is so superstitious that he refused it; he is afraid to have the Eye put on him. Specially as he is hunting for the treasure of this Order – or rather Quatrefages is hunting for it, for him. So I'll take it back. If I tell the Egyptians that it is a Prophesying Head my enemies will go pale. Egyptians are just as superstitious as you English, more so."

He popped the cover of the silk-lined hat-box with its grisly remnant and ordered his servant Hassan to wrap it up softly in tissue paper and convey it to the wagon with all the other effects. "Phew! It is hot," he said, fanning himself with a reed fan of brilliant hue. "Egypt will be a furnace still. Never mind. Sit down, my dear boy, and let me tell you a funny joke. Laughter makes one cooler, and Hassan will bring us some jasmine tea and some crystallised fruit. You laughed, remember, when I told you about the Egyptians throwing up their clothes and showing their private parts as a greeting, *n'est-ce pas?*" Blanford said, "Indeed. It sounds delightful." The Prince, whose mind slipped from perch to perch, from branch to branch, like a bird, suddenly was diverted by a twinge of rheumatism in one of his fingers. "This damned arthritis deformans," he cried, and started to tug at the joints until they cracked aloud. When he had done he resumed his theme. "About the greeting I can tell you a funny tale which makes Egyptians laugh – it shows that we are not devoid of humour. It concerns Sir Charles Polk, the last British Ambassador. This fashion of greeting so worked upon his mind and upon his imagination that he became an insomniac. I have it from the Embassy doctor, Hassim Nahd. Poor man, if he slept he always dreamed that the peasants were greeting him in this way, and he had an irresistible impulse to throw down his trousers and return their greeting! It put him in a fever of anxiety, Hassim was all the time prescribing sedatives, but to no avail. Then one day the blow fell. London told him that the King had decided on a state visit to Egypt and that he even proposed to travel the whole length of the Nile. Sir Charles had to start making all the necessary arrangements. Naturally the Palace offered him the classic old steamer *Memphis* which had always served for this kind of state journey. The problems were not insoluble. Or rather there was only one that stuck out – if I may use the phrase without indelicacy. It was the traditional greeting. It is a long way up the river, and there are thousands upon thousands of peasant *felaheen* – in fact for such an event they would probably line both banks solid. Poor Sir Charles went pale as he thought of what might happen. He tried to reason White-hall out of the visit, but no, it was deemed both advisable and apt on political grounds." The Prince gave a tiny snort or chuckle and, banging his knee softly, went on, "One imagines the dilemma of poor Sir Charles. What should he do? Well, you can say what you like about the British public servant, but there is nobody like him for probity and unflinching devotion to duty. He explained his position and offered his resignation. The thought of exposing his Sovereign to such an outrage had been too much. The F.O. was so impressed by his dignity and firmness that he was transferred at once with promotion to Moscow, while the Egyptian trip duly took place under the aegis of a Chargé d'Affaires, who was afterwards put on the shelf and held *en disponibilité* for nearly ten years until all was forgotten. I sometimes see old Charles in London and we talk over old times; but I never ask him what the unusual peasant greeting is in Russia!"

With such pleasant exchanges the morning wore on until the mayor called for the usual pre-prandial glass of *pastis* which enabled him to resume the state of the world for the benefit of the Prince. He, the mayor, was in constant touch with

Paris and with every bulletin of news or rumour things seem
to be deteriorating further. It must end in war and yet . . .
"*Drôle de guerre*," said the mayor, quoting the current slogan
of the day. "They will never attack us, for they know that the
French army is the best in the world. It would be madness. And
then the line, the Maginot line!" On such ephemeral delusions
they based their hopes for peace. "They have given us some
air-raid sirens," went on the mayor with pride, "and today the
pompiers are going to have a rehearsal at three o'clock. Do not
be afraid when you hear them. It will only be for a few minutes.
But we must be prepared for anything with the modern aero-
plane." There was so much sunlight on the terrace and so much
laziness in the air that they had the greatest difficulty in treating
this sort of conversation with the seriousness it deserved.
Blanford lunched at the hotel with the Prince and afterwards
they sauntered across the glowing town and climbed the
Rocher de Doms, the sharp spur from the platform of which it
was possible to see the even sharper snout of Mont St. Victoire
raising its dogged crest, bare and mistral-tormented. There was
no snow now, of course, but the cold afternoon mistral had
furrowed the green Rhône and bent the bushes and cypresses
on the dry garrigues around them. They spent a while looking
down on the town with its brown pie-crust roofs and its
crooked dark streets. Suddenly the sirens started to wail, and in
spite of themselves they were both startled – the more so because a real plane passed over the town in slow gyres. "One of
ours, I hope!"

Had things been different, Blanford thought, what a
pleasure it would have been to saunter away an evening thus in
the sunny city, watching the pigeons turning and hovering
among the soaring belfries, gossiping about nothing very con-
sequential, just unpacking their idle minds of their dreams and
thoughts. . . . But one felt guilty of enjoying such a luxury with
the world coming apart at the seams.

Hilary unexpectedly joined them in the main square for a companionable *tisane* of *vervaine*, urged upon them by the Prince. He had not been seen all day at Tu Duc because he had come in to attend early Mass at the Grey Penitents. Now he was deeply despondent, though he tried to hide it – a mood brought on by a long talk to the curé who had assured him that France would not lift a finger to fight and would be over-run whenever the Germans wished. It was all the fault of the Jews, he had added, with all their infernal radicalism. Hitler was right. France was *pourrie jusqu'à la moelle* – rotten to the marrow with it. Hilary sighed and lit another cigarette. "A young Jewish couple committed suicide in the Princes Hotel last night, so the tobacconist told me. They were refugees from Berlin. Very young, too. He heard the shots."

They took leave of the Prince, who promised to get in touch with Blanford the moment he had made up his mind when, if ever, he was going to move. Walking past the tall doors of the Museum, Blanford peeped into the courtyard and instantly felt an almost physical blow upon his heart, so vivid was the memory of Livia standing there. In the half light of dawn she had recited a line of Goethe in her "smiling voice". He walked on now to overtake Hilary, thinking to himself, "What beautiful wind-washed days we lived this summer. I feel like an old king whose favourite cup-bearer is dead." For he knew that it was definitive, her departure, and that though they might meet again they would never again live together. The thought was not unmixed with gratitude, for hers had been the kind of magnetism which matures men. He closed his eyes for a second and saw her turn the corner ahead of him. She had learned to walk like a Roman slave – that is how he put it to himself – and turning a corner she would keel and hesitate, like a hawk about to stoop. Hilary started to hum a tune from *Bitter Sweet*, and because the melody moved him Blanford hummed in unison, to disguise his emotion. So they strode over the famous bridge towards the hillocks and the winding road which led to the domain of Constance, who at that moment was aiding Sam in the business of stuffing pimientos with forcemeat and garlic against the evening meal.

After they had walked in friendly silence almost to the gates of the old house Hilary said, putting his hand on Aubrey's wrist, "I don't want to pry, Aubrey, but what the devil were you tearing up last night? It lasted ages, like in Chekov."

"Aptly said," replied his friend with a sardonic downturn of the mouth. "In fact old notebooks, bits and pieces. I wanted to clear the decks before leaving." He paused, and then went on a trifle defensively, "Even a bit of a novel. I invented a man I called Sutcliffe – for lack of anything better – and he became altogether too real. He started following me about like gravity, as well as riding on my back like the Old Man of the Sea. I had to stop!" Hilary laughed. "I see," he said. "You should have left them to the Museum. The papers, I mean."

They turned the last corner to find Blaise the carter standing proudly outside the house, on the balcony steps, chatting to Constance and Sam, for he had come up from the station to deliver the old leather sofa which had been sent them for safe-keeping by Pia. *It had arrived!* It was covered in a clumsy skin of thick brown paper. Constance gazed at Aubrey with narrowed eyes and said accusingly, "I thought you told me Sutcliffe was invented." She held the end of the invoice which contained the name of the sender. "We will see about that later," said Blanford evasively. Together they picked up the shabby object and placed it in the conservatory among the palms, where it looked not inappropriate. Blaise did not take part in this, but stood and coughed on the balcony until the girl came back with a tray full of brimming *pastis* glasses. This cough of his was no stage effect – he had been gassed in the 1914 war. Constance had managed to secure the services of his wife as a cleaner as well as laundress, which was a great help to them.

So they all chatted awhile in the course of which, inevitably, the subject of the war rose again to the surface. "The President spoke last week – *quel con*!" said Blaise without undue animosity. "He has never seen what war is. He spoke of freedom!" It was the usual mental rigmarole without any form of pith – how could there be any in a country where the leaders themselves were so confused and so pusillanimous? As for freedom . . . The Prince had indeed remarked at Lord Galen's dinner table, "Freedom is an evanescent thing – you only remark it by its absence, but you can't define it. That is why the British refuse to understand us Egyptians with our desire for freedom. We will make a mess of things, no doubt, but it will be an Egyptian mess, our own personal mess – and what a mess it will be! But an Egyptian mess!" He had raised his head proudly and gazed fondly around him.

Sam set about undoing the string and tearing off the wrappings in which the old couch was swathed. "It's Emily Brontë's sofa," he said. "No," said Hilary, "guess again." Constance said, "No more impiety, please. It's the chair of prophecy, the sofa of divination. I shall spend the afternoon reading my psycho-whatsit pamphlets upon it and praying for guidance."

Blanford had collected a Poste Restante letter from a school-friend, bookish like himself, who furnished a bewildering description of a Paris not so much frivolous about the war as totally unbelieving in its reality. "Sitting at the Dôme you feel that it simply *cannot* take place, not in this century, after all we've seen. Yet the danger gives a strange unreality to everything – the quality of amnesia. Actions become automatic. Look, sitting here on the *terrasse* I am watching the evolutions of some hirsute porters in uniforms trying to hoist an appalling statue of Balzac by Rodin on to a pedestal; finally they have waddled it up, like a penguin on to an ice-floe, where it will soon be almost invisible because of foliage; this week it is the turn of Georges Sand whose bust will appear in the Luxembourg accompanied by speeches which give one gooseflesh. Such rhetoric! Yet so highly appropriate for a people which can solemnly put a notice *Défense d'uriner* on the railings outside the Chambre des Députés! They are the true inheritors of the Anc. Gk. sense of civic anarchy. . . . And yet, like a douche of icy water, reality suddenly steps in with a *fait divers* like 'René Crével commits suicide'. (He is a poet friend of mine you don't know.) I was bemoaning this tragic fact to a painter at the Dôme, but he cut me short, saying: '*Ce que je lui reproche* . . . What I reproach in him is that he had good *reasons* for so doing. *C'est pas ça la suicide! C'est pas sérieux!* He has brought suicide into *disrepute!* ' "

Blaise the carter, rosy as the setting sun, took his leave now, and his cart crunched its way back towards the town. Sam cleaned the paraffin lamps against nightfall and cracked open some packets of candles which they would set up in old saucers on the terrace table. This week Constance and Sam had been elected to perform all those tasks which come under the heading of "fatigue" – and some of the fatigues like the blocked lavatory had been distinctly onerous ones. Sam groaned and swore, but it was rapture to be alone with her. "They lived forever after," he said as they worked, "in a faultless domestic harmony which gave people quite a turn to see."

They dined early that eve – *entre chien et loup* as the French say, to indicate a "gloaming" – and afterwards the boys grew restless and elected to go for a swim in the cool waters of the weir, leaving Constance the washing up. Nor did she mind this – she wanted to be alone for a while, and the mechanical actions soothed her and enabled her to think of other things like, for example, those enticing pamphlets, so many of them with their pages uncut, which lay beside her bed. Love had rather got in the way of her studies and she had a bad conscience about the matter. So once she had put everything to rights in the kitchen she went upstairs and secured a couple which she proposed to read there and then, and in the most appropriate of places: the verandah with the conservatory. This involved some juggling with candles to obtain adequate light, but once all was in order, she lay down with a sigh and plunged into the labyrinth of suggestions and speculations which had completely altered her way of looking at things – given her an extraordinary new angle of vision upon people, upon individuals and cultures, upon philosophies and religions. It was as if her mind had been released from its cocoon of accepted verities, released to take wings on this extraordinary adventure into the world of infantile relationships, of demons and gods of the human nursery, and bestiary. God, it made her rage to find how lukewarm everyone was about these matters – the insufferable conceit of the male mind! Sticky old Aubrey blowing hot and cold down his long supercilious Oxford nose; bigoted Hilary; silly Felix . . .

She read for an hour, listening abstractedly with half an ear to the noise of their laughter, and the splashes as they dived. Then on a sudden impulse she got up, took her pamphlets and a branch of candles, and mounted the stairs to her room, which was now filled with rosy shadows reflected back from the giant old-fashioned cupboard with its full-length mirror. She sat down upon the edge of the bed and arranged her candles upon the floor so that they threw their light forwards and upwards towards her. Then she slipped out of her clothes and sat upon the edge of the bed, stretching her legs to their greatest extent and keenly gazing at the slit between her legs as reflected in the tall mirror. With her hands she spread wide the two scarlet wings of the vulva and stayed thus, staring at this terrible scarlet gash between her white thighs – a horrible gash, as if hacked out by the clumsy strokes of a sabre. Her vagina, her vulva – what a horror to contemplate such a primitive and horrific member! If a man saw this, why, he would go mad with disgust! She gave a small sob such as a bird gives when the shot strikes its breast in mid-flight. "My cunt," she said in a low voice, still staring at it, "O my God, who could have thought of such a thing?" She was filled with a barbaric terror as she stared at the red gash. He would never stay with her if he should once glimpse this terrible bloody sinus between her two beautiful and shapely legs. She craned back, spreading the scarlet cretinous mouth wider so that it assumed an oval shape with part of the hymeneal net still across – it gaped like a whale in a Breughel painting. Poor Sam! Poor Jonah! She felt quite weak with despair and horror. In her imagination she seized him by the shoulders and clutched him to her while her heart cried out to him: "Hold me, suffocate me, impale me! I am dying of despair. What good can come of poor women with this frightful handicap?" She rose with such impulsiveness – gestures winged with despair – that she overturned the candles and had to plunge after them and set them upright again. She could have wept with vexation, but she thought it would be better not to let herself go so far until he was there to comfort her. Nevertheless she did weep a little so that should he come very late he would see the tears upon her cheek and realise that she had suffered from his absence. He would be very contrite. She would forgive. . . . She drew a veil over the scene of reconciliation.

At that moment Sam himself was experiencing a wave of despair of roughly the same calibre; a chance remark of Blanford had set it off like a firework. Aubrey had said, in his gloomiest tone: "The power that women have to inflict punishment on men is quite unmanning, quite terrible; they can reduce us to mentally deficient infants with a single glance, make us aware of how shallow our masculine pretensions are. With their intuition they can look right into us and see how feeble and infantile and vain we are. My God, they are really terrifying." Listening to this wiseacre of twenty Sam felt a sympathetic wave of horror pass through him as he thought how superior Constance was in every way to himself. Yes, what good were men? The role of Caliban was the best they could aspire to! He hated himself when he thought of all her perfections – a whole Petrarchian galaxy of qualities which made her, like Laura, supreme in love. And now they would soon be parted. He jumped to his feet. Here he was wasting valuable seconds talking to these fools when he could have been with her. How like a man! What idiots they were! He took one last plunge and rose panting like a swordfish, with arms extended. How delicious the water was, despite the desperate fate which lay in store for men! How he longed to feel her in his arms once more! *He must try to be worthy of her!* He was so intoxicated by the thought that he fell over a tree stump and ricked his ankle quite severely.

And when he did arrive at the bedroom door it was to find her asleep with the marks of tears upon her cheek. How callous, how thoughtless men were! They were just ogres with a sexual appetite, and apart from that quite unfeeling, brutal, philistine! He crawled into bed with wet hair and snuggled up close to her warm body, stirring now in sleep.

Despite these emotional polarities he was at once soothed by the physical warmth of her, and like a diver immediately plunged back into those refreshing innocent dreams of his early puberty, which always figured, like some mystical *mandala*-shape, in the form of a brilliant green cricket-field upon which the white-clad players, like druids, performed their slow reflective evolutions until the evening bell sounded four from the clock on the pavilion. The deep grass which bordered the field was where the schoolboys lay with their books and cherries. A population of rabbits almost as numerous had stolen to the edge of the field to watch as well. (The same rabbits now on many a secret airfield had tiptoed to the edge of the mown runways to watch the Spitfires as they rehearsed, landing and taking off.)

He groaned a small groan from time to time in his sleep, and automatically she folded him in her arms without waking up herself.

Two floors below, a long-visaged and weary Blanford was completing the destruction of his loose-leaf notebook which seemed to him now insufferably priggish and threadbare with all its wide-ranging sonorities. "A throw of the dice must decide whether the mates magnetise or not, whether they click and whether their product is a clear-eyed love or a mess – a mess transferable to their children." He sighed and watched it burn among the other slips, for he was using the fireplace for his *auto-da-fé*. Later they would scold him and force him to clean up his room. He had said as little as he could about Livia, it was too painful to discuss; as for news of her, speculations about her, and so on, he left all that disdainfully to Felix Chatto.

"Europe's behaviour was appropriate for those who drank symbolic Sunday blood and munched the anatomy of their Saviour." So thought Blanford's Old Man of the Sea – about the C. of E. It was pungent stuff – was he himself as pessimistic as all that? He thought and smoked and thought again; and decided that he was, and that he had done well to cleanse his bosom of such perilous stuff.

> Unhealthy couple full of sin
> Witness the mess that we are in!

Then, further on, another note which was destined to have a longer life among his speculations. "If real people could cohabit with the creatures of their imagination – say, in a novel – then what sort of children would be the fruit of their union: changelings?" He laughed helplessly in Sutcliffe's voice and took a turn upon the terrace. The night was fine, like blue silk, and the stars were on parade in force, twinkling away like mad upon the operatic blue dark.

He got into bed and sought his restless slumber, head buried under his pillow, which smelt of newly ironed linen which had been hung out in the rain. The rain! He was not awake at four o'clock – the dawn was just hinting – to hear the swish of a light shower on the trees and on the stones of the verandah outside his room. The summer heats, rising from the brown parched drumskin of the earth, had given rise to a customary instability of temperature – little summer fevers which suddenly produced large ragged sections of free-flying cloud, so low that you could almost touch them. They were quite isolated, surrounded by summer blue, and they bore small showers or sometimes even hail which slashed at the vines and drummed on the grassy ground.

Bang! The report was so loud that the lovers started up; so did Hilary and Felix Chatto who was on a camp-bed in the kitchen. "What the devil!" exclaimed Sam. Could they be shelling the city? And who? Bang! This time they were awake enough to orient themselves towards the sound; it appeared to come from the densely wooded knoll above Tu Duc where they had once been to hunt for truffles in a holm-oak glade. But who could have got a gun up that steep hill, and for what reason? *Certes*, the whole town of Avignon lay down below it, across the river, with Villeneuve at one side turning the sulky cheeks of her castle towards the left. It had sounded like a light mortar, but there were no answering shots fired and no sound of aircraft, so, puzzled and disturbed, they started to make coffee and question. "We must go up and have a look," said Hilary in an alarmed voice. The wet grey dawn was breaking through the forest. "Of course," said Sam: so they gulped their coffee, and during this time two more shots were fired by the invisible artillery. They hastened, bolted their drink and food, and started the short but steep climb towards the summit of the overhanging hill. It took a quarter of an hour, but when at last they emerged upon the green platform it was to find that the weapon was only an old *paragrèle*, or cloud-cannon, which was firing shells full of salt crystals into the black stationary clouds above them. There were two old men alone to charge and fire this small mortar with its cartridges – the charges hissed upwards into the clouds which were swollen like purses with rain; yet after half an hour the trick worked and a light rain fell like smoke upon the slopes. One of the old peasants uncorked a bottle of *eau de vie* and passed round a sip after the success of their last shot. A watery sun struggled out and turned their faces to grey and then to yellow. They toasted each other with an Eviva, and then one of the old men remarked in an offhand manner, "They have gone into Poland! *L'après-midi, c'est la guerre.*"

The cloud had burst at long last.

TWO

The Nazi

THE LANDS OWNED BY THE VON ESSLINS MARCHED WITH the sealine in a desolate corner of Friesland, but without ever actually opening out upon it. Thus they shared the high winds and foul weather without in any way sharing in its picturesqueness, its refreshing breathlessness of spray and grey cloudscape. It was brackish land, poor land, encircled by shallow ranges of low hill which gave a deceptive profile to them, hinting at their penuriousness and the pains which they must inflict upon those who tilled them. Hills bent like pensive brows; thick yellowish loam, poor in limestone, which clogged under the plough, being too clayborne for rich crops. Winter came almost as a relief here, the land sinking back into its secret silence among the frozen dykes and ponds where the ice-cocked speargrass suggested armies of swordsmen. The trees dripped noisily in the night thaws, letting fall their icicles.

It had been theirs since the early seventeenth century when the first Von Esslin – also an Egon – had entered the profession of arms and won himself some dignities and a small fortune from a lucky marriage. The large, ugly feudal manse had in some way inherited two incongruous towers and a small moat, now in use as a duckpond. It was uncomfortable and impossible to heat. Moreover, as for most military families hovering on the margins of being considered nobility of the sword, finance was a perpetual trouble. The land offered them an income from two gravel pits and a seam of very fine white clay which they sold to potters in Czechoslovakia. The old General's pension was quite substantial, while Egon himself found his staff pay just about adequate for the life he led, which did not allow him to indulge himself in gambling debts, horseflesh or actresses like many of his brother officers of the same caste but with greater means. He did not regret the fact, for he was of a serious, almost pious bent, as befits a Catholic whose origins on his mother's side had been Bavarian. But as a family they were stylised now as being of the Junker breed, and they had acquired some of the massive obduracy and obscurantism of that class – retaining, however, a special weakness, a seasonal weakness, one might say, for the music that took them each year in the direction of Vienna, a capital they had always loved and where they had always kept an apartment with lovely views out upon the famous woods. But Gartner, the family house in the hamlet of that name, was a grim place, a difficult place to love, and now that his mother spent nearly the whole year there Von Esslin himself had begun to feel the strain: he was rather ashamed of the fact that he felt almost glad when the army called him away to his duties and gave him an excuse to live elsewhere.

These were some of the half-formulated thoughts and sensations that passed through the soldier's mind as the squat staff car lunged north and east along the dunes where the sea sighed among its summer calms and the sand lilies showed their pretty summer flowers; he had, by making some specious excuses, achieved an unheard-of luxury – twenty-four hours of leave – at a time when everything, every stitch of armour, every man, was grouped upon the borders of Poland. With so much impending he wanted to bid his mother goodbye – for who knew where the decisions of the Führer might send them? The telephone had been under blackout for some days now, except for army messages, but he had managed to signal her by asking a colleague in a northern unit to detach a motor cycle despatch rider to warn her. So she would be there, waiting for him as always at the end of the long green salon, her fingers upon a book, smiling. It was her invariable pose when it came to one of his visits – it tried to suggest that all was well, life was calm, and everything to do with the property taken care of. The Polish maid who never spoke would open the door to him and curtsy silently with that shy, downcast smile on her swarthy face. Well, but . . . they had much to discuss. Things were moving so fast that everyone felt out of his depth; they had been outstripped by the speed of events. Peace was not yet mortally stricken – but it was like a patient unconscious on a table, bleeding to death.

The summer had been exceptionally hot; warm rain in August, if you please! Everything was steaming; and now the real harvest weather had come, stilly blue with appropriate sunlight. (Ideal for a campaign in the Polish marches.) Von Esslin frowned and touched the edges of his short moustache as he watched the house come into view at the end of a long winding road lined with gracious lindens. This was his home – he repeated the phrase in his mind, but it evoked no pang of pleasure, simply the dutiful anxiety and affection which he had kept for his mother. They were very close in a way, and yet a mortal shyness ruled over their behaviour; to hear the tone in which they talked you might imagine them to be mere acquaintances, so without animation and lustre was it. It had grown, the shyness, since they were left more together, following upon the death of his twin sister Constanza, and of his father, the General. The old man had worshipped Constanza, and he never really recovered from her death; he had pined away like an old mastiff, filling the salons with photographs of her as a young woman before the slow wasting M.S. – sclerosis – had declared itself. How beautiful she had been; Egon himself had been stricken down with despair at so cruel a fate. They never discussed it, or seldom, and then gruffly.

It was different when they were separated, for then he permitted his warmth of feeling to evoke his childish attachment for her; in letters she became Katzen-Mutter, and as he wrote the words he felt the picture of her rise in his heart as a benign cat-mother, always with a great Siamese rippling at her side. They were still there, the cats; they were a passion with her.

The staff car drew up at last before the culvert covering the moat, and then gingerly crossed the plank bridge to arrive at the tall oak door behind which the Polish maid stood already waiting for his ring. She heard the driver open the door and heel-click, and then the voice of the Major General telling him to take his dressing-case inside and to be prepared to move off on the morrow at first light. This brief, barking exchange was succeeded by the jangle of the bellrope. The Polish maid opened and muttered something guttural as always; she bowed her head and sank into a half-curtsy. Von Esslin grunted something which bore a vague resemblance to a greeting and walked past her to place his cap upon the marble table and turn aside to where already the girl had opened the door into the green salon where his mother rose to greet him with a little cry of pleasure. "I did not quite believe it," she said, with her brief scentless embrace. "But how wonderful." He stepped back a pace to take her hands and kiss them with a suggestion of affectionate homage. "I haven't very long," he said, and then cleared his throat harshly as he added, "We are on the edge of war." She nodded swiftly, a bird-like nod. "But how brown you have got," she said. "It makes your scar look whiter than ever." He smiled, the joke was an old one. Once a horse had run away with him into a wood and he had cut his cheeks open by riding into a coil of barbed wire which for some unknown reason had been tied upon a tree. The wounds were clean and he did not think to have them dressed or stitched – the result being the neatest simulacrum of duelling scars you might imagine. Despite his explanations his mess refused to believe that he had not in secret indulged in the old samurai-style duelling match which had been for many a year banned in the army, but which from time to time tempted young officers to practise it in secret. The more he denied this, the less he was believed. Was he not a

Prussian? Such cases were rare but they did occur, just as from time to time someone had to be court-martialled for fighting a duel. The scars remained, grew whiter as his skin browned in summer. He was rather proud of the implication in a childish way; and at the same time ashamed. They were like stigmata to which one was not entitled but which could not at the same time be expunged. They laughed together at the absurdity.

"Come and sit beside me," she said, "and tell me what is happening. Here we know nothing, the wireless is broken."

He obeyed her and sat himself down on the sofa, sighing as he did so. "Things move so fast," he said, "that I risk being out of date. That is why I must be at my post tomorrow. The Führer is making lightning decisions."

The Polish maid came in with a tray of drinks and a silence of lead fell between them as the girl crossed the room. Usually when she was present they spoke in a wooden and stilted French for the sake of privacy. So his mother said now, "The Czech contracts for the clay have lapsed, but I think we have found another buyer closer at home. I am waiting now for a response." He nodded and replied, frowning, "It was bound to happen, events being what they are." As the door closed silently behind the servant his mother said, "She asked for leave to visit her parents. I thought she would not come back. I was surprised that she did." He expostulated, "*Ach* why, she has always been with us, even if she has never learned a word of German. She must feel more at home than in some Polish hovel – her parents are farm labourers, no?"

The fate of Poland cast a momentary shadow over their conversation; both hastened to inter the subject along with the sentiment of regret – it would have been too much to call it shame. He became hearty and sentimental. "It's good to feel the country flexing its muscles, facing up to its detractors. Germany has been patient for too long, the Führer is right about that. Too long."

In sympathy with the mood she altered her expression to one of suitable sternness; she bowed her beautiful heart-shaped head a little and allowed her mouth to settle into its cat-form. It was straight and hard – the expression of a soldier's wife used to confronting bereavement and sudden loss with courage, if not with a resigned equanimity. He liked this in her, this expression of indomitability. There was much left unsaid behind this façade of normality, much that as Germans they could not say. There were paradoxes – for example the German expansion into Austria had put the music festival so dear to her temporarily out of reach. The festivals went on, yes, but she felt inhibited about visiting her beloved Salzburg and Vienna as a member of a master race. . . . It was awkward; happily the Führer had shared no such feeling of inhibition. He had consecrated a whole day to the convulsions of Wagner's music, and solemnly had himself photographed with the Wagner children for the benefit of the press. He apparently wished it to be clear that the intellectual and emotional foundations of the present German postures and actions were to be traced to the artist. The spiritual justifications of the new faith were there.

And then of course there were other matters upon which they could not smear self-justificatory conversation like a salve; matters too dark, too floating in ambiguities, to form a substance upon which they might base talk not hedged with reservations. "You realise, mother, we must be *positive* now." He had a special plosive way of expressing the word, accompanying it with a short gesture, as of a man driving a nail into a door. Positive. His thoughts turned with schoolboyish pleasure to those dark tanks of his, now so peacefully browsing in the fields and pastures, the rolling lands which led towards the border. Some might have seen them as obscene steel beetles manned by men dressed in helmets shaped like ugly turnips of the same steel. But no, for him the thought of them

and of their crews was one of joy unredeemed by any reserva-
tion. The 10th Brigade, the 7th Panzers – this vast grouping of
steel was breathtaking in its battle-power, its beetle-power. The
slither of mesh as the caterpillars cackled across the asphalt of
major highways, the roar and slither of the engines – all this
was a Wagnerian paeon of malevolent power which would
soon be unlocked. His heart rose at the thought and yet he felt
somehow tearful inside. He repeated the word "positive" again,
giving it a touch of grim relish. So they sat staring unhappily
into their drinks.

When he got to his room to change for dinner he found
that the girl had already set out his dress uniform on the bed
and had passed an iron over the braided trousers. A little touch
of formality was suitable to his first evening at home with his
mother. It had always been so. The silver-backed brushes and
the phials of cologne had been taken from their leather slipcases
and disposed in the bathroom against the shave which he
always gave himself on such occasions. How well this spindly
Polish girl knew the routines of his life. It was curious to think
of her as soon to be formally declared a slave. . . . He thought
about it, frowning, as he lay in the hot water. Then he dressed
and went downstairs again to the picture gallery where he
would wait for his mother to join him. The tall windows, the
little bow window at the far end with just room for a sofa and a
grand piano, gave it intimacy. There were a few indifferent
portraits of the various members of the family, one fine Klimt,
and a few glass-covered cases which held various family relics
deemed worthy of exhibition. There was some vague relation
by marriage on his father's side to the Kleists, and in some
mysterious manner they had inherited a couple of his love
letters and a manuscript copy of a play. This was perhaps the
most important exhibit, apart from a couple of letters from
Hindenberg to his father about military affairs. The Kleist
archive was rather an ambiguous trophy, despite the poet's

34

admitted genius. But . . . he had, after all, insulted Goethe in the
most rabid fashion; and then his suicide (after all he *was* of a
military family) . . . that was also somewhat awkward, in a way.
Von Esslin had quite a vivid picture of the handsome couple
setting off for the fatal picnic with their hamper full of cakes
and fruit. Underneath nestled the loaded pistol, waiting like
Cleopatra's asp. He closed his eyes the better to visualise the
lake scene with its sunshine and drifting swans; he heard the
sharp crack of the discharge upon the sunny silence, he saw her
fall sideways upon the bench, folding down into the poet's
encircling arms . . . No, one could not help but feel distaste.

When dressing he had extracted the coveted order called
Pour le mérite and pinned it beside his own Iron Cross and the
other service marks which his brother officers always referred
to as "confetti". The *Pour le mérite* (which was the German
Victoria Cross) had been won by his father at the end of the
First World War. Naturally he treasured the medal, and since
he could not wear it in public he always pinned it on the inside
of his breast pocket, reserving the outside for his own more
modest prizes. It gave him pleasure and a certain confidence – as
a sort of talisman. He knew she would notice with pleasure
though she would make no allusion to it. He poured himself a
drink and, sitting down at the piano, forced his fingers to play
a few airs from Strauss. How stiff they had become! He always
longed to be somewhere within reach of a piano; but it was ages
now since he had had the chance to play. When his mother
arrived he took her arm and led her in to dine without preamble.
He did not wish to make a late night of it for the morrow
promised him exceptional fatigues. They dined by candlelight
and spoke in low tones so that there was no chance that their
conversation would be listened to – despite the firm conviction
of the Pole's total illiteracy. His mother told him of the visit
of a young security officer from a local unit who had asked if

he might wire a microphone into the kitchen. Von Esslin was at first incredulous, and then overtaken by laughter at such block-headed service behaviour. They were so far away from the Polish border. . . .

"That is what I told him, and after a time he went away. He had not been told who you were, either."

"So!"

They talked on until the clocks chimed ten, and then she bade him rise and prepared herself for bed. It was goodbye, for she would not be up on the morrow when he left. They embraced. "Please take care," she said, and he promised that he would as he saw her to the door before turning out the lights and following her up the old-fashioned staircase. He looked round him slowly, a little mournfully. In his room the bedside light was on and the covers were turned back.

He undressed and got into bed, thinking that he might read a few pages of the detective story he had brought with him, but he found his mind wandering back to his men and machines and all the excitement associated with this entirely new form of warfare: the use of aircraft as artillery, the concentrated masses of armour. Such force could not help but burst apart any enemy by its sheer concentrated impact. How had the democracies not seen it – for apparently they had not produced a shadow of tactical reorganisation to meet the threat? It was rugby against tennis, a powerful toboggan against a *fiacre*. . . . He sighed and laid down his book to stare at the wallpaper. And then the total secrecy of command offered by the astonishing scrambler coding machine they called Enigma. No, nothing could miscarry, despite the cautious saying of his old father, namely that on the battlefield chance always ruled. Chance!

He lay quietly breathing, allowing these vagrant thoughts to pass through his mind until they slackened speed, dimmed. He fell asleep lightly now. He had just enough self-possession to turn off the light.

When he awoke it was around one o'clock; it was as if a hand had been placed upon his shoulder in a gesture at once soft and confiding. The hand of a woman. At once he rose, one might say obediently, for it was in response to a wordless call like that of some animal or some bird. The gesture was quite unformulated; he walked down the corridor like a sleepwalker and then climbed an inner staircase which led to the maid's room. It had been like this for years now, since around his fortieth birthday. No word was exchanged. She lay with her face to the wall, but with her eyes open – she did not even pretend she was asleep. He stripped naked and climbed softly into bed beside her, lightly touching her flanks with his fingers, giving the signal which repetition had made customary. And she turned slowly round, quietly but ravenously arching her skinny body to accommodate his own sturdier, taller one. They were locked in silent combat now, like two experienced wrestlers, and he felt in the spider-like grip of her thin thighs and arms a kind of helplessness, an agony of submission and sexual abasement. She bowed before him as if she desired only one thing: to be trampled, to be spurned. Yet it was only a ruse, for she felt his mounting excitement as he trod her with ever-increasing violence, with a powerful, determined passion which mounted towards a climax which would sweep them both breathlessly away into the marvellous amnesia of their double lust. With no word said, no gesture of complicity offered on either side. They were like insects answering a rhythm, a wave-length of light or a sound. Her eyes were closed in the death-mask of her little dark face with its helmet of hair – so dark as almost to suggest the hair of a Japanese doll. The sort of tresses which grow on Eastern corpses after death. Her face was pretty but terribly emaciated, terribly thin. It was the head of an adder, though the details which made it human were quite fine, good eyes and teeth. When younger she might have made the impression of being a *petit rat de l'Opéra*.

She was his, she submitted, and the thought excited his cupidity; he overwhelmed her as his army would soon overwhelm her country and people, raping it, wading in its blood. At last the climax came and in his muddled exhaustion he fell asleep on her breast to dream of his big, playful tanks nosing about like sheepdogs in the dust and clutter of the farms they had knocked down, pushing their squat steel noses through walls and hedges as they fanned out into the attack. She lay as if dead, though her lips moved as always at this moment. But he could never catch what she whispered so very tenderly while she cradled his head. It was not in German that she spoke.

Two storeys above them his mother lay with open eyes, staring into the darkness and thinking as she listened with furious concentration to the silence which from time to time blurred into the small sounds of congress which they made. A chimney-flue conveyed whatever sound there was up to her room; but that was little enough, so she must supplement it with guesswork to imagine clearly what she had already imagined so often in the last years of his father. Then silence came.

It must have been just before light when the girl woke him with a touch, herself sliding out from the circle of his sleeping embrace and into a wrap. He took no formal leave of her, simply rose in heavy silence and made his way back to his room. He took a hot shower and dressed with circumspection. Then, taking up the locked briefcase, he walked downstairs once more to where, on a sidetable in the dining-room, a coffee-pot steamed over a bud of alcohol flame and some buns of brown oatmeal lay warming in a chafing dish. He helped himself and sat down, knowing that while he ate the servant would be packing his affairs at lightning speed into the two suitcases, and then bringing them down to await the chauffeur in the hall. After that she would no longer manifest herself unless there was any precise need – she would wait behind the green baize door until the front door closed behind him. It was a time-honoured routine.

As he drank his coffee he unlocked his briefcase and flicked through the documents it held, to refresh his memory of things outstanding, things to be done when he returned to his unit. They were for the most part unclassified field-orders and annotated map references: with things moving so fast there was hardly time for signals to linger about on the secret list. Operation White, *der Fall Weiss*, had already been formulated and allowed to mature in the mind of the General Staff for some time – the Nazis were nothing if not thorough.

Then came the plastic folder which imitated a superior pigskin, but in a flashy and debased fashion which gave the show away. This contained the two pamphlets which Dr. Goebbels had issued to them after the latest staff briefing by the Führer. They lay side by side in the pouch, one red and one blue. What was it the little crippled doctor had called them? "A cultural and intellectual justification apparatus": *Ein Kultur- und Intelligenz-Rechtfertigungsapparat*! *There* was a phrase to gobble on, and gobble he had had to with his slight impediment of speech. But what a momentous experience it had been to sit there among some two hundred or more of his fellows, his colleagues, in the new study which the Führer had built for himself in the newborn Chancellery.

They had cooled their heels for a good hour before he came, *der Kleinmann*, sidling almost shyly through the great doors with an air of preoccupation, almost of vagueness. With a fine synchronisation they rose together, stamped once and heel-clicked – echo-smack of boot-leather was like a giant licking its lips. In unison they greeted him with a hoarse, carlish roar of "*Heil!*" and an outflung right arm. To this he responded with a vague gesture of reply and an even vaguer glance, an almost embarrassed glance. Then he released the spring with the words, "Be seated, gentlemen."

They settled once more like a flock of pigeons and leaned attentively forward to catch, in its most intimate and exact sense, the purport of the words which flowed now from his lips. They began slowly at first, and then gradually gathered speed as his ideas fired them, the obsessional ideas so long harboured and polished in silence and exile. But he looked tired, as well he might, with so much upon his shoulders, so many wrongs to right, so many scores to settle with the world. He was pale also and there were times of near aphasia, as if he were still coming out of an epileptic "aura". They listened with a kind of fearful emotion to the long trailing diatribe.

And while they listened they looked around them at the immense room, memorising as well as they could the details of this pregnant encounter with the man-god of the future who was delineating for them the spiritual frontiers of the new estate. The prospects of the freedom these ideas offered made them feel buoyant and shriven; for all that they were going to do now the Führer offered them an absolution in advance. Belief – that was all that was necessary for them; the rest followed automatically. One could become drunk on such rhetoric. Many of them felt moved, their faces flushed, their breathing quickened. So it went on until suddenly, abruptly, like a motor running out of fuel, it ended and the silence flowed in upon them all.

It had taken only nine months to bring to birth this huge edifice of a Chancellery with its nine hundred rooms, plus the great operations-room and study – the cavern in which the Führer was going to live and work; to guide this huge battle-ship towards the new millennium. He had worked long and lovingly on the plans with the architect Speer. It was massive, subdued, theatrical, but of a classical theatre suitable to the age. As for the lion's den, it had all the middle-class allure of a classicism such as would satisfy the criteria of an architect used to building cafeterias. But it was impressive, because its owner, the slight man with the moustache-tuft and the side-saddle hair, was impressive. One asked oneself how he had arrived at this point. Then one noticed his eyes. . . .

Von Esslin, normally no sycophant, leaned forward and pretended to take notes; the eyes distressed him, and he disguised his anxiety in this fashion. From time to time he looked about him, taking stock of the place. The acoustics were really excellent.

The monumental room was twenty-seven metres in length, fifteen in breadth, and ten metres high. The air moved tepidly and sluggishly about it despite the well-studied ventilation of the place. The windows were six metres in height and framed in heavy curtains of grey velvet. And then everywhere there was Greek marble, specially ordered; the workmen had been generously rewarded for working overtime at Pentelikos to cut the slabs for their future monarch. Marble grey, rose and coral. Then, to offset the delicacy of these tones, there were tapestries – admirable Gobelins. The ceiling was carved into two hundred and twelve equal caissons, each one offset by mouldings of a rigid geometric style. A sculptured frieze repeated unto infinity, as it were, while upon every column flowered six double torch-holders of unctuous bronze above the initials A.H. cut in a style which hinted at a Doric order. On the cool floors glowed oriental carpets of impeccable pedigree. Three tall standard lamps of bronze presided over the massive, gleaming, walnut-wood desk and four high-backed chairs before the work-desk. It was more than convincing, it was overwhelming.

There was a sense of anti-climax when all of a sudden the discourse stopped and the Leader rose to leave them. Once more they repeated the ritual heel-clicking and the hoarse cry. Then he was gone, and the cripple came into the room and took his place, while uniformed orderlies distributed the little plastic pouch with its two pamphlets. Goebbels waited until the distribution was complete, and until the tall doors had closed behind the orderlies. Then he cleared his throat and in a quiet, unemphatic voice began his exposition; it was pitched in a low key as if to form a contrast to the harangue which had preceded it. Here they were on more familiar ground, for most of what he had to say was orthodox and free of surprises; it was what one read every day in the newspapers: the wrongs of Germany which would soon be righted, the intolerable provocations they had suffered from inferior breeds. The tone, however, was reasonable and expository. Germany had now found her true path and was going to go forward with the building of a new world, a new order of things which would be more in keeping with the order of nature. *Ordnung* – he almost sang the word; it clamped together the whole edifice of his thought. It was a rivet in the flanks of this huge steel battleship which would soon be rolling across the land and the sea, promoting the new Golden Age. But here the speaker reined and with uplifted finger warned them to keep always in mind the two basic foes of all they stood for – the two forces of darkness which they must overthrow in order to achieve their objectives. They would find the documents of the case in the little plastic pouch. They must be studied with care for they contained the whole truth of the German mission; every field commander should study them. These and only these two forces stood between them and the new Aryan order. That was the germ of the matter.

One might perhaps have expected an anthology of Nietzsche quotations, expressing all his vehement anti-semitism (sentiments which, forty years later, would prove to have been forged and inserted by the philosopher's sister and her husband); but no, the two documents which nestled in the little plastic pouch were, respectively, the text of the celebrated Protocols of Zion, which outlined the Jewish plot to conquer the world, and the extraordinary Will of Peter the

Great,* equally a plot to redeem it through Pan-Slavism.

The terrible thing was that there was nobody with whom one could discuss such matters, except hypocritically, for to express reservations about such apparent trash would at this stage have been taken as a treasonable act. Each was locked in the private cell of his doubts and fears – with no hope of an exit this side of the war. The position was an intolerable one for men who could still regard themselves as men of honour. Von Esslin sat in the corner of the staff office with these documents on his knee, staring at the sunshine upon the trees and pondering. Army folk were so innocent of all political instinct. It was best to think nothing, to say nothing – to throw oneself into the marvellous liberation of blind action; to become part of this vast steel juggernaut aimed at Poland, and leave the thinking to others who knew more than he did. These were the thoughts which filled him with elation – the promise of glory and the fulfilment of his professional curiosity in the matter of tanks. Could they be directed from division, or would the general staff have to ride on their backs, so to speak, in order to control the pulse-beat of the battle as it unrolled? He would soon find all this out, unless by some last-minute chance the wind turned and the French and English changed their orientation. Yes, but even then . . .

He was impatient to get back to his command post, to his staff unit, to his professional friends who were all as keyed up as he was; he was keen to sanction the last signal before battle, the "Last Letters Home" which would tell the troops, if they did not already know, that the die was cast, the attack ordered. When these thoughts passed through his mind he was seized by a sort of vertigo – a desire on the rampage. It was at such moments that he longed for a piano with which to assuage all the confusion of his thoughts and impulses.

How slowly history evolves! Each drop from the icicle

* See Appendix.

takes an age to form and to fall -- or so it seemed to those who, like himself, waited for the definitive signal. He motored up by night, through a country of forests and marches where now the chief vegetation seemed to be of steel. At a turn in the main road, by a bridge, he came upon some sort of accident, to judge by the flare of headlights and the silhouettes of figures busily occupied around a couple of lorries which had turned turtle and lay in the ditch with their wheels in the air, like insects turned over on their backs. "An accident," said the driver. With so much traffic, in so many complicated formations moving about by night, it was hardly to be wondered at. But there seemed to be nobody of rank about to direct whatever operation might be necessary to free the road and Von Esslin jumped out and made his way to the scene. Then he saw that the lorries had contained crosses, thousands of wooden crosses which filled the ditch and the field beyond, gleaming white in the sterile lights of the halted cars. Crosses! For some reason the sight threw him into a towering rage; he began to give orders with a hysterical violence which surprised even himself. The soldiers on the scene, aghast alike at his eminence and the febrile fury of his rage, began to buzz like an overturned hornets' nest themselves. Von Esslin all but screamed. He ordered the drivers to present themselves and berated them. All three were put upon a charge at his behest. Then, still fuming and feeling almost faint with the force of his emotion, he returned to his car and resumed his journey.

He soon forgot, for the mighty rhythm engendered by the Grand Army in movement is irresistible, is all-engulfing. They were all diminished as individuals, shorn of their personal responsibility by the power of its motion. Its coils and meshes held them fast while its gathering momentum rolled them irrevocably down, as if on the breast of some great river, towards the fulfilling ocean. But a river of chain-mail, a river of meshed steel. Von Esslin, once he had regained his place in all the warmth and tension of friendship with his fellow adventurers, found himself as if upon the bridge of some great raft, rolling with ever-gathering speed down towards the deeps which beckoned them; towards the new human order which they had been set to build and to inspire with their presence. He looked around the map caravan at the brown, intense, beefy faces and the big red hands; his heart swelled with emotion, with affection for them all. From the depths of the night they were setting out towards a new dawn – by the time the sun was up the whole face of history would have been changed!

The edges of the darkness trembled and here and there the horizon flickered with light, as if from a distant storm's sheet lightning. But they knew it was the first rumour of engagement, the armoured units in their delving had already locked horns with the enemy scouts. The whole symphony had been set in motion within two hours of dawn; the great animal was uncoiling itself, at first gingerly and then with increasing confidence and speed, unfurling the darkness with its few points of necessary light as it got into gear, with only the suffused roaring of an ocean grinding upon shingle to herald its advance across the plains.

At first light the air bombardment was to begin – an innovation in tactics which blasted vast ragged holes in the front. They might have been forgiven for imagining themselves to be taking part in some great historic saga, were it not for the distasteful bearing of the special units which were attached to them. The prisons had been scoured to brim their ranks. They would follow the fighting men and start the task of pillage, rape and extermination which was so carefully embodied in their official directives, issued on the field-grey signal paper which the para-military Schutzaffeln affected. "Fear of the Reich must be instilled at whatever cost. No effort must be spared." They were a special breed, these men, furtive and monosyllabic and withdrawn. The officers smiled without unclenching their teeth; they exuded guilt and unease as do all people who enjoy inflicting pain – jailors, inquisitors, shop stewards, executioners. The concentration camps had allowed their choicest disciplinarians to gain prestige in the hated and feared death's-head uniform of these modern centurions. The regular knew them to be lackeys on whom the authority to murder had been conferred; their shame ignited his own, for he knew that their task was to turn the whole of Europe into one smoking knacker's yard.

They moved forward now from darkness into light and soon came to the edge of those endless plains of yellow harvest wheat, still under a cerulean sky which would soon be full of small black specks swerving and chattering like distant magpies. Then sound came, volumes of it, varieties of it all mingled into one earth-trembling concave weight upon the flinching ear-drums; they could not hear themselves speak. Their mouths worked. And slowly, from two ends of the horizon, the world began to burn, the wheat began to burn, racing as if to meet them.

Seventh and Tenth Panzers had been unkennelled like hounds and directed deliberately across this flaming prairie, racing to make contact with the invisible foe. They had supposed that their speed would carry them through, but a sudden ambush supervened, the fires elongated, unrolling before them as they raced, and they found themselves encircled by the flames. Von Esslin saw his cherished tanks going off like chestnuts, their petrol tanks exploding in the heat. The command car turned back, hesitated. He swore at his driver and urged him to continue, to follow the armour, but by now they were at the edge of the flame area and more vulnerable than the exploding tanks. It was only a minor incident in an uninterrupted chain of successful actions – they were almost bored with the reiterated signals which told of objectives attained, objectives over-run, enemy units bypassed or completely encircled. A small setback, yet it played upon his *amour-propre* and he felt culpable as well as cheated of something – what he did not know. He was relieved to discover that he was sitting in a puddle of blood; a nasty cut in his forearm had soaked him. In his excitement he had experienced no pain; now the wound began to smart. He called for an orderly and stripped off his coat, the better to present his wound for bandaging. Dense smoke had succeeded the panorama of flame. Units were poking about in the black charred stubble for his exploded chestnuts of tanks. There was a bit of shrapnel in his sleeve; the orderly picked it out and handed it to him saying, "A souvenir, sir." Von Esslin's humour was restored by this trifling expiation. At this rate they would soon be in Warsaw.

THREE

Into Egypt

THE EMBARKATION WENT OFF WITHOUT A HITCH AT DEAD of night and by morning the royal yacht was well out to sea en route for Egypt.

In his notebook Blanford wrote:

Immortality must feel something like this for a poet. Suppose I were to tell you that here, in perfect peace, we sail eastward under cloudless skies upon a windless cerulean sea with not one Homeric curl in it. . . . The *Khedive* is the royal yacht which is carrying us into Egypt and safety. No, it is totally unreal to find myself here under an awning of brightly striped duck, lounging beside the calm Prince, drinking a whisky and soda with grave reflective delight. Contemplating the abyss which has opened at our feet – the war. The Prince himself has been transformed into an imposing maritime figure, for he has put on yachting *tenue* complete with white trousers of some magnolia-soft tissue, set off by a blazer and an old heraldic yachting cap bearing the insignia of both the royal house and the Alexandria Yacht Club. The blazer is all Balliol, Oxford.

From time to time, so pure and so encouraging is the air, we doze off for a few moments; then we awake and continue the Arabic lesson which is going to transform me into a linguist If there is world enough and time.

(My darling, these lines, somewhat to my surprise, are written to you and not to Livia. I write them because I feel freed by the probability, nay certainty, of never seeing you and Sam again in this lifetime! I write them from the part of myself which has slowly and secretly turned to you. Typically enough

I did not recognise the situation at first. But Livvie did. I noticed her jealousy but not its cause. I did not realise the truth until I was on the very brink of kissing you goodbye. But Livvie did and hated you accordingly – as much as one permits hate for a sister. I simply did not know or did not realise until the train bore you away.)

And so here I am, like a younger version of Tibullus without the sea-sickness. My poetry is crowding on sail. My mother is dead, my friends dispersed, my future uncertain, my solitude a delicious weight. One feels in all this a sort of affirmation for some early promise made by the good fairy. She must have said: "This one will be introspective, cut off from ordinary life, proficient in solitude but subject to enchantments because of his insight."

The old yacht has been provisioned in the most imaginative way – caviar, champagne, whisky, nothing lacks. We sit down to meals of fervent Frenchness served by great bronze servants with the tones of gongs, clad in booming white and gloved spotlessly to the forearm. Unruffled in their dignity and truth, like great aristocrats, they disburse kindness without servility. It is my first taste of Egypt, the marvellous hieratic servants of the Prince, serving our food on matchless plate. It worries the Prince sometimes. "I suppose that if we were to receive a plebeian torpedo I would be asked to regret the loss of all this stuff – even though it isn't mine. Farouk would be furious of course. I suppose he is insured." I had never thought upon the matter. Kings get given everything – do they need to insure? I yawn and stretch like Cleopatra's pet cat.

The ship's library is full of Victorian fiction amassed by Farouk's English nannies. But among a small yet choice Arabic section there is a play which the Prince considers to be an excellent introduction to his country. "It is by a friend of mine," he says, "and it is entitled *The Death of Cleopatra – Masra Kaliûpâtrâ* – it is very suitable for you, yes."

It is pleasant to know that Cleo was known as "Kaliû-pâtrâ" by her subjects. The collapsing world she knew could not have been vastly different from this one – a question of scale merely. Catastrophe is catastrophe, whatever the magnitude.

All around us, according to that scratchy oracle, Ship's Radio, a war rages. The fleets of France and England threaten to cross swords. Somewhere lurks an Italian fleet, showing great discretion, thank goodness. Meanwhile (as if at the fabled heart of some great hurricane, the core around which it has moulded itself), we float onwards, serenely, in untroubled silence save for the quiet purring of the motor and the languid plume of smoke from our great funnel. Onwards towards the white cliffs of Crete and then Evnostos, the harbour-home of the Alexandria basin. It is too good to be true.

"Mr. Blanford, I would like to ask you a favour on behalf of myself and the Princess."

"Certainly, Your Highness."

"May we call you Aubrey? It simplifies things."

"But of course."

"Thank you, Aubrey."

"Not at all, Your Highness."

So the Arabic lesson winds slowly on its way, interspersed with a hundred and one interruptions and interpolations by the Prince. Among them he urges upon me a book about Egypt written by his own nanny, a Mrs. Macleod, and entitled *An Englishwoman on the Nile*. He says that it is full of striking observations; it lists many of the queerer things about Egyptian life. I open it as he talks and see that it begins admirably indeed, with the words: "In Egypt one acts upon impulse as there is no rain to make one reflect."

In the cocoon of this fine warm air it seems a sin to go below, so we order our dinner to be served us upon a tray, and eat it while we are still idling on deck. From time to time a typed news bulletin comes our way with the compliments of the radio operator, but its contents sound mad, inconsequential, out of all proportion to this grave sinking sun and still sea. We had, however, contacted Alexandria and were to expect an escort to join us before midnight in order to see us safely to port. The great harbour with its immobile battleships and cruisers, both French and British, would have been an impressive sight, I suppose, but we were to be spared it; for after dinner the Prince was summoned to the bridge where he was able to make use of the land telephone to call someone who would relay his message directly to the authorities and obtain permission for him to land, rather unorthodoxly, at the Palace of Montaza rather than in the Grand Harbour. He explained that this would lighten the journey a great deal and enable us to get ashore without fussy *douaniers* and security officials. "The English will be obstructive as usual, and won't like it; but they will have to lump it if Farouk says so, and now he knows he will jolly well say so!"

We retired early to get some rest, leaving everything to these grave brown beadles of servants, who spoke so thrilling deep and smiled like pianos among themselves. And sleep I did, to be woken by a brown hand on my shoulder, shaking me with extreme reverence while a brown voice said, "Master he say you to go uppy stairs now. He waiting." I dressed and made my sleepy way on deck, where I found the Prince in high good humour presiding over all our baggage. "I was right," he said joyfully, "the English are most furious with me."

We went ashore in darkness in a large motor launch belonging to the Egyptian navy and landed at the water-gate of a palace plunged in utter darkness; then, after much chaffering, somewhere a switch was thrown and a sort of combination of Taj Mahal and Eiffel Tower blared out upon the night.

It was my first exposure to Egyptian Baroque, so the simile is surprisingly apt. To blare, to bray – so much light in so

many mirrors of so many colours – the effect was poly-
morphous perverse, so to speak. . . . I realised that I was going
to fall in love with the place – I saw that it was a huge temple of
inconsequences. Silently pacing these matchless Shiraz carpets
which paved the vast saloons my spirit was intoxicated by
scarlet leather, golden studs, lapis lazuli, cat's eye, and everywhere mirrors spouting light like deserted fountains. For the
reception rooms were empty, not a soul was about. The state
lavatories were the size of Euston, but the chains clanked on
empty cisterns. We hesitated, irresolute.

Then the Princess manifested, coming down the great
staircase half-asleep, wrapped in a white kimono of soft feathers
like a small, yawning swan. They stood gazing at each other,
expressing such a wealth of desire and delight that it was
exquisitely moving to the onlooker. Etiquette prevented them
from embracing in public after the plebeian style made common
by the cinema. They behaved birdfully, like birds, which have
no arms to grab hold with; they spread their wings, so to speak,
and whispered each other's names with humble rapture. The
Prince kissed the tips of her fingers; then, with a little sob, like
an excited child, she rushed away to dress for the journey.
While we waited, a sleepy palace servant encouraged us into
the vast dining-room where the chandeliers now shone upon
tables laid for breakfast with coffee and chocolate and fresh
croissants and cream. I felt extraordinarily heartened to see
people who could love each other so devoutly; it was so unlike
Europe where serious thinking about passion has really come
to a standstill.

We embarked in two dark limousines, leaving the staff
to disengage the Prince's affairs from the yacht; there was some
concern, for a fresh wind was springing up and the anchorage
was not a sound one. However we got our bags, and I travelled
in the second car piled high with them. A vague impression
of the Grand Corniche with the sea slapping and the wind

knuckling the palms. Then dark ribbons of road across the desert. I fell into a troubled slumber, lulled by the smooth engine and the feeling that time had no joints.

I write these words some days later, seated upon a shady balcony overlooking the Nile which runs as smooth as a razor across the garden's end; it is sulphurous hot, I trickle as I write. My wrist sticks to the paper, so clammy is it, and I am forced to press it upon a blotter in order not to smudge. But I am happy. A whole new world opens before me. I have fallen on my feet. I was rather dreading the Princess – I felt sure she would instantly divine all my deficiencies. But she took my hand and held it for a long moment while she gazed earnestly, thoughtfully into my eyes, with a deep preoccupation as if she were listening to sacred music. Then she sighed with relief, dropped my hand, and said, "He is all *right!*" Whereupon the Prince gave a small chuckle and said, "She *never* trusts me."

I am all right! What more does one need to hear about oneself? A wave of confidence swept over me, and I realised that I would certainly make a success of this rather vague assignment as English secretary to the Prince. It is also pleasant to begin to feel part of a family – my upbringing had not accustomed me to such warmth. Nor are my statutory duties very onerous; the correspondence is fairly heavy but will be easy to despatch in a longish morning of work. Remains the social side – I feared this; but here I am treated with great consideration. I am not forced to hand round drop-scones for the English tea parties of the Princess. But I do it. A complete wardrobe was being supplied to me by the centenarian tailor of the house, in beautifully cut mint summer silk.

The town house of the Prince (for they also appear to own an abandoned palace at Rosetta and a summer villa at Helwan) is not exactly a castle. It is the size of a medieval prince's hunting lodge with extensive dependencies, indeed a sort of nabob's country seat. Parts have been shored up against ruin, parts have been allowed to subside gracefully and melt back into the primeval mud of Egypt – the black viscous element from which everything seems to be fashioned. One wing is full of corridors boarded up as a safety precaution against floors which have been ravaged by termites. The furnishings are modest compared to those of the palace of our arrival, and all is a bit dusty, decorations, furniture, mirrors, everything; but very faintly, like powder in a wig. Time and neglect and the river-damps have hazed the clear outline of things. On the other hand there is distinction in the quality of the paintings and bibelots, the plaster mouldings. They had not just accumulated, one felt, but had been individually chosen and desired and cherished for their aesthetic feel. Though they were various, not matching in a uniform way, they lived on in harmonious and coherent discord. The whole place felt nice, smelt nice. Extraordinary cats abounded. The dissonant shriek of peacocks made one jump. The Nile smelt old and sad and disabused, turning green like oxidising copper, but imperishably itself, unlike any other river in the world. At dawn I saw a fisherman standing in quiet expectancy by the river bank, as if waiting for the sun to rise; presently it did, and the whole insect world began to buzz and bubble in the warm ray which burned the last mists from the water's surface. The fisherman took up a mouthful of water and blew it out in a screen of spray against the sunlight, revelling in the prismatic hues of the water-drops.

In the morning I heard moans from an outhouse and the sound of strokes and swearing; I enquired of the Princess what this might be, and she informed me demurely that it was Said, their young major-domo, receiving what she described as a "smart slippering" for some domestic fault. "Ah," added her husband, "you no doubt recall that the royal sceptre of Egypt was always the rod. And with our servants there is no way to combat the progressive amnesia which comes over them, gradually accumulating until they seem quite mental, quite unable to hold anything in mind. Then they begin to forget things and break things and it is time for a kindly reminder. About every six months I reckon. You will see the difference in Said tomorrow. Today he will sulk because of the insult to his honour, but tomorrow . . ."

"And your secretaries – do you have them slippered?"

The Princess clapped her hands and chirped as she replied, "I told you he was all right." But the Prince cocked an eyebrow and said, "We have much worse reserved for the secretaries!"

I am not the only secretary – there are several others, each with his own domain of activity; but they all vanish at the end of the day while I stay on to dine *en famille* or else alone in the magnificent suite of rooms I have been allotted. Everything is new and curious, so that for the moment I do not find this padded life of an honorary attaché becoming wearisome. But I have always enjoyed being on my own and I indulge the bent several evenings a week in order to write letters or scribble notes such as these sporadic annotations on the margins of history. For the moment I feel cut off from the world, almost from the human race. Egypt is like some brilliantly coloured frieze against which we move in perfect ease and normality. The country has declared itself neutral, and its cities are "open cities" – shimmering pools of crystal light at nights, of choked bazaars and traffic-laden thoroughfares by day, of lighted shops and brilliant mosques – a parody of the true Moslem paradise. We read of blackouts elsewhere; in the City of the Dead you can practically read a newspaper at the full moon. I feel at once exhilarated and lost, exultant and despairing. The world has been cut off, abbreviated to the confines of this lighted city between deserts where all is comfort and plenty. But for how long? Nobody dares to think about it.

The disturbance of the mails has called forth new conventions like the air-letter; I have armed myself with a package of them, but to what end? Will England still exist by the time my letters arrive? A profound despondency rules over this underworld of forebodings and hidden fears – I speak as much for my hosts as myself. They are beginning to realise the depths of their affection for the misty island where they had spent so many happy summers hating the English. And France, too. "France, *halas!*" It sounds somehow sadder and more absolute in Arabic, like an overturned statue. It has in it a hint of the wailing Aman-Aman (Alas-Alas) songs of the radio which scribbles over the silences of every café with the voice of Oum Kalsoum, the nightingale from Tanta. . . . I suppose *kaput* would be the translation of *halas?*

I was formally presented to my fellow scribes by the Prince himself. Professor Baladi was tall and slim and spoke fluent English. He had blue eyes and a fresh colouring and wore his red fez at a jaunty angle. He had an endearing desire to represent himself as a man about town and hinted that he would be available to assist me in exploring the city – a most useful offer. He carried an ebony-headed walking stick with great care, like a sceptre of an inconceivable preciousness. We clicked. So it was with a slower and muddier gentleman, Khanna, a Copt, who seemed at first a little shy and taciturn. Confluent smallpox had given him a skin like a colander. He had a preference for speaking French, and to express an opinion cost him a great effort. He was a brilliant soul in strict hiding; he trusted nobody. There was reserve here, but none of the animosity I had feared.

Yet the power behind the throne, so to speak, was a young and quite disarming Syrian, by name Affad. He was, I gathered, a millionaire in his own right, and only appeared upon a number of boards to support the Prince, out of pure affection. He was a remarkably attractive character with rather misty, glaucous eyes and a helpless appearance; slim and tall, he gave a curious sort of androgynous feel upon first meeting. I thought he must be some brilliant homosexual of the ancient ilk, for like Alcibiades he had a faint lisp. His line of talk was most amusing, self-deprecating, satirical; it was clear that nobody could long stay immune to his deadly charm. In dress he was of a negligent elegance which almost suggested a fashion-plate. His English was faultless, he possessed the language fully and his apparent incoherence and almost ineffectual mildness was really a ruse in order to call forth affection. When he wanted to make it so, his talk was brilliantly incisive. "Well, but I have been expecting you for some time," he said, to my surprise. "It has taken him an age to find the right sort of secretary for his work, and once he met you he cabled me that you would be ideal and that he would try and make you an offer." I wondered what I could have said to create an impression upon my first meeting with the Prince back there in Provence. As if he read my thoughts, Affad smiled and answered the question for me; the solution could not have been more surprising. "The Prince heard you say something most interesting about Apollonius of Tyana, and it made him realise that you would find yourself at home in Egypt." What could I have said? I racked my brains to remember. Yes, perhaps I had mentioned something about gnosticism in Egypt in relation to the Templar heresy – to Quatrefages or perhaps to Felix. It was nonetheless astonishing. The Prince himself was far from being an erudite, an intellectual, so why should such a remark... ? I thought idly of the dried and resined head in his red hat-box. I wondered what had happened to it.

Meanwhile Affad poured me a drink and assured me that I should find my post a deeply satisfying one from several points of view. This I was beginning to believe. Never had I fallen among such agreeable and gentle folk. To work for them, with them, promised to be easy and pleasurable.

There remained my compatriots; we spent a morning and an afternoon upon them, since form decided that I must at least register at the Consulate and fill in an availability form in case I should ever be called up. My passport was examined by a disagreeably lordly little grocer's assistant (it would seem) called Telford – *Mister* Telford, sir, if you please! He was thus addressed by his sycophantic pro-consul. "You will have to stay on call for the present. I can guarantee nothing."

The Prince was nettled by his tone. "Well, I think I can," he said icily, "we are seeing H.E. this afternoon and he is aware that Mr. Blanford is engaged as my secretary." Telford shrugged and handed back my passport with disdain. "So be it," he said and waved us away into the noisy street where the Prince's car waited.

In the afternoon we went up to the Consulate to sign the book and to make our obeisances to the Minister. He was sitting in a deck-chair far out upon the dusty lawn, a thin, tall, rather attractive man in his shy way. He had chosen a strategic spot midway between a couple of large water sprinklers which were hard at work in the heat keeping the paper-dry lawn alive. The water pushed large blocks of tepid air about around his chair, giving the faint illusion of freshness and coolth. We stepped between the columns with care so as not to get our trousers sprinkled, and were received kindly enough by the Minister, whose servants came running with further deck-chairs which were placed with equal strategy round about us; also a table upon which appeared in due course a large English tea complete with rock cakes, ginger biscuits and drop-scones. How strange it seemed to find this in Egypt! I commented on the fact and our host smiled and said, "You should find it reassuring, should you not? With the present situation on our hands we shall need all the morale-building tea we can get." Then he added as he stirred his cup, "I have had you officially 'frozen' for a year, as the saying goes. This means that H.M. regards your job as a privileged one and essential to the war effort." I did not quite follow how and was about to ask, when the Prince turned to me and did the explaining himself. "It's because I am a Colonel on the Military Mission, and also head of the Red Cross in Egypt. That is why H.E. wants you to keep an eye on me and see that I don't get into mischief by inviting Mehar Pacha to lunch one day, eh?"

The Minister did not rise to the jest but on the contrary looked rather pained. "You will soon know," he said, turning to me, "just how lucky we are to have someone like the Prince to consult on policy. Egypt is terribly tricky politically, and doubly so at the moment with the present options."

The talk then generalised itself into gossip about the war situation which, despite some lucky strokes on our side, was still appallingly full of hazards; it gave a highly provisional air to these orders and dispositions and it was obvious that the Minister was weighed down by these fearful contingencies which hedged us in between the deserts, still with inadequate forces and armour to confront the worst that the enemy might think up. He did not say any of this, but his tone implied it – and of course the facts of the general situation were so widely reported that there was nothing secret in the matter that any newspaper reader might not know. Our tea-party ended on an amiable but subdued note. "I know that you will be in and out of the Chancery on business matters," said the Minister as we rose to shake hands, "I will tell my social sec to see that you receive all standing invitations. But if you ever need to see me personally, don't hesitate to ring up and come round." We thanked him for his warmth. A swerve of the water sprinklers sent a gust of cool air towards us; it dislodged a leaf from the bundle of despatch-paper on the little wicker table. I picked it up as it fell to the ground and handed it back. It looked at first to be a cipher. Then I saw that it was a game of chess described in cablese. He thanked me as he took the paper back and said, "I see you caught a glimpse of the positions. Do you play chess?" But there I had to disappoint him. "Canasta, bridge or pontoon – nothing else." We took our leave.

So the long days of my secretarial engagements outlined themselves, full of variety and novelty. The interests of the Prince were multifarious; as president of the Red Cross he had a fine set of offices in the centre of the capital, where I was accorded a small room by the teleprinter from which I had to harvest a huge correspondence; then there was the dusty, agreeable Consulate which he so frequently visited – though here he had no foothold. We wandered about the Chancery at will. My palace office was the central one, the key to everything else. But the Prince, as an honorary Colonel of Regiment to the Egyptian Field Artillery, was also entitled to an imposing office at headquarters which he adored visiting in his uniform – a British colonel's outfit topped with a traditional fez. He wore a spray of service decorations on his breast and it was obvious that they gave him immense pleasure, for he stroked them unendurably during formal conversations with the obsequious young officers of his regiment.

Yes, this new world is full of colour and sensation; nor would it be possible to overpraise the beauty of this gorgeous, dusty city with its bubble-domes topped with new moons, its blazing souks, its brilliantly lit riverside suburbs, its bursting shops. The whole of Europe is in darkness and we are here in a night-long incandescence permitted only to the cities which have been declared "open". No bombers snarl out of this velvet-blue night sky. There are no signs of the war save the soldiers on leave. Occasionally, just before dawn, a stealth of tanks and carriers might emerge from the barracks and rustle across the deserted roads, making for the desert on tiptoe, as it were; but so circumspectly that they make less noise than the thudding of camel pads on the asphalt – for just before dawn long columns of camels bring in the vegetables to the town markets together with other loads like cotton, reeds, *bercim* – clover for animal fodder.

"The Princess rather mocks my uniform," said the Prince, "but I keep it for it enables us to picnic in the Western Desert when we want; without it I would be a civilian and the desert is out of bounds to ordinary civilians. That reminds me, I must have you gazetted to the Egyptian army as a volunteer second lieutenant. Then you can come as my aide." An alluring prospect – to wear British service kit with a scarlet flower-pot on my head. Strangely enough, both Prince and Princess were deeply moved when I walked in on them, dressed in full fig complete with tarboosh. "Now you are really one of us," she cried, and tears came into her eyes. I looked an awful fool in the flower-pot.

England was an occasional pang, an occasional twinge of conscience away; the new life was all-engulfing in its variety, while the information which it profferred so liberally was persuading me to see this ancient country not as something exhausted by history, existing through its ruins, but as something still thrillingly contemporary, still full of an infernal mystery and magic. Of course I owed most of this to Affad, though at first, while I was settling in, I had little to do with him; my fellow scribes occupied the centre of the stage. Professor Baladi, for example, with his quaint Victorian-novel English, could have earned music-hall renown had he so wished. "Mr. Blanford, I esteem that there is nothing more sublime in nature than a glimpse of an English lady's bubs." He watched me curiously for my reaction, head on one side. "Really, Professor, you are making the blush start to my cheek." He laughed airily and said with a certain archness, "I only said it to make you chortle." And so I obliged him with a chortle – or what I took to be such a thing, something between a chirp and a giggle.

"I have been told that the Egyptians are mad about pink flesh, hence the pimp at Port Said who offered his little daughter, crying 'all pink inside like English lady'." It was a very old joke, but he had not heard it, and it threw him into a silent convulsion of decorous laughter; tears poured out of him. He mopped them with the sleeve of his coat. But we had put our foot in it. We realised this when we caught a glimpse of our fellow-scribe's face – the face of poor Khanna the Copt. He was crimson with anguish and evidently deeply shocked. Baladi did a wonderful toad-swallowing act as he saw this, and his laughter abated somewhat, subsiding away into sighs touched with contrition, though from time to time a small seismic convulsion seized him midriff, and at the thought of the jest he hid his face for the space of a second in his sleeve. I thought the best way to atone was to go all silent, speechless and industrious for a full quarter of an hour, in order to let the dust settle. Outside on the green lawns the sun shone, the sprinklers played, turning and turning their slim necks like sunflowers. Somewhere in the palace the telephones rustled – their bells had been gagged, for their sound was judged indecorous. I pondered the war news in the *Egyptian Gazette* and allowed England a slight ache of nostalgia; but secretly my heart turned to the Pole Star of Provence – a Provence now forever peopled by Felix, Constance, Hilary, the vanished friends of that last summer of peace. Where might they all be now? Dead for all I knew. And the most painful evocation of all, that of Livia. Last heard of in Germany – the girl I had insisted on marrying, like a fool.

When Khanna withdrew to soothe his ruffled feelings and relieve himself in the ornate lavatory by the reception hall, Baladi jerked a thumb at his retreating back and whispered, "I think we pipped him rather." I agreed solemnly.

"If you are free on Saturday night," said Baladi, with the air of wanting to compensate me for my sparkling conversation, "I will ask you to accompany me to a house of joy for a little spree." I accepted, but faint-heartedly, for I had just drifted into an affair with a young officer of the Field Transport Corps, a volunteer unit of rather over-bred girls which supplied the army with drivers, secretaries and field-messengers. One of these had taken a fancy to me and invited me to dinner at their mess. Anne Farnol, a Slade student, was a girl of about twenty-eight with brilliant blue eyes which kindled with bright intelligence and sympathy at the slightest excuse. She was unusual among the rather frigid dollies of her unit, for she exuded warmth and femininity which sorted ill with her martial attire. Yet when she sprang to attention and saluted before my desk the gesture had great charm. She brought the Embassy despatch-case which contained Red Cross minutes of which I took possession on behalf of my liege lord the Prince. For a moment, while I sorted the papers out, she accepted my invitation to sit down and smoke half a cigarette, which I cut for her with the office scissors. This pleasant little ritual and the idle, friendly conversation which accompanied it had become a feature of my existence on Mondays and Fridays. I had warmed under the smiling gaze of this military young woman who wore her small lifeboat hat (these were, I afterwards discovered, known as cunt-caps among the girls themselves) and smoked her ration of tobacco, though she always refused coffee.

So the invitation to dinner fell naturally into place; and one evening I found myself in front of a smart apartment block of buildings in the Sharia El Nil, negotiating a lift which took me to the fourth floor where her small apartment was. The door was ajar and there was a note on it to say that she had just slipped out for a moment, but that I was to make myself at home and await her, which is what I did. I spied upon her in her absence, examining the poor meagre treasures around which she had woven her new nomadic life – postcards of Hastings, a family group, father and mother and then a handsome young man with hurt eyes clad in a sculptor's smock. He held a mallet. The husband, I supposed, for she wore a ring on her marriage finger. A sudden sadness, inexplicable really, came over me. I riffled

her sketchbooks. The room was deep in the scent of flowers –
where else do flowers smell like they do in Egypt, as if they had
just passed through the Underworld and across the breath of
an open oven?

I sat for a while so, smoking and reflecting, upon her
balcony above the buzzing thoroughfare beneath. She was
beautiful and self-possessed and I desired her, yes; but my
infernal English upbringing stood in the way of any enterprise
which might bring about a fitting conclusion to this chance
meeting of exiles so far away from the beleaguered island. She
came at last, looking somewhat pale I thought; she had been
back to the mess to draw her ration of whisky in my honour. I
was ashamed, for with what the Prince was paying me I could
have brought her a case of the stuff. I made a mental note to
have one sent. She was as sensible as she was beautiful, and
thanks to her my stupid diffidence which so often gives the
impression of sulkiness, was thawed out, and I began to tell her
a little about my life and ask her questions about hers. As a
married officer she was entitled to a flat of her own, while the
other girls of the unit, or those not in her position, had to be
content to live in a sort of Y.M.C.A. with strict hours and
visiting rules. It was quite late when I rose in awkward
desperation and made a gesture to simulate departure. I walked
out on to the cool balcony; the night all round was deep, furry
and dark, while directly below us the street blazed with light.
We stood there in the darkness looking down, like gargoyles
on the leads of some medieval church – just two heads sculpted
in darkness. I had at last the courage to say, "I would like to
stay with you," and she put her hand on my arm, saying, "I
hoped you would – I am so homesick, I sleep badly and this
town makes me restless."

With the lights turned off, the flat became a dark burrow
lit at one end by the theatrical flaring light of the street. We
made love suddenly, precipitately, with a sort of involuntary

desperation. She was still in uniform, I felt the cold buttons of her tunic on my flesh. It was terribly exciting – so much so that she began to weep a little bit, which increased my lust for her. Afterwards we lay side by side on the bed in the darkness and I could feel the steady drumming of her heart and the little shudders of pleasure slowly diminishing. I lit a match to look deeply into those steady blue eyes, which stared at me through their unnecessary tears. "It is the first time I have made love to an officer on active service; it's wildly exciting to do it in your uniform. Let's repeat it." But she was already slid from her clothes and lay naked in my arms, smelling gorgeously of some Cairo perfume and our own delightful rankness. Our kisses grew steady, we composed and aimed them with more love, more direction, less haphazardly. All night we lay in each other's arms, too excited to sleep more than fitfully, in short snatches. And we talked in whispers, sometimes falling back into sleep in mid-phrase.

The next day I watched the dawn come up over the desert from her balcony while she lay buried in the heaped bedclothes in an abandon of quiet sleep. The night had brought us both a wonderful animal happiness and a new calm. I felt a disposition to sing as I put the kettle on in the tiny kitchen and prepared the table for an early breakfast, for we both had offices to attend before the heat of the day declared itself. In her tousled, sleepy awakening she looked divinely beautiful and vulnerable. Yawning, she joined me and let me help her to coffee. "Strange what contentment," she said, shaking her head, "and yet nothing we do has any future, any meaning. Everything has become sort of provisional and fragile. I mean, next week I may be dead or posted. So may you – no, I forgot, you are not really in the war as yet, so you can't feel the strange posthumous feeling about things. Does it matter what one does? It has no future, no substance."

"If you go on philosophising at me like this, so early in

the morning, I shall quote Valéry to you."

"What did he say?"

"*Elle pense, donc je fuis.*"

"Unfair to my sex."

"Sorry."

A wonderful feeling of physical well-being possessed me; I had not realised that, despite my present colourful and delightful activities, I could be a little lonely – simply for lack of the sort of company which I would, for preference, keep. I hoped that this bond would continue and strengthen, despite the threat to it posed by the chance of postings to other war theatres, like, for example, Syria. I had, in my optimism, even ventured to sketch in a few possibilities as to our spare time. I knew that my hosts (I could not bring myself to think of them as employers, so kind and familiar were they) would be delighted if I were to discover a personable English girl to visit museums with, or make desert excursions with. . . . It seemed that fate had put a lucky experience in my way, perhaps to make me forget the harvest of bitter memories I nursed of Livia and the Provençal summer she had virtually ruined by her behaviour – that of an *allumeuse*, to put the matter plainly. Now she had diminished in size, so to speak, though not in poignance; but this new experience might help me to qualify the pain of the old. Perhaps I was too forthcoming, for my companion did not respond to my suggestion with anything like my own exuberance; indeed, there was something rather lame about her responses, though she agreed in principle, and even allowed me to suggest taking tickets for a recital of native music.

Two mornings later at my desk I awaited her arrival. I had already halved the statutory cigarette which she accepted. But no Anne manifested herself. After quite a longish interval another girl appeared – indeed, Anne's commanding officer – and it was she who bore the despatch-case. Placing it on the desk before me she said, "I suppose you have heard about Anne?" I looked blank, as who might not, and shook my head. The girl drew up a chair and sat facing me across the desk as she said, "It's been a bit of a shock to us all. She's dead. She was discovered on Thursday morning."

"But I went to dinner with her."

"I know you did; she told me where she could be reached if need be."

"Was it an accident?"

"No. Suicide."

She had taken the big estate car which formed part of the unit's car-pool, tanked it up fully, and then parked it in front of the garage, as if to await a duty call. There was nothing suspect in such a gesture; their work often fell at irregular times, irregular hours – they were, after all, on active service. But after dinner, when the mechanics went home and the Arab watchmen locked up, she borrowed the keys of the night watchman and sent him home. Then she drove the car into the garage, and into the hangar where cars were washed – it was practically hermetic when the sliding doors were shut. Indeed, when they were you could not tell there was a car inside at all. She locked the garage from the inside, turned out all the lights, and started the engine of the big duty car. In the morning of course she was found dead in the driver's seat, a death by carbon monoxide poisoning. "She left no messages for anyone. I have the unpleasant task of writing to her mother, who lives in Hampshire."

"But why on earth?" I exclaimed in an outburst of chagrin. It is absurd, but I have noticed that one often does this – it seems such a personal affront! "She seemed so well and so happy." The commanding officer eyed me for a moment and then said, "She said nothing to you, then? When she came to the mess to fetch that bottle there was a service signal for her saying that her husband had been lost at sea. He was in minesweepers apparently. She just put it in her bag and went off to join you for the evening. Nobody but I saw the signal. I think it's the reason why for the suicide at such short notice. What do you think?"

I could think nothing. I was speechless, in a daze.

To have appeared and disappeared with such startling suddenness . . . I felt absolutely bereft, not only deprived of her warm physical presence but also of the future of meetings which might have been in store for us. It was as if she had over-turned the desk at which I was working. If my business associates found me distracted and thoughtful that day they did not remark on the fact. I felt completely dumbfounded. And it was with an effort that I picked up the threads of my daily life in the city. Fortunately there was plenty of work to do; indeed my sleeve was being plucked at almost half-minute intervals, so that I could at least use the excuse of my duties to occupy my attention. I thought the image of the girl would fade quite soon, for I knew so little about her; but on the contrary she continued to exist in memory with a remarkable clarity of outline and focus. She was like a statue in a niche, corresponding to nothing else, cut off from space and time, yet quite complete and separate. Anne Farnol! The modest name vibrated on in my memory for whole months which succeeded her disappearance from the scene, from the war, from time.

The war! The Prince was much preoccupied during this period with the economic affairs of his own country as well as those which menaced the structure of European affairs. The Red Cross, which at first seemed to me to be a time-wasting repre-sentational job, proved on the contrary a most valuable source of information, a veritable port-hole open upon the new Nazi Europe; moreover, it was based in Geneva, and the traditional neutrality of the Swiss had not been violated. Nominally at least the Germans were still signatories to the Red Cross convention, and the servants of the organisation still enjoyed a quasi-diplomatic status which was everywhere accepted. I was surprised to hear the Prince announce one day that he proposed to visit France one day soon, when "things had settled down a bit". And suddenly my own world, the lost world of friendships and youthful happiness which I had interred in the fastness of my memory, returned vividly to me in the form of a letter addressed to me which tumbled out of the scarlet despatch-box one day. It was from Constance. From *Constance*! I could hardly believe my eyes as I gazed upon that familiar handwriting, which I had never truthfully expected to see again. In a flash the whole vanished reality of things reasserted itself; I was deluged by memories. It was only a short note, a "trial" note as she put it, in order to see if she could locate me through the Prince. She knew of his Red Cross connection, and the postal link through Turkey was still holding. But there was something more important she had to tell me, and that was that Sam had been posted to the Middle East and would soon be here, if indeed he had not yet arrived on the scene. I sprang up from my chair, almost as if he stood already at my elbow. Sam! It was fantastic news; for he must certainly know how to go about finding me. The very telephone directory would have the Prince's number listed.

"Tell him from me what a sod I think him, for you know he has never written at length; he hates writing like you all do. The last thing was a picture postcard of a fat woman from Worthing on the back of which he had scribbled:

> The weather here is mild and balmy.
> I'm awfully glad I joined the army.

"Just wait till I get my hands on him. I will prove Hilary's contention that marriage is a martial art. O Sam, you low-down swine, hiding your laziness behind the pretence of security regulations!"

I carried the letter about like a talisman, excited beyond measure by this sudden rekindling of the past; my loneliness had burst into a blaze, so to speak, and I was moved as well, for she had also mentioned me with affection. "You down there, alone in silence like a rising moon, building up your poems out of selected reticences, please, *please* write!" I did better, I sent the Red Cross a deft telex to be transmitted to her with a few scriptural passages signalled by references, all of which ran to a decent-sized letter; the superficial impression created was of a confidential letter on Red Cross matters coded out thus in quotations from the Bible. But the important thing was to spark the contact, and indeed within a week or two a bundle of letters for Sam arrived on my desk through these semi-diplomatic channels. It remained for Sam himself to manifest, and when he did I was surprised to learn that he had been in this theatre for some little time. Indeed, the bronzed young officer who one day sprang to attention and saluted as he stood in the doorway of the Red Cross office was clad in full fig as a Desert Rat, bush-shirt, suede ankle boots and all. He announced himself as "Captain Standish of the Bluebell Girls". We hugged each other like Turkish delight, with tears in our eyes, so deeply did we feel the fatefulness of the meeting. "How marvellous to find you sitting here quite unaltered, old gloom-bag Aubrey, with your eternal notebook and slyboots expression; it restores my faith in nature, if not in the army, which got me out here so safely. And all to meet you again. O, let's start a quarrel about something trivial shall we? Just to celebrate? You and your old Zen Cohens" – this was his version of *koan*. "The only *koan* I've learned is the British army one – shit or bust. It's terse and to the point."

"What!" I cried. "I must not forget!" And opening my safe I took out the treasure trove of her letters and placed them before him on the desk in a triumphant fashion. "Good God," he said fervently, and it seemed to me that his face fell a trifle. He looked sort of abashed – perhaps with guilt for not having written to her. He stood and looked at them, but did not fall upon them as I would have done had I been in his place.

He took them up awkwardly and instead tapped the package softly on the knuckles of his left hand as he talked. Perhaps he wanted to be alone to read them? Of course, that was it! I dismissed the matter from my mind. "I didn't come before," he said, "I wanted to wait for some *real* leave – like this, a whole week. Besides, I was posted off to Greece briefly with some odds and sods of units and guess where I have just come back from – you'll never. *Thermopylae!* The Hot Gates themselves. I was visiting fireman to the New Zealanders. Then back here. And at your service. Now can you put me up, or shall I go to Dirty Dick's?"

The palatial dispositions set this doubt at ease for I occupied a veritable apartment with several separate but inter-connecting bedrooms, and one of these was made ready for my guest, who sang and whistled joyfully in the shower, picked fleas out of his vest which were, so he said, ancient Greek fleas, and borrowing some civvies from me sent all his own clothes to the cleaners of the palace. They would all be back at dusk, spotlessly cleaned and ironed. Such was the luxury in which I lived. It created, he said, misgiving about my writings – the worst thing for a writer, he had been told, was soft living. "This way you'll never succumb to absinthe or syphilis or something, which I gather is absolutely necessary to meet the case." I shook my head. "On the contrary, every vice is open to me, and every drug from hashish to scarlet cummerbunds – which, by the way, I have been talked into wearing with my white dinner jacket. Promise not to laugh if we dine with the Prince – he will be delighted to see you again, and the Princess equally to meet you."

He agreed somewhat sombrely, anticipating perhaps a social evening, but was relieved when we dined alone with the couple in the vast echoing dining-room. He had supposed that we should have to be tactful about the Prince's rather questionable behaviour when he was in Provence, but to our surprise we found that the Princess seemed to be fully informed of his various "sprees", and completely understanding about them. One realised her great strength in this, and also the reason for their marvellous attachment. It was really a marriage, not an artifact. We drank, in our excitement, rather too much champagne and elected to go to bed at a decently early hour, to lie in adjacent bedrooms with the doors open, talking sleepily far into the night about everything under the sun. I noticed that Constance's letters lay unopened upon the mantelpiece and speculated vaguely as to why they had stayed that way so long. Perhaps he was shy about being unable to answer them as they deserved? He had always accused himself of being tongue-tied and paralysed by shyness. But now they were married. . . . I found the matter something of a puzzle, but I was not disposed to probe for mysteries which might not be there. In due course we would speak of her.

In due course we did; I woke well after midnight to see my friend standing naked on the moonlit terrace on which the full moon blazed, staring down into the garden, completely still. He must have heard me turn, or known in some way that I was awake, for he turned at last and crossed the brilliant terrace to stand at my window and talk to me as I lay there in the dark room. "The thing is this," he said, and I instantly divined that he was about to explain his reluctance to open his wife's letters. "I feel a complete traitor to Constance, to all she believes in, to all we both believed in. That is why I hesitate to open her letters. You see, Aubrey, I don't hate the war at all, I like it; and it's marvellous to have a good moral excuse to wage it. Our war against the Hun is just, and we must win it. Of course some wars can be bad, but some have been of the greatest use to the human race, like the Persian War fought by the old Greeks. You simply do not know what an engagement is like, going into battle. Your blood freezes, your heart trembles to its roots. I have had no experience comparable to it. Beside it, love-making is a charming adventure, nothing more. I know, what I am saying is horrible, but it's the truth. Adventure, I was born and trained for it; I know it now. And if I survive this lot of thunder I shall join the army for life!" He stood quite still now, with hanging head, as if abashed and waiting for the reproof which these sentiments must certainly evoke. I did not know what to say. I was disgusted beyond measure at such glib propositions. "I know what you will say and think; but I am only describing what I see. The lack of individual responsibility is so wonderful – it enables the whole race to act from its functional roots, in complete obedience. Hardship and danger are splendid medicines for softness. And the girls are available now in a way they never were. They smell the fox, smell the blood like packhounds. They are so happy that you should be torn from their arms and flung into the pit – still alive, so to speak. It's like being a baby torn from its mother's arms. What kisses we are reaping! How can I explain all that to Constance? I shall come back to her changed in quite unforeseen ways, but without the power to describe it all, and feeling a traitorous shit – which of course I am now from your point of view." I groped my bedside table and found my cigarettes. We both lit up and started smoking furiously, deep in thought, like two mathematicians beating their brains out upon a problem in physics. "How can I tell her that?" he went on. "All that I have seen would seem to justify what she feels about war, what you feel about it. I have seen some horrid things, things which freeze your mind. But this desert war is marvellous – you engage, and if you lose the toss you fall back forty miles and re-form. Glorious! I have seen some fearful accidents on all sides, some suicides. I saw a bayonet charge by the Essex which was of such scrupulous malevolence that I couldn't believe I belonged to the same race as them. I have seen chunks, whole arms and ankles literally flying off a column being machine-gunned at low level by a fighter. They fire slugs the thickness of a child's wrist in sharp bursts like a spray. They use up the oxygen by their speed and leave you gasping in the middle of a litter of human spare parts. It's horrible, it's wrong . . . what can I say? I wouldn't have missed it for anything. O Aubrey, say something!"

But I was dumbfounded, thunderstruck. I was also rather shamefaced at having been caught out in a moral dilemma which I had never resolved; perhaps the slick moral judgment was mine, and mine the condemnation? Inevitably, and without quite meaning to, I found myself becoming sententious. "My experience has been limited so far as a non-combatant," I said. "And surely humanity's mishaps suffice – do we have to add to them by wars? Last week I was asked to go down to Port Said and read for a weekend to some remnants of the Australian Div. There were about two hundred young men, all cases of blindness. They were waiting in transit to be repatriated. It was terrible to see their white, shocked faces and fluttering eyelids, and their panic, for they were new to this world of blindness. I felt sort of ashamed, as if I had no clothes on. I read to them from *The Bible Designed to be Read as Literature*, etc., etc., the gospel according to Gollancz. It was a strange experience to hear the 16th psalm in the atmosphere of the first-class saloon of a cruise-liner. Instead of looking down as one does when poetry is read or music played, they raised their faces like chickens, as if the words were pouring down on them from a cloud. I was glad to beat a retreat after an hour. Despite the profuseness of the education officer's thanks I gathered that my 'pommy accent' offended some and spoiled the experience for most."

While I talked he had put the light on in his room and unearthed a decanter of whisky; we had a drink there in the theatrical moonlight of the Egyptian night.

"There's one thing I want to ask – a favour," he said at last. "I took the liberty of putting your name on my blood-sheet, you know, the next-of-kin sheet we all have to fill in."

"But why?" I said.

"Well, just in case I get stopped in my tracks by something, I would like to feel that it was you who would break it to Constance; you would be able to explain it better than anyone and offer what consolation one can in such circumstances. I felt it sort of kept the good tension of the last summer in Provence – as was appropriate. Is it all right with you? Unless you don't want the responsibility of announcing the dismal fact of my departure for the land of shades . . ."

"Of course not," I said, getting back into bed and switching off the light. "Let's catch a glimpse of sleep before the sun comes up."

"Done," he said with an enormous healthy yawn. "Done!"

Turning and tossing restlessly, eager to achieve sleep before the dawn with its first mosquito rendered it almost impossible, I heard him muttering on, pursuing the same line of thought which had caused us such an amazing exchange of confidences.

"It's awful how we all want in one way or another a certificate for glory," he said sadly, and groaning, fell asleep.

He was up well before me, and was sitting on the terrace reading his correspondence with affectionate attention – our talk had dispersed his doubts and fears. Somewhere a soft breakfast gong sounded and I groaned my way to the shower.

"Awake at last," he cried, with a revival of his usual high spirits. "I saw you lying there, dauntless as a sausage, snoring your head off, and I could not help but appreciate your contribution to the war effort. It sounded like distant gun-fire."

The Prince was up and in a somewhat testy mood, unlike his usual lark-like good humour. He was reading the war news in the columns of *Al Ahram* and shaking his head over the non-committal communiqués issued by the staff. It was one of those rare periods of stalemate where nothing particular was happening. But it was not of this that he wished to speak. "I sometimes wonder," he told us, "if the British really want to win or not; they behave in such an extraordinary way. You know about our agent? Well, we have a Nazi agent living in the summer-house at the bottom of the garden; the gardeners found him and he offered them money to leave him alone. Can you imagine – a German archaeologist who speaks perfect Arabic? As you may well imagine, I rushed to the Consulate and told them, expecting they would send someone to sweep him up and shoot him. Not a bit of it. That detestable and supercilious Brigadier Maskelyne said, 'We make a point of never disturbing a nesting agent.' And now they are even proposing to supply him with equipment. Is *this* war, I ask myself? If all the agents are going to be left alone and even kept supplied . . ." He did not appear to imagine that it would be very much worth our while to try and infiltrate German or Italian Intelligence, and as he was almost hopping with irritation it was wiser to leave him in ignorance of the facts of life.

The conversation turned upon the few days of relaxation he had immediately accorded me with the appearance of my friend; no effort must be spared to make Sam's leave as agree-able as possible. A marvellous series of alternatives was proposed – excursions to the four corners of Egypt, visits to countless ancient sites. Only time was the enemy, circum-scribing this little holiday. "Nevertheless," cried the Prince with energy and determination, "between the lot of us we shall certainly see that he has a good time." His vague gesture took in not only his wife and palace staff but also the various secretaries and his friend Affad.

Indeed, the banker Affad was the most charming, diffident and resourceful of the Prince's associates, presenting himself as an eager host, and his invitation was made the more tempting by the fact that he was about to set off on a journey by water – a Nile journey: moreover, in a well-appointed little ship belonging to the French Embassy. We hardly realised the magnitude of our luck until we had been two whole days aboard this pretty pirogue travelling up-Nile, a water world which is like no other. It was all too brief, for halfway up to the nearest big town we were to be dropped in order to return to Cairo by car, since my friend must not overstay his leave, or even risk such an eventuality, while this return would enable him to enjoy a little of the company of the Prince and Princess to whom he had taken a great fancy. But this little journey proved delightful as a sort of extension of our untroubled Provençal summer – the links formed there still held. Indeed they seemed almost forged anew, so ever-present seemed Constance and Hilary her brother, seemed Felix Chatto the consul . . . seemed even in ghostly form the dark shade of Livia. Where would she be, I wondered? And Avignon with its looming skyline against the blue sky – the cathedrals which Hilary had always referred to as "disused prayer factories, with no noise of bumble like turbines coming from them". The thrilling swish of mistral in the pines. It was all these, it was all here.

More piquant still was the fact that Affad's other two guests proved to be a French couple, of meridional persuasion; "*les ogres*" they were christened, for their family name was LeNogre. They were brother and sister, twins to the hour, inseparable – Bruno and Sylvaine by name. The boy was a young attaché in the Free French Embassy; his sister kept house and entertained for him. They owned, or so he said in his calm, studied English, an old derelict chateau in the village of

Villefoin, not very far from Tubain where "our" chateau, the house of Constance, was situated. Why, they had been there that summer – we could all have met! There was a gleam of sorrow in the dark eye of Sylvaine as she stated the fact. The expression on her face, the shape of her features, her way of holding her head, reminded me most acutely of someone, though I could not for the life of me think whom. The thought was troubling, like the attentions of a fly one could not brush away; but my obstinate memory refused to yield up the key to those dark features. Her brother was deeply preoccupied and ashamed of the way France had fallen, and of these base chicaneries of the French Mediterranean fleet which refused to join the Allies. However, the Free French movement was now a fact, and within the year De Gaulle would have twenty thousand Frenchmen in the field under his leadership . . . so that all was not lost. Yet it was touching to see so young a man wounded in his national honour by the collapse of his country and its wholehearted espousal of a Nazi peace. But, he added ruefully, "I am surprised at the strength of my own feelings – I did not know I had any. I am just the average French intellectual, and you know how cynical they are!" Sam reassured him in his tactful way by saying that something very similar had come about in England. "I was very much criticised for joining up," he added, with a side-glance at me, "as Aubrey will tell you." All of this was true; we had all been living in a fool's paradise. It has taken Hitler to blow off the tent top and show us what a circus the political world really was.

These young people were hospitality itself, and soon the large centre cabin with its enormous table and hanging petrol lantern was well and truly taken over – our belongings were disposed upon and around the bunks which lined the walls. The big central table with its sanded benches was where we sat and ate or played cards, or spread out our maps and writing materials. We were staying with them too briefly to have accumulated much luggage, for they were planning a trip of some two weeks and were very well equipped with everything in the way of tinned food and ammunition for their sporting guns. But the mood was so tranquil, the coilings of the great river so suave and dense with beautiful islands and groves, that we quite forgot that the pastures which bordered it were thick with quail and turtle-dove. While we were with them there was no shooting by common consent. That would begin, said Affad, when they arrived in the true north, the crocodile reaches. One ached to be going with them. Not the less because their visit to upper Egypt was to end with a ride out to a distant oasis where a famous country fair was to be held, and where a clairvoyant of renown was to be encountered who would tell their fortunes. "I don't mind about the fortune-teller," said Sam, "but the oasis sounds everything one has read about. What a damned shame." But the two "*ogres*" professed not to be unduly superstitious and would, they said, be delighted to offer themselves to the fortune-teller as subjects.

We dined that night by lantern light, while high overhead the night sky spread its carpet of brilliant stars and a frail new moon shone. It was quite chilly on the water and the freshets of evening wind rapped upon our prow as we drew into shore to anchor for the evening meal. Our consciousness had already been lulled and subdued by the thump of bare feet upon the wooden deck and the quavering, trailing songs of the watermen as they guided us southwards. The river opened and closed like a fan – suddenly enlarging its confines into whole estuaries or small lakes, only to fold back into its own narrow bed for a space. Kites hung in the higher airs, keeping up their steady relentless patrol, but all along the banks we met brilliant rollers and kingfishers, and the little rock-doves of the desert fringe with their plaintive small cry: "Too few," they seemed to say, "too few."

The ever-changing light all round expanded and contracted solid outlines and distances so that the eyes, travelling in pursuit, were mesmerised by the apparent make-believe. "Lord bless you," exclaimed Sam, inappropriately crossing himself and repeating the Latin grace in use at his Oxford college. "You couldn't describe it to anyone because you can hardly believe it yourself."

Palms and tombs, tombs and waterwheels and palms. Islands rising and subsiding in the mist. A river which flowed like smoke between the two deserts in a luxuriant green bed full of paradisiacal plants and trees. "No wonder dervishes dance," Sam went on, and Affad smiled his approval. "Who wouldn't?" But with the rising light came also the glare and the parching heat, so that at midday the sky weighed a ton. "Tell me what surprised you most about Egypt," said Affad curiously; he was genuinely curious and not merely in search of compliments. To have replied, "O everything" would have been at once too easy and not sufficiently exact; for my part what had assailed me was an extraordinary sense of familiarity. To throw open one's shutters at Mena House and find oneself with, so to speak, a personal Sphinx squatting outside one's window, patient as a camel . . . They seemed great playful toys, the Sphinxes, and despite the complete mystery which surrounded their history and meaning, curiously warm and familiar – domesticated animals, like the water-buffalo or the camel. And then of course the desert itself had been a complete surprise. One came upon it, came to the edge of the carpet of human plantation and there it was like a great theatrical personage, waiting serenely. It was at once a solitude and also homely as a back-garden. But as much an entity as the Atlantic; one could not just walk into it for a stroll, for its shapes were always changing; at the least wind all contours changed, and one's tracks were expunged at a breath. No more could one decide to go for a row in the Atlantic without misgivings. The desert was a metaphor for everything huge and dangerous, yet without so seeming. Parts were slick as a powdered wig, parts shallow with pretty coloured rocks and clays, striated with the marks of vanished caravans; parts were like a burnt-out old colander full of dead cinders. Rosy winds sighed about it at dawn, or when the desert wind called *khamseen* set upon it, pillars of rusty blood-coloured wind raced as spume races ahead of the waves in an Atlantic storm. But riding across it one found certain animals quite at home, oriented and self-possessed; the rat, the *jerboa*, a kind of jack rabbit – how did they manage it when there was no cover at all save scrub? Packs of wild dogs wandered about with the air of living off the land – but what could they find to eat? Heavy dews at dawn and at midnight provided moisture of a kind for insects like mantises and locusts. But dogs? The desert offered a different sort of providence; its terrible frugality engendered introspection and compassion. God!

Some of this I managed to say and Affad listened keenly, with interest. The desert fringed our present skyline, but here we were gliding upon the glazed reaches of the Nile which offered the contrasts of cool surface wind and sparkling water, not to mention the gorgeous panorama of river-craft with its thousand eye-coaxing sails of different hues. Here the felucca came into her own, dominating, like some great queen of antiquity, the river upon which she had been built to travel. The beauty of function, the elegance of purity and stress. No one could see a felucca and not feel it to be a symbol expressing the unconscious essence of womanhood. But feluccas have no need to be fashion-conscious. The way they press their cheeks to the river wind is as invariable as the wind itself, which imposes on them a formal geometrical precision of trajectory. They run down river upon a few sweet angles of inclination – and they surprise one with the feeling that they are among man's choicest and rarest creations, which indeed they are. Their field of action is limited and more exacting than ocean navigation. The Nile flows directly down out of the heart of

Africa into ancient Greek history – like the spine of a cobra. Its feluccas are controlled by the river winds which arrive and depart like soft-footed servants whose work is dedicated to these swallow-cut, pouting lateen rigs. A shivering goes through them like an electric current all day long, and they slide down river as if on a cord, then abruptly come to a halt and everything is becalmed, frozen in the middle of a tactic; the feluccas bow their heads as if the wind when it comes will behead them. Instead the glass floor starts rolling again, and quietly they turn to left or right to resume their journey. Here and there you might encounter one ferrying sugar-cane and wearing an eye like some apt Aegean echo; but the eye will be an Egyptian eye – the eye of the camel, in fact, with its double set of eyelashes. One will recognise the ship as a Greek vessel manned from the Greek colony at Edfu. The whole of Herodotus gazes out of that kohl-traced eye!

The people of the river too are special and apart, different from the mundane and banausic town Egyptians. On the banks they superintend the criss-crossing water-channels and tend their dates and their vegetables, but always with time for a salute and a hoarse cry of welcome which invites the wayfarer to sit and sup with them. The women strike one more than the men – their magnificent carriage upon the treacherous river banks. They are black-avised as warlocks and wear their black cowls with formality and disdain. But their smile, fuller of ivory than a male elephant in rut, flashes out of toil-worn faces packed with all the majesty of hunger. They glide along like the unconscious patricians which they are, and their bear-like, gloating walk seems to draw its rhythm from the pace of the Nile's green blood, flowing steadily from some distant wound in the heart of Africa.

"For me," said Bruno, "it was chiefly the tombs, dug so deep into the ground, and yet so snug. I have never seen anything comparable to the tiny kings lying there in their painted

cocoons surrounded by their toys, as if the world of childhood
also passed with them through the barrier of death. But what
am I saying—'barrier'? I was struck by the facts of that
marvellous workmanship, all those frescoes so brilliant in their
colouring, were to lie there unobserved by human eyes
through the centuries. The little kings and queens with their
toys, slowly drying out in their awkward sarcophagoi (the
word means flesh-devourer in Greek, no?); their attitude to
death was quite different from ours, or indeed from their contemporaries the Greeks' with their asphodel-splashed underworld expressing all the sincere and open regret which the
thought of death brought. They had no impassivity about
death—it was terrible and sad and uprooting, and the end of
every happiness. They refused to allow themselves any
factitious consolation. And yet they were also naive, they felt
if they wailed enough, made enough noise they might make
death relent. But the Egyptian? This massive, slumbering,
vegetal life of silence and vacancy, strapped into one's swadd-
ling clothes, the mummy wrappings . . . Then I realised that the
word eternity really meant something to them—an eternal
waiting—but for what they did not know. Time existed forever
in massive extension—to the very confines of the human
consciousness. It was frozen, their thoughts as well as their
tears were frozen by the sepulchre, but there was no repining
for death was real, and it existed like the next room exists while
we are talking in this one. I got a shock off these strange little
mummies, planted like vegetables in the shaly valleys. Even to
sit beside them in the tombs and hear one's own heart beating
was a strange experience. And the toys? Reaching out one
could actually touch their touch upon them, the touch of
children's fingers! But the quality of immobility, of waiting
without thought, without hope, without desire, is something
you can see in the peasants today as they wait for the sun to rise
or set, or for the station to open, for the first train to come. They

wait like inanimate objects, like sacks of grain, like chunks of marble. There is no buoyancy in them – just the enormous load of their waiting. One can read into their posture some of the immobility of the little kings in their brightly painted tombs. The word 'eternity' comes into the mind, the whole field of consciousness becomes one eternal waiting-room. Even the dust does not gain upon one in these bright tombs, for they are sealed and the little kings exist now in a tepid vacuum of eternity. They can get no older now, nor will they ever get any younger; but at least they have achieved a perpetual immobility, a perfection of non-being beyond moon or sun."

"How beautiful the women are!" cried Sylvaine. "They don't seem to fuss very much about the veil either."

"It's hard to work as they do and wear it."

"I hope they abolish it one day. What eyes!"

"What eyes!" echoed Sam and added, in garbled quotation, "She walks in beauty like the Nile." But it was an apt enough paraphrase for what one felt watching the women upon the banks, their tall frames moulded from the darkness of water and clay, brown as terracotta. In them you felt the great river with its sudden eddies and slow oozings, its lapses and languors. Yes, the river was her clock-time, she walked in time to river's green blood, the Nile-pulse which throbbed in that velvet smooth element. The warmth of these villagers was inspiriting, smiles of charcoal, ivory or magenta, sudden flashes from the turret of a veil; and then the hoarse, bronze laughter of the man, brazen heads laughing, bronze arms raised. All suddenly cut off by a bend in the river, decapitated: their voices drowned by the shrieking of waterwheels whose wooden squeak is the most characteristic sound of the Egyptian night.

The pilot smiles as he answers the wave of a whole village – but the smile passes like a breath over embers and then is gone, lost in his dark abstraction, his nilotic amnesia. Slowly the villages pass out of sight; night is falling, soft as a great moth. These big lumbering men and women have all the humbling dignity of dispossessed monarchs. They are paupers, ravaged by want and illness. The old stand about in attitudes of deafness, like so many King Lears. And yet their land is a paradise – nature's exuberance has gone wild. You see cork oaks ravaged by ants, honeysuckle climbing into palm trees, water-laved rock carved into the heads of elephants. But everything enjoying a seeming aloneness under that burning sky. Dusk to darkness to starlight. A fish jumps. Then another. Then a sudden shower of silver arrows. It is to be our last night aboard.

A faint river wind favours us, keeping the night insects at bay, so we are able to have our dinner by candleshine on deck – a smoky flapping light which we would soon extinguish in favour of a young rising moon. We grew sentimental and spoke of *après la guerre*. The French couple unhesitatingly expressed their intention of returning to Provence to spend the rest of their lives in the old tumbledown chateau of their ancestors. Bruno wanted to write a book about the Templars – apparently there was a mass of unpublished matter in the muniments room of the chateau.

"You will come too," he cried warmly. "I feel you will. I know you will. We will be happy living there with just each other for company!" I hardly dared to extend my wishes so far, though Sam seemed ready enough to promise so far ahead. I could not envisage any end to this war, and a deep sadness took possession of me. I thought of Anne Farnol and wondered how many like her would be forced to abdicate in the face of fate. Then, with a jolt, I "recognised" the face of Sylvaine; it is strange how small things stick. I had seen her for a while in the lunatic asylum of Montfavet near Avignon. I had been taken there by Lord Galen to visit a friend of his and I had glimpsed a dark girl, a patient, walking in the rose garden. So very like Sylvaine, the dark, bird-headed girl – they could have been twins as well. I told her this and she smiled and shook her head. "Not me," she said, "or me in another life – who can say?"

We had become such close friends now that it was quite a wrench to envisage this parting; just round the corner was the little town where tomorrow our car would wait to ferry us back to the capital where we were expected to dine with my Prince. Another small sadness too was that soon Sam would be going back to the front – and everyone knew that there was a big battle impending in the Western Desert. My heart turned over as I thought of Constance and watched her handsome, insouciant mate packing his kit bag.

On the morrow it was all goodbyes and regrets, unfeigned enough, for the whole voyage had been a miracle of comfort and delight. Yes, we would all meet again, we swore it. Then with a melancholy thoroughness we packed our affairs into the big camouflaged staff car which bore the Egyptian army crescent. The return journey was a whirlwind of dusk and clamour as we swept through the villages on the river bank, scattering livestock and villagers alike by the noise of our triple horns. There was some point in this speeding, for the capital was a good distance away – and indeed we only arrived at the palace with half an hour to spare before dinner. As my servant wound me into my cummerbund I heard Sam in the shower talking, half to himself and half to me: "So Constance doth make cowards of us all, eh? As a matter of fact I wrote her a long letter from Greece; but God knows if it will ever reach her through the army post office. Anyway, I feel the better for having talked to you. Will you write her about my visit? You have so many more nouns and verbs than I." I agreed to do this.

The servant brought in a parcel of clothes and started laying out a desert uniform with Egyptian army tabs. Sam watched this curiously, wondering what it could mean. "I have been created an honorary lieutenant in the Egyptian army for tomorrow. Apparently the picnic place is technically out of bounds except to troops." It was some time later over whiskies in the scarlet leather salon that the Prince himself added the details to this explanation, smoking a hashish-loaded cigarette in a long yellow holder.

"It has always been our favourite picnic place, an old Coptic monastery in ruins, Aby Fahym. Now since that corner of the desert has been cleared of the Italians I have asked H.Q. for permission to revisit it. You will see how pretty it is, though mostly knocked down. First the Italians took it, then the British kicked them out; then they came back, then were kicked out again. Each time they knocked a piece off it. There was one old monk who refused to move; he lived in the ruins, crawling about like a lizard. Both sides fed him, he became a sort of mascot. Finally he disappeared in the last British attack which took the place, and since then has never been seen. He will obviously become a legend in the Coptic Church; but meanwhile you will see how pretty it is."

Next morning we set off by car and motored to the desert fringe where we were met by horses and a string of camels: slower moving traffic, so to speak, but more adept when it came to carrying heavy baggage, tents and suchlike. Everyone was in high good spirits. The party had been joined by two young staff officers from the Military Mission, an Egyptian liaison officer and an R.A.M.C. doctor who seemed to be on good terms with the Prince and Princess and answered to the name of Major Drexel. He professed himself to be "swanning", very much as Sam himself was. The Princess with some hauteur refused the horses and camels which she described as "Bedouin folklore" and elected to lead us in her comfortable estate car with its special tyres. So we set off in a somewhat straggling party to complete the first part of the journey which was undertaken with circumspection, for the route led us first through a network of minefields until we hit the final wire with its command cars and straggling tanks on duty. Here we provided our permits and documents and were ushered into the desert as if into a drawing-room by a ceremonious staff officer who took the trouble, however, to compare map references with the liaison officer and insist that we went no further than the feature mentioned on our permit. "At least, we take no responsibility for you beyond that point."

The Prince puffed out his cheeks with a proud and disdainful expression. "There is no danger at all now," he said, "I have it on the best authority."

"Very well, sir," said the ruddy staff officer. "On you go, and a happy picnic to you."

A light wind sprang up, not enough to create sand, yet enough to cool the middle hours of the day. The light with its dancing violet heart outlined this strange primeval world of dunes and *wadis* through which we wound our way; quite soon, like a ship which clears the horizon, we would be moving by the studied navigation of the compass, or the stars. It gave one a strange feeling of freedom. Once a small arrowhead of planes passed overhead – so high as to look like a formation of wild geese, and far too high to let us read their markings. Sam rode with the Princess, and I on another horse with the Prince. The whole journey only took about an hour and a half. We came at last to a small oasis and a series of grey escarpments, forms of striated rock, which shouldered up into the sky. "Look!" someone cried as we rounded a shoulder of dune. We saw a small oasis and within a few hundred yards the Coptic monastery came into view. Aby Fahym must once have been very beautiful, though now it was rather knocked about; one had to decipher its turrets and crocketed belfries anew to rediscover its original shape and style. But almost any building in that strange, romantic site would have seemed compelling to the imagination. The two main granaries were joined by a high ramp in the form of a bridge. The Prince was highly delighted and gazed at the old place through his glasses, exclaiming, "Well, it's still there, the old Bridge of Sighs. They haven't knocked it down after all." He superintended the setting up of a shady marquee with childish pleasure, even going so far as to knock in a tent peg or two himself with a wooden mallet, until a shocked servant snatched it from his royal hand and reproached him in guttural Arabic.

Carpets were spread, divans appeared, as also the latest creation from Italy, a portable frigidaire which held countless bowls of sorbet and iced lemon tea. We were all thirsty and did justice to this initiative, seated in a wide semi-circle around the Prince. The conversation had turned to politics so that, excusing ourselves in a whisper, Sam and I set out to trudge up to the monastery. "We might put up the missing monk, eh?" said my friend with boyish elation. "There may be cisterns or cellars below ground – there's little enough cover above," I replied. We had both had a good look at the place with the Prince's binoculars. On a ridge quite close to the monastery I had seen some red markers planted in the sand and wondered if somebody was surveying the place – I thought them to be for theodolites, perhaps. Somewhere to the right, upon a profile of sand dune and sky, moved a line of light tanks and command cars engaged on some obscure military manoeuvre. We turned back once or twice to wave to the colourful party in the oasis below. The camels were groaning and being bad-tempered. Then we addressed the last part of the slope and entered the baking gates of the little place. It had been built with a mixture of straw, brick and plaster which gave the walls, or what was left of them, a strange appearance of wattle-moulding in brown hide. But there was no sign of the monk, and no sign of any subterranean cellars where he might be hiding. Disappointed, we lingered a moment to smoke a cigarette, and then retraced our steps – or at least began to do so.

Then it happened – as suddenly and surprisingly as the

capsizing of a canoe. The suddenness was quite numbing, as well as the immediate lack of sound which gave the illusion of a whole minefield going up silently around us. A series of giant sniffs and a crackle of splinters followed a good way after the first seismic manifestation – the desert blown up around us in picturesque billows and plumes – a whole running chain of puffs, followed after a long and thoughtful pause by the bark of the mortars, for that is what they turned out to be. "Christ," shouted Sam, "they must be ranging." Another series of dry crackles followed by puffs seemed almost deliberate, as if to illustrate his remark. We began to run awkwardly, stooped, hands spread out like startled chickens. The red poles I had seen must have been ranging markers. We tried to set a course away from them, running sideways downhill now in the thick sand. Out of the corner of my eye I saw that the party in the oasis had also been alerted. There was a stir of alarmed recognition. They pointed at us as we ran stumbling downhill towards them, and the servants in a sudden access of solicitude started running towards us, as if to avert the danger from us. There was a tremendous burst now – it went off between my teeth, my whole skull echoed, my mind was blown inside out.

With scattered wits and panic fear we raced, Sam and I, along the side of the dune, in the hope of cover. But before we reached our objective we were overtaken by the whole solid weight of the desert. It was flung over us like a mattress. We collapsed like surfers overtaken by the rollers of the ocean, like ants overwhelmed by a landslide.

It seemed as if huge fragments of this shattered desert composure were blown about on all sides of me; my brain swelled and became full of darkness and sand. I felt my tongue swell up and turn black with heat, I felt it protrude. All this while falling sideways into space and vaguely hearing groans and whispers magnified on my right. Then thump – someone or something buried an axe in the middle of my back and the pain spread out from this centre of crisis until it reached the confines of my body, tingling in the fingertips like an electric current. I tried with all my might to rise to my feet but there was no traction to be had. My companion had fallen too, propelled skidding by the same sandspout as my own. And now in a lull came the crackle of shell splinters among the hot rocks, the sizzling spittle of the invisible guns.

From this point on everything becomes quite fragmentary, broken up descriptively like strips of cinema film, with just a frame here or there showing an image, indistinct and alarming. And even more alarming were the shattered fragments of conversation, or of voices calling. Guttural Arabic shouts and sobs – the servants in their devotion had shown great bravery. They reached us as we fell half rolling down the sandhills, in a welter of bloody smears which had begun to print themselves on the new khaki drill of our uniforms. I suppose we were picked up, joints all loose like rag dolls, and transferred bodily to the canvas tarpaulin which allowed Drexel to examine us, but only perfunctorily for the firing had become nearer at hand, and the whole party was retiring in the utmost confusion, leaving half their possessions behind in the oasis. In a moment of lucidity I heard the Princess say, "God! my veil is covered in blood." Sad and reproachful she sounded. And then Drexel saying, "Give me a chance; I want to examine them." And the Prince suddenly petulant says, "He is a doctor, after all." I was moved about moaning and thumped down on canvas; I heard the clean clicking of scissors and felt air where my clothes were being cut away from me. Then in a lower register a voice I could not identify said, "I think the other one's gone." There were groans of vexation and the curious whimpering noise of the servants – to echo the anxiety of their employers was a formality of good manners. They did not fear death as much as blood, black blood which oozed like the Nile, or spouted darkly from a severed artery, or inundated a whole section of the skin with wine-red smears. "There's a field dressing station by the wire," said Drexel. "We can clean them up a bit there; but for the rest . . . what can one do?"

"I shall never forgive myself," said the Prince in a low, hissing voice. "The whole thing is my fault."

A smatter of Arabic voices now took up the tale, cajoling, excusing, explaining, or so it seemed. The sun seemed to be playing upon my very eyeballs. The pain was one continuous even throb now, with its own anaesthesia – when it reached a certain degree of intensity one fainted away for a moment.

Now the shuffle of car wheels and the grinding of gears; we were heading back for the wire. Somebody suggested whisky and water but Drexel said, "Not with such bleeding please."

"I shall never forgive myself," said the Prince.

A sympathetic group of voices hovered like an overturned beehive at the wire. We were treated with kindness and despatch. The officer was disposed to crow over our mishaps, but the Prince bit his head off with a crisp, "That's enough. Can't you see we have two casualties? Where is the dressing station?"

Dust and whirring sand, and flies settling on blood in swarms. A needle, a drink of cold water, sleep.

I was not to know till later that Sam was dead.

Nor that the guns responsible for the accidental assault on us had been our own – Cypriot mule-borne mortars at target drill.

In the month-long agony of lying half insensible from shock – both the shock of my friend's death, and the post-operational shock from all the spinal excavations I had had to undergo in the "cleaning-up" process – much else had happened. Cade had appeared from nowhere, to my dismay and consternation. Thanks to the Prince he had succeeded in getting himself transferred to the Egyptian mission and appointed to me as a batman. It was intended as a kindly gesture on the part of my hosts. How could they have divined the depression and horror I felt to wake and find, sitting at the end of the bed, the yellow weasel of my mother's last days – her manservant and reader of the Bible, Cade? He sat there in expressionless silence, with an air of profound disapproval of everything – Egypt, the war, the Prince, my disposition – everything. It took less than nothing to start him off whining about the army, the Germans, the war, the peace, the weather. He wore his puritan life like a dead crow round his neck. Every day I was tempted to sack him, and yet . . . He was useful to me. He had once been a male nurse in an asylum and he knew how to wash and change me, and how to massage my splintered limbs. Also my eyes seemed to have been affected by my other tribulations, and I allowed him to read to me – the new correspondence which flowed out of Geneva: the letters of Constance, who by now was fully abreast of events, in possession of the truth. "So Constance doth make cowards of us all," I heard Sam's voice in my ear as Cade read her brave letters, so full of a contained hysteria, so free from bravura. "I am puzzled, for it has keeled me over: yet in a way it was to be expected. Aubrey, send me every scrap of detail, however horrible. I want to experience as deeply as possible this terrible yet perhaps most valuable experience. Did he speak of me, did he miss me? Why should he? He loved me, and was as free as a butterfly, his wings turned sunward. Here in the sleet and snow it all seems unreal – down there by the Nile. By the way, I thought for a long time your Sutcliffe was imaginary, but I find he is all too real. What could you have meant by that? I am treating his wife – standing in for a colleague on leave of absence. What a *ménage*! He asked to see me, I complied. He brought up the question of Freud's sofa without my prompting him and I knew he was 'your' Sutcliffe. I told him it had arrived safely.

We are friends now, close friends. He is a weird man. Strangely enough, the sort of man a woman could love. An old wart-hog with dandruff – so he says of himself. It has meant a lot just now, with Sam, having someone like this to talk to. Aubrey, please recover, please tell me all."

Cade folded the letter with distaste and looked at the wallpaper with a mulish expression devoid of emotion. I was tempted to sigh. "If foreigners did not exist the English would not know who to patronise," I said angrily, and I asked him to take a letter back to Constance. He seated himself at the desk with the portable typewriter before him, waiting, his pharaisical hatred of everything flowing out from him into the room in waves, in concentric circles. Horizontal, I drew a long breath and hesitated peevishly, for Constance had now made a coward of me: I simply could not tell her the truth. I would certainly report that he had died instantaneously with a bullet through the head. After all, what did she really want to hear? "His spine was shivered, his organs splattered with thorns of shrapnel, the works of his watch shot into his wrist? Nothing could stop the flow of blood, our blood. The car cushions were daubed, the canvas sheets on which we lay were smoking with flies. Rib-cage stove, thorax broken and bruised, ankles snapped like celery . . ." It was disgusting. Moreover, what was the point? Worst, it was selfish. It was not part of her loving, it was a medical therapy to test her professional composure. No, I could not tell her the truth.

Every day now the contrite Prince came to sit by my bed, for the most part with the Princess; but usually they separated these visitations. She came in the afternoon to have tea with me, he just before lunch to discuss any work problems which might have arisen in the morning, for we kept up the pretence that I was still in his employ, neither side wishing to let the relationship lapse.

For the rest, it was Cade who waited upon me now, who

dressed and fed me; why did I tolerate this man whom I found so detestable? His insolence – examining the fillings in his back teeth with the aid of my shaving mirror, doing his hair endlessly in the bathroom with my combs and brushes! Sometimes he did not answer when I spoke but just looked at me, his head on one side, with a benign contempt. But when I raised my voice his assurance wilted and he became a slave again, cringing though still loitering. Was it because he had witnessed the death of my mother? Or because it was to her that he had read the Bible every night? Nowadays he kept up the same practice, spectacles on the end of his nose. His lips moved as he read. ... He sat now before the machine, his head bowed, waiting. I simply could not bring myself to write to Constance through such an emissary. "That will be all, Cade," I said, much to his surprise. "I am beginning to ache. I'll record a letter later." He looked at me keenly for a moment and then got up, shrugged, and removed the typewriter. They had loaned me a little magnetic recorder, and this meant I could have my recording typed out in the Red Cross offices and so keep it from the prying eyes of Cade. "You can go now," I told him. "I am going to sleep for an hour."

The unhappy conventions of grave sickness – I had not known them before; you become a burden to those who nurse you. The dressings and the drugs and the tiptoe people only emphasise what you would be only too glad to forget – your utter helplessness. The world closes in, one affronts it from a lowly horizontal position; those who help you you come to hate. For me at this stage the future had vanished as inexorably as the past – even if the war lasted a century it would not modify my condition. And how ignominious to be put out of action by one's own side! Drexel came in sometimes in the afternoon to talk to me, and showed me the pictures he had taken on that fatal afternoon. The Bridge of Sighs, so-called, in the far distance, with Sam and me in the foreground turning to wave –

within a minute of being blown up! I was glad of his presence, for he could examine and talk about my wound; Cade had simply held up a doubled fist and said, "You got an 'ole this size in your spine, sir." Drexel for the first ten days assisted at night with the dressings and bindings. "You will have to be re-strung like an old piano, I am afraid; thank goodness we have a first-class orthopaedic unit with the Indian Div. But you will need at least two more ops which I don't think can be performed here – so delicate; unless the Prince has some foreign talent up his sleeve. Ask him." But the Prince had nobody except competent local doctors – Egyptians of his class were used to being treated in Zurich or Berlin for any malady graver than a common cold. I entered the dark tunnel of this illness with a tremendous depression, for my whole life seemed to have been compromised by it. Sometimes in the shuttered afternoons with the white ripples of the Nile reflected on the ceiling of the tower-room into which I had been moved for convenience, I awoke in the blaze of fever to see my valet's face bend over me to take thermometer readings to log my progress. Then there came as well exhausted days of remission and coherence where I found I could speak and craved company. The Prince's children came and played in my room sometimes: I tried to get them to pass me the holster on the mantelpiece which contained a service revolver – part of my Egyptian army kit. But they refused, and must perhaps have told someone, for when next Drexel came I noticed that he broke it and tilted out the cartridges. Neither of us said anything. "Different sorts of fever," he said once, quietly. "My own is a girl with dark hair and black eyes." I did not know it then, but the reference was to Sylvaine, the dark sister-*ogre* with whom we had travelled up the Nile. The information came from Affad, who also dropped in regularly with papers and presents of chocolates. "It's a strange love trio," he said, "quite worthy of Ancient Egypt. They have great plans of retiring from the world after the war and locking themselves up in their Provençal chateau."

After the war! "Have you seen the news?" I asked him, and he replied, "Yes, I know." How could anyone dream of an afterwar state? He lit a cigarette and quoted some Chinese sage: "In this life they are only dreaming they are awake." Yes, it was true—we lived like parvenus, like vulgar provincials in the city of God. And now to be helpless in a foreign land, far from love and its familiarities, strapped down to an ironing-board with a pound of lead on each foot and the plaster sticking to the hairs of the skin in an agony of heat . . . I had been assured that it would not be for long though. I closed my eyes and saw Constance walking by the grey lake, a whole landscape of iron-black trees quivering under snow. I would have given anything to be walking beside her. "I took them to the oasis of Macabru—you should have come. There is a little sect of gnostics who meet there at this time of the year; they carry on ancient rites and beliefs. They admitted us, and we took a good deal of hashish and had visions." He laughed softly. I asked him, "How would you define gnosticism?" but he only shook his head doubtfully and did not answer.

The coming of Theodora changed everything. She was the new nurse from the Greek Hospital in Alexandria who had been drafted to Cairo. The Prince without telling a soul had engaged her to live in and look after me. One morning she was simply there. She stood in the doorway divesting herself of her shawl and eyeing me a little sideways with her yellow goat's eyes, as if she were listening to some invisible pulse-beat. She said good morning with complete assurance in French and Greek—her accent sounded very plebeian in both languages. Then she rolled up her sleeves and came towards me slowly, stealthily, as one boxer approaches another to deliver a blow. At this moment Cade came in, and turning to him she gave him a long yellow look and then pointed at the door, saying,

"*Moi massage le Monsieur. Sortez.*" The manservant slunk out of the room without a backward glance.

"*Ego eimai Theodora,*" she said in Greek, tapping upon her own breastbone with long capable fingers. "*Je suis votre infirmière Theodora.*" And with that she started to massage my ankles and toes which felt as if they had been buried in the ground for a century. She turned me deftly this way and that with the voluptuous air of a small girl playing with her doll; and finally when she made her way towards my midriff it was dolls indeed; I felt a whole surge of new life awake in my loins, new oxygen enter my lungs. The massive vascularity of the big blood vessels was invoked by her strong fingers in their apt progress. "*Et comment ça va là?*" she asked at last, taking up my faltering tulip in strong fingers and kneading it as if for the oven. "Did they not check if it worked?" She was both outraged, and at the same time delighted by what she had accomplished, for brave tulip was the size of a Montgolfière and still growing. "*Assez,*" I cried, but my voice must have given me away; the truth was it was delicious. And bending down over me she brought me to a climax so thunderous that I thought I had burst all my stitches. Never had I experienced such an immense slow orgasm – its ripples ran like the tributaries of the Nile throughout the whole nervous system. With this bold stroke she restored me to life and I knew that I could only get well. It was so intense that I started to cry, and bending down tenderly she licked my tears away, dabbing my eyes with a handkerchief. "*Enfin!*" she cried triumphantly, "*C'est ça. Tout va bien.*" And then added in Greek, "*Sikoni monos tou,*" which later I learned meant "It stands up without prompting." Indeed so it was to be, for every day she took tulip for an outing, and every day I waxed in vigour with all this delightful target-practice.

Later, as I grew stronger, she straddled me with her long lean legs and repeated the miracle even more slowly, sharing in the pleasure herself this time. It was rape, the infantile dream of being tied down and raped forcibly by someone who smelt like your mother and had the eyes of a goat. Tall, lanky Theodora was, like her great namesake, a gem. With her I rose from the dead.

FOUR

Paris Twilight

THE GERMAN OFFENSIVES FOLLOWED SO FAST, ONE UPON another, that they left the German General Staff almost breathless with exultation. It was as if all they touched turned to gold – they had difficulty in catching up with themselves. They lived with the unexpected, each victory seeming so easy and so inexpensive that life had the signature of a great adventure. Their own casualty lists were so ridiculously low that it seemed almost beyond belief that within a few months they had shattered and dismantled all the powerful armies surrounding them. They were left sole possessors of the field – a field which now seemed to be expanding itself limitlessly, effortlessly, with only the distant Caucasus mountains as a boundary to German ambitions. All reservations were gone. They were madly in love with the Leader who seemed to them now to have righted every wrong, to have subjugated the traditional enemies of the Reich. The feeling of invincibility made them drunk. The future of Germany was opening before their bemused eyes as if on a huge screen. History had turned turtle and a new German Empire had come into being overnight.

Von Esslin had never been so certain of the appropriateness of his emotions. It was almost with tears, which he uncharacteristically allowed to grip his heart, that he stood to the salute on the sunny Champs Elysées and watched the Leader gliding down through the silent crowds, standing upright in his triumphal car, pale of face, distraught of mien. No wonder he looked pale after the strain of plotting all these vast manoeuvres, directing whole armies like clouds to do his bidding. The giant brain of that little figure had launched Von

Esslin like an avenging catapult first into Warsaw, and now sheer through the Ardennes into a France taken so much by surprise that resistance was nil. The French General Staff had been knocked off their perch. Chaos now reigned. Von Esslin's tanks had behaved with exemplary skill and force – but with such unexpected speed that they had run out of petrol and lost touch with command; had been forced to hold up ordinary commercial petrol pumps like gangsters. It had been great fun. At every halt he could hear the laughter of his "young lions" as they stepped from their machines. Sometimes in sheer exuberance they would burst out laughing and pummel each other playfully. Resistance? There had been a little light skirmishing, that was all. A few *franc-tireurs* had been summarily shot against the walls of village *mairies*. All's fair in love and war! Instructions to the German troops were to administer swift and fatal justice to any who might stand in their way or hesitate to acclaim their triumphant passage. The terrified inhabitants of the towns and villages they entered were in no state to withstand the murderous élan of the Nazi advance. They sank speechless before this grey tide of men and machines. God, but it was beautiful to watch the panzer divisions fan away at speed down the country roads – not unlike the start of some speed trials, say the opening of Le Mans! The dust and whirl of their passage shook the earth and reverberated throatily in the sky. They passed strings, groups, columns of dispirited and disoriented prisoners aimlessly walking in every direction of the compass. They had no point of reference in a world where both morale and communications had failed them. The encircling German forces might appear from anywhere. Of course the heavy fighting was taking place far away to the West, but even here the catastrophe had already declared itself; the defeat was unequivocal. The sunny weather made the run-in on Paris almost a holiday event and Von Esslin felt himself to be getting quite brown from the sunshine; he sat in the back of the staff car with the hood down. Yes, it was not perhaps very wise, but there it was, victory is like strong drink. There had been some light machine-gunning from the air, but it seemed to the Germans in their present euphoria as light as spring rain merely; it rippled the corn and knocked branches off the trees. Von Esslin found himself humming an air from *Don Giovanni* as he read the coded messages which ordered him to group his armour around Belmoth. There was some resistance in that area and once or twice they crossed the tracks of some heavy artillery moving up that way. But no trace of a real road block, no ambushes, no gross air movement. It was wonderful to be alive. They ate ravenously under an oak tree and monitored the crackle of messages coming in; all the real hard work was being done away on the right flank.

While they were eating there came a slow drift of motorised infantry moving up to clear the sticky villages and a great friend of Von Esslin hailed him: "Klaus!" They were enchanted to meet, and overcome with laughter at this piquant encounter so near to Paris. The young officer elected to spend a few moments sharing a sandwich with Von Esslin and exchanging such news as he could mobilise after a night and a day of speedy advancing upon a non-existent enemy. "I can't believe it!" he kept exclaiming. "I hope there is no catch in it!" The elder man patted him on the back and assured him that there could not be. "In one week, when we are billeted and organised, I shall meet you in Paris, at Feydal on the Champs Elysées, and we will drink a vintage champagne in honour of the Führer."

The young officer took the challenge as seriously as it was meant to be taken. He stood up and clicked out his salute, and then took the General's hand in his, saying, "Seriously?"

"*Ein Mann, ein Wort*," said Von Esslin with an explosive

good humour. "My word of honour!" And indeed the somewhat rash promise was redeemed exactly on time, for the two
of them met on the appointed day and hour and found a table
in the sun at which to drink the promised toast. Moreover the
Leader himself was there to look in upon the drinking. It was
unforeseen, but it gave the toast significance.

But there was still some resistance ahead; Von Esslin felt
the tanks and infantry gradually building up behind them like a
wave. A staff officer reproached him for travelling thus in so
very vulnerable a car, and though nettled he accepted the
greater safety of a command car with a turret. All that night
they were bogged down with this invisible resistance ahead,
and then towards dawn it eased; it was as if someone had
pulled a plug out of a bath. Everything started to flow again
and a new momentum was achieved.

What surprised him – yet war is like that – was that he
seemed to have missed all the major engagements of this
period. They felt almost like holidaymakers. He had a confused memory of his young bronzed giants stripped to the
waist, wading about in the ripe corn. It was beautiful to see – in
his heart bourgeoned a renewed love for Germany. But what
the devil was actually happening? He called for operational
signals and a field orientation, and in doing so made contact
with another of his cronies and contemporaries, a General
Paulus who telephoned him to sketch in the background, the
backcloth against which, like a blind man, Von Esslin was
advancing. It was from Paulus that he learned of the tremendous exodus of the civilian populations of Belgium and the
northern sectors of France – the thousands upon thousands
who sought an imaginary safety in the southern parts of France
which they believed would be behind the lines.

"What lines?" The German advance had been so hectic
that frequently these marching hordes arrived in towns and
villages only to find that they were already in German hands!

Confusion was total – their victory was more than just physical, it was quite as much psychological. All the little towns in the southern sector were already swollen with itinerant refugees for whom no sort of preparations had been envisaged. In Toulouse and Nîmes people slept on the pavements like gypsies. And during all this period of turmoil and upset Von Esslin's forces advanced without undue stress or strain until they lay not far from the open road to Paris. It was unbelievable. Nightingales were singing in the woods. They had captured the contents of a wine cellar and the General sipped some wine and ate a biscuit for his lunch, though he spoke long and earnestly to his troop leaders. They must spare no effort to contain any disposition towards drink in the ranks of the tank-troopers. But how marvellous, how warming victory was! Terrified peasants here and there gave the Nazi salute in a cringing sort of way; then, delighted that they had not been shot at, they smirked. "The French will welcome us," he thought, "for their heart was never in this war, and we have much to offer them in the New Order." He nodded with a frown, as if he had need to insist on this point, to convince himself.

The world unrolled itself around him with a grand polyphonic flamboyance; he was dazed with the march of affairs. Moreover one of his tactical ploys had come to the notice of the Chief of Staff and earned him commendation! It was a lucky accident. Yet it had seemed to him self-evident, obvious – just the sort of thing that improvises itself in the heat of battle. In the general surge forward they had here and there met with road blocks and some spasmodic disposition to delay them. He had passed his panzer on to the adjacent railway line and let it crackle down the permanent way, to turn the flank of these obstacles. The use of railways . . . it would go into army manuals on tactics. It had been vastly amusing to watch the tanks hopping on and off the main line in order to let trains go through – the French Railways system simply could not admit to the existence of a war, much less to German tanks flopping in and out of their railway stations like so many rabbits. Here and there they fired a few bursts at a train, but it was largely for the fun of the thing. Once they even emptied an express – the people came scuttling out deathly pale with their hands above their heads. "What to do with them?" asked a bronzed patrol leader as he nudged them amiably towards the waiting-room of the station. "There was a French officer – that one over there – who fired at us with a pistol." Von Esslin turned curtly away with a bark: "You know your orders." As he got into his car again he heard the ripple of a machine-gun inside the station.

The rest of the tank brigade turned right across fields and joined the general advance upon a main road now littered with abandoned farm wagons and personal belongings. It was a great temptation to stop and examine all those burst suitcases from which protruded every sort of gear. Thank goodness, they were on wheels and moving fast – he would not have to read them a lesson about looting. That was to follow, of course, but in systematic fashion, in a punitive manner. Indeed the whole philosophy of their campaigns had already been laid down for them. They were to be just like Napoleon's: campaigning *à la maraude*, as the French would soon find out. For a moment Von Esslin swelled with pride, and then the sentiment was swallowed up in a sort of guilty fury. France was finished! He struck his boot twice, hard, with a cane and immersed himself in deeply gratifying memories of the noise his steel-meshed caterpillars had made upon the railway lines. A flight of planes ahead of them swooped down and started chattering like magpies. Their advance slowed. Thick smoke and a series of thuds spoke of an engagement ahead; a burst oil drum had flooded the road and the hollow tanks swished about, as if in heavy rain. He pulled them off the main road and into the green fields on either side of it. It was late afternoon, soon dusk would come; they must gain as much ground as they could before bivouacking for the night. He called back for a few bus-loads of infantry to support the tanks as they combed the forest, firing odd bursts into the greenery in order to flush out troops which might be hiding there.

Once it had become fact it seemed so obvious, so inevitable, the total victory which had already altered the fate and disposition of so many nations – the British rout, the French collapse, the Low Countries . . . So many and so diverse were the successes that it was impossible to sketch in the boundaries of a future – for it spread out in every direction. He was not simply being Junker when, in response to the question: "In your view what should we next consider doing?" he had replied acidly: "I am a soldier of the Reich, I have no views. I simply do what the Leader says." His interlocutor, a staff officer in the map caravan section, looked disgusted. Nevertheless he saluted and bowed in agreement, trying to keep his look free from irony. But the truth of the matter was that Von Esslin was rattled – events had outdistanced him and he had genuine difficulty in marshalling them into coherence. He hoped that he might soon find himself back on the Eastern Front – a vague sense of *malaise* haunted him, something at the heart of the French collapse. Nor did the cringing, hysterical reception afforded his men by the citizens of Paris do anything to allay his sense of disorientation. They kicked some police units out of their billets in Avalon and took possession of this sensitive entry to the capital. But pretty soon the general efficiency of their forces had carved out a reasonable way of living – which afforded Von Esslin frequent short leaves to Paris where he found that the girls eyed his uniform with great respect. Once a young *fille de joie* asked him if he would care to come with her and give her a good beating with his cane. She would consider paying him, she said, which was at least original. He was

shocked, and contemptuous of the French race for taking their
defeat so contentedly. He muttered some opprobrious epithet
and hurried on over the bridge to the *quais*, where he found
many German books which he bought and sent home to his
mother. The mails were now getting through and he heard
from her every month or so; in exchange he wrote to her to
retail his adventures and to describe Paris, which he had always
found so fascinating, and which was now, in defeat, almost
more so.

When he had drunk a cointreau or two he became
flushed, heavily sentimental, and in these moods he would
sometimes escort a street walker to her grubby lodgings. But
the period in question was brief, like the withdrawal from the
southern sector of France, and within a few months he found
himself posted with his armour to Tulle – on the edge of the
occupied zone which he himself had always been convinced
could not co-exist peacefully with the occupied north. France
was like a Christmas stocking – everything had been pushed
down into it, refugees, Jews, criminals, and members of a hypothetical Resistance; not to mention the fact that the Allies were
sending in agents the whole time in an attempt to gather
information and to promote insurrection. It was rumoured
that Von Esslin was to have a new command, and he pondered
deeply whether it might not be something to do with the push
into Russia, for nobody he knew had believed in the factitious
pact that had been signed – it had been a manoeuvre to free a
flank against Russian perfidy while France was dealt with. Nor
could one be very much in doubt about future possibilities, for
the armoured build-up in the north hinted of such preoccupations. Meanwhile, the absurd *drôle de guerre* had given place
to an equally *drôle de paix*! The French really believed that it
was only a matter of time before the two million French
prisoners were released to them, to be accompanied perhaps by
a general German withdrawal from the country after the

signing of some sort of peace pact and the payment of an indemnity. It lingered on for months, this fatal misapprehension, in spite of the desert battles, the battles for Greece, Yugoslavia, and so on. People clustered round the symbol of a France which would retrieve her freedom and greatness, though the old Marshal Pétain, with his avuncular speeches and ineffectual acts, was hardly the man to inspire such hopes. Anti-British feeling was at its height, for the English by their ill-considered bombings and hostile activities risked upsetting the Germans who would then obviously punish the French civilians. In the midst of all this confused and incoherent sermonising they managed to establish for a few months a life as quiet as any seminarist's, with frequent Paris leave for troops, Avalon being so near, and plenty of time to refit and rekit against the next round – whenever that might be.

In the meantime, as Von Esslin wrote to his mother, some new units had come in to anchor alongside them and he had found four or five bosom cronies whom she knew well – old Keller and Le Fals and Kranz; they made up a four for bridge in the mess of an evening. They also made their descents on Paris together in jovial Bavarian style, and all being of a Catholic persuasion they attended many services in some of the great churches and cathedrals of Paris. "The music is marvellous," he wrote, with real feeling, "and I am often reminded of Vienna where we so often heard an unfamiliar mass, only to discover that it had been written by a Mozart or Haydn for that particular church!" But though this period was rich in its enthusiasm and carefreeness there was an invisible preoccupation growing up in the back of his mind; it seemed like an ever-lengthening shadow over the future. At first Russia had opened up before their eyes like forest fire, like a volcano erupting – the scale of the assault was dumbfounding. But now new elements had begun to intrude – resistance in Africa, in Russia, in the Balkans, in Norway ... It was slowly thickening, like a dish of lentils from too fast a cooking! He brushed the feeling aside as somewhat of an illusion, but it persisted.

Nevertheless ... a thousand bombers over Cologne! And the B.B.C. radio programmes from over the water gathering self-confidence and density – always with that ominous drum-beat taken from Beethoven! He was impatient now for some action, in order to avoid such reflections.

The new Government of Vichy was all smarm and affability, but it was obvious that without the weight of German forces watching over it its life would have been a precarious one, so evenly were the French divided between those who genuinely favoured Nazism, and those who found the occupation intolerable. For the moment the public had not felt the full weight of the German yoke. But it would not be long before the shortages and the ration-cards brought home the sombre reality. But such general considerations hardly touched the fringe of Von Esslin's preoccupations at that moment; his speculations about the future were crystallised by the visit of three Vichy functionaries who arrived in an old car one morning and demanded audience. They were, so they said, attached to the French Second Bureau and they announced that within a matter of weeks the German army would move into the unoccupied zone as a sort of unofficial police force for the Vichy Government. Von Esslin was to be part of this operation.

It threw him into a frightful rage to hear these shabby Frenchmen deliberating upon his future, and he was almost tempted from spite to put them under arrest. His face flushed dark as he told them, between clenched teeth, that he took his orders from the German High Command only – from nobody else; they were abashed by his vehemence and apologetic for the gaffe they had perpetrated. Nevertheless one of them showed him a letter of appointment signed by the *Reichsführer S.S. und Chef der deutschen Polizei* – no less a personage than Himmler himself – and Von Esslin's heart sank. As a soldier he resented being a tool of the politicals and a weapon used by them in their secret wars. Nor would it have been any use to ask the rank of the new appointee – he might simply be a modest colonel-general and yet still have the power to report directly to Berlin behind his back and manipulate the armed forces by remote control. Besides, Von Esslin did not want a quasi-civilian posting in a backwater, with no possibilities of promotion. He applied instantly for a posting to the Russian theatre, but the message remained without answer. Silence fell. Perplexity grew. He heard no more of the dark-suited Vichy functionaries. Then one day his orderly told him that someone was waiting for him in his office and he found Fischer there, installed in a swivel chair, cap tilted back, paring his nails with a paperknife. "Good morning, General," he said with his lazy and insolent smile, but he made no move to rise. Von Esslin remained standing and gazed at him silently. He wore the S.S. uniform, but with a shiny black greatcoat that hid insignia. He had very light blue eyes of great brilliance and weakness. It was as if you could see pieces of the sky through his skull, for the eyes did not join in the smile. "Pray be seated, my General," he said, smiling, showing perfect white teeth. An incandescent smile but without any heat. "You are in my chair," growled Von Esslin. He did not want to take the suppliant's seat in his own office. The younger man shrugged and rose. He was tall and thin. He had rings on his fingers. At first blush this might have hinted at an innate effeminacy, but the impression was rapidly dispelled by the empty eyes. They might as well have been the empty sockets of a Roman statue, so little did they convey of sensibility or intelligence. He turned slowly towards the window and briefly traced a pattern on it with his forefinger. Then he turned round once more and again flashed Von Esslin that brilliant smile, empty as a neon sign. "You will get marching orders on Monday. I will go on directly and be waiting for you when you arrive."

Von Esslin sat down massively and treated the young man to a grimly bad-tempered smile intended to express his disdain and resentment of such cavalier manners. "But of where do you speak?" he asked, and the young man answered, "Avignon has been selected as the headquarters of the force, you will group there. The S.S. will quarter quite near at hand. All this is to help the Vichy régime – they fear the situation is sliding out of control; too many communists, Resistance groups, Intelligence groups. We shall have to begin with an impact. You will receive a list of villages where hostages are to be taken and liquidated." He looked suddenly sick and sad, like a sort of blond Mephisto wounded by a memory. Ruminating, his tongue travelled round his teeth, as if to gather fragments of something he had eaten. Then he said abruptly, "I look forward to working with you. General, do you play chess?" Von Esslin said that he did not, though in fact he did. "Pity," said Fischer, and once more gave that dazzling, disconnected smile. His skin was very pale, his cheeks bloodless and anaemic-looking, his eyelashes of a lightness that was practically albino. "Pity!"

"What is your rank?" asked Von Esslin in a heavy, boorish tone; of course it would make no difference to the day-to-day issues. From his accent he thought he detected a sort of clever Munich garage mechanic in uniform. Fischer pulled down the collar of his greatcoat sufficiently for Von Esslin to see the characteristic insignia of the Waffen S.S. "I thought so," he said. Fischer nodded with satisfaction. "We will work together very well," he said, and added, but in a much politer tone, "May I see your hand, General?" Caught by surprise Von Esslin laid his hands out before him on the desk and the young man leaned attentively over them for a second, though he did not touch them. Then he straightened up, smacked his lips and said, "I thank you." He went to the door, and standing by it, with the doorknob in his hand, he allowed his right hand to sketch a formal salute of great punctilio, at the same time bringing his heels softly together. Was it mockery? It was hard to decide, with that dead, smiling face gazing at him. Technically he should have risen and responded, but he was still full of anger, so he contented himself with a curt nod. The door closed behind Fischer, and Von Esslin turned with despatch to his telephone. He must find out from Paris what was brewing, what the future held for him.

When he managed to contact operations he was told that movement orders had already been despatched, that he would have them within a few hours, together with details of the units engaged. So! He felt a touch of perplexity and unease grow up inside him as he listened. It was to be a take-over, no resistance was to be anticipated; he would consolidate around key towns and pave the way for the French Milice – the recruited Nazis of French origin. One of his oldest cronies was high up in postings, and Von Esslin broke the rules of military etiquette in telephoning him to say testily: "Forgive me, but do you know any reason why my transfer is being passed over? This is almost a civilian command they offer me! Why?" His friend's suppositions were not very elaborate. "Passed over?" he said diplomatically. "That is hardly the word *surely* – you have been *mentioned* quite recently and that means despatches. It's just an administrative bungle which will sort itself out in good time. Be patient."

As a matter of fact Von Esslin found these blandishments anything but reassuring; his mind once more began its hovering around a private thought which had for some time been troubling him. Was his Catholicism going to tell against him professionally? The idea had already presented itself to him more than once, though so far there had been nothing to confirm it. Well . . . once or twice he had heard ironic phrases fall from the lips of S.S. officers which hinted that one could not compromise between God and Hitler. Once he heard a young

man say: "When a Nazi goes to confession . . ." but the rest of
the phrase had been lost in ironic laughter. Then again, on
another occasion, there had been a reference to a Nazi storm-
trooper on church parade which had also led to strenuous
guffaws. Was this new posting a tacit indication that his
religion had come to the notice of his superiors? Shaving in the
mirror, he went guiltily over the last few times he had been to
church with his friends – *they* would hardly have informed on
him? Why "inform"? "You are being stupid and suspicious,"
he told himself aloud, and stepped into his bath with a sigh and
a shrug of the shoulders.

That night the detailed orders came and he read them
through with cynicism and distaste; those Waffen units, why so
many? They were going to break civilian morale, he supposed,
in the traditional way; the Waffen units were Himmler's
personal toy, and consequently almost a law unto themselves.
On the other hand Von Esslin's own command had shed a lot
of tanks – they were wanted for Russia perhaps? But there was
no doubt that as a command this was going to be a backwater of
little importance where nobody could expect to earn glory and
advancement. It was not exactly a slight, yet he almost felt it to
be one. There was nobody to protect him up there at the
General Command, nobody to whom he could appeal
privately.

He felt suddenly very much alone.

FIVE

In Geneva

THE STREET IN GENEVA AT THE END OF WHICH THE OLD
Bar de la Navigation stands runs back from the lakeside
with its bulky Corniche and scrambles up a steepish
slope. It is an undecided sort of street, it seems at cross-purposes
with itself, for it begins as a modest side-street, becomes for a
block or so a wider boulevard, then breaks off abruptly to
become a narrow dog-leg passage giving on to an evil-smelling
court full of lidless dustbins. It was precisely this air of
lugubrious secrecy that endeared itself to our hero (heroes,
rather, for Toby had appeared in Geneva to join forces with
Sutcliffe). It seemed to them the ideal place for those confidential mid-morning potations and games of pool for which
the Foreign Office had invented the phrase "elevenses", after
the hour of the morning when one feels one most needs a short
swift drink, or a long "unwinder", to use slang.

They were both engaged on what was then known as
"war work". In the damp basements of the Consulate (below
lake level) a flock of new temporary offices had been created,
each separated from the next by a wooden partition. Services
of the most heterogeneous sort rubbed elbows. Oxford had
sacrificed Toby to the needs of M.E.3 (counter-espionage),
while a disgruntled Sutcliffe, pushed out of Vienna by the
troubles, translated confidential German documents for the
Military Attaché's department and waited angrily for his wife
to be restored to him by the psychiatrists. It cost the earth. She
was housed at the Prangens clinic across the lake. (Every
morning he used to go out on the balcony of the small flat
which he shared with his friend, and shout aloud, "I want my

wife" in German; but it appeared to have no effect on the unimaginative Swiss.)

The two huge men, so like ninepins, shared as best they could this ugly flat which was impossible to keep in decent order. Chaos reigned; neither was tidy, neither could cook. They heated up tinned food in a saucepan of hot water and ate it with sadness and disrelish, under the belief that they were economising. On Mondays a desultory charwoman did what she could to restore some order in their lives. In the evenings they often sat down to play poker, wearing pyjamas with broad stripes and eyeshades of yellow celluloid like the croupiers at Las Vegas. Their raptness might have persuaded one that they were playing for higher stakes than matches. Ah, the nights of the early war, fading down into the blue lantern-lit dusk with their dense fogs smearing visibility on the lake! The Swiss army was on "alert", the country mobilised, the towns blacked out, though not entirely. It was almost a curfew, with most bars and bordels closing early. The world lived in a tension without remedy. The authorities had tried the air raid sirens and found they worked. The noise was deeply depressing and reinforced an innate tendency to stay at home and drink tea laced with applejack or plum brandy. Toby called these confections "spine-twisters" from the shuddering caused by the first mouthful. Aptly.

The potations of mid-morning, however, were different, consisting of hot grogs with brown sugar (despite the muggy climate) in a vain attempt to defeat the chronic bronchitis they shared, the result of smoking too many Celtiques – the *tabac gris* of over-run France. This affliction rendered the morning cacophonous, due to a joint symphony of coughing so violent that it brought the Swiss couples who lived below out on to the landing, wondering if they should call for help. Sutcliffe imitated a young cat being tried for size, Goddard a surly Turkish porter being mauled by a bear. Sometimes they united to imitate the national anthems of various nations, or else to repeat in musical coughs the phrase "*Le docteur Schwarz est un pot de chambre*". Schwarz was the analyst who had fled from Vienna carrying with him his choicer and richer patients – for not all could find the money to move with him. (Sutcliffe's overdraft did not bear thinking upon.) It was Schwarz who had been bitten by a paranoid patient and granted a month's leave to recover and attend to his infected ear-lobe. "Such are the love-bites analysts receive," commented Sutcliffe bitterly to Constance when she answered the phone. "I wish my wife would react as positively." But Constance was not there to be made fun of; she turned the jest coldly aside, saying, "I will certainly see you if you wish for any information. I am abreast of the dossier, but I am only standing in for Dr. Schwarz, holding the fort. I am not treating her, though I have established contact with her and had several talks. You may come at ten tomorrow." She was disposed to be rather priggish, and received a rather unfavourable impression of him due to his dirty fingernails and lack of physical spruceness. Sutcliffe was intimidated by her beauty, but had only the faintest idea of who she was. Then came an accidental reference to Blanford in the conversation and she saw his eyes widen. "Goodness!" he cried and sat staring at her. "You must be Constance, the other sister."

"Then who are you?" asked Constance with hesitation, for a sort of feeling of familiarity had begun to grow up inside her, vague as a cloud. His name fell with a thud upon her ear. "It's not true!" she exclaimed. But it was, it was he. They sat silent for a long moment, staring at one another, and then she began to talk rapidly, erratically, still not quite sure of her man. But the sofa of Freud clinched the matter – for she had seen his name on the invoice. "So after all you are real!" Sutcliffe laughed and said, "Everybody is real."

It was a crazy thing to say, if you were someone who did

not believe in fairies, but then he was given to immoderate optimism when in the presence of beauty, to which he remained forever susceptible. But he smarted under her coolness, he found her a right bitch and he told Toby so. "*Une garce,*" he said, preferring the French word with the broad vowel sound spread like legs: like those satisfactory words and phrases he treasured – "*gâtisme ou le relâchement des sphincters*".

His friend looked at him with interest and asked, "Why are you so much up on end?"

Sutcliffe replied soberly, gravely, "I am sure that Aubrey will end up in love with her and I understand why. It's those sea-green eyes and the snow tan. But she's a real Swiss prig."

"But she's English."

"She's both: a double priggery."

She had initially refused to meet him on social terms, outside the consulting-room, and he supposed this to be a question of medical etiquette, mixed with the evident distaste she seemed to feel for his company. So he was surprised when she telephoned to his office and said in her rapid, rather strained way, "I feel I was rather uncivil to you, and probably hurt your feelings; I am sorry if it is so. I would like to repent and also accept your kind invitation to a drink. This evening, if you wish." He was both elated and nonplussed by the sudden change of wind. "Good," said Toby when informed, "if she's medical she might give us some tips about geriatric aid. I am putting up feebler and feebler performances with the typists' pool. Little Miss Farthingale is languishing, and I am heartily ashamed of the poor motility of my product. The damn stuff can hardly swim, it turns over on its back and floats. The girls are right to protest." Sutcliffe clicked his tongue disapprovingly. "We can't ask her that. You will just have to live with your humiliation, Toby. But come to think of it, why don't you try a Diplomat's Aid?"

"What's that, may I ask?"

"Get a nice thick office rubber band and make a tourniquet for your closest friend; place it rather high up and fairly tight. It will work wonders. I learned it from the little Indian typist. She says that in the Foreign Office . . ."

Toby was elated by this information and unearthing a series of rubber bands from his briefcase he retired to the lavatory in order to find something suitable for his troubled circumstances. Sutcliffe walked down to the lake to meet the ferry, for he despaired of anyone finding the little bar, just on a set of telephoned instructions. It was tea-time and the day was fine. Constance waved to him from the deck and he replied.

She was not at her best, she looked tired and strained. Indeed her general appearance, for a girl who liked to be well turned out, bordered on the unkempt; her white mackintosh was not too clean and a missing top button had been replaced by a safety pin. Her hair had been badly cut and was all puppy dog's tails. The truth was that she was still in a state of semi-shock, almost collapse, due to the news of Sam's death. It was simply amazing – for they had both imagined that they were strong enough to face up to such an eventuality, that the life-giving power of their magnetic love would resist even this sort of separation. Love makes you naive, she realised it now; they had been acting a part, the part of two golden immortals from some romantic opera. Now here they were, under the wheels of the Juggernaut – or rather, she was; in a sense he had escaped and left her to gather up the remains of the thought "death". No, that was not all, for some days after the news she had received to her surprise one brief letter duly transmitted by the Army Post Office to the Consulate. It had made an elaborate journey, the voice of her dead "husband". Yes, all of a sudden the word had resonance, an old-fashioned gravity and pith. The whole of her small apartment by the lake seemed impregnated with it. That is why she had taken to sleeping at her office in the clinic, on a camp bed against the further wall.

Everything, even her work, seemed suddenly insipid; the chance collision with Sutcliffe now filled her with conflicting emotions. She wanted to avoid talking about Sam with half of her: with the other half she realised that it might help her to find her way out of this temporary numbness, the way back into life. So here he came, patient as an old dog, to ask for news of the pale slender girl, who was now sliding away down the long slopes of melancholia which would lead only to mania.

"I should not visit her at the moment. She will only start wringing her hands and weeping again – all day long."

"But you know as well as I do, she holds me responsible for everything, and it is not fair."

She shook her head. "Nothing is fair with the insane." Sutcliffe placed his hands on the top of his head like King Lear and said, "I destroyed her dolls. How could I have been such a fool?" But the trouble went deeper than that, much deeper.

"The negress calls every day, and with her she seems a little better. They play noughts and crosses."

"It's appropriate to the day and age," he said bitterly. "Indeed when one sees the state of the world one wonders why one should call her back to it – supposing we could."

Before going to join Toby in the bar they walked a while in the gardens which border the lakeside and she told him of Blanford's wound, which made him, rather unaccountably, chuckle.

"I must get in touch with him again," he said, nothing more. But when she mentioned Sam's death – as a therapeutic measure in order to take its pulse, so to speak – he looked at her with sympathy and a certain rough affection. "It's just the beginning," he said. "Have you seen what they have reserved for the Jews?" Who had not? "Anyway," she said, "Freud is safely away even though all the books are lost; but copies exist here, thank goodness." He looked at her with interest and said, "Did you know him?" She nodded and smiled, as if at the memory of a pleasant and rich meeting. Indeed it had been the great turning-point in her life and she was prepared to defend the old philosopher to the death. Sensing this, Sutcliffe was prepared to tease her a little; under his breath he sang a stave of "Dear old Pals" in an amended version.

> "Dear old Fraud, jolly old Fraud,
> We'll be together whatever the weather."

"O cut it out," she said, "I am sure you don't believe it." He grinned, for he did not. "I got to know him quite well," he said, "and he was no humbug. He gave me several interviews and outlined his system with great elegance and modesty. He emphasised its limits. He gave me half a dozen consultations on the couch to show me how the thing worked, which was jolly decent. The thing is it doesn't – not for anything really serious, anything like psychosis."

"He never pretended it did."

"But Schwarz did, and it is his messing about that aggravated the condition of my wife; but that's not your affair, I suppose, since you are only a locum."

"Well, I can't pronounce on his cases," she said with the light of battle in her eye. "But I am glad you met Freud himself."

"He was very amusing with his Jewish moneylender touch. I teased him a bit about love being an investment – invested libido. But the old darling was serious. Jews can never see themselves from the outside. They are astonished when you say that they are this or that. They are naive, and so was he, very much so. The way his hand came out for the money at the end of the hour, when the clock struck, was a scream. I asked him if he would take a cheque but he said, 'What? And declare it to the Income Tax?' He insisted on cash and when he put it in his pocket he shuffled it until it tinkled, which put him in a great good humour. He looked just like Jules Verne at such moments; indeed there was a sort of similarity of imagination between the two fantasists. Anyway the idea amused him for he had read and admired Jules Verne. But when I told him that the whole of his system was a money-making plant, to be paid for just listening, and by the hour, he chuckled. 'People want to suffer,' he said, 'and we must help them. It's the decent thing to do. It's not only Jews who like money, you know. Besides, the hand-to-hand payment is an essential part of the treatment. You feel the pinch or the pain in your infantility.' "

Constance mistrusted the depth of his knowledge in the clinical sense. It was one thing to talk all round a subject in terms of philosophy; it was quite another to adapt it to a therapy. "I am boring you," he said, and she shook her head. "No, I was thinking of other things, of that whole period when I started medicine. Tell me more."

Sutcliffe, when they had retired to the bar once more, called for drinks and said, "There is little more to tell. I was with him for such a short time – sufficient however to foster a great respect. The biggest pessimist since Spinoza. For the last session I brought him the fee in coin of the smallest possible denomination. I had a little leather bag with a drawstring round the mouth, which I filled with farthings or their equivalent. He was quite surprised when I presented it and told him that it was his fee. 'Good Lord,' he said with a laugh, 'you've got diarrhoea!' "

Toby drew on his pipe and listened with half an ear; he was not really abreast of the subject and knew little of the personalities under discussion, but Sutcliffe seemed well enough informed. "And then we left Vienna, and old Fraud moved back to his flat to a new consulting room, abandoning his gloomy rooms and the old couch where she had set out all the elements of our married life like someone sets up toy soldiers for a battle, or dolls for a picnic. But when I spoke to the old boy

about us he simply shook his head and said, 'The story of
narcissism is always the same story.' I felt an absurd temptation
to weep for myself and wring my hands, but to what end? He
told me that I must sublimate the distress in a book, which God
knows I have been trying to do from the very beginning – even
before I felt the distress, so to speak. I have from early adolescence suffered from *Schmerz, Angst,* and for good measure
piles. My first publisher gave me an advance to write a cookery
book about Egyptian food. I was wild with joy and took ship
for Egypt at once. But the very first meal I had – there was a
French letter in the salad. And things have gone on like that
ever since." Under the rather lame banter she felt the massive
depression and the stress. In his rough lumbering manner she
found something comforting and helpless; he was like an old
blind bear tied to a post. For her own part she had her own
share of distress to cope with; she realised that she did not want
to go back to her cold sterile little flat with its over-flowing
bookshelves and undone washing-up. Since she had received
the letter from Sam she had suddenly taken it into her head to
flee across the lake; at least at the clinic she had the company of
other consultants and nurses, while even the presence of the
insane all round her seemed to afford a paradoxical sort of comfort. But now the evening was drawing on and Toby had a
dinner engagement. He bowed himself away with solemnity,
hoping to have the pleasure once more . . . The seventeenth-
century sentiments became his vast form very well, he was
made for awkward bows and gawkish scrapings. That left
Sutcliffe. She thought: "It must be strange to exist only in
somebody's diary, like Socrates – we only have Plato's word
for his existence."

He was thinking: "And this book which I have always had
in deep soak, when will it be finished? When I stop breathing?
But the idea behind this furtive activity has always been that
ideal book – the titanic do-it-yourself kit, *le roman appareil.*

After all, why not a book full of spare parts of other books, of characters left over from other lives, all circulating in each other's bloodstreams – yet all fresh, nothing second-hand, twice chewed, twice breathed. Such a book might ask you if life is worth breathing, if death is worth looming. . . . Be ye members of one another. I hear a voice say, 'What disease did the poor fellow get?' 'Death!' 'Death? Why didn't he say so? Death is nothing if one takes it in time.'"

She was thinking: "To be instructively wounded is the most one can ask of love. What innocents we were! Now I see it all so clearly. Some marriages just smoulder along, others chime by couples, but in ours we were blissed out. What luck! But how hard to pick oneself up after such a knockdown blow. What now? I shall live alone like Aubrey, sleep alone, on my right side, pointing north-south; yes, quite alone."

He thought: "To commingle and intersperse contingent realities – that's the game! After all, how few are the options open to us – few varieties of human shape, mental dispositions, scales of behaviour: hardly more numerous than the available Christian names used by the race. How many coats of reality does it take to get a nice clean surface to the apprehension? We are all fragments of one another; everyone has a little bit of everything in his make-up. From the absolute point of view – Aristotle's Fifth Substance, say – all persons are the same person and all situations are identical or vastly similar. The universe must be dying of boredom. Yet obstinately I dream of such a book, full of not completely discrete characters, of ancestors and descendants all mixed up – could such people walk in and out of each other's lives without damaging the quiddity of each other? Hum. And the whole book arranged in diminished fifths from the point of view of orchestration. A big switchy book, all points and sidings. A Golgotha of a book. I must talk to Aubrey about it." He bowed his head while an imaginary audience applauded lengthily.

She thought: "To wake up one day with a vision of Absolute Good! What would it be like?"

Sutcliffe, who sucked a pipe in order to supply a substitute against smoking cigarettes, threw it down and lit yet another Celtique, snapping his fingers defiantly at his own reflection in the gloomy café mirror.

The drink was beginning to tell on them; she felt quite unsteady and all-overish. "We must eat something," he said and bade the taciturn waiter produce his dismal menu. He read it through, groaning: "*Plat du jour*, baked beans on toast. Let's have that."

She was too weak to resist for they must eat something or be completely dismasted by the alcohol. Besides, it prolonged the evening, for she had not yet decided whether her courage would permit her to resume residence in her flat which was hard by, or whether she would need to go back to the clinic across the lake. This at least set a time limit upon the decision, for the last ferry left at eleven at night. Her heart was beating much faster and from time to time she felt flushed and a trifle incoherent. The food was produced and they fell upon it with zeal. "What a swiz life is," said the big man between mouthfuls, "I saw an advertisement for a smart secretary for my office, and I answered it only to find that the girl in question – O dear! Masses of dirty hair attached to a broomstick. So I sent her to Toby's department where they are all colour blind." She was not listening. She was thinking: "How intensely one dreams of the past." She said aloud, "I keep dreaming of the last summer we had in Provence – it is so vivid. Small things come out so clearly. Sometimes very trivial things about Hilary my brother and Aubrey. Do you know, when Aubrey became absolutely insufferable with his preaching about how superior to us the French were we set up an ambush for him. The one subject which he always brought up at the end of one of those futile arguments about Art or Sex was the richness of the French language. It had many more pejorative epithets than English, he would assert loftily. It got on our nerves so much that we rehearsed a little act and whenever he brought this up we used to chant in unison, with terrible facial grimaces, the half dozen or so which he always cited. It doesn't sound funny but if you saw the grimaces and his own crestfallen blush . . ."

"What were they?"

"*Cuistre! Mufle! Goinfre! Rustre! Jobard! Goujat! Fourbe! Gniaf!*"

"Good. I didn't think his French was up to much."

"At any rate we cured him that summer."

"Good."

But she sighed and said, "I wonder what he is doing now, all alone in that palace with the Nile flowing on his ceiling."

"I can tell you," said Sutcliffe, "but it's only a novelist's guess. He is listening with ever-increasing irritation to the nasal whine of Cade, his servant, who is massaging him reproachfully. Cade has found out about the goings-on with the Greek nurse and he is saying, in his lugubrious Cockney accent, 'For my part, sir, I never go with a girl without wearing a conundrum.'"

"I must try and get home," she said, "but I need help after all these drinks." They negotiated the gloom of the place with its vast dusty clumps of furniture and arrived in the street only to find that it was raining – an autumn drizzle for which neither was prepared. "The quickest is my flat," she said, glad that the issue had been decided for her by an extraneous factor. "It's just around the corner." They scurried with as much despatch as their condition permitted and reached the house in somewhat unsteady shape. Here she had a struggle to find her key, but find it she did and they took the lift up to the second floor. The place was very dusty and had clearly not been inhabited for a while; there was washing-up about and through an open door one saw an unmade bed. But the little studio room over the lake was pleasant and the sofas were comfortable, which invited Sutcliffe to relax while she went in search of further drink. There was only vodka left in the drink cupboard and this, she realised, was going to be fatal to him; but it was obvious that he had already decided to fall where he stood – he had shaken off his clumsy shoes and was examining the big toe of his left foot which protruded from a torn sock. "I like these Swiss suburban flats," he said, "they are homey. There is always a *membre fantôme* on the hallstand and a Valéry open in the loo. They are inhabited by psychoanalysts and abortionists."

"Thank you."

"Not at all."

"I see you don't believe in science."

"I do, though; but in the poetry of science."

"And happiness?"

"Has nothing to do with the matter. You cannot create this obscure and marvellous field of energy – *le bonheur* – by advocacy or the whip, by force or by guile, but only by pleading. Poetry begins there, and prayer also; they lead you to a thought, and science comes out of that thought. But the pedigree is long." He broke off and erupted in a string of hiccoughs which rather alarmed him. Then he went on: "The sixpence in the plum pudding must be taken on trust. We must believe. It is really there. It is the holy Inkling."

"You are babbling," she said reproachfully, and he shook his head sadly over her, saying, "You have received a tremendous shock with Sam's death." And at this, quite involuntarily, they both burst out crying simultaneously, joining hands. It was such a relief to discover that she could produce so human a reaction at last; he cried like an old horse, she cried like a humble adolescent, awkwardly and noisily. And while she cried she thought: "The arrival of death on the scene brings an enormous sense of the sweetness of things – the richness of impermanence which one has always avoided, feared. 'The dying fall' is true for all of us: clowns, heroes, lovers, cads, fools, freaks, kings, commoners, the sane, the mad, or the silent."

She laid her distraught drunken head on his shoulder while he, unmanned by emotion and exhausted by his potations, stroked it with his coarse palms and repeated helplessly, "There, my dear, there." And all the while she was thinking: "The long studied suppuration of confessional analysis! The fatigue and intricacy! The weeping wall of the Jewish spybrain hovering around schemes of investment; picking the scabs off wounds and wondering why they bleed. Scar-tissue of un-assuaged desires!" Then she burst out: "He wrote me such a foolish letter with nothing in it but schoolboy jokes and just one good sincere passage. Wait, I'll get it. I left it in the loo."

She had wanted to tear it up and flush it away but instead had put it beside the bath where the steam had gummed half its leaves together. Now she picked up the flimsy mass and peeling it like an onion found a sheet. She read out: " 'Connie, death is nothing and that is the truth. Pain of course one fears a bit, but amnesia comes with it. Our great weakness, the place where we all cave in, and can't take it, is love.' "

"But the letter," said Sutcliffe, "it's all glued together." She replied: "I know it by heart. But it came too late. That is why I am so terribly upset. In it he told me that whatever happened I must keep the child, for we both practically knew for certain that I was pregnant; at that time I told him that I would certainly not hold him up by having one, in case when he came back he no longer felt keen on me."

She knocked on her forehead with her knuckles. "I was being noble. I did not wish to risk that he might stay with me against his will because of a child begotten in haste and by accident during the war. After all, I thought, when our love re-establishes itself there will be time enough to have another one.

So I made away with it. I made away with it. And hardly had I done so than the news of his death came, and of course the child became infinitely precious – if only I had kept it!"

He realised now the full extent of her distress and guilt. She stood in the centre of the room with hanging head and relived that cold afternoon in the little apartment of the old doctor – lying spreadeagled in a dentist's chair hoisted against a white pane of glass where the clouds from the lake surface reflected themselves. Lying with her legs apart while the old man talked rapidly, confidentially. Pain and anaesthesia melted and blended. Then the mountains of wadding to stay the bleeding. The old man came with a slop-pail in which the foetus lay, the fruit of their love, like a little greenish tree-frog, with perfectly formed fingernails and toes. It was still alive but tremendously exhausted. It lay like a half-dead swimmer washed up on a forlorn coast.

Realising his role as confidant, his therapy, Sutcliffe plied her with questions, made her spit the whole poisoned lot of it out into his lap. They talked on and on in the darkness and in the intervals between the sound of their voices they heard the whewing of gulls or the bray of a ferry-siren mixed into the simmering noise of rain on the windows. The topic of their conversation, their common distress, united them in a har-monious web of shared emotions; but the slow spirals of alcohol in the blood led them further and further towards in-coherence, and at last into the fastnesses of sleep. His snores replaced his sobs, and gained in splendour as he slept, his head on her companionable shoulder. It was dawn when she woke with a start – the night had folded itself away like a screen. On tiptoe so as not to wake her confidant she betook herself to the kitchen and set going a copious breakfast which she knew she would need as much as he; though it was early she made haste, for she had work to do across the lake. Sutcliffe slept on, quaking into a snore from time to time, his frame wobbling jelly-like and then settling again into its mould. He too had work that morning and would be glad of the hot shower and the plate of bacon and eggs when he awoke. Nor were the promptings of reality unhelpful, for the telephone rang and cut through his sleep like scissors. Constance answered it briefly and turned to her guest who was beginning to stretch and yawn his way back to life. "It is Schwarz," she said with relief, "he is back on duty again and I can return to my own cases at last. Is there anything that you would like me to tell him when we consult later on this morning? Or to tell her for that matter?"

Sutcliffe pondered heavily. "I was once promised that she could go for walks round the lake in the afternoons; what has happened to that idea?" Constance shook her head. "I did not hear of it. Perhaps she showed a disinclination to meet you? I will find out." He lumbered to the lavatory, having selected an old copy of *The Times* to read there, leaving her to clear the place and lay their breakfast table which she did with despatch and care, for the extent of their alcoholic abuses had rather alarmed her in a medical sense. The murdered bottle of vodka lay there, showing its teeth, so to speak. Had they really put away so much? Noises from the lavatory answered her question. She tapped on the door to ask if he was all right. "Yes, thank you," he said. "I was just lost in the liana of my lucubrations as I unwound the *Times* leader. Rigorous, cleansing prose. After this I shall totter to my office, as pretty as a virgin with horns. Ah, my head!"

But the weather had cleared and a fragile sunlight enhanced the lake mist with its gleams. They embraced warmly as they separated. "O thank you, my dear," she cried impulsively and he spread wide his arms in a gesture of resignation. "Fifty-fifty," he replied.

It was no more than the truth. "And do remember that if you wish to send Aubrey a message I can have it sent over the

Red Cross teleprinter." Sutcliffe chuckled again and nodded his head vigorously. "I certainly shall," he said with a smile. "But above all, Connie, please keep in touch with me now and help me if you see any way."

"Of course."

The little office smelt of Turkish cigarettes rather than French, and he knew at once that his partner Ryder had been in that morning; it was equally obvious from the litter of press cuttings and half-typed pages which adorned the desk next to his own. That week there had been an awful lot of technical articles to translate from Swiss and German periodicals. Laboriously, in a frenzy of tedium so to speak, they were wading about in search of the scrambler device which rendered the codes of the German "enigma machine" so impenetrable to their own Intelligence. Thousands and thousands of articles had been combed, and thousands awaited them. Ryder and he were building up a "scrambler file" which would contain almost all that was known on this abstruse topic. Ryder – astonishing for a regular officer – was a brilliant German scholar and had been delegated to this pedestrian task, which he performed with discipline and good humour. A small peppery young man with a toothbrush moustache, he was always on time; he drank and smoked most moderately and lost his temper infrequently. Sutcliffe hated him, because he always felt that Ryder's professionalism showed his own behaviour up for the lackadaisical sort of article it was. Sometimes when Ryder criticised a passage in a translation he would feel that he was steadily turning blue with rage. He gritted his teeth and felt the muscles at his temples squirm with irritation.

But he had to accept these strictures for what they were – observations from someone with superior knowledge; and bow to circumstance, for Ryder was head of the section, and their translations went in under his name and signature. Sutcliffe was only a clerk. How hateful it was to be a subordinate!

He slumped down at his desk and felt his gorge rise as he turned over with one finger a clump of cuttings from the German press. He was about to address himself to his file when Ryder himself walked into the office, beaming and holding two champagne glasses in his right hand and a bottle wrapped in a wet cloth in his left. His springy bantam's walk was made more pronounced today by his obvious good humour. "Today," he said, "is a day for a celebration. So I brought the necessary. A drink is in order. H.E. yesterday sent us a strong commendation, and is putting me in for a gong." Sutcliffe groaned with disgust. He was about to say, "Is that all?" when his companion went on: "But that is not the reason. Last night I got through to London and I gather that at last they have started to get the hang of the damned scramble device on the model – the only one – we've squeezed out of Jerry so far." That was indeed great news and worth celebrating, for it implied being delivered from any more articles of scientific purport in the near future, and the thought made Sutcliffe happy. But . . . much as he would have liked to toast Ryder's "gong" his overwhelming hangover with its waves of deafness and nausea made the prospect something of a dilemma. Nevertheless, he did not wish to seem churlish. "Just a little," he cried feebly, but his companion, full of goodwill, filled him a brimming glass and pressed it upon him saying, "Come along my lad. Here's to us!" Ironically, too, the wine was a yeared Bollinger of almost carnal subtlety and while Sutcliffe's stomach quailed his palate hungered for the treat. He closed his eyes and with a sort of lustful despair, like a man diving off a cliff, he thrust his nose into the beaker and took aboard a vast draught of the precious stuff. How good it tasted, yes, but as it whorled its way down into his stomach it set up all the foreseen reactions, at first slowly, then in more explicit spasms. Retire to the lavatory he must, and in haste; to his intense fury he was disgracefully sick. It seemed somehow symbolic of the whole mess they were in – the mess the world was in: the mess in the heart of reality itself. "First free drink I get on Hitler and look what happens!" And with the news so bad, the future so dark, it was not possible to hope that there might be another. Ryder said, not without admiration, "Some hangover, I must say!"

Sutcliffe groaned and resumed his place at his desk, pale as rice. "It's the Grand Climacteric," he said, "I knew I would reach it one day." And in answer to Ryder's question as to what that might be he replied with dignity, "The Grand Climacteric is the moment at which the problem of when to die takes precedence over that of how to live." The lavatory mirror had deeply reproached and dispirited him – his eyes appeared to be poached in liver extract. Nor was the burden much lightened when Dr. Schwarz telephoned and told him with unction that the afternoon walks for his wife had been sanctioned on condition that they took place when he was not about; he must not see her lest she feel that she was followed or in any way persecuted. "Persecuted!" he lunged out the word contemptuously at the good doctor, who for his part added, "She will be accompanied by her friend – the negro one – who has agreed to come and fetch her between three and four in the afternoon." He hoped that this would meet with Sutcliffe's approval.

So began the afternoon ritual which from now on would dominate his life in the afternoons; the pale blonde girl and the slender vivid negress (so often clad in violet, magenta, orange) walking slowly arm in arm along the shores of the grey lake. Behind them at a great distance came Sutcliffe in dark glasses and hat, coat-collar turned up in a furtive manner. He did it in order to see her; he could not resist the urge to do so, for she still ached him and dominated his restless imagination. The illness, uncoiling as slowly as a python, poisoned his self-possession by its remissions and labyrinthine metamorphoses. He followed the two of them as one might follow a funeral, muttering to himself, sometimes suddenly striking out to left or right with his cane, as if to strike off the heads of imaginary flowers, for none grew on the bitter grey concrete reaches of the Grand Corniche.

From time to time the dark girl might pause, point at something, and speak, often with laughter and buoyant gestures; she had a ringing sane laugh and a big mouth like an open umbrella. Her pale companion never smiled, however, for she had been shocked into silence. Yet sometimes she echoed a word here or there in a small and precise tone, puzzled by its unfamiliarity. Her whole manner suggested that she had regressed in panic to the age of ten.

Far, far behind them walked the solitary bondsman of this unholy trinity, nursing in his mind murderous thoughts about destiny and the treatment of Dr. Schwarz. "You know damned well," he might tell the absent doctor in his mind, "you know damned well, Schwarz, that the subconscious is fished out — there's hardly a sprat left. So you are driven back to base, my lad, with the old fashioned mind-fuck machine of an electro-convulsion-therapy jag. Any poet will tell you that the basic illness is the ego which, when it swells, engenders stress, dislocating reality. Then the unbeknownst steps in with its gnomes and *Doppelgängers*; but once you realise this simple fact your positivism falls from you like a cloak. The penny drops, the *jeton* engages, and you have the Dalai Lama himself on the wire; what comes out now is poetry — that highly aberrant act of nature! It lies the other side of a crisis of identity, stresspoint, flashpoint, turnstile. Once in these calm waters one reads new meaning into things." So, lumbering along in his operatic disguise, he might stop to stare hard at the back of his wife as he resumed his monologue. "Thus and only thus does one become a great lover, shedding the scar-tissue of old dried up love-poems; despite my chain-smoked eyes and lamprey's smirk I have become at last the One I really was all along. A lover made for the intensive care ward of some great asylum on the lake, where Connie in her white smock with her bunch of keys moves gravely among the toys they give to lunatics in a vain attempt to curry favour with them. Schwarz, when you step outside Christianity and look back at it through the bars your blood runs cold!"

The girls ahead of him paused at a stall which was selling fresh *beignets de pommes*, apple-fritters, and bought one each; suddenly Sutcliffe felt violently hungry from all this pious cerebration. He could not wait for them to continue their walk so that he might himself approach the stall in sneaking fashion. He watched them wolfishly as they bit into their hot fritters, happily licking the icing sugar from lips and fingers. The simple gesture had transformed them into schoolgirls enjoying an afternoon off. The pale one almost smiled, as if the sweetness of the sugar dust brought back vague and long-vanished memories. Once more they resumed their quiet stroll while Sutcliffe's stomach contracted with desire and the saliva rose in his mouth. It was an agony to wait for them to take themselves off to a reasonable distance, leaving him free to hurry to the stall and snap out an order for a couple of these delectable comestibles. He watched their retreating backs against the grey mountains, himself standing still, holding a fritter in each hand, his eyes full of tears. Guilt overwhelmed him. He ate ravenously, astonished at his own febrile lust. Vanished scenes came to mind – of when she lay in his arms with her eyes closed, sleeping like Ophelia among the lilies; even then her mind was fraying and he had an obstinate notion that if he managed to make her pregnant it might condense her wits. But she behaved as if she did not understand what his desire might mean. She obeyed him like an animal but without emotion, according him every sexual liberty but without a hint of participation. Their kisses expired in air, and no child came of them. He wrapped his coat more closely around him now and resumed his prowling monologue with the absent Schwarz – the eminent Black, which symbolises death to the psyche of the Christians. Death, the old specialist in unhappiness, always there, un-hurriedly waiting for the phone to ring. The while over grey Geneva the soft pornic clocks choked out their chimes: at night old teeth ached in the fragile mouthscape of the indented coast. "What precautions *can* one take against the suicide of a patient?" Schwarz had asked humbly; he spread his hands to suggest the vastness of utter impossibility. "None." The Christian mind is a wonderland of smut, so thought the un-happy writer as he lumbered along. Why was it so hard to imagine a reality without qualities, and an illusory soul? The whole of Europe was dying of blood-poisoning because of this inability. As indeed they both had been, long before she ab-dicated and renounced the safety-nets of logic and reason. It was all very well to be clever – how bitterly he regretted all those self-consciously ironic propositions he had advanced in his conversations with her, stupidly imagining that she might through them admire the brilliance of his intellect. As when he remarked that the whole paradox of love for him lay in the fact that one wanted something permanent but which did not last too long. He had been well repaid for his lack of sincerity in his loving! The white-coated doctors had gathered around them in clusters, their voices softer than moths.

Thus had opened the Vienna period with Freud and Jung – the sweet-and-sour pork of psychoanalysis, so to speak. Taking apart the clumsy old folkweave Unconscious with all its terrors and aborted ardours. He got the hang of it fairly quickly and was dazed by the suggestions it opened up; in those enthusiastic early times nobody knew that these mar-vellous vistas ended in a *cul de sac*. If there was a dropped stitch in the folkweave there was nothing that could be done – unless of course by suicide which unravelled the whole cloth. Never-theless he had learned much from this stay. It had been a test, and a stern one. Drink and cream cakes had done for him. Someone, perhaps Freud himself, had assured him that strong characters are nearly always constructed around some grave central weakness, a central flaw. We live in a state of over-compensation for this flaw; our tears of pain solidify into jewels of insight. "The sickness of the oyster is the pearl." But after a drink or two had cooled him he realised always that if happiness had not come his way it must have been because he had never really prepared himself to receive it. Now, after such a long period of misadventure, he realised in what sense Western Man had got his priorities wrong; the target was not between the thighs, but between the eyes – the pineal gland of the white vision.

Other memories surged in upon him as he watched the two receding figures of the women ahead of him. Soon they would reach the end of the Corniche and it would be the signal for him to turn aside and scuttle into the side streets, safe from recognition. Trash the negress was very animated today, but he was not near enough to hear that robust laughter; happily, for it would have put him in a rage, by reminding him of how she had provoked a scene of violence in a Sapphic club in under-ground Vienna, and all because he had followed them, wistfully hoping to detach her companion, to reclaim her, so to speak. In his rage he had shaken his fist at Trash and promised to beat her up; he had received a box on the ear which made his head sing. The door was slammed in his face, and the Judas clicked shut, leaving him alone in the draughty street, now smelling of night and approaching snow. He turned aside into a café and drank his wits into a curdle of incoherent shames and loathings. Trash was not a woman, she worked on batteries, so he told himself. On the coat-hanger in the café entrance he had noticed a walking stick hanging on a peg. It gave him an idea. He would burst in upon them and administer the necessary punish-ment to the negress who had thrust herself between his sick wife and himself. When he went wandering back with the stolen weapon he found to his surprise that the door was ajar. He entered somewhat unsteadily but with the gleam of battle in his eye and slowly negotiated a corridor lined with heavy damascened curtains which smelt suffocatingly of dust and the piss of cats. He had hardly got inside this high-ceilinged saloon when the lights went out with a snap and he realised he had fallen into an ambush; for from all sides naked figures leapt through the curtains and started to belabour him with sticks and umbrellas. His hat was pulped, his tie torn off at a single wrench; he was beaten to his knees and forced to defend himself wildly with his stick, and though he got in a smart cut or two he was soon disarmed and overwhelmed by the invisible girls – for he smelt they were women, for all that he could not see them. It was lucky that they did not break anything apart from his spectacles which were expensive ones. He drew himself together as best he could from this rain of blows and thumps. He retreated slowly, ignominiously, on all fours in the direction of the passage which led to the front door, and once outside they were content to let him go in peace. He scrambled out into the street covered in bruises and sweating with humiliation. He stood for a while swearing at the sky but refreshing himself with the prickle of light snow on his face . . .

Ah! But now the women had turned to begin the return journey; it was his cue to make himself scarce, and this he did with alacrity, hopping across the main road and into the anonymity of the side street, making his way slowly back to his office, where he might stay until six before joining his donnish friend at the flat, or heading directly for the homely old Bar, so ill-lit and gloomy and full of sombre furniture. It was the appropriate cocoon for the two bachelors. Here he ordered a drink and sat down with the Geneva newspaper which was so clumsily compiled and written that it seemed to him to be the work of an analphabetic moron from the nearby snows. Even the war news which was enough to strike a chill of despair into any citizen's heart somehow emerged from its smudgy paragraphs as without significance; it was partly due to the French written by Swiss – like porridge poured into a guitar.

Finally Toby appeared, stalking gravely into the establishment; he so much enjoyed being a spy, albeit a desk-bound spy. He wore dark glasses and a hat with a huge brim; he looked over his shoulder all the time, sure that he was being "shadowed". He looked under the table for gunmen and under the bed for kidnappers. He was the fully fashioned operational secret service man. Sutcliffe was bored with all this absurd behaviour and had started to play tricks with him, to give him something substantial to fear instead of these fantasies of power.

He told him lies about odd phone calls, and spoke of the mysterious presence of a black saloon car, a German Horch with bullet-proof windows which patrolled their street sometimes after dark. It was full of armed men; he strongly advised his friend to ask the service for a bullet-proof waistcoat, lest he be attacked on his walk back from the office. At this however Toby demurred – the waistcoats were heavy, he said, and might give him a hernia. However he was impressed by this propaganda and wore an air of nervous precaution when he walked the open street.

Now he entered the old bar in high good humour, hanging up his coat and hat as he boomed a welcome full of gratitude. "My dear fellow, how to thank you .. ? Your rubber bands ... a wonderful contrivance worthy of the best civil service in the world . . . secret service too . . . saved my honour this very lunch hour . . . Miss Farthingale was able to say with Galileo, *eppur si muove* . . . it obviated the need for her to wear spurs, thank goodness, and carry the good news from Ghent to Aix . . ."

He placed his briefcase in a strategic place where he could keep an eye on it, and motioned Sutcliffe away to the pool table for a game of French billiards, switching on the lights and checking over the balls which clustered in their wooden triangle, a formation suggesting the symbolic properties of the Grand Pyramid's square root of five: symbol which faraway Blanford was even then thoughtfully contemplating in a big book of engravings concerned with such abstruse matters. From time to time they talked a small bit of shop, but for the most part they pursued this wholly absorbing occupation in silence, enjoying the long meditations between strokes, between remarks. Then once they were relaxed they replaced their cues in the rack and resumed their places at their customary table where Toby looked at his watch and said that there was just time for a stirrup-cup before they must face the awkward problem of a dinner neither knew how to cook. "I see your Ryder is in for a gong," he said. "It won't do him any good; the damned military don't like civilian gongs being dished out to their people by poor old ambassadors." Sutcliffe said, "He could hardly refuse." Toby wagged his head and added: "The man has a poorly aspected Saturn I suspect." The door opened with a clink and Toby exclaimed: "There you are! I was wondering what had happened to you." It was Constance! Sutcliffe looked reproachfully at his friend, since he had obviously expected this visit – doubtless she had telephoned him. "You could have told me," he growled.

Toby looked haughty and said, "It was all top secret – so she told me – and I respected her confidence, didn't I, my dear?"

Constance looked more rested and better groomed than upon a previous occasion, or perhaps it was simply that with the familiarity of their friendship she had flowered. On the other hand it may have been that expurgating her conscience with Sutcliffe through alcohol and conversation had acclimatised her feelings of reticence. But whatever it might have been the warmth and simplicity with which she took her place between them spoke of an affectionate complicity. Moreover she now had a topic of interest, of burning interest, to discuss. To Toby she said, "I am sure you have heard my news independently, because for some reason not clear to me everybody seems to suspect the Prince of being a double agent." Toby nodded gravely. "It is absolutely false," she said. "He criticises us very harshly at times but he is completely pro-Allied in sentiment. Anyway, he is the topic of my chatter – because I have just had a long communication on the teleprinter saying that he wants permission to land here for discussions." All this Toby knew, as the old Prince had been the subject of some highly confidential exchanges with Cairo, from which it had become clear that his movements were causing concern and alarm since he threatened to return to the unoccupied zone in France for reasons unspecific enough to be described as "business consultations". Toby had no fast views on the matter himself but he was in honour bound to echo the sentiments of his office, which in turn relayed the sardonic suspicions of Cairo, whose saturnine Brigadier Maskelyne could see no virtue in the old man, nor any sense in letting him gallivant about Europe conveying, no doubt, military appreciations and perhaps even coded messages to the Germans. Maskelyne wanted his journey blocked if possible, and proposed that once in Geneva he might be snowed under with prevarications and visa problems. But this was easy to say, harder to execute, for the Ambassador in Egypt was very much on the side of the Prince and, if appealed to, would certainly try and facilitate his request in the teeth of Army Intelligence. The only thing to do to achieve the desired end was to cause muddle and as much bureaucratic confusion as possible around the matter in the hope that the discouraged old Prince might get bored and renounce the journey. This Toby expounded to Constance

with care, watching her ever-growing impatience as he outlined the business. "You don't know the old man," she said,
"he is not only an absolute darling but also very pig-headed;
and he has plenty of people who would be on his side and
against your detestable short-sighted Intelligence Branch.
Mark my words."

Toby sighed and called for drinks, in order as he put it to
himself to give her time to cool off; but she returned almost at
once to the attack with: "Anyway, the die is cast, for the Swiss
have given him a visa and the Red Cross have cabled the
Ambassador." Toby nodded and sighed. "But the army controls transport on a priority basis. If they pretended that there
is no room for two months . . . that is what Maskelyne is
wondering . . . How much power does the Red Cross carry, I
wonder, in Cairo?"

She chuckled. "You will soon see. The old boy will be in
the air tomorrow and through Turkey by the weekend. He has
already asked me to call a meeting, and I have alerted Felix
Chatto to convoke it."

"Another name I seem to know," said Sutcliffe, feeling
rather out of his depth. "Isn't that the consul? I thought so."

"Of course, you know perfectly well. I have no further
doubts about your identity. You were with Aubrey in Vienna
when Livia, my sister . . . She who disappeared just when war
broke out."

"Did Aubrey really love her?" To her surprise the girl
found herself blushing as she replied hotly, "Of course he did.
Who else?"

"And Felix also?"

"You can ask him that yourself. He is here in the Consulate, open to the public all morning."

"And Livia?"

"Vanished. I saw her in a newsreel film of a great Nazi
rally. She was in uniform. After that no news. I don't dare to

speculate, Robbie." He was delighted by this mark of intimacy. "Yes, do call me Robbie, that is what Aubrey calls me; it brings me closer to him. After all we owe you a great debt, your Freud sent us to Vienna. Poor stricken Pia! Not that it did any good, alas!" She put her hand on his arm and squeezed. "I am sorry," she said. And now Toby called them to order. "We are wandering from the point, which is this: is the old bugger going to get through and start up all sorts of conspiracies and projects? I have no one to shadow him." She laughed and replied confidently, "He won't need it. I can guarantee his *bona fides* if you wish. He is staying at the Orion where he has always had accommodation set aside for him since he left Egypt years ago."

"And he will have the latest news of Aubrey," said Sutcliffe, and then stopped short, confused, for the remark seemed to raise up between them the ghost of the vanished Sam. The girl nodded. She looked a trifle pale. She added that the Red Cross was anxious that whatever proposals the Prince might have should receive the attention of the security authorities, "Therefore I ask your department to send a representative to the first general meeting where he will give an account of our work in Egypt and then raise whatever else he has in mind. I only come into it as a medical adviser to the organisation for the Swiss area. I have no sort of jurisdiction outside it. But I have been invited to form the meeting in this way so as not to waste time."

"I can't blame Cairo for being thoughtful about the old boy," said Toby. "If I had Farouk on my card index, working day and night to help the Germans, I would be very thoughtful too. Yes, of course we'll send someone, probably me, since I know something about how you spent your summer before the war, and we are having quite a business getting agents into the unoccupied zone before the door shuts, as it soon must."

"Why must it?" asked Sutcliffe and his friend replied,

"There is too much going on. Finally they will get fed up and occupy the whole place. Meanwhile we are making hay despite the French who are making things hell for us and collaborating very nicely with the Boche."

Sutcliffe was secretly piqued that Toby should have kept the arrival of Constance secret from him, and in revenge felt bound to make them laboriously explain everything to him – to expiate their sin of collusion. His friend, feeling the reasons behind his testiness, resolved to take them all out to dinner at the Lucrèce where, despite rocketing prices, good food was still to be had. The question of the Prince was for the moment shelved, and the evening passed in friendly persiflage and banter.

SIX

A New Arrival

BUT CONSTANCE'S PROPHECIES CONCERNING THE PRINCE and his powers proved well founded, for within the week they found themselves standing on the windy airfield in a darkness punctured only by the runway flare path, waiting for the aircraft which was bringing him to Geneva. He had evaded every obstacle with ridiculous ease. "My boss is in anguish," said Toby. "He has forbidden me to mention the Prince's name in the office as it gives him toothache. Cairo is furious."

"Everyone is always furious with him," said Constance, "but it does no good." The reception committee consisted of Constance and a ventripotent Swiss banker, representing the Red Cross, Felix Chatto from the Consulate, Toby with his elaborate air of spycraft, and the Egyptian Chargé d'Affaires, smooth as an egg. They could hear the noise of a plane droning about among the mountain peaks, its note altering with altitude and position – presumably it was the old English Ensign crammed with passengers. So they hoped at any rate. The airport buildings were in darkness except for a few dimmish lights in the lounge. It was cold, the smell of autumn was in the air. It was not hard to imagine the dark freezing cities of Europe which must already, due to curfews and food shortages, have huddled themselves down to sleep or watch through the silent friendless hours of the Nazi night. The bar was not open in the lounge or they would have drunk a defensive coffee or whisky against this notion of vicarious misery. At last out of the darkness of the sky a plane materialised and they realised that it must be theirs. It rolled quietly to a halt at the end of the runway to disgorge its passengers, for the most part military or diplomatic figures, but among whom, very sprucely clad, and with a fresh buttonhole in his lapel, walked the Prince with an unhurried gracefulness. The little group formed a semi-circle into which he came smiling from face to apparently familiar face; but he stopped when he saw Constance and gave a sudden little leap of recognition. In a moment he had his arms round her, squeezing her shoulders until it hurt her. At last when they disengaged and he had freed her she saw with emotion that his eyes were full of tears. "There is no doubt that it was our fault," he said under his breath, "the Princess said to be sure to hide nothing from you. It was my fault and hers, that dreadful picnic. His death, *aïe!*" He raised his finger and tapped it softly upon his forehead.

She squeezed his hands, as if to comfort and exonerate him from so much feeling, so that he at last felt free to turn his attention to the others, to greet each and every one of them with the punctilio due to his condition. He had a special word of acknowledgement for Felix Chatto, whom he remembered from Provence. The young man was delighted to meet with acclaim for his political percipience. "I remember your political judgements," said the Prince, "and I took good note of them while your foolish uncle made one bloomer after another." It was music to the ears of Felix. Having done his duty thus the Prince then made his excuses for the lateness of the hour and for the fact that he was too tired to prolong the evening. If he was to be fresh for the meeting on the morrow he must really get a little sleep – and who could begrudge him this?

The flock of official cars followed the dark Red Cross limousine bearing the Prince and the banker to the former's hotel, and then as they approached the town, dispersed in their various directions. Felix dropped Constance off at her flat and kissed her cheek as he said goodnight. The Prince had given her a large envelope from Aubrey Blanford containing messages and manuscripts for her to read and she was anxious to examine them before going to bed.

On the morrow they met in the Consulate ballroom which was so often used as a boardroom of a temporary kind, and here the Prince, freshly laundered, so to speak, presided with aplomb. He had recovered his twinkle and the suavity and crispness of his professional manner. He began by giving them a brief account of the state of the war from the point of view of Egypt. "I am irritating the British very much," he admitted, "because my Intelligence is so much better than theirs; you see, being neutral we still have diplomatic representation behind the German lines and normal confidential bag facilities. So it's not to be wondered at that I know a good deal. Naturally we pass on all we can as Allies, but often we are not believed, they think we are double agents and passing planted information to them.... Goodness, how suspicious and mistrustful they are as a race!" The central heating was on full blast and, finding it a trifle too much for him, he pulled out a small Japanese fan from an inner pocket and fanned himself as he continued his exposé. He was lucidity itself, and beginning with the rape of Poland he went through all the succeeding events in order; it aged them to hear him. Each great battle or disaster sank into their consciousness like a nail driven home. Dunkirk, Sudan where France fell, the Battle of Britain, the fall of Paris. "What is to be expected now?" he went on. "I can tell you, though I don't know the date. And don't tell the British, they won't believe it. But all my contacts agree and all my sources insist that an attack on Russia is imminent. This will relieve pressure a good deal, but not in the desert where Axis forces are building up again."

He now turned aside to purely Red Cross matters concerned with budgets and balance sheets and appointments. "My journey has somewhat intrigued everyone but in fact there is nothing specially confidential about it. I am bearing messages to various people, and I must briefly visit Sweden and if possible Paris. I hope to get the necessary exequatur this week for both; but while I am busy talking to the Germans, I

want to propose that we have some representation in the unoccupied zone of France. Aix? Marseille? Avignon? I don't
know. You may think it not very urgent but in fact my own
guess is that the zone will not remain unoccupied very long; it
is too easy for the British to filter agents into it, and whatever
there is of dissidence and resistance to the Germans can form
down there more easily than in the industrial north. And you
know what the French are like. They won't obey orders and
they are completely selfish; sooner or later there will be a gaffe
and the Germans will come in with a heavy hand and take over
the zone. We need someone there to make sure that Red Cross
supplies get through and are properly distributed to the medical people. I cannot see that the Germans will refuse such a
request since they are still signatories and we have not been
repudiated." The Committee heard him out with quiet respect;
nobody had specially clear-cut views about their field of operation, nor were there any very thorny budget problems. In
Egypt all appeared to be going well and even the new Axis
build-up was being faced with confident determination.
"What would you?" said the Prince. "The war will last another four or five years, then peace will come; though what
sort of peace and on what *sort* of terms I cannot tell you! Even
though I appear to be a know-all . . . there are limits. You will
have to consult Nostradamus!"

That evening there was a reception given for the Prince
at the Consulate to which only Felix was invited. Constance
had work of her own to do, while Toby's department never
figured on the social secretary's invitation list because of its
confidential nature. The Prince was in great form. "Felix!" he
cried, "if I may call you so, for we are old Provençaux, no?
Felix, I want to speak to you frankly about your uncle, Lord
Galen. I fear he has been misplaced by the British and will
commit incoherences." Felix Chatto groaned and threw up his
hands. "I share your views alas," he said. "The appointment is

disastrous. The P.M. must be out of his mind!" Lord Galen was the new Minister of Culture and Information, and had taken up his new post with great style and an elaborate incoherence special to himself.

From every point of view the appointment had been regarded as extraordinary. It was not that Lord Galen lacked all culture – except such as might be acquired by someone who had spent a lifetime on the stock exchange: there were other objections as well. The fact that he was an eminent and widely known member of the Jewish community would give Nazi propaganda an easy topic of comment about the culture of the Allies; moreover the appointment had irritated all the intelligent Jews already involved in the struggle. "And then, your uncle made an inaugural speech at his first press conference which was of fantastic inappositeness." Here the Prince got up on tiptoe, spread his arms in an imitation of Lord Galen's public manner and said, in broken tones, overcome by emotion, "Culture . . . our heritage . . . we must . . . do everything to preserve it . . . it's so precious . . . we can't ever do without it . . . precious heritage . . . I mean to say, what?" The Prince shed his imitation like a cloak and pursed his lips, shaking his head reproachfully the while. "It is not possible. He is drawing ironic applause everywhere, like Ramsay MacDonald in his heyday. And you know he gave Aubrey the fright of his life; poor Aubrey woke from a siesta to find Lord Galen standing at the end of his bed with outspread arms like an eagle, intoning: 'O my dear Aubrey, the first victim of our culture . . . the first young writer to be wounded by enemy fire . . . I will get you an O.B.E.'" They both laughed at the thought, imagining the face of Blanford waking to find this dark cultural apparition at the foot of his bed. The Prince went on: "I pointed out that Aubrey had been shot by his own side, and he was extremely irritated. No, I don't think the appointment can last long. There is not enough culture to go round with him in charge.

And you know, Felix, I am an old friend and love him dearly, so I am not just being malicious about the matter. He is a *disaster*!"

Felix was delighted by the sincerity and familiarity of the old Prince's conversation; it somehow set the seal upon his own new maturity, for he himself had changed very much since the outbreak of war. First of all he had secured a vastly superior posting to Geneva – ironically enough he had moved heaven and earth to get himself called up for the Air Force, but with no result. The Foreign Office had "frozen" him in his new duties which were not too arduous and only mildly confidential. Best of all, Lord Galen had been so impressed by the eminence of his new rank that he had offered him a rather handsome allowance upon which he could not only live in good style but also run a small car, which greatly aided the image carried by his rank. The change in him was rapid and very much for the better; he became quite at home in the more famous *auberges* of the town, and indeed in the more respectable night clubs. He even managed to conquer his innate timidity enough to invite the occasional dance-hostess back to his flat for the night. He had grown taller and very much more handsome and assured the Prince that he would be happy one day to accept a Cairo posting if it could be arranged. "Of course it could. The Minister is my friend," cried the little man with vehemence. "He would do anything for me. It's thanks to the Mount of Olives, as we call him, that I am here really, in the teeth of those old Arab Bureau slyboots. I will start work on it as soon as I wind up here and in Paris and go back to Egypt. We will speak more of this matter – this is not the place."

Everything, for the Prince, had a place and an appropriate time; it was amazing how he kept things so sorted out in the filing cabinet of his memory. Most people in his position would by now have succumbed to the role of "delegating" to an assistant. It was this quality which made Constance sure that he would devote some of his private time entirely to herself –

there was a whole sea of conversational matter between them which had not yet been taken into account. She quietly stood back and waited for him to complete the first social evolutions on his agenda. Sure enough after a week during which he had sent a bunch of red roses to her flat every morning, he proposed lunch and a drive round the lake in the afternoon.

It was a brilliantly sunny day despite a fresh wind off the distant snows – for already the traditional autumn decor of Switzerland was beginning to assert itself; the Prince, compensating for his short legs by a prop in the form of a cushion, was at the wheel of the office limousine. They set off in a sort of bemused silence due to a sudden attack of shyness which took them both by surprise. "How strange," he said at last in a puzzled voice, "I feel that I don't know where to begin. . . . Isn't it strange? Help me, Constance, will you?" She smiled, and shaking her hair out of her eyes said, "I know. What a strange sense of inhibition! Dear Prince Hassad, forgive me. Let us begin with him, with Sam." He recognised at once that she was correct in her assessment of their mutual reluctance to talk of the death which nagged them. He began to talk now, quietly but with emphasis, about the fatal picnic party and the Bridge of Sighs, and he could feel her physical tension, the timbre of her anxiety, as yet hardly even translated into physical form, though her fingers trembled slightly as she lit a cigarette, and she turned away from him rather abruptly to gaze out of the car window at the fleeting lake scenes they were passing. Once launched, however, he spared no detail, for all the world as if he were anxious himself to unload the full burden of his guilt, to expurgate the whole incident for which he knew himself to be responsible. Indeed he was paradoxically a little hurt when she said sharply, "There is no real question of guilt. I think we should drop that notion, it leads nowhere. The same thing could have happened in Piccadilly with a runaway taxi, you know that as well as I do. Only . . ."

"Only?" he echoed, gazing at her.

"The thing has filled me with impatience and anger and the sensation of uselessness. I have been seriously thinking of going back to the U.K., shelving all my commitments here and finding something useful to do there. After all, there something real is happening, they are being starved and bombed. They are in the thick of it, while here we are skulking on the outskirts of reality. The Swiss get on my nerves, they are so dull and gluttonous."

"I know what you feel," he said thoughtfully, "but I think you should not act in too great haste. You are doing valuable work here; and if you did move I can think of more useful places for you to occupy. No, I don't agree." He shook his head somewhat sternly. It made her smile affectionately and putting her hand fleetingly on his arm she said, "You sound reproachful."

"No, but for someone so clever not to recognise that you are only acting out of a sense of guilt. You want to be punished, that is what, so you seek action, fear, discomfort."

He was right, of course, and she knew it. "I am just run down," she said. "I'm tired of the insane, I need a change. But a radical one." They drove on in silence for a while. Then she went on: "I've got so jumpy, and that is a bad sign in my line of business. Yesterday a dying patient threw his slops at the nursing sisters – they are nuns in my ward – and screamed, 'You don't love me at all. You love Jesus, you hypocrites! I want to be loved for myself! Take your hands off me, you bloody masks!' To my surprise I burst into tears – a poor advertisement for a doctor."

"Well, you will need a change; how would you feel about a visit to Tu Duc? I have to visit Avignon quite soon; I saw the German Mission yesterday and they have agreed to get Berlin's authority to have Red Cross representation in the unoccupied zone – though I don't think it is going to remain unoccupied long. What do you say – a trip into enemy country, so to speak? It's a rather *unSwiss* remark, I am afraid."

"Back to Avignon?" she mused, for the idea seemed quite chimerical, unrealisable; the rail system was dislocated and the frontier closed, this much she knew from the steady flow of visitors which passed through Geneva, as often as not to call upon friends and relations taking treatment in various clinics. The city has been from time immemorial a vast sanatorium as well as a political cross-roads. Its present neutrality was nothing new; a spycraft and international banking were still flourishing, and the buzz of loans and mergers was always in the air. The Prince found all this delightful, suggestive, invigorating.

"In fact," he said, "when the post is approved I will offer you first refusal of it. It might suit you for a year to work there for us, and come back to Geneva every other week. To keep on your flat and continue your present job in a less exacting sense. What would you say?"

What could she say? The prospect was such an unexpected one that she could hardly visualise it to herself, much less take a decision involving it. When they had left Provence they had envisaged saying goodbye to it for years, perhaps forever. In the case of Sam it had become indeed a case of forever; she closed her eyes and conjured up the battered old balcony upon which they had spent so much of their summer, the woods dripping now with the first winter mists and heavy dawn-frosts. The melancholy road winding down past Tubain towards the silent town with its assemblage of belfries and towers, its cruising walls still hairy with stork's nests, its gypsy-infiltrated bastions.

"I don't know. I must think."

"Of course you must," he said, "and the post has not yet begun to exist, so you have time ahead of you to consider it."

"I shall do so," she said, and with that the car which had

stolen back into the grey town, took an abrupt turn and entered the drive of the Egyptian Legation. On the steps under the portico a young man was alerted and came towards them. He was a tall and extremely handsome personage. The Prince tooted softly at him and said, "Ah there he is at last! This is Mr. Affad, my conscience, my guide, my banker, my confessor – anything you wish. I know you will like him." He was indeed an extraordinarily attractive man with his quiet and well-bred air, his attentive serviability. He opened the door of the car and offered her his capable brown hand, saying as he did so, "I am by now a friend of Aubrey, a firm friend, so I have no hesitation in asking you to please accept me too as a friend. I have heard a great deal about you, and have been hoping to meet you. There! I have said my piece." She asked if he was with the Prince and he replied that he was. "I am supposed to be his business adviser and to keep him out of mischief, and I try to. But it's not always possible."

It was nearly tea-time and the Prince led the way to the garden where in a glassed-in verandah full of hot-house blooms there stood an elaborate tea-table prepared for such as wished with cakes of every sort. A servant also appeared with water for the tea-pot and they seated themselves comfortably around the metal garden table to have a cup of China tea. Affad seemed about to embark on a remark involving some of the Prince's business when he caught himself up and lapsed into silence; noticing this the Prince said, "It's all right, Affad, you can talk in front of *her*; she is a close friend." Affad looked pleasingly confused and replied, "You read my mind wrong. I was about to start talking shop, but it was not for security reasons I braked: it seemed to be impolite to talk shop before a third party – that's all." The Prince wagged his head impatiently and said, "Hoighty-toighty, what a pother! She won't mind if we speak freely, eh my dear? I thought not."

He turned to Affad and said, "Well."

The banker produced a small red notebook from his pocket and turned the pages. "Very well," he said, "first the journey to Sweden and to Paris is fixed. Communications are so haphazard that it may take longer than you think. I have had a long talk with the astrologer Moricand. It is true that he was invited to visit Hitler but he could not get through the lines with all the fighting, so he returned here to wait."

The Prince was absentmindedly feeling in his own pockets for a memorandum book with the manifest intention of jotting down some notes, but he came upon some snaps of his children and began to study them carefully, with a pleasure that was almost unction. He listened to his adviser with only half an ear, so to speak. "Astrologer!" he said vaguely. "What next?" The children stood staring into the camera with their doe-like regard. "How beautiful they are, little children," mused the Prince. "Each carries its destiny in its little soul — a destiny which slowly unrolls like a prayer-mat." He was suddenly overcome by guilt and came to himself with a start. He put the photos away with despatch and turned back to Affad who was saying, "You know, he lives by predictions, like a sort of Tiberius; there is great competition among soothsayers to capture his ear. We may turn this weakness to our own profit later on. I am glad you brought your Templar head on the off-chance. It's the kind of thing . . . we shall see. But what seems imminent is Russia; the whole machine has wheeled round in that direction. I suppose with Greece defeated and the English pinned back in Egypt by Rommel the little man feels free to move: no flank problems."

"I have so many irons in the fires," sighed the Prince to Constance. "I must also arrange a trip to Vichy. The Jewish community of Egypt is offering vast sums to ransom their own kith and kin in France and I must find someone who has the ear of Laval. That is why Avignon, you see; then also the British have unearthed some new intelligence which informs us that the Nazis believe that the Templar treasure still exists somewhere in the Provençal area of France, indeed that Lord Galen's team had actually pinpointed the place but were forced to decamp before they could dig it up. Two members of the staff who stayed on have been arrested already, and one has died under torture. Ironically enough a secretary who was dumb, and could not speak to them! They thought he was just being obstinate and tortured the poor chap until he died. What a world, what vermin!" He stood up and said, "Well, I have things to settle before I leave." Tenderly, reluctantly, he took his leave of her, promising that he would contact her directly he got back, perhaps in ten days or so. "Affad will drive you home. He is going to stay on a while here, and has messages for Aubrey's friends."

"I can tell you where to find them," she said, "with a fair degree of certainty; they foregather almost every evening about this time at a rather disreputable old pub. I can show you where it is if you are going to run me back to my flat, which is quite near."

"With pleasure," he said, and the three of them crossed the rotunda and descended the marble stairs into the drive where the old limousine waited for them. The Prince did not make heavy weather of his goodbyes, for he did not think he would be long away. Time proved him to be mistaken but this was not to be foreseen now, as they parted company among the green lawns and gravel stretches of the Egyptian Legation. Affad drove very slowly and carefully, talking to Constance in a low voice about ephemeral, indeed frivolous, matters until they reached her flat, after they had passed the bar and he had duly taken note of its address. He was really an extraordinarily attractive man, or at least she found him to be so; but as she did not approve of this feeling she frowned upon it and upon him and informed herself sententiously, "Charm is no real substitute for character. There!" Nevertheless she stayed chatting to him in the car for a moment, telling herself that she must be nice to the friends of the Prince. But she found herself admiring his brown hands as they rested on the wheel of the car, and the easy negligence of his dress; for his part he found her very beautiful but slightly mannish – he mentally tried divesting her of all that beautiful hair and crediting her with a moustache. It was a trick he often used when he wanted to "see" into the character of someone, to change their sex mentally. Often it was quite a revelation. But in this case the moustache didn't really fit, and even as a boy she made a very pretty Narcissus. He gave up at last and said, smiling, "The Prince says you are now an analyst. I suppose you treat our dreams as bottled wishes." She laughed and replied, "More or less."

And on that note, with a laugh and a warm handshake, they agreed to part, though he asked if he might ring up and keep her informed of the Prince's movements. "Of course," she said and wrote down her number. The car drew away, and turning the corner, came to a stop outside the old Bar de la Navigation, where Sutcliffe who had just missed an easy shot was using very bad language. Seeing the car he cried to his friend, "There's the black car, Toby. Look out. There's an armed man just crossed the road. He's coming in here." That performance was so lifelike that Toby almost bolted to the lavatory to hide. It took a moment to reassure him, though Affad did not look at all like a gunman; but when he said that he had just come with messages from Blanford everyone raised their heads and expressed great interest. Affad obtained a drink from the gloomy bar-tender and joined them round the billiard table, to talk while they played on. It was his first introduction to the little group of which he was soon to become an inseparable part.

SEVEN

Orientations

THE HARSH WHITE LIGHT OVER THE GREEN BILLIARD
table outlined the massive forms of the two stout men,
making a contrast with the more slender silhouette of
Constance, who had agreed to form a trio with them. It was a
restful way of spending the twilight – nobody had spoken for
a full ten minutes. Seated in an armchair by the cue-rack sat
the negligent and elegant form of Affad, who was watching
intently and drawing from time to time upon a cigar. The balls
clicked contentedly as they rumbled about the green cloth.
Sutcliffe paused to take a swig of his beer and said, for the
fourth time that evening, "I'm blowed if I know what has been
eating you; why, I mean, you have come to this decision, which
seems futile, romantic, dramatic . . . I mean to say?" He chalked
his cue petulantly, as if to alleviate his perplexity and annoyance.

Constance showed signs now of creating a "break", so
that she did not answer directly; she pursued her advantage
until a missed stroke halted her progress. "I have told you why,
but you won't grasp it. I want to do something more active.
What good is a poor psychiatrist when the whole world has
gone out of its mind?"

Toby failed to exploit a lucky shot now and whispered a
very abrasive epithet to himself. "It's just maidenly vapours,"
he said disagreeably. "Believe what you please," she snapped,
"but at any rate I am going into France to see for myself if such
a posting wouldn't be just what I need at the moment. I know
what you are thinking – that all this is a backlash from Sam's
death; but that only catalysed things! My dissatisfaction with
medicine has been going on a long time, and it's not connected

only with that, it has also to do with being a woman. Yes, damn it, being a woman."

"How is that?" said Affad curiously, for she had sounded quite specially intense. "What has being a woman got to do with the matter – and specially this journey?" Constance chalked her cue with robust determination and said, "A woman doctor is no good. The masculine shaman is too strong for her, she will never be taken really seriously even though she is twice as good as any man. When the door opens and the doctor is announced the appearance of a woman doctor creates anti-climax. The patient's heart sinks when he sees he has to deal with a woman when he needed to see her husband. Woman can cure, all right, but only the man, her husband, can *heal*. It is all rubbish of course but the patient's soul *feels* this, his infantile soul feels it; for when illness comes one becomes a child again, helpless, passive. What can a woman do? O yes, she has learned a trick or two from her husband about chemicals; but she can't convey the massive authority and warmth and paternalism of the man-doctor." Toby shook his head firmly and said, "I think you are exaggerating, Constance." The girl pursed her lips as she played on, letting her theme elaborate itself in her mind.

With compressed lips and concentrated eye she bent to her strokes, while her sigh of exasperation filled in the moment or so of respite. "I know what I am talking about," she went on sadly. "After all I've been in this business for years, some of them in general practice before I specialised. I can only say that, however good you may be, and I reckon I'm good, being a woman spoils everything." Pausing, she transferred her cue to her other hand in order to give a thumbs down sign in the Roman manner! "Even if you perform miracles of healing! We are working against a shaman of great antiquity and great tenacity. It will take several hundred years for us to come to terms with it – if we ever do. It isn't possible, is it, to imagine

Hippocrates as being a woman – though God knows, why not?"

Toby seemed about to launch indignantly into a tirade in response to this pessimistic formulation, but Sutcliffe motioned him to be silent so that she could continue; he was genuinely puzzled, while the silent Affad was deeply touched and looked away, as if what she had said had had the effect of wounding him. How beautiful she looked at this moment of doubt and contrition! "Tell us more," said Sutcliffe quietly, "It seems so strange."

"Very well," she said, "let me give you a simple example. It is not possible to examine a male patient without making him undress and actually palping him all over. Just the classical routine examination, I mean. Well, I don't know any man who can respond to this elementary routine without getting excited sexually, and in some cases even getting an erection! This should not be so, but it is. I have had to evolve a technique in order to get over this situation – which is as embarrassing for the patient as for myself, for neither of us wish to let sex intrude upon such a transaction. I talk to him all the time, telling him what I am doing, localising his interest so that he forgets his risk of excitement, often by pure shame or funk. I say, 'Now I will examine your liver, so! If it hurts just say.' So I talk on and he takes an interest in his liver. As for touching him with my hands, which can be powerfully exciting, I have adopted another ploy. I bought the short drumstick that bassoon players use in orchestras. It's stubby and has a rubber head. I plant this cold instrument on the organ in question before following up with my hand! But in God's name what a bore this whole thing is! Now in psychiatry the sexual game is only verbal and one can counter male or female susceptibility more easily, or so I imagine. Also one does not have to *see* one's patient, which helps."

"Is beauty no help, then, in healing?"

"It's a great hindrance; it's only in loving that Beauty is a help, in my opinion. And when you are dealing with science there is no place for it."

All three men echoed the word "Science!"

"Yes," she said defiantly, "Science!" Affad lit another cheroot and murmured, "In an ideal world science should be love!" He stared curiously at the girl; she had a way of concentrating her eyes as she stooped to a shot which fairly made them shine with blueness. "But you will still be connected with medicine," he said, "even if you take the Red Cross posting, no?" She nodded and said, "In a sense. But it's purely administrative – distributing medicines and food. What a relief that will be! But first I must go and see for myself."

"A descent into the pit," said Toby dramatically. "I hope nothing goes wrong."

"What could go wrong?" But Toby shook his head and did not answer. In truth he hardly knew. Constance, when she thought of this journey with the Prince, felt a sudden little wave of exultant excitement. It must have been, she reflected, much the same for Sam when he put on his uniform and let a train carry him away towards a war. It was stupid, of course, but one could not help it.

She was meeting the Prince for dinner that evening in the old Hôtel Orion where he was always pleased to lodge because of the mirrors. "Wherever you turn, wherever you look, *there you are!*" he said exultantly. "Sometimes you are taken by surprise because you didn't know you were there, but you *were*; and then sometimes people can watch you without you knowing, or you can watch them. When one is alone there is nothing like a lot of mirrors to make you happy!" He busily counted the number of his reflections as he attacked the smoked salmon. Constance followed suit, wondering how long the Swiss would manage to live in such luxury, ringed about as they were with battlefields. "When do we set off?" she said and the Prince replied, "Tomorrow afternoon. Remember, no very heavy baggage as we have to change trains at the frontier and walk with our valises. And wear the grey uniform with the markings. I thought of abolishing my tarboosh for fear of being shot at or taken for a spy, but I think on the whole it's better to stay natural even though distinctive! And after all we are to be met. And then, finally, we are *only* staying for ten days or so initially, eh?"

"Very well," she said, and returned home to pack her exiguous possessions which included stout walking shoes and tweeds and a heavy overcoat, for the season was late, and despite the marvellous summer the winter was upon them. Then, as she tested her two little valises for weight, she felt some of the excitement wear off, to be replaced with a mixture of curiosity tinged with dread. It was not necessarily going to be specially tough – just different, that was all: or so she told herself. Her taxi brought her to the station at the prescribed time, just as the Red Cross car drew to a halt with the Prince sitting upright in the back. He waved gaily.

After many a delay they were shown to an unheated train which promised them ample discomfort. It went slowly, too, and the Prince, a true Egyptian, groaned as they mounted into the snowy alpine passes on the way to the frontier. He worked his toes in his polished boots. Their breath turned to spume, whitening the air; they shrank into their coats and buried their hands in their pockets. "Well, we mustn't complain," he said with an attempt at cheerfulness. "Nobody invited us." This was somewhat obvious, for apart from their own presence aboard there were no other civilians – everybody else had an apparent function. There were a few railway officials, some police and soldiers, and a *douanier* in bright uniform. Moreover their speed was funereal – it was as if they feared an ambush or explosives planted on the line. Soldiers swarmed in the country-side, and the signals seemed heavily guarded. And so at last, somewhere at the level of Culoz, with its double helix of line, the train came to a halt and all the lights went out. This was apparently the temporary frontier. The uniforms changed with the language and everything became much louder and more imperative. "*Schnell*!" cried voices, and feet trampled the dark confines of the railway sheds. Their hearts sank, it was so dark.

They had to navigate by the light of lanterns and torches and to carry their baggage for several hundred yards of dark permanent way; then at last round a bend they came upon the new French side, a brightly lit station full of soldiers and officials. There were long wooden forms in a customs shed, presided over by officials and soldiers, aided by a group of French Fascist Milice, looking sinister and depraved in their dirty mackintoshes with distinguishing brassards ornamented by swastikas. Eyeing them with distaste the Prince said, under his breath, "When the sewers are flooded up come the rats!" It was most apposite, for the swarthy line of faces, insolent and rapacious, were indeed rat-like. Their papers were scrutinised with an insulting thoroughness; as if these riff-raff were trying to memorise their very passport photographs. After this they entrained once more and this time they had a carriage to themselves, albeit once more unheated. After another delay they moved off into the night, but with an elaborate stealth, and with no lights on, sometimes drawing to a halt, sometimes accelerating: the whole impression created was one of indecision, as if they were now travelling through unmapped country in which anything might happen. Around them spread the white snowscapes of this winter land – they dared not hope for more clement conditions much before Valence where the olives of the French Midi began. It was eerie. Aloft there was a dazed-looking moon. It looked as if it had been bled white. Constance dozed, or tried to do so, while the Prince produced a pocket torch and a thriller and proceeded to read for a bit, nibbling at a ginger biscuit the while. "I am trying to put myself into a good mood," he said. "One *must!*"

It was the right attitude, at any rate, and she tried to compose her mind to influence the quality of her sleep. She was in a bad humour, though, and obscurely enough this passing irritation had been provoked by the fact that at the frontier she had heard a group of French soldiers, but regular ones for all their grubby disarray, discussing with great earnestness whether snails were tastier if simply roasted, or whether a sauce improved them. It was so very French that it made her want to laugh and swear at one and the same time! The French attitude!

"Tell me more about Affad," she said.

"He's a strange fellow, a queer fellow," said the Prince, thinking with great rapidity like a bird, his ideas beating in his breast—but at the same time remaining absolutely motionless on his branch, so to speak. He was seeing his friend "in his mind's eye", as the saying goes. "You see, his wife's mother was a friend of ours, still is, in fact, an old school-friend of my wife. It is she who lives here in Geneva and looks after the little boy. She has a vast house on the lake and is still very beautiful, tall and dark like a statue, and never speaking, just huge dark eyes. Affad was between the two Lilies, as we used to say, to tease him. Both mother and daughter were called Lily: there was no father, it was something of a scandal at the time. But they were absolutely alike, both dark and statuesque and un-speaking, with the power of looking at you as if they looked down a well. Uncomfortable, their silence and their regard. First he was friends with Lily the mother; he says she often used to ring the bell of his flat and when the servant let her in would come into the sitting-room and stand by the fireplace looking at him, never saying a word. Sometimes she lit a cigarette and smoked thoughtfully for a moment, but silently. Then, as if a new impulse stirred in her, she turned and left the room, just as unsmiling, just as vague. He got used to these

visits, but they hardly exchanged greetings even. It was un-
canny, he said. Then he met the daughter Lily and to everyone's
surprise he married her. She was a striking beauty like her
mother, severe as an Egyptian goddess, selfish as madness but
of great purity and justness. Many men were after her, but she
was unaware. One day in her hearing Affad said something
like: 'There is a certain kind of independence in piety,' and the
remark – I'm not sure it's right, but something of the kind –
had an extraordinary effect on her. She fell hopelessly in love
with him. I repeat what he told me. It was at a crowded cocktail
party. She said to him, as if to confirm her bursting heart,
'Would you say those words again, please?' and he did. So
she stayed with him, true as a magnet until the break. That is
how our Egyptian women are – tuned to the mind like
feathers."

"And the child?" she asked with curious sympathy.
"Where is he?"

"Here. That is why Affad comes so regularly to the place.
The boy has the same eyes as his mother, indeed also as his
grandmother. Lily's eyes, violent deep eyes, wounded eyes,
they burn in his little head like suns, Constance, like
suns."

He paused for a moment, deep in thought, caught in an
abstraction of memory as he re-enacted these scenes in his mind
and tried to evaluate them.

He went on: "In English poetry they say 'orbs' for eyes –
yes, that is what he has, two black *orbs*!" The word took on an
extraordinary colour as he rolled it out. "I think they all hoped
that some medical treatment might cure him, something new
like your analysis, whatever that is. . . . But so far nothing has.
Orbs!" he repeated, thrilling to the sound.

"Analysis!" she quoted hopelessly, overcome by the
realisation of her professional helplessness. It worked in such
a limited field, this cherished analysis of theirs. You could only

reach a certain depth; after that your penetration was compromised and involuntarily you began to invent, you began to start reading in Braille; distortion set in. The vision grew turbid. Limits were reached, the ship grounded on hidden reefs. Intellectual insolvency set in – the so-called cure was really only a promissory note. "It would not work," she said, "that is not the sort of thing to do any good."

"It is like a culmination of the two women's speechlessness, his . . . what d'you call it? Yes, autism. O dear, such sorrow we have all had for poor Affad, such sadness when you thought about his reality. At first they seemed to have found a unique relationship, they drifted about like clouds together. They gave the impression that they thought the same thoughts, even that their breathing synchronised. It is a long time now and he has recovered his calm, I suppose. But he still comes here to see about the boy. He told me that before going to the house he goes down to the Corniche – he knows the hour – to watch the great black car pass along the lake. Lily takes the boy for a short drive every afternoon, still looking sincere and beautiful, without a crumb of discontent, staring ahead of her just as the child does. He sits beside her in his sailor suit from Harrods with H.M.S. *Milton* lettered on the hat. You see what I mean? Once he took me to watch them pass. Afterwards he asked me what I thought and I did not know what to answer. What was the sense of his question, I wondered? The boy's eyes were full of energy, he seemed to see everything, he turned from side to side. Why would he never speak? Affad told me that only once did he hear Lily – the mother – take the initiative and speak before a crowd of people. That was at the theatre during a performance of *Phèdre*. She all at once stood up very gravely and raised her hand, crying out in a deep hoarse voice, yet calmly: 'No! It must stop. It is too much.' Then, turning round just as calmly, she left the theatre with her hands over her ears. People are so strange, don't you think? Her beauty was phenomenal and her gravity was like a charm, it silenced people." Constance found herself dozing at last.

The train jogged on across the snowlit fields with the sleeping girl and the reading Prince. They trailed through Grenoble which was in darkness, and thus down into the plains which led them onward towards Valence. It was late when they finally drew into the silent and empty station. The city around them was asleep, though here and there shone sporadic lamp-bulbs in tenement rooms. By now, too, they were tired, and hardly realised that the train was no longer moving. Indeed the dawn was breaking when once more things started to warm up again. A covey of grey soldiers clanked down the platform at the double with their equipment and embarked, but in absolute silence, which seemed to them very singular. But now, as if stimulated by the new arrivals, the train gathered speed and in the icy dawn they found themselves running through a countryside as yet untouched by the snow, along the Rhône of "hallowed memory": the catch-phrase came into her mind as she watched it gliding beside them, and recalled their own youthful descent of the river – now it seemed a century ago. The willows, the fortresses, the vines – they were all still there, then? It seemed inconceivable. The consciousness of distance and separation suddenly afflicted her with a pang of sorrow for that last memorable summer. Superficially, then, nothing had changed, Provence was just as it had always been.

As if to celebrate the cold sunrise in an appropriate way the Prince produced a thermos flask of hot coffee and poured her a cup. It was delicious, as were the ginger biscuits which he always carried with him against emergencies. "How clever of you to think of it," she said. "Like a fool I imagined there would be drinks and sandwiches available." She had somehow not associated war with shortages, she realised; yet it was obvious. "I shall have a good deal to learn, I can see," she told herself, settling more deeply into her overcoat. Thank goodness for the sunlight on the plains, glinting among the mulberries and the olives. But her education in war was not complete – there was more to come.

Some way before their destination they came upon an old-fashioned railway viaduct which spanned the line, and gazing absently up at it she saw, turning in slow evolution at the gusty tugs of mistral, six faraway swinging forms which some part of herself instantly recognised as human. They had been suspended from the iron balustrades which spanned the viaduct arch, and then allowed to tumble into the void beneath. Brought up short with a jolt, they must have endured a brief moment of agonising discomfort before paying the price for whatever offence it was that they had committed. They lay there against the sky, hanging from the reddish spars of the old viaduct like dolls, turned by the wind as if on a slow spit. Their heads were set crookedly enough on their shoulders so that they looked like quizzical members of a Greek chorus, or else perhaps like strange birds. Their presence there, so high in the air, served as an elaborate warning – but for whom and against what? Once she had seen dead magpies nailed to a barn door with a similar intention. She felt cold. "Look!" she cried sharply on an imperative note and the Prince looked, studying them for a long moment before saying, "Signs and portents of the master race! Six human beings!" To himself he thought, "Their long quibble with reality, circumstance, contingency is over, and so quickly and direly! A small, small click, a tiny bone displaced." Suddenly he felt very old and very vulnerable. He went to the window and watched the swaying figures intently, following them until they went out of sight, as if to steep himself in the notion of war, the reality of war. "I see the Germans have made themselves quite at home," he said bitterly and took up her hand to kiss it before sitting down once more. They fell into a gloomy silence which was only broken when the engine shrieked and slowed down – they had reached the station of Avignon, their destination.

The station was almost empty except for the troops who had travelled with them, and it was not difficult to pick out the little group of civilians who had come to meet them. They stood in a dispirited circle, eyeing the train and chatting to each other; then they caught sight of the visitors and broke into smiles. There was Bohr, the Swiss consul, who was representing quite a number of belligerent nations apart from his own country – for example the interests of Britain and Holland as well as Belgium. Beside him, looking resigned and sardonic, was the doctor who acted as liaison between the medical corps and the Red Cross. He seethed with provincial gallantry when he saw that he had to do with a pretty woman – the wearisome French skirt-fever was her own diagnosis. He would obviously have to be put firmly in his place! The third member of the group was a small and extraordinarily pretty women in her thirties, with hair almost as blonde and lustrous as Constance's own. Her style, her smile, were gallant and spontaneous, and immediately one felt in her presence that one had made a warm-hearted friend. At least this is what Constance recognised at once.

The reception offered them by the little party was cordial if a trifle restrained – as though invisible witnesses somewhere out of sight might have been observing, taking notes. Bohr had already been introduced to Constance by Felix Chatto in Geneva; he was a large heavy man with an unimaginative expression and a thick dark suit. He was heavily polite but monosyllabic. The doctor was called Bechet, the girl in the fur coat Nancy Quiminal. Constance knew from her files that she was a married woman with two small children; her husband was a musician in the city orchestra who was bedridden at present with some unspecified disease. For some years Madame Quiminal had busied herself in representing the Red Cross in a southern province of which Avignon was the principal town –

the *chef lieu*. Her manner was so cordial and persuasive that Constance immediately fell under her charm, as did the Prince. It was almost arm-in-arm that the two women turned to leave the station. Military guards sniffed at their papers like mastiffs but said nothing and waved them through the barrier. Superficially nothing had changed: but then yes, for all the little horse-drawn *fiacres* had disappeared to be replaced by a couple of ancient taxis and two or three buses. The palms looked sick and mildewed. "How sad," said Constance remarking upon the change, and the doctor said sardonically that he thought the horses must have been . . . he made a large and comprehensive gesture . . . eaten to compensate for the defective meat supply. Yes, meat was in great demand and fetched astonishing prices; but recently it had been impossible to find any at all, even on ration cards. Constance was all contrition. "O please forgive my lack of tact." But Nancy Quiminal only squeezed her arm and chuckled as she said, "We are starving slowly; you will see for yourself. Yet everyone thinks that Marshal Pétain is a god and trusts the Nazis." There was bite in her way of expressing herself, and perhaps the doctor found it too sharply pointed as a remark for he added, "You must look on the bright side, my dear. The doctors are worried because with this shortage of food nobody will be ill any more, and they will be out of business. Starvation if it is not pushed too far has its uses for the public."

"You have no children, doctor," said Nancy, with a grimace. "As for Pétain and Laval . . ." but she did not finish her phrase. They managed to secure places in the largest taxi for the brief run along the outer circuit of the ancient walls. The river looked turbid and uneasy. The Prince rubbed his hands with anticipation – he was looking forward to a hot bath and a drink. But the old Europa looked hopelessly unkempt. Its pleasant inner patio was adrift with unswept autumn leaves. Its dim and makeshift lighting arrangements argued a power shortage. Moreover it was unheated; the main lounge was cold and damp. The manager came to greet them – he knew them of old, but it was with sadness that he advanced to take the hands of the Prince. "Excellency," he said sadly, and made a vague gesture which somehow expressed all the unhappy circumstances with which they would have to come to terms in this new world. "O dear," said the Prince, "all those nice wood fires!" The manager nodded and said, "All the wood has been sent away, trainloads; not only firewood, Excellency, but all kinds of woods used in carpentry. *Kaput*! And one wonders why. So many trainloads. Meanwhile we are here . . ." The bar was lighted with candles and looked rather like its old self. They were given drinks and sat down for a moment of briefing before surrendering their new friends. The Swiss informed them that they were expected for dinner at the Military Governor's villa. He turned to Nancy Quiminal and the doctor and said, "Unfortunately you are not included in the invitation, I don't know why." Their alarmed faces at once cleared and their upthrown hands registered an immense satisfaction. "Thank God," said the doctor, and set about taking his leave of them. It was clear that Nancy Quiminal felt a certain relief when he went; there was a sort of constraint in her manner which now vanished. It was as if she had been unwilling to talk freely in front of him. This, Constance recognised, may have had nothing to do with the situation – it was probably just a meridional convention – for in the Mediterranean countries nobody trusts his neighbour; he suspects that he is plotting against him, or talking ill of him behind his back. Quiminal was a Protestant from the rugged country around La Salle, whereas Bechet was from Arles and probably Catholic. Now the two women felt free to speak, and under the quick sympathetic questioning of Constance Nancy picked up her courage and told them just what it meant to be living under very stringent rationing of food, fuel, clothes; and under curfew also which made the nights seem interminable. In full summer they would be stifled alive in the airless habitations of the lower town. And then, of course, there was the ever present danger of being denounced to the Milice; its members would invoke the Gestapo, and anything might result from such a thing—deportation, imprisonments, or even ill-treatment at the hands of these thugs. After half an hour of these exchanges the Swiss looked at his watch and said that it would not be long before the staff car came for them—they might perhaps like to wash their hands and prepare for the ordeal. "Well, I shall be on my way," said Madame Quiminal briskly. "You can give them all my love, I don't think." With a bitter little grimace she shook hands all round and walked briskly off into the dusk, saying that she had to prepare dinner for her two children. Apparently she had somehow managed to come to terms with the Germans and find ration cards which enabled her to feed them. One hardly dared to imagine how . . .

The staff car with an escorting adjutant was duly waiting for them in the little square with its half-stripped winter trees. The three of them entered it with rather the feeling of being diplomats about to present their credentials—which was roughly the case, despite the ambiguities of the German position. It was gratifying that as yet the Red Cross had been overlooked, had not been repudiated by the Nazis. They might still have some sort of tenuous influence over them, then—or so they imagined. This grimly social event hinted as much.

Constance's heart beat faster as she saw that the car, after crossing the bridge, took the curving narrow country roads which led through the foothills towards the villa where once Lord Galen had held court with his absent-minded pronouncements on life and art: where the violet chauffeur Max saw to everything, protected his Lord against every encroaching reality. It had been taken over for the nonce as the General's residence, as well as the senior officers' mess – an arrangement which suited Von Esslin not at all, and made him feel more than ever slighted by the Party. He felt as if he were a sort of local concierge, for he alone lodged there, but he was forced to eat and drink and fraternise with a crew of senior Waffen S.S. officers, including the one who was in overall control of the Gestapo, Fischer. This dire situation in which he found himself made him gloomy, monosyllabic. To assuage his mutinous thoughts he had resurrected an ancient monocle with a golden rim which he hardly needed any more, and which he usually reserved for special occasions of military weight. He planted this object grimly in his right eye, aware that it made him seem aristocratic and forbidding. At the mess table he sat upright, as if deaf, rolling breadcrumbs; he was cold as an iceberg. It was into this somewhat frosty situation that the Command signal had fallen, ordering them to "permit and assist" the implantation of a Red Cross official who would be coming in from Geneva to make contact. It was rather vague – whose responsibility was it, the civil arm's or the military's? While they debated the matter there came another signal, this time from the Consulate in Geneva, telling them to stand by to receive a Prince of the Egyptian ruling house who was representing the Red Cross! Egypt! The business began to take on a vaguely political hue, for the Eighth Army was locking horns with the Africa Corps in the desert and something useful might be gleaned from such a visitor. Von Esslin decided to shoulder the responsibility, though he could not have guessed how apposite it was for them to receive their guests in Lord Galen's old villa with all its memories.

Constance pressed the Prince's hand and his own gave an answering pressure of sympathy, divining her excitement as the car turned into the familiar ravines clothed in *maquis* which tended towards the secluded glades where the iron fences began to mark Lord Galen's old boundaries. "There's the house!" she cried and the Prince took her hand once more, though this time he did not let it go until they stepped out upon the gravel which fronted the villa; indeed he went further, for he held it as they mounted the steps of the portico with its hollow Greek columns and together entered the spacious drawing-room, like actors entering on stage. Behind them lumbered the Swiss consul, a trifle out of breath, and slightly intimidated by the circle of silent officers who rose to greet them. They were for their part astonished, for nobody had told them to expect a pretty woman to dinner, and the Prince suggested an intriguing exoticism with his tarboosh. The Swiss grunted some fairly approximate explanations concerning them, and the officers approached formally, one by one, for the ritual handshake of welcome. But the stark astonishment of the General was the most marked of all; he let his monocle fall with surprise, it tinkled against the buttons of his dress uniform. He turned red, and seemed half disposed to bow rather than touch her hand. Nor was his confusion dissipated when her name was pronounced, for he saw in her the near-double of his vanished sister, Constanza – the same reserved beauty, the same tilt of mind, independent and serene. He withdrew his hand from its contact with hers with a sudden impulse, as if he had been stung by an insect. She had the impression of someone large, shapeless and somewhat guile-less; he was rosy and touching – as so many of the brutes were! He mastered himself, but inside he felt quite overcome, for they had started to speak now and he heard her crisp Hanover accent with its stylish intonation. She was of good family!

The Prince spoke somewhat halting German, though it was serviceable enough for his present needs. Fischer now came forward, full of assurance, but strangely tongue-tied. Von Esslin quite understood why – the lackey had been brow-beaten by the girl's accent and her masterful social insouciance. She saw with disdain a sort of gigolo with heavily greased hair brushed back from a high forehead. He had the flash good looks of a tailor's dummy. Somewhere no doubt he must harbour some deep social resentment against life – she tried to sketch in his disposition as women always do with men, so terrifying and so unpredictable do the creatures seem. It was the self-defensive gesture of her tribe. She felt more at ease with Mahl who was a blockhead and silent, and with short-sighted Smirgel who wore dense pebble spectacles over eyes which seemed made of bluish tweed, with no reflection in them. But he had a certain donnish distinction, and she was not surprised later to hear him referred to as a "Professor" – for that is what he proved to be. Drinks were brought on the scene to accompany the politenesses now exchanged. The officers drank heavy sweet wine or else whisky. Constance chose the latter to allay her fatigue and to stay her hunger, for the journey had made her quite ravenous – hunger could not be stayed with sandwiches and biscuits and such scraps. She hoped that they had had the sense to procure a good dinner.

While waiting upon the event she politely answered questions and blithely accepted compliments on her German – they had never heard an apparently Swiss girl talk such an aristocratic version of the language; it was hard to believe that she was not German, with her blonde colouring; it was harder to believe that she was designated to become the representative of the Red Cross in Avignon where very few people spoke the language. At dinner, which now followed and which proved to be quite eatable, Constance and the Prince flanked Von Esslin who acted as host. Fischer sat at the far end with the consul. On his left there sat a tall saturnine officer of rank called Landsdorf. He was very deaf and conscious of the fact. In the middle of the dinner the Prince let it be known that he was familiar with the house, that he had often been here to dinner during the years of peace. This roused the interest of both Professor Smirgel and Fischer, though it was the latter who

said, "You mean Lord Galen?" The Prince admitted as much.
"A rich Jew who was trying to locate the famous Templar
treasure?" He was all attention now, tense as a cat, as he
waited for the Prince's response. "Yes, though with no luck
I believe. Or so he told me, for he is in Egypt now. I saw him
last month." Smirgel put his head on one side and stared with
his tweed eyes for a long moment before he put in, "But he
located something – a possible place, no? Luckily for us, his
clerk and his secretary stayed behind to help us in our own
researches. You know the Führer is actively interested in the
project in which he deeply believes. It has been prophesied
more than once that he will find it." He depressed his cheeks
and bent his head down until he was staring at the white table-
cloth, in order to hide the faint smile which played about his
lips. It was not sardonic, the smile, but shy and uneasy. The
Prince said boldly, "I personally think it is all rubbish, it is
just local folklore." They looked at him curiously but said
nothing; they went on eating in silence, waiting as if to hear
him continue; but he too fell silent now. Mahl coughed once, a
sharp bark, and Landsdorf, believing himself to be addressed,
looked up and cupped his ear to receive the message.
"Nothing," Mahl told him. "Nothing."

Constance was frankly puzzled by the obvious disarray
of the General who seemed hardly to dare look at her directly –
except once when the Prince announced that she might become
the Red Cross nominee and he stared fixedly at her for a brief
second before timidly replacing his monocle.

"In my case," said the Prince airily, "I am from a neutral
country and have several propositions to put before the
responsible people here – if I can find who they are. For
example . . ." he drew a deep breath before embarking upon a
subject to which he could not foresee very clearly the German
reaction. "The Jews!" There, the word was out! "With whom
do I discuss the Jews? I have proposals of the most far-reaching

kind from the Jews of Egypt to present to someone. Who is it?"

They looked at each other, the five German officers, with an awkward complicity disguised in a stylised hauteur; it was as if the introduction of such a subject had been a gross breach of good manners. Von Esslin stared at the far horizon and cocked his ear in the direction of Fischer who, after a moment of thought during which one could look into his features as if into a well and see right back into his childhood, smiled and moistened his lips. Constance was amazed for none of them looked really hangdog, really guilty. They all believed in what they were doing! The most troubled was the General, and he had the air of ruminating over matters far removed from the present exchange. "You must see Vichy," said Fischer, "Laval – the bureau for Jewish affairs. Remark, it won't do any good. It won't stop this – he calls it *prophylaxis*!" He gave a smile, a snake-like grimace in which the eyes did not join as he resettled the cutlery beside his plate. Mahl chuckled lazily and added, "Now the French Milice has arrived with its new uniform all will be well." This released a spring and everyone felt disposed to smile in agreement. "What new uniform?" asked the Prince curiously, and was given a description of it by the contemptuous Fischer. Khaki trousers, blue shirt and beret. "No doubt they will wish us to salute them in the street!" he said, his voice full of merriment, and his audience of uniformed men guffawed in polite fashion. "Very well, I shall call upon Laval," said the Prince, "since you have no powers, since you are simply the instruments of the old Marshal." They did not quite like this; as a diversion Constance who smelt the hostility in them said, by way of a palliative, "*Aber*, my own problem is one you can solve, General, I am sure. I own a house just outside the village of Tubain. If I accept this Red Cross post will I be allowed to live in it while I work in Avignon? I used to spend the whole summer there once, and it would be easy to open it up. Would you permit me?"

All at once everyone felt relieved, for here was something they could comply with easily enough. They felt suffused with archaic gallantry. "I see no reason why not," said the General amiably. "Indeed we have the very man with us – hey there, Landsdorf!" The deaf officer cupped his ear and had the situation explained to him by Professor Smirgel who had not ceased to cast hungry and admiring eyes upon Constance ever since he had heard her patrician accent. Landsdorf looked surprised for a moment and then nodded quite vigorously to indicate that the eventuality was well within their scope. Constance's heart rose with pleasure. "It will however be very cold, and perhaps not really safe," said the General as an after-thought. "But I am sure you can arrange things to suit you; perhaps to share it? And the Red Cross will have transport, no?"

They surmised as much and Mahl became very know-ledgeable on the subject of black market petrol as compared to the rationed variety. They were still canvassing the subject when the signal was given for them to retire into the comfort-able cretonne-covered armchairs which adorned the dining-room. Smirgel managed to sneak himself into a seat beside Constance with an eagerness which at first she took for sexual attraction – it caused her misgivings that she was admired by this goat-like creature. But it became rapidly clear that he had other interests in mind. "Did you also know Lord Galen?" he said at the first opportunity, and when she replied in the affirmative went on, "Did you know what he was doing?" It was rather a thorny point and she hesitated for a moment before saying, "Very vaguely. He was a businessman. Perhaps the Prince here would tell you more." But the Prince was disposed to be modest. "I was his sleeping partner; he was trying to find the Templar treasure – we found almost everything but that . . . Greek and Roman statuary, medieval ware, ancient weapons . . ."

They looked at him with respectful attention. "But treasure there was *none!*" he said emphatically. "*None!*" There was a long silence. Everyone had half-inclined towards Smirgel, as if he perhaps was the oracle who alone had the right to pronounce upon the subject – as indeed he had, for his sole task was to do just that. He looked quizzical now, as he lit a cigarette; then, watching Constance closely as if for a reaction, he said, "That is not what we hear from the chief clerk Quatrefages, who is our prisoner and whom I have interrogated myself. I must add that the question is an important one for us as the Führer has a particular interest in the matter. I am here on his special instructions to try and solve the mystery."

The Prince looked rather peeved at this, for his suspicious mind toyed with the idea that perhaps after all Galen had unearthed the treasure but kept the secret to himself; perhaps he knew, Quatrefages knew, the whereabouts of the orchard with its fabled quincunx of trees? But no, it could not be! Lord Galen was too much of a fool to be able to manage a double-cross like that without giving the show away. He shook his head in a decisive manner and said, "No, it is impossible! At any rate, *we* did not get it. Nor did we ascertain whether it really existed. Quatrefages had been dismissed already when . . . you gentlemen crossed the border into France."

Smirgel was lying, in order to find out how much they knew – that was how the Prince summed matters up. It was obvious that the Nazis knew nothing either. But they had the task of convincing Hitler of the fact, and that could not be easy. He sighed. He would take up the matter again with Lord Galen when he was next in Egypt; could something be done for the poor clerk? "Where are you keeping the boy?" he asked, but no answer was forthcoming and the Prince let the matter slide, busying himself with preparations for a visit to Vichy with its notorious bureau for Jewish affairs. Meanwhile Constance agreed to show Landsdorf where the house was – he would call for her on the morrow and motor her out to Tubain, simply to familiarise himself with the spot and decide whether such a scheme was feasible so far from the town and the protection of the armed forces. This sounded somewhat disingenuous. "I am not likely to be shot by the *French*, after all!" she said, and Landsdorf turned a trifle red. "Nevertheless!" he said, and they shook hands on the deal.

The duty car duly motored them back into Avignon later in the night; they were stopped on the bridge by an armed patrol whose task was to enforce the curfew which had been declared for eleven o'clock, but their shepherding adjutant made himself known and assumed responsibility for them. The hotel was in darkness, but as they tapped upon the front door the manager rose from the depths of an armchair where he had been dozing against their return. He had prepared a tray of something hot, and also hot water bottles for them to take to bed. They were glad to turn in, both being preoccupied and tired by the journey – a fatigue and depression that lingered on in irritating fashion. It was reinforced by a vague impression of unreality as if everything were swathed in cotton wool. The depression and sadness of the whole community seemed to be leaking out into the atmosphere, infecting it; even with the brief glimpse they had had of the town they had the impression everywhere of faces crashed down into depression. They had smelt the stench of war now; it was more than the smell of folly, of disaster. It was the smell of intellectual disgrace, of human deceit. Constance sat on the side of her bed, warming her hands round her coffee cup, and thought back over the evening she had just spent. A lighted candle puckered the darkness about her. She found herself recalling the conversations, she went over them meticulously, as if to come upon some clue as to what made these soldiers perform their acts. Suddenly the thought came to her: "*They are not ashamed of what they are doing!*" And of a sudden a chill of pure terror entered her heart.

She got into bed and turned out the light, blew it softly out, to settle back in the cold sheets which smelt of damp. In her restless sleep she dreamed of the blue gaze of Fischer, its fixity and its mineral-like quality as of some worn-out gem. It was a gaze full of unconscious sexual information. He could deprave, this man, simply by smiling. In him she felt some buried puzzle which had never been deciphered yet. And yet there was magnetism, compared to the others who were easily understood, easily classified. The General was a harmless fool as apt for good as for evil – provided it came in command orders. He had looked quite confused by her beauty, he would be easy to handle if need be . . .

The subject of this somewhat unflattering judgement had, for his part, also retired to bed – or, more accurately, retired in search of sleep which was to prove extremely elusive on that particular evening, coloured as it had been by the strange new visitor – in the guise of an apparition, almost. Constanza! He bathed in the memory of her blondness, of her warm blue regard, and the sentiment permeated his sensibility with tenderness made the more rich because its object was someone long since dead. But there were confusing cross-currents, rapids and shallows, which perturbed him, prevented him from sinking into his usual heavy slumber. There had been the letter from Katzen-Mutter, for example, which had stung him to the quick with remorse. It was a brief sad letter about the family house but which, halfway through, recounted the suicide of the Polish maid; she had stabbed herself through the heart with the old dress dirk belonging to some forgotten regimental outfit, and which had always been on the wall in his room, over the writing desk. On the desk itself she had left a message in clumsy German which read: "I do not wish to be a slave." His mother did not expressly reproach him, nor in any way suggest that she might have known what the relationship between them had been . . . yet! It was as if she had known, and he felt a profound shame for something of which he could not be accused of being guilty.

It came, too, hard upon a field episode which his rank obliged him to witness – the "judicial execution" of twenty citizens in a small village near which a *franc-tireur* had fired upon his panzers, killing two troopers. It made him feel old, indeed mad with fatigue, but he behaved with a dutiful sternness, walking up and down the line of dead with determined step. There was hardly any blood. They had fallen in all kinds of positions. They looked, with their shabby black winter clothes, like a clutch of dusty fowls lying beside the tiny war memorial. He returned to his office in the fortress with a splitting headache, feeling the two separate emotions of the two distinct events blend inside him and trouble his composure. He wondered if he was perhaps getting influenza. But that night and the next he dreamed of the Polish maid, and on waking he realised that he must find some way of attending confession. He must find a priest. And here once more the cursed ambiguity of his position as a Catholic came upon him like a huge weight. Why not the Cathedral? Indeed why not – but he could not, as force commander, move without escort for fear that someone might take a pot shot at him. Kidnap a priest, then? He laughed gruffly. Simply join a congregation for mass, then? He spoke very bad French!

The situation worked upon him. He became a prey to constipation and colitis – childhood illnesses which no longer responded to senna or castor oil. And now, miraculously, after meeting Constance all was well. He knew he would have the courage to insist on being shriven somehow – he would go to the Grey Penitents' chapel, he would go out to Montfavet with Smirgel; what did an escort matter? Nobody would notice, after all. He felt elated, as if this strange meeting had been an omen of a favourable sort. Constance! He had nothing to read and he felt the need of a calm half hour before sleep claimed him. He turned with renewed perplexity and respect to the little official booklet—the intellectual absolution offered by Dr. Goebbels. It was hard going, the Protocols of Zion, and he was not too sure about the historic role of gold in the matter; he felt an exaggeration somewhere but, after all, the document was an official one: who was he to question facts endorsed by Rosenberg? Rosenberg, himself a Jew—so he had learned! It was even more perplexing. Yet he was in a sudden mood of relaxation, almost of euphoria. Proof: his blocked entrails performed their duty now with rapture, with profusion, as if to make up for days of costiveness. Overwhelmed by the feeling of relief he slept, having made a mental note to visit the chapel of the Penitents on the morrow.

But to Constance sleep did not come so easily, troubled as she was by the memories of the dinner and the empty stare of admiration from the blue eyes of Fischer. It made her impatient, she tried to analyse the dynamism of the glance and came at last to the conclusion that it was his capacity for cruelty and mischief which gave him an almost sexual radiance. She was angry with herself for feeling such a thing and reflected ruefully that at any moment the woman keeps in mind, like undeveloped negatives, several sexual possibilities, several choices which circumstances might put in her way. She turned with impatience to a more troubling topic—Affad; when she had called at the hotel the Prince had asked her to see him, for Affad was indisposed and in need of a prescription from a doctor. "The simplest is to ask you," he said, "though he is dead against it, doesn't want you troubled." She took the lift up to the elegant suite which Affad occupied and found him lying quiet, staring at the ceiling; he blushed with vexation when he saw that it was Constance, and expressed his displeasure with the Prince. "Nonsense," she said briskly, "it's much quicker for me to make out the prescription." "Very well," he said unhappily, "I have run out of Paludonin, that is all." She sat down by the bed and said, "I shall get you some." But she took his wrist in order to feel his racing pulse, and at once remembered her conversation about medicine in the bar with the two friends Sutcliffe and Toby. Perhaps he did too, for he turned scarlet and turned his face away to the wall, with a womanish gesture of shyness. She was, so to speak, left alone there with his pulse and her science – and bereft of words. It was as if he had slipped off a glove. But what came into her mind was a thought which confused her in her turn. She did not quite believe it, but she felt certain that he had fallen deeply in love with her, and the thought was both chastening and elevating. It forced her really to consider him, to evaluate him as a possible person she might love in her turn. A woman is a creature who keeps all her options open. "You have a blazing fever," she said, because saying something filled an awkward space, and he nodded at the wall, keeping his eyes closed. "If you could just give me the prescription," he said, and it was clear from his tone that he was anxious to see the back of her. But she had not brought her printed prescription block, so she elected to slip down to the pharmacy at the corner in order to fulfil his request. "I will send the bottle up with the *chasseur*," she said. "It should pull down the temperature dramatically – but you know that." He nodded once more, and lay as if asleep. "Thank you," he said. "By tomorrow I shall be up once more."

She thought this episode over very carefully as the lift swung her down to the main hall; trivial in itself, it nevertheless vibrated inside her like the echo to something long wished for, ardently desired. At dinner she asked the Prince to tell her about Affad, and followed with great concentration an account of his business life and his education in three countries. "He is really a sort of strange mixture of businessman and mystic. Perhaps he is a homosexual without being aware of it – I don't know." The Prince made a face to express his amusement at this hypothesis. "I certainly don't think so myself," he added more vehemently.

All this and the emotional indecisions provoked by the encounter with Affad she recalled with great vividness bordering indeed on a sort of anxiety because of its ambiguousness. She was not ready to love anybody. Turning and tossing in bed she squashed the tepid water bottle against her toes to try and warm them. But even though sleep came, it was late and unrefreshing. At dawn she was up and dressed, anxious to take a walk across the town. Her feet on the stairs woke the night porter who had overslept and he let her out of the front door on request but without approval. "What will you do?" he said in a wondering tone. "Just look," she replied, and set off for a brisk walk to fill in the time before the planned arrival of Madame Quiminal who was coming at ten to take her to the offices which had been proposed as a centre for Red Cross operations. The town had always been somewhat dirty and dilapidated, so that at first blush little seemed remarkably different about it. Then the smell of rotting garbage became pronounced and she observed mountains of it, overflowing from dustbins and packages everywhere – the stray dogs had enjoyed a field-day in dragging all this stuff about the main square where it mingled with the drifts of fallen leaves. No café was open so early, and the only public phone booth opposite the post office had been used during the hours of darkness as a sort of urinal by persons unknown. There were wall-portraits of the Marshal in a number of places but they were mostly defaced or covered with impotent graffiti. More imposing, for they reflected a history more recent, indeed of burning actuality, were the large command posters attached to walls and trees around the main square; they recorded the death sentences pronounced upon captured *franc-tireurs* by the German High Command. In some curious way the letterpress, crowded together as it was, gave a faint hint of Gothic script most appropriate to the subject, while the red ground upon which the whole was printed was precisely the dull red of arterial blood which had been, from time immemorial, used on the bullfighting posters. The dark red of bull's blood, upon which the crooked cross had been overstamped. Sighing, she read through these condemnations, heavy in spirit, wondering how human beings with so short a span of life at their disposal should seek in this way to qualify and abbreviate it with their neurotic antics. It was a mystery. A deep-seated self-destructiveness was the most one could diagnose about such a state of affairs. But it involved everyone. You could not opt out. Even those comfortable neutrals up in Geneva, though they thought themselves out of reach, were involved in this calamitous historic process – it would reach them in time. Her absorbed steps led her in and out of the medieval cobweb of streets, past the Princes Hotel, where once (so Felix Chatto had averred) Blanford had spent an afternoon with a girl in a room belonging to Quatrefages the clerk. She had completely forgotten this incident until now. She followed the curving walls of the outer bastions, past the little bread shop which had always been the first to open in the mornings because it supplied the buffet of the railway station. But now there was no light in the interior and on the door there was a notice which read *Plus de pain,* which must have struck a heavy blow of dismay at the French soul: such an idea was unthinkable. Maybe it would bring home to the citizens of the town the reality of the New Order. On she walked and the north wind rose and sparkled through the bright sky.

Back at the hotel the Prince sat in the breakfast-room with a bad-tempered expression on his face, spooning up the meagre fare provided for him while opposite him, with an ingratiating expression on his goat-like face, sat the Professor of last night, Smirgel, who seemed to have taken a great fancy to this new friend. "We could not speak freely last night in Von Esslin's mess," he said, "and I wanted to ask your help with the question of the Templar treasure." The Prince in a somewhat irritated tone said, "I've told you all I know." Smirgel made a soothing gesture with his hands and said hastily, "I know, sir, I know. But I have only recently arrived, sent by the Führer specially to deal with this problem and this has put me in rather a delicate position. For example your clerk, Quatrefages, has been very difficult; first he lied and then he pretended that he was tortured, while now he is pretending that he has lost his reason. I say 'pretending', but I am not sure."

"Why should he be pretending? He will probably die under interrogation like the secretary of Lord Galen – he was 'pretending' he was a deaf-mute, I suppose?" Smirgel hung his head and allowed the Prince's high indignation to sweep over him in a wave. He even nodded, as if he accepted full weight of the incriminating charge. Then he said, "All that was before I arrived; now things are different; we are proceeding in another manner now, with caution and sincerity."

The Prince looked as if he were about to throw a plate at him. He swelled up for a moment, filling his lungs with air, and then said, on an expiration, "The last information we had from Quatrefages was that we now knew the names of the five knights who were in the secret. It was a question of trying to trace through them the famous orchard with its quincunx of trees – I ask you! A hopeless quest, I should say."

"You do not believe it exists?"

"I did not say that. Lord Galen seemed quite convinced that it did; but he is a strange whimsical man and could, I should think, be capable of believing anything. But Quatrefages offered us hope, and that is as far as it went. Clearly your inquisitors have driven him out of his mind, thus ruining any chance of getting hold of such information as he might hold. How typical! Where is he now? Is he to be seen?"

The Professor deliberated for a long moment before answering; then he said, "In the asylum at Montfavet – where he can receive treatment and follow a sleeping cure to try and straighten out his mind. He was in the fortress but there was an attempt to help him escape by the gypsies – he was always their friend, no?"

"Of course he was; they were doing a lot of the digging in the part of the town known as Les Balances – they found most of our statuary. We bought it for very high prices."

The Professor gave an elf chuckle. "Our people thought it was Foreign Intelligence which wanted to free him because of the secrets he knew. Hence the interrogation. But you have confirmed my own surmise – it was just a friendly act by the gypsies who were his friends. Thank you, Your Highness." He stood up, for in the mirror among the clustering palms in tubs he had caught a glimpse of Constance returning. "I don't wish to disturb you any longer. But if there are any other afterthoughts please let me know – here is my number. I could arrange for you to visit him, if you so wished – either of you." For Constance had seated herself and after nodding good morning, was looking from one face to the other to try and seize the thread of their conversation. The Prince explained, "It's about Quatrefages. He is in the local asylum. This wretched treasure – now it's Hitler who is after it, one can't imagine why. He can't need the money I shouldn't suppose!"

The Professor permitted himself to say, with a becoming unction, "The Führer's motives are not pecuniary, I can assure you; his interest is a mystical one, to trace the roots of the Templar beliefs, the secret of their downfall. German freemasonry was also involved in their history – I suppose you would know that?"

He seemed anxious to justify himself and indeed re-open the conversation, but he received no encouragement from the Prince, who nodded curtly and with a dismissive air said, "Ah, I see Madame Quiminal coming into the hotel. Let us order some more breakfast for her, shall we?" The Professor accepted his cue and made his departure but not before giving Constance a card with his phone number on it. "In case you might ever have news for me, or information for me," he explained hastily and saluting turned away to make room for the newcomer who came smiling to their table. She was grateful to spend a moment with them before the office opened. "I will be frank," she said. "I have been told that the hotel can afford real coffee because its patrons are army people." But though the coffee was good the hotel seemed completely empty. Although Nancy Quiminal was handsome in her unusual fair-skinned way she was clad in rather a perfunctory fashion, and her shoes were very worn. She caught Constance's eye as it roved over her attire and she said, "*Eh bien,* I know. You are looking at my shoes with surprise." "On the contrary," said Constance, "I took a walk this morning to look at the shops – there is nothing in them! And when I think how *chic* the town was as a shopping centre." Quiminal made a grimace. She did not comment further. But when they rose to go she asked if they might take the bread and croissants with them because one never knew . . . She wrapped them swiftly in a paper napkin and placed them in her much used shopping bag. Then she led them to where their new office was to be created in the back block of apartments which adjoined the handsome central Mairie which looked out over the famous square with its formal Monument des Morts wreathed in metal tracery of breath-taking flamboyance, and contrasting so definitively with the sobriety and ampleness of the theatre. The great central court of the Mairie with its fat classical columns was swept with icy draughts, for a traditional mistral had begun to blow. "We will call on the mayor," said their mentor, "but don't say much to him; he is one of them." She jerked her head with contempt and looked as if she were about to spit. They climbed the beautiful staircase in silence, digesting this information. But it was only to be expected that the Germans would appoint people they could trust, and Constance said as much, *sotto voce*. But Nancy Quiminal said, "No. He was here before. Anyway it is for you to judge." And she threw open a door on the first landing and ushered them into a handsome high-ceilinged apartment where M. le Maire sat at a vast desk, his shoulders bowed under a quilt whose function was to keep him warm enough to sign the documents which issued from his department. He looked both pleasant and quite intelligent, and offered them chairs with courtesy and a certain dignity. "I have heard nothing official, but I gather from common gossip that you are going to come and install yourselves here for the Red Cross. I would say welcome, if things were not so difficult. My poor country!" He saw them eyeing a portrait of Pétain on the wall behind his desk, and made a grimace of distaste and sadness. "Ah, the Marshal," he said tenderly, "without him it would have been worse – a *total* defeat! He is saving as much as he can, but even he is not superhuman." There was an awkward pause; Madame Quiminal rose and excused herself, saying that she would precede them to the offices which had been set aside for them. "I think M. le Maire will want to talk to you for a moment by himself," she added tactfully.

For the mayor it seemed an unexpected idea. He asked them a few questions about the sort of organisation they were minded to father upon the town, and seemed quite pleased at the idea that through the Red Cross they might have access to medical supplies and food parcels for the new prisoners. "All is chaos," he said, "for the moment. There are new camps being used as transit camps for prisoners. . . . Supplies are always short." Then, somewhat to their surprise, he said that while all knew that Madame Quiminal was indispensable to the Red Cross she was not . . . here he paused to seek the right phraseology: she was "not a woman to whom one could say everything". Constance showed her surprise so plainly that the mayor went on to explain that he had nothing against her personally, she was very good at her job. "But there are ambiguities. They say, for example, that she accepts the favours of a German officer, indeed the head of the Gestapo here!" This really took the wind out of Constance's sails; she felt her nascent indignation subside in astonishment and sadness at the thought. "She must have her reasons," she said with asperity and the mayor agreed with his gestures that there was no doubt about the matter. "Nevertheless," he said, "it makes one hesitate. You see, there are many people who are frankly on the side of the ... enemy. One has to be rather careful. But there, I don't want to depress you with such matters. Come, I will take you to your offices myself."

Together they negotiated several corridors until at last tall doors opened upon a pleasant suite of rooms in one of which sat Nancy Quiminal at a desk devoid of paper as yet, knitting and reading. The mayor made his adieus with a formal correctness full of reserve.

Outside in the square there came the tramping of boots as a contingent of infantry crossed it on the way to the fortress where they were quartered. It was a strange sight. Constance stood at the window watching the soldiers, lost in thought; the town was all but deserted. Where, one might wonder, were all the inhabitants of the famous city, normally so eager for diversion that the faintest hint of marching feet, or of drum and trumpet, impelled them immediately into the open streets and squares, keen to mingle into a procession or join a dance-measure? A few shabby housewives skulked here and there like mangy cats, holding empty shopping-bags. Members of the new Milice – *les barbouzes* as they came to be called – strutted awkwardly about in their newly minted apparel. Latins are always conspicuously dangerous when they are serving an unpopular cause for money. It would have been folly to smile at their get-up for they were armed with out-of-date but still quite serviceable weaponry.

They had taken an oath to save the French nation from a besetting Jewry and on them was beginning to fall the onus for the rounding-up of the victims; it had become almost as familiar a processional feature of the town's life as the dustbin round had once been, and would again be when they got it going. The air of solemn legality was absolutely breathtaking when one understood the issues at stake. Constance could hardly believe her eyes as she watched them pass down the boulevard upon their appointed errand, flanked and headed by motor-cycle combines.

The most important thing, she reflected, as she stood on the balcony of the Mairie which formed a most useful belvedere over the town, was to make her appearance as commonplace and down at heel as possible, so as not to appear conspicuous in so much shabbiness. The Prince, who stood beside her, stirred uneasily in his cold shoes and said, but without much conviction, "I suppose it will all settle down one day." He had spent an active and not unsuccessful morning in taking up old contacts dating from his Provençal sojourn, and he was relieved to find that many had gone to ground in strategic positions — some in the *police des moeurs,* some in the Milice, some in road-haulage and land speculation. With their help he had even made a brief visit to the brothel where he was accustomed in the old days to pass an occasional evening, but he found the girls somewhat dispirited and depressed. Their clients were now a superior officer class, but mean with the money. All the girls had been issued with ivory swastikas which they wore over their tin crosses and birthday medallions. They were pleased to see the Prince, though they at once concluded that he was pro-Nazi and this somewhat dampened their elation. Nothing he could say would convince them of the contrary. Nor was there time to do much more than distribute some sweets to the pallid rachitic children. It was with something of a pang that he said goodbye.

There were days when one felt like this – that all was lost, or that the war could not be finally won in under a decade. How could one blame people for not believing in the Allies, for picking up the shattered pieces of their lives and trying to reassemble them again, even in the shadow of the black swastika? He sighed and she looked at him affectionately, saying, "You are in a mood today, aren't you?" He nodded. It was true, and there were a number of reasons. He was not happy about leaving her here in order to go north for discussions over the Jews which he now felt would be fruitless. He had thought at first that the French were simply hostages to fortune, forced to do the bidding of the invaders; he had been disillusioned and disgusted to discover that, on the contrary, quite a number were active anti-semites at heart and only too glad to assist in the persecution of this gifted and ill-fated tribe. He had heard stories of the French concentration camps which froze his blood with indignation and horror – places with such poetical names as Rivesaltes and Argelès, as Noé and Récébédou in the Haute Garonne; but nearest of all was the camp of Gurs in the Pyrénées, which had become a byword for its open brutalities. He became quite pale as he retailed these stories to Constance. "I have been wondering what we could do, if anything; could we ask to visit them? I know, it's premature. I'm jumping the gun. Let us get established first. O my dear, things are much worse than I imagined. These Germans, they are not only foul, but they revel in foulness for its own sake. What have we done to deserve such things in this century?"

She did not know what to say to console him. Almost every day now the buses went the rounds of the old town, openly, industriously, like bees from flower to flower, combing out their human prey with all the appearance of solemn legality. A uniformed officer presided, holding a typed list of names of the wanted Jews. Nor did the victims ever seem to fly, they waited in a kind of paralysed apathy for the green buses to draw up at their door. There was never a struggle, a protest. The Gestapo was using the familiar green buses known to Parisians, with the broad balcony astern, secured by an iron chain and bolt. This made a characteristic click as it slipped into place. Years afterwards Constance was to remember that little click in the post-war Paris, for the same type of bus was still in use.

She was thinking of other things. She said, "Tomorrow I am to visit the house once more!" She squeezed his arm as she said the words in order to make her voice sound even and natural. It was hard, for emotion and excitement welled up in her when she thought of that bleak little manor-house in the woods, with its high windows and dormer roofs set at ungainly angles. It stayed in her memory like a human face – the face of some meek old housekeeper worn down by a life of household cares. She recalled the last look back at it, as the gate clicked shut – clicked shut upon what had now become the last summer in Eden before the Fall. She had some vaguely stirring pre-monition that much would be decided by this visit, though in telling herself this she could not exactly explain in what sense, nor fully account for the heightened sense of expectancy. It was as if she might meet her lover there once more, by accident – or something of that order. What rubbish!

The chilly airs at last drove them back into the bright high-windowed rooms of M. le Maire, but not before they had become aware that down there in the almost deserted square a new sort of movement had begun to come into being; by slow seepage a crowd was forming and advancing gradually down the side streets towards the Monument des Morts. It increased in density as it slowly pushed its way through the narrow arteries which all led in the direction of the Mairie with its wide central square. Yet the pace was slow, almost leisurely, like that of a flock of sheep being coaxed along; in this case, though, the shepherds were uniformed men armed with automatic rifles, a sight which stirred their every anxiety. Their thoughts turned to reprisals, punishments, massacres – the last months had conditioned them to expect the unexpected. But no, apparently, for the mayor took his place beside them inside the sheltering windows, and said, "Ah! It's the bicycles." She echoed the word at him in surprise and he smiled reassuringly and said, "It is for today, together with the handing-in of shotguns."

They saw now that the crowd indeed consisted only of cyclists wheeling their machines; they were ushered, urged, guided into the main square where under the tutelage of the soldiers and the Milice the bikes were abandoned on the ground while the owners were motioned back to the perimeters of the square to become no longer actors but spectators of the scene which was about to take place. It took a little time but gradually the thick carpet of bicycles spread over the ground; many of the owners, now watching from under the trees, were schoolgirls. They were in tears. They felt that something dire was to befall their machines and they were not wrong. Quiminal caught sight of her own daughters in the crowd and asked to be excused so that she could descend and offer them her comfort against the loss they were to suffer. She slipped across the square towards the pretty young adolescents, herself as graceful as a doe. She put her arms comfortingly round their shoulders and spoke to them smilingly. A silence fell for a moment.

Presently there came a stir and some senior German officers made an appearance, obviously to preside over the proceedings and to emphasise their significance. They climbed up on to a dais, whereupon a signal was given at which, with a rustle of steel meshes, two light tanks wallowed into the square, like bulls into a ring, and commenced to devour the bicycles with great zest. Like minotaurs they addressed themselves to the fallen bicycles and reduced them to shivers with their jaws. The officers watched with approval, the crowd with disdain and sadness. The operation proceeded with speed and method.

The carpet of bicycles was gradually rolled back, and as gradually the Milice started to dust the residue of steel towards the centre of the square, forming it into heaps for disposal. Here and there a bicycle which had arrived late on to the scene was fed to the tanks like a Christian being fed to the lions. "It's unbelievable," cried Constance, watching. "What unbelievable spitefulness!"

"*Au contraire,*" said the mayor, who had come back to her side after taking a telephone call, "it's a calculated military move to prevent messages being carried to the Resistance in the hills – supposing that there is such a thing!"

"In what way?" she said, and he smiled as he replied, "A bike does some ten miles an hour. They already control petrol and the cars. It would be hard for me to send a message to the hills, and harder now without bicycles. They are very thorough, our friends."

Together they watched the systematic destruction for a long moment, the conversion of the bicycles into mounds of dusty steel fragments. By now, too, brooms had been produced and the watching crowd was invited to sweep the débris into the middle of the square where a lorry might gather it all up. "*Ainsi soit-il,*" said the mayor sadly. "For those who live in the villages and shop in town it will be very cruel indeed. Horses would come back into favour – but I fear the majority have already been eaten! What more can I say?"

There was nothing to be said. The performance was over and now the shepherds began to manifest impatience with the sloppy, tearful crowd which still surrounded the square, as if unable to disperse, to tear itself away from the sad spectacle. Those who had come from the villages were indeed wondering how they would get home. Now they were ordered to disperse, with gruffness; they obeyed slowly and reluctantly – too reluctantly for the Milice in their new get-up. There was a menacing clicking to accompany the orders as the firearms were primed for action. Those with brooms started to sweep literally, at the feet of the crowd, driving it back into the side streets from which it had emerged to form this assembly – now riders sans steeds. Nancy Quiminal had rejoined them now, still smiling but albeit somewhat tearfully – on behalf of her daughters, so to speak. "It's too much really," she said. "Every day something new. The poor *lycéens* are stricken to the heart, for their bikes were gifts for first communion or good work or whatnot. Thank God we live in the town."

When it came to taking their leave she elected to walk Constance back to her hotel, and together they crossed the icy marble halls of the Mairie and descended the broad stairway outside which a lorry was busy sweeping up the litter left by the bicycle episode. A chill wind stirred the trees and Constance thought with distaste of the unheated hotel and her cold bed which awaited her. As they fell into step Quiminal said, "I would have liked to have you home for some tea – I managed to get some fuel for the old wood central heating today: but I am expecting a visit, alas! I suppose the mayor has told you about me?"

"Yes," said Constance, surprised and relieved in a way that there should be no secrets between them. "He warned me against you!" Quiminal smiled. "Good," she said. "It's his duty and his right. He is for Pétain – what can you expect?"

"But I was surprised."

"Were you?"

"Yes. I wondered why; and moreover I wondered why Fischer of all people. But it's not my affair, after all."

They walked in silence for a while and then the French girl said, "It isn't much of a mystery really; I have a husband I love who is dying of a rare spinal complaint. He is bedridden. A musician, an artist! At all costs my two children must eat and drink – no sacrifice would be too great. My job as documentalist with the municipal library vanished with the war. My work for the Red Cross earns me a pittance as you know . . ."

"I see. Therefore!"

"Therefore!"

On an impulse the two girls embraced and said no more. In the window of the bookshop which angled the narrow street they saw a cluster of slogans and pamphlets and portraits of the Marshal which suggested that the bookseller had responded to one of the "warning visits" of the Milice. Yet on the outside of the window, written perhaps with a moist piece of soap, were the words "*le temps du monde fini commence*". It was like a douche of cold water, life-giving and sane and truly French in its cynicism and truthfulness. Quiminal laughed out loud, her composure completely restored as she said, "*C'est trop beau*." It was as if a ray of light, a glimpse of the true France, had peeped out at them through the contemporary murk of history. They walked on awhile before the girl said, but almost as if talking to herself, "It is he who controls the lists of the taken." Constance guessed that she was speaking of Fischer. An expression of weariness and sadness settled on her features. "Sometimes he 'sells me lives' as he calls it. I buy as many as I can!" For the moment Constance was silent, though she did not quite understand the purport of the last words. But she felt great warmth and sympathy for the girl and admired the world-weary resignation which was so very French, and so very far from everything that she herself might be, or might wish to be. The basic Puritanism and idealism of the north held back from such an open acceptance of life with all its hazards. But there was no knowing how she might have reacted under similar strains, similar circumstances. Much later Nancy Quiminal was to describe her strange harlot-like relation with Fischer. The names of the Jews and other undesirables gathered up in the weekly list of *battus*, as they were candidly called by the Gestapo "beaters", were transcribed on long spills of paper and in this form were delivered to the Mairie where the

Etat Civil of the victim could be checked and his or her name transcribed in the register. There was nothing underhand about all this, it was legal and above board – it satisfied the Nazi sense of self-justification for what they were doing. But then Fischer would arrive with these lists, unbuckling his belt and throwing it upon the hall table like a wrestling champion making his claim, issuing a challenge. She had to wait for him there in a kimono of silk which he had sent her – ready for business. But sometimes they sat and talked and drank some stolen liquor, a bottle lifted from the house of one of his victims. For the most part, however, the Gestapo did not loot; they gave a note of hand for everything they took, for they revelled in the intense legality of their actions. Naked on the bed with her, he would become heavily playful, touching her body and her lips with the long spills of parchment-like paper, and asking her whom she would buy from his list. It was the sexuality of the satrap – he allowed her one or two, sometimes three, slaves of fortune. Their names were crossed out and were not transferred to the great official register. Such victims were surprised to be released the next day. But it did not always work, sometimes he was captious and capricious; after promising her he withdrew his promise and reinstated the names. It was a curious way to redeem these unfortunate hostages – by her very embraces. It was queer, too, sometimes to come upon them alive still and walking the streets, unaware that they owed their good fortune to her. But even this sacrifice did not always work, for Fischer went through variations of mood; sometimes he was full of vengeful thoughts and desires and she found him hard to handle. Once he asked abstractedly why her daughters were never present when he visited the house, and she did not answer, though a cold thrill ran down her back. She had to beg for every sou, to plead, to wheedle, and he would gaze at her with that bright dead smile, anxious that she should grovel; sometimes half-playfully she did, sinking to clasp his ankles, and he stood there with his hands on her shoulders, suddenly switched off, his attention elsewhere; he gazed into some remote distance and went on smiling from the depths of this complete abstraction. She described him as *"un drôle d'animal"*, and mixed with the distaste and disgust for this relationship there was a certain pity – an inbuilt French regret at the spectacle of someone who deliberately chooses the road to unhappiness, who revels in self-immolation and the misfortunes of others. Sometimes he fell asleep and had nightmares during which he cried out and wept, and once after such an occasion he discovered the adolescent sources of much of his instability based on shame – for he wet his bed. It was a shock, and he did not reappear for some time – it was she who, needing money, set about finding him. But all this information came later; on that first evening the two women merely shared a coffee at the bar of the hotel before saying goodbye and promising to meet on the morrow for the visit to Tu Duc.

The Prince was in a poor humour that night, and not at all disposed to travel north as he must; he felt he had a cold coming on. His room was cold, his feet were cold. "And yet I must," he said gloomily, "the General's movement permit specifies times and days, and I mustn't miss the connection since we have to cross into the northerly departments. Damn! I saw the old boy coming out of the church at Montfavet; he looked very sad and weary, perhaps the Creator gave him a talking to . . ."

"What were you doing there?" said Constance.

"I went to try and get a glimpse of Quatrefages; they gave me permission – Smirgel, the slimy one, took me. My dear, Quatrefages is really floating, really *dingue*. Walking about like Hamlet. He was sure I had come from India with special private information for him! I ask you! No, he's not all there. Perhaps it's the drugs, though Smirgel says not. They are keeping him most preciously in the hope of discovering . . . what rubbish it all is, I must say!"

EIGHT

A Confession

I N THE CASE OF VON ESSLIN MATTERS HAD FALLEN OUT
somewhat differently, for he had not been slow to act upon
the wave of optimism occasioned by Constance's visit. It
was almost with euphoria that he motored down into Avignon
bound for the Grey Penitents, for he had been visited by a new
idea concerned with the problem of mass and confession. His
boots clicked firmly upon the pavements of the little causeway
which crosses the bubbling waters of the canal, with its old-
fashioned wooden paddle wheels. He went with only a modest
escort, so as not to draw too much attention to his exalted rank,
and also because he did not like to fill the street with armed men
unless it were on a professional basis, so to speak. The great
portals of sodden wood sighed open and he stepped from stone
on to wood, and from daylight to the fragile light of candles
burning everywhere. The little chapel was deserted though
ablaze with light, as though the time of a service was approaching. The three wooden confessionals, so like telephone booths,
were open. Beside them was an electric bell and a card with the
name of a duty priest who, apparently, could be summoned in
case of need. Von Esslin sat down in a pew for a moment, then
knelt in prayer, as if to prime his gesture, to purify it, before it
was executed. Then he pressed the bell and listened with bent
head until the echoes died away in the depths of the church.
Outside one could still hear the hushing of the waterwheels as
they spooned away at the dank canal of the ancient and now
vanished tanners. At last from behind the altar, moving very
slowly, very sluggishly, there came a burly priest with a
massive square head on which the shock of greying hair was cut
en brosse. Von Esslin sprang into a salute as the figure advanced

and then, relaxing, said in his halting French, "Father, I would like some information. On behalf of many of my officers, where can they hear mass and attend confession?" The insolent dark eyes stared at him with a toad-like composure; the priest's face stayed expressionless as he reflected. He looked the General up and down with no trace of servility. "There is only one priest who knows German," he said at last, "at Montfavet. I will telephone to him and you can go there when you wish and arrange with him. When would you like?"

"In an hour," said Von Esslin, elated to find that he might shed his burden so summarily. "Is that possible?" The square-head bent his chin to his breast and said, "Very well. In an hour. I will telephone to Montfavet now." It seemed almost too good to be true. The priest turned abruptly on his heel and went slowly back towards the altar. Von Esslin watched for a moment, a trifle put out of countenance by his cursory attitude. Then he too turned and made his way out of the candle-gloom into the sunlit street where his escort awaited him. He had one or two official calls to make and he undertook them now in order not to present himself too early at the little church of Montfavet – he wanted the priest to have ample time to contact his German-speaking *confrère*. So that it was a good hour and a half before he broached the winding tree-lined roads which lead towards the ancient village. Everywhere the streams were in flood, they ran hissing and gushing among the green meadows. Larks flinched in the blue sky above. His spirits rose again and he heard himself humming a tune from an opera under his breath. How long ago, how far away, the world of music seemed!

The car with its escort rolled across the green sward in front of the old church and came to rest. Von Esslin got out smartly and with springy step made his way into the gloomy interior. He no longer felt timid about the matter – he had convinced himself that he really was acting on behalf of his brother officers. But the church was empty and there were no lights on – only such light as filtered through the tall windows on to the big, undistinguished holy paintings. After a moment of irresolution he entered the side chapel marked IV and sat himself down in patience for a while; then, thinking to improve his hour, he took to kneeling at a *prie-dieu* and ventured upon some propitiatory prayers to the Virgin which might serve as a sort of scaffolding to the more important confession which was to follow. The sound of footsteps – a strange shuffling footfall – brought him back to himself. The priest had entered from behind the altar and was halfway across the church to where the confessional stood, its oaken doors invitingly ajar. He was a tiny figure, stunted and swart as a black olive, and his eyes glimmered with intelligence. But from the waist downward he was grievously twisted, his whole haunches thrown out of symmetry so that he walked half-sideways with a laborious swaying rhythm. All this happened so fast, however, that there was hardly time to form a clear impression, for the little priest with open arms beckoned him into the confessional with an air of kindly complicity. Von Esslin obeyed and found himself in semi-darkness now, facing an empty slot in the wood, for the priest was not tall enough to reach it. He heard the little man's rapid exhausted breathing as he began with the opening flourish of his *peccavi*, "Father, I have sinned."

The responses and interventions of the little priest came back in German all right – but with so rich a Yiddish accent that for a moment the General nearly burst out into an imprecation. It was as if the gods were making a jest of him! Had they set a Jew to shrive him knowingly? No, it could not be, yet was there anything to stop a Jew from becoming Catholic? Was there? Was there? No, nothing. He was nonetheless briefly possessed by a confused sense of outrage and involuntarily his hand sought the butt of his revolver, his fingers fiddled with the safety catch in a futile, aberrant manner.

The accents of a Viennese psychoanalyst, forsooth! It turned his conscience sour to hear that unmistakable slurring upon certain words. Yet how silly all this was! It cost him something to proceed with his confession, but he managed to stumble through it and receive the expected admonition and mock-punishment which would, according to the strategy of the faith, absolve and pardon him. Yet the contretemps almost made him feel that the performance lacked real conviction. It set him arguing with himself. It was in something of a state of perplexity that he had himself driven back to his headquarters in the fortress. His staff had taken over a regular warren of interconnecting chambers, all giving through one central door on to the main corridor – a security officer's dream. And here on the wall, leaf by leaf, they were laying out the maps which delineated not only his somewhat ambiguous command but also its relation to general troop dispositions further north. He supervised all this with undiminished élan and good humour. The news from Russia, though not disquieting, nevertheless hinted at diminished momentum, of halting to regroup, of stiffened resistance. Well, with such extended lines of com-munication an occasional pause for consolidation was only to be expected.

That evening Fischer was alone in the mess, reading and re-reading his one and only intellectual possession, Kropotnik's *Chess Problems*. The younger man seemed moody and dis-inclined to converse, which was quite in keeping with the General's own mood. He ate his dinner with a haughty silence. In his memory he still lingered over that singing, swaying Yiddish intonation, as in words or phrases like "*Welch einen Traum entsetzensvoll . . .*" He wondered if the little priest might figure one day upon a Gestapo list? There was disrelish in the thought.

The next day dawned chill and misty with skirls of fine rain; the German officer appeared on time, sitting rather stiffly upright in his duty wagon – the posture somehow seemed to illustrate his deafness. He was full of a shy punctilio, but was not unhappy to be escorting two pretty women – for Quiminal had elected to join Constance for the visit to Tu Duc. There was mist on the swollen river as they traversed the famous bridge, leaving behind them the flock of churches and belfries and taking the road to the hills. Constance sat in front beside the driver, eagerly reading off the landmarks which memory rendered precious.

NINE

Tu Duc Revisited

AS FOR AVIGNON, SHE HAD NOT AS YET REALLY MADE UP her mind whether to stay or leave – her resolution had been somewhat sapped by the obvious disgust and distress of the Prince who was dismayed by the thought of leaving her behind when he took his own leave. All the sadness and barbarity of the place with its medieval sanitation – how would she face all this alone? He asked her this, and Constance herself did not quite know how to answer these questions. It was as if she were waiting for a sign or portent which would decide the matter for her. But meanwhile the rich tapestry of her memory spread itself all round her, illustrated by these fine forests and sweet limestone hills full of pure water. The German officer drove stiffly but carefully, walled up as he was in his deafness; Nancy Quiminal had fallen silent, though from time to time she shot a thoughtful glance at her companion. How silent the roads were! The countryside looked, in such wintry light, ominous and beleaguered – as indeed it was. It was not far to go, but Tubain was tucked away in a secret hollow of its own, so that when they arrived the seclusion of the place gave them the impression of having travelled many leagues.

The German switched off the motor and the sound ebbed away from them into the forest. There stood the little manor, damp-stained and unpainted, its gutters swollen with fallen leaves, overflowing upon the front steps and the broad stone verandah with its climbing rose trees. They sat, the three of them, and said nothing.

"Is this the house?" said Quiminal and when Constance nodded, went on, "I came here once, very many years ago, as a small child; an old mad lady lived here? Yes. We brought her eggs!" Constance climbed down and said, "I must just see if everything is the same." The familiar click of the gate greeted her. Everywhere gutters oozed and dribbled for it had rained that night, though now the sky was clear. The garden lay, as always, in its own atmosphere of ruinous isolation, waiting for the burden of summer bees, for the song of blackbirds or cuckoos. The kitchen window was still broken; she peeped in upon the table at which they had so often sat to eat or play cards. But the hearth was piled high with vine snippings and paper – a suggestion of habitation which made her heart leap. Was someone living here? She turned abruptly aside and cried, "We must go down to the village and get the key; I must see the inside." The French girl shrugged and said, "*Bien sûr.*" But as Constance turned, her eye caught a ghost of movement amid the forest trees and following it discerned a man hovering about in the distance, obviously hesitatingly, haltingly wondering if he dared approach. It was Blaise the carter who, together with his wife, had played the role of caretaker for them during that last summer. She beckoned him urgently and at last, with misgiving, he approached, though he only recognised her when he was quite close. Then with a bound he came to her side and took her hands. "They have arrested you, then?" he said in a low anguished tone. But she smiled and disclaimed the fact, and they were far enough away from the car for her to whisper a brief account of her fortunes, and an explanation of what she was in fact doing there. He followed her explanation with narrowed eyes, urgently and with a sort of fearful concern. But when she hinted that she was all but thinking of returning to live at Tu Duc he threw his head back and gave a harsh laugh of pure rapture. "Wait till I tell my wife," he cried, "she will be mad with joy."

"But first I must see what state the inside of the place is in," she cried, for she was still hesitating, and taking the key from his pocket he said, "Come. Enter. All is as you left it. It is perfectly habitable."

It was strange to step into the dark kitchen with its ceiling-high cupboards and scoured white table marked by the cutting knives of past cooks, among whom she could now number herself. She ran a finger along the white mantelpiece and saw that it gathered no dust; who continued to clean and tidy here now? His conversation supplied the answer – it was his wife. But leaping over all these considerations he asked impulsively, "And the boys? How are the boys?" She was caught unawares, and felt all of a sudden assailed by shyness. "Well," she said. "Very well." He insisted, "And Sam?" She realised with a sudden shock that Sam was still, for him, alive on this earth – it gave a strangely relative colour to the fact of his death. She went on to volunteer the fact that he was in Egypt with his friend Aubrey, on active service. She was suddenly swept away by the luxury of having him, her husband, restored to her in this factitious way. She positively drank up his impulsive "Bravo" and squeeze of her hand. The echo of Sam went on repeating itself in the empty room, the empty house; she could talk freely about him because he was still alive! The psychologist in her reproved this weakness, but the lover rejoiced; just to talk about him as if he lived helped her surmount the agony of deprivation which she had been forced to bottle up by her false professional pride. Moreover this was the signal for which she had been waiting. She would stay on in Tu Duc with the shadowy mythical Sam, sole possessor of the truth of his death, so to speak, until her sorrow and hunger were worn out; she would work through the rich vein of his death and Blanford's incapacitation – the horrible accident which had encapsulated itself inside the greater and more wounding accident of the world at war.

"I am coming back here to stay," she said, and when they were back at the car she repeated this in a more excited tone to

Nancy Quiminal who nodded brightly and said she saw no reason why not. There was just enough of the old furniture to make it livable; the rain droned and drizzled on the glass roof of the verandah with its coloured panes. The old analytic sofa stood there, silent, passive, patient as an ideal analyst. She sat down upon it for a moment in passing and heard the twang of a spring. "In dreams begin responsibilities," she quoted to herself; it was a dream with which she would have to deal – a past Sam and a future Sam, transformed and assimilated, and all bound up with the memory of a dead child. It was terribly rich and painful still, this material; but also fecund as only sorrow can be. She would live it all out here on this hillside with its good memories and bad. The wife of Blaise now appeared and added her cries of surprise and welcome – and incredulity at the thought that Constance might come back once more to live at Tu Duc. They promised to have it all ship-shape within days; Quiminal said that her sister's vacated house was full of linen and cutlery and furniture. "I must get permission first," said Constance, "and see the Prince off. He will be angry with me when I tell him." After lingering goodbyes the car bore them back towards the town, Constance craning to catch diminishing glimpses of her "chateau" amid the green screen of woods. They were silent on the way back, completely silent. It remained for the Prince to be voluble, to argue with her; but arguments only strengthened her resolve. "The loneliness *alone*," he said. "What on earth will you do there alone? No telephone, no radio, winter, snow, curfew . . . My goodness, Constance, *soyons raisonnables*!"

"I am staying," she said, taking his hands in her own strong ones. "When you go I'll move up there; I feel the need, don't you see?"

"Just like a woman!" he said, for he was in a real huff. "Come," she said, "you knew it was a possibility when we set out. You yourself suggested it indeed. That is why I packed my affairs in the two suitcases which you are going to send me with the first courier." He made a growling noise and cleared his throat. She pressed his small hands and went on, "I will arrange the whole matter, residence, transport, and so on. The farmer and his wife will look after me. I'm two minutes from town with a duty car."

They parted sadly to go to bed, and next morning when she came down he had disappeared. A car had called for him before first light, and he had taken his affairs with him, leaving her a brief and angry note. "I'm taking my things as I may decide to return to Geneva direct. If you wish to stay I can do nothing. I will send on your things. *Please* arrange to come back *frequently* for consultations at least with Affad."

She felt suddenly bereft, abandoned, and consequently sad; she had counted upon him coming back to give her his support until she was settled in. Now . . . But from other quarters the news was better. The mayor had won the right to have a Red Cross duty car at his disposal with a uniformed driver, though it would have to fly a swastika. And the deaf officer came one day to announce that a villa further up the road from Tu Duc had been earmarked as a strongpoint. This meant that there would be frequent patrols in the vicinity and that Constance could use the duty car to be fetched each day and lifted home each night. This was a great convenience, and they marvelled at their luck. Everything was turning out well — save for the disapproval of the Prince. Nor did she know whether he would come back this way – or had her insubordination driven him away for good?

"I don't care," she said. "I think we have the General to thank for all this. I hope there won't be any strings attached to it." There did not seem to be, for the General himself did not manifest; he was making his own personal arrangements to move, for at last a suitable villa had been found as a residence for him; at last he could vacate the mess which so weighed on his nerves. He did not so much as deign to mark the event by a dinner or an announcement – he simply disappeared one day with his batman and the half dozen or so valises which housed his affairs. He had inherited Lord Banquo's old residence, where he would have the ministrations of batman, cook, A.D.C., and a signals officer who functioned as a shorthand-typist. His responsibilities had grown, his command had become more "critical" in the professional phrase. All this coincided with the first battle definitely lost in Russia and several small but sharp reverses in the Middle East. The plot was thickening, the wind of victory was blowing less strongly. He was glad now that he had left the old mess, for these factors would certainly have caused constraint. Something was changing, had changed; the old cocksureness was no longer there. But the anonymity of his swift departure from the mess had angered the susceptible Fischer who celebrated the occasion in his own way by giving a beer party at which he himself became hopelessly drunk. They felt a sense of release, like schoolboys when the master has left. They sang songs and ended the evening by shooting at candles, having set up a branch upon the mantelpiece, before the tall mirror which gave back their reflections as they stood to aim; the heavy slugs made a satisfactory crunch as they buried themselves in the glass or in the wall. Hardly anyone hit a candle-flame – the object of the game. They were so drunk. But they laughed immoderately, and in the intervals shouted out songs and war-cries. When his pistol was empty Fischer sat exhaustedly in a chair, leaning against the wall, and said to his nearest companion, "You know what I like? Hostages! When you stop a bus or workmen's train. You see their faces and you say: 'I want you, and you, and you'." He set his face to imitate himself in ruthless mood. A pause. "I say: 'Get down.'" He allowed the command to sink in and then continued. "They say, 'Who, me? I've done nothing. I've done nothing, why me?' And I say, 'I know what you've done. You get down and quick.'" He swept up his pistol to support the commanding tone. Then his face crashed, disintegrated into a smile which became a guffaw, expanding into a paroxysm of loud laughter as he slapped his knee and repeated, for his own private delectation, the phrase: "Who, me? I've done nothing." He would never forget the look on their faces when they said the words. And he went on laughing in a maudlin delight. The party wound its way to a slow ending, past midnight. A young Waffen officer decided to imitate the Russians by breaking empty glasses in the fireplace. They were invited to imitate him but few did; the gesture left them very thoughtful. The thought that it might be ill-timed, however, did not affect Fischer who loyally disposed of two beer tankards in this fashion before somebody took his arm and cajoled him back to his normal sober sense. He looked haggard and ghastly when at last the party broke up to go to bed. It was their farewell to Von Esslin with his excruciating aristocratic ways, with the reserve that froze. Naturally his name was not mentioned, though the fact was tacitly accepted by them. Only Smirgel the intellectual had remained quiet, had taken no very active share in the proceedings, contenting himself with a quiet smile from time to time to show that he did not disapprove.

But to be alone suddenly is another matter, alone in a town which in its new guise was no longer the sun-golden, leisurely town she had known. The winter wind, the whirling leaves, the seething river below the ramparts all went to make up a revised image against which she now had only the fact of her loneliness to place. It was true it was desired and willed and self-induced – nor would she ever have repudiated it for she felt it to be necessary. Yet with the departure of Prince Hassad a twilight fell, a winter twilight populated by Germans, and the bitter world of shortage and curfew which they had brought with them; a world of ration-card and movement-order which slowed down the course of everyday affairs and made all of them apathetic and ill-tempered, cold and underfed as they were. And supplies were short, or had to be hoarded if they were not simply appropriated by the Germans. Here she knew how to use both force and tact – and her knowledge of German helped her in her numerous altercations with supplies officers or small functionaries trying to curry favour with the German authorities. For a while she even managed to invoke Pétain and plead for a shallow margin of independence, but the image of the old Marshal had tarnished so rapidly in the light of the forced deportation of Jews and the drive for manual workers for the German war-industry that it conveyed little force; already public disgust with his antics and malpractices had become marked, and the present discontent was soon to be followed by despair as it finally dawned upon people that their boasted independence was completely hollow. Yet in a sense the resulting shame only made them hate the English more for having refused to do as they had done. Above all, *they* should not be encouraged to create incidents here in the "free zone" for which they might all suffer – for the German reprisals were swift and not too selective. Nor did it take much to annoy them. In one random machine-gunning they could, and often did, account for a whole village. The posters with their rusty blood-coloured texts proclaimed the fact quite clearly: "The German High Command will extend no clemency to *franc-tireurs*. They will be punished ruthlessly."

The day she chose to move was a Sunday, and she had invited Nancy Quiminal to come and help her make the change-over. If she had any fears or imaginings about a life in Tu Duc which might be one of loneliness and privation they were rapidly dispelled by the warmth of her welcome, by the evident relief of Blaise the carter and his family, not forgetting the three children he had fathered. The whole house had been scoured from top to bottom; a fire of vine snippings blazed warmly in the narrow hearth, its flames twinkling among the copperware hanging on the wall – they had left behind a serviceable *batterie de cuisine* for some future visits unspecified. Cutlery, table linen, sheets and blankets – all had been reverently locked away by the good man's wife, only to be revived now for Constance who was astonished by the transformation. There was even a drum of paraffin in the outhouse with which to fill the small lamps with their warm gleam. She felt quite tremulous as she sat at the scoured kitchen table and watched the fire blaze up and felt the heat turn her pale cheeks to rose. Stray thoughts of Sam did not help her composure and though Quiminal felt the temper of her emotion – she pressed her fingers – she could not guess the reason behind the mood. It was the secret poignance of Sam's invisible presence – he had once polished the little lamps with pieces of newspaper and carefully stacked them in the cupboard against a future summer – they all had believed obstinately in *that*. Blaise had found a hidden bottle of wine at a good degree of alcohol and they were each given a small beakerful to toast the "success of the house". It was so marvellous – the leaping fire, the smell of food already cooking (a *ragoût*) on the old-fashioned range with its coal bullets, the chatter of the children … all this was a good augury for her stay, Constance felt. She would live and work in the kitchen, would use the big barn-like pantry as a dressing-room while at the same time keeping on her own bedroom – the one shared with Sam, because it turned its back to the north wind. In fine weather she could emerge on to a kind of verandah conservatory which, though water-tight, was so smothered in rose creepers that it filtered the light and one felt almost as if at the bottom of a pool. Here the old sofa lay at anchor, waiting for happier days.

They had brought modest rations with them – some rice and vegetables, some coffee and cheese. She had persuaded Nancy Quiminal to stay the night after much cajoling, and now the wife of Blaise delightedly made up the bed in Blanford's old room. "It's almost like being on holiday!" cried the girl. "One simply doesn't feel the Boche up here – and yet we are only a few kilometres from the town."

It was true, the Germans had hardly shown their faces in this small hamlet; the fact had enabled Blaise to make his dispositions for winter as he had always done, behaving as if there was no war, no Germans, no shortages. In Tubain he had done what he had always done at the end of the year; he had bought two geese, a couple of piglets, and half a dozen chicks. His backyard gave out upon pure forest. It was easy to dissimulate and disperse these modest purchases in such a way as not to excite the cupidity of any passing patrols. In an old Provençal chest he had hoarded up some flour, rice, tea, and a collection of dried herbs for medicinal teas – *tisanes*, so beloved by the French as a defence and counterbalance to a too rich cuisine. He made his own wine every year in a modest enough quantity but at the expense of the neighbouring vineyards where, after the harvest, a free-for-all is permitted to make a clean sweep of inferior grapes which the harvesters have rejected or missed. This is called *grapiller*, and everyone of modest means goes a-graping after harvest and with what he gathers makes his own home-made brew. So Blaise. His wine was of good colour – like a good Frenchman he held his glass up to the light before drinking it off: and it had "nose", just the very faintest wraith of a trace of earth-coolth, cellar-warmth, odourlessness of human hands which have plucked the fruit, redolence of the magma of decades from the great vine-presses . . . *presence*. All this romance and folklore seemed immortally true and real in the warmth of the leaping fire and the rosy light of the lamps, lit well before their time to lighten the dark kitchen. The wife of Blaise was called Colette, and she was a proud and robust woman from the Protestant sector of the Cevennes, slow to kindle "like holm-oak" as the saying went, "but once alight, burning forever". She had long since adopted Constance, and was genuinely thrilled to think that she might spend the dreaded winter ahead with them in Tu Duc. This vivacity and sympathy was not withdrawn from Nancy Quiminal either, for it was almost impossible to resist her good looks, sincerity and forthrightness. They found themselves bringing the "latest news" from Avignon to this couple for all the world as if they lived a hundred miles away; but it was sombre news of punishments and arrests – and in some cases gratuitous brutalities for which, illogically enough, they had been ill-prepared. Sights they had not been prepared for: like civilians hanging on the branches of a plane tree opposite the Papal city. Or in another part of the town a dog and a youth hanging from a first floor balcony. There were stories attached to all these bloody incidents and Nancy Quiminal told them in her low melodious voice. A pained silence followed, while the gaze of Colette, with all its dark intensity, passed from face to face, as if questioning them as to the meaning of such events. "You will not be afraid here?" she said at last to Constance, and seemed reassured when she shook her head. "Much less than in town I can assure you." There was, indeed, no curfew here and no patrols, which sometimes took a pot-shot in the direction of a forbidden light during the obligatory blackout. Nevertheless like true peasants the family turned in early, but not before Blaise had crept down to the cellar and tuned in his ancient radio to listen to London for news of the war. This was very dangerous and might one day have dire consequences, but he could not resist this one link with the outer world; it made their Crusoe-like existence up here, perched over the village of Tubain, tolerable. "One thing," said Colette. "There is a good deal of movement on the road after dark. If someone knocks don't open. It's safer. Many people are escaping to the hills, to avoid forced labour, you see. From the end of this road, they turn aside into the forest and gain the hills like that. This is the last point. They pass at night, sometimes one hears them talking. Once I saw cigarettes in the dark. But I always lock fast and so far nobody has tapped at our door."

However they dined very early, for the winter dusk fell betimes at this season, and then the children were sent up as warming pans to warm the beds made with fresh, rain-smelling sheets. The little boy insisted on performing this service for Constance's bed, for he had been hopelessly in love with her since the beginning of the last summer. He lay still and thoughtful, gazing open-eyed at the ceiling, remembering how she looked when almost naked, in her old-style bathing costume. He groaned. He had been so jealous of Sam. He put his hand upon himself and imagined how it would be if he could get Constance to make free with him as his sister so obligingly did when they played in the barn. He groaned again and turned from side to side in a small paroxysm of desire. (And to think, thought Constance to herself, nobody noticed such things before Freud discovered infantile sexuality. It is quite unbelievable.)

Then she admonished herself by saying, "Dear me, being schoolmarmish again. Every mother must have known it, seen it; but social convention gagged her, she couldn't speak about it." Yet she was not so sure. As for the famous infantile sexuality there had been an incident during that memorable last summer which had been anything but equivocal. It had happened one morning when Sam had forsaken their nest-warm bed, to brave the cool of the weir and gambol among the water-lilies, leaving her half-stunned between love and sleep. The sun would soon be up. So, lying there, dozing dazedly, she felt the sheet drawn back enough to admit the smaller body of Blaise's son who slid down beside her, into the circle of her arms, to shower kisses upon her sleeping face. She awoke surprised and lay there nonplussed for one long moment, unable to formulate a form of conduct to suit this forbidden intrusion which at the same time seemed almost innocent because of the youth of the young

Tarquin, who did not seem able to help himself. He was in an agony of love. Emerging through the barrage of tiny bird-like kisses she found herself saying, "*Non. Non. Arrête!*" but even as she uttered them she felt his small throbbing penis tremble and discharge like silk against her warm sex. What should she do? It was a quandary! The speed of the assault had taken her by surprise.

She managed to utter the saving words without undue priggishness but it was already too late, the deed was done, and the boy's transfigured face spelt out the innocence of his emotion. His weapon had now started to shrink and wilt, he uttered brief smothered cries of pleasure and buried his face between her breasts. This would not do, and she was about to take a more forceful and definitive line when providentially they heard the latch of the kitchen door down below click open, and a step fall upon the kitchen flags. In the most miraculous way the boy disappeared – as if into thin air; it was an act of the purest de-manifestation! He slipped out of sight and sound so swiftly that she could not even formulate her aroused reproach, and even began to wonder whether she had not dreamed the whole episode. But no, the little pool of semen was there, proof positive, with droplets caught hanging in her bush. She dozed again, or tried to, until the reappearance of Sam and the renewal of his caresses, his cool flesh turning warm under her responses. They made love once more and slowly, a little wearily; and because the incident and her own arousal made her feel a little guilty she felt overburdened with the truth and the desire to confess – or nearly as possible! She needed to feel a vicarious absolution in this richer, deeper coupling with her mate. "I've been raped," she said, but in such a way as to make it sound a jest. Obligingly he took it as such and said, "By what – by a dream, or a wish, or a clergyman's thought?"

"Yes," she said, but not specifying.

"Well, you are pretty warmed up," he said, with a mock

sigh of sadness. "One always has to thank the other, *l'Autre*, the Lodger, the sod . . ."

"Homosexual ploy, that," she said, proud of her new analytic skill. "Ah, the public school."

"If there were world enough and time," he said, most unexpectedly, and bit into her bottom lip until it hurt intolerably. "Constance, you as my *ideal* girl will always keep a gilded dildo for doldrums – as when I go to the wars, like." She felt him deeply, deeply sad.

"You authorise me, my Lord?"

"Anything you do is fine," he said. "Only because it's you, that's how I feel it."

"Only because it's me?"

"That's it, that's how I feel it."

They lay staring into each other's eyes as if mesmerised for a long moment before he turned on his elbow and groped for a life-saving cigarette. "My dear," she whispered, and put her arms upon his shoulders which were still cool from the waters of the weir. He did not mean a word of it!

As absolution that was all there was and it would have to do. . . . And now, remembering these past events, so sharp in memory's focus, she told herself the real reason for her decision to stay – it had not even been clear to herself until a moment ago. The truth was that for all these people Sam was not dead, he was still in an unspecified somewhere which would one day divulge him again and restore him, blithe and unharmed, to this landscape, to these people. It made her a little shamefaced to realise this, for she had rather strong views about sincerity; but she needed time to herself, time to stare Sam's death out of countenance. Here she could live without having to give an account of herself or of him. For how long she could not tell, but evidently one fine day, when she could resume life to the full, there would no longer be the need to cheat. She would assume his death before the world.

The fire in the range blazed up now, and their dinner which consisted of a large *ragoût* of various palatable scraps, conjured from God knows where, and eaten with that rarity, a home-made loaf, smelt marvellous. The children came down and announced that the beds were blazing. Their mother despatched them to bed betimes to save fuel, but they refused to go unless their father gave them a glimpse of the family of ferrets which he had just managed to acquire. They were kept in a large wooden mousetrap of the old-fashioned kind, one with several compartments, almost like a small apartment. Blaise said, "To call in the farm-guns as the Germans did could have spelt starvation for many – perhaps it still does, who can say? But I thank God for the warrens of rabbits in the forest, and for these little fellows. I had ten conies yesterday. Aren't they pretty?"

The ferrets were sleek as very tiny greyhounds; they slid about their cage with an evil composure, their eyes gleaming as they made a queer little clicking sound. The children were given their glimpse but not encouraged to caress the little animals. "To bed," cried their mother. "Kiss the ladies goodnight and off you go!"

Constance did not fear that the son of Blaise would risk renewing his addresses as she had successfully quelled him by hinting that if there were any renewal of such behaviour she would inform his father of it. The boy turned pale and from then on avoided her stern eye whenever chance brought them together. The threat weighed heavily upon him, as well it might. Nevertheless now, after such a lapse of time, the event itself did not weigh so heavily, and she kissed him lightly, giving his shoulder a squeeze. They locked up the little duty car in the great barn of the Bastide where Blaise lived as caretaker to absentee tenants; it would not do to let the motor freeze in the whirling mistral which had risen upon the night, like an outrider of the coming snow. They said goodnight and locked themselves in the kitchen, having blacked out the room with scrupulous care. Nancy Quiminal played a hand of solitaire on the kitchen table in order, as she said, to calm her spirits before sleeping. Constance brewed a *tisane* of sage – she had picked some in the field outside the house.

When they crawled into their tepid beds and bade one another goodnight Constance felt that for her the war had really begun; this was her first night of it and Sam was still alive, had been unobtrusively salvaged from the wreck of the world.

Both girls slept badly, unaccustomed to the sense of emptiness engendered by the country noises which came to their ears from the garden with its sombre greenery and tall pines and chestnuts, and from the strip of forest which lay beyond the high road. It was not fear, but strangeness which bade them rise before first light and set the old oven going to brew morning tea. They had begun to move imperceptibly into winter – the dawn showed it with its sullen crimson gashes, its clouds wind-scarred from the fitful mistral of the night before, its ringing frost upon the highroad leading to town. Quiminal remarked upon it when the little duty car rumbled and skidded downhill to the town, and added, "Now our troubles begin; the cold will soon strike." But they were in good heart after all, the trip had refreshed them, and they supported the insolence of the soldiers at the checkpoint on the bridge with a vexed resignation. Now they could see the point of having a uniformed driver to conduct them, for he would bear the brunt of such encounters with the soldiery. It was as good as having an armed guard. "Paradoxically enough, our dangers will come from the *maquisards* when once they form – if ever they do." The loathing and despair engendered by Vichy was apparent from her tone.

But good news awaited them in the form of permission to travel about the area replenishing medical stocks in hospitals and clinics, and this task was delegated to Constance, as the newcomer, a fact which rejoiced her. Here was a chance to move about, to restore her contact with the Provence they had once known as a playground; it was as yet not quite a cemetery, despite the depredations of the Germans. Even in chains, like this, denied all the brilliant trappings of its bullfights, Corsoes, village fêtes, religious or secular foregatherings – its life-giving ethos of pious joy and unbridled paganism: even now as it was occupied and defeated, it emanated life and hope. So long as there was one point of light in the bleak world there was hope. And Constance was irrationally proud that it was England which had fed this flame. Though the defeat and the betrayal hung heavy, people had begun to feel that it was redeemable. It was sufficient to hope for the moment. And in the final analysis hearts rose to realise that already France Libre under its youngest General had twenty thousand French volunteers under arms ... None of this could be said; but in every look cast at a German soldier or at a member of the Milice there was a buoyancy which conveyed the thought. The insult was there to be read, which is why both the Huns and their instruments took special pride in their routine cruelties. It was their reply to the silent reproach of the public's charged silence. A new kind of hate had been born, and it was with anger that they filled the trains to bursting point with poor half-demented souls from the camps, bound for the better equipped camps in the north. It was with deliberate pride that they ordered them to go slowly, at a walking pace, through the town and over the famous bridge, so that everyone could see their captives. In olden times they would have impaled them and stuck their heads on pikes to be exhibited along the walls, over the gates of Avignon. Yes, but the enormous numbers of such quarry precluded such a medieval gesture, or else certainly the Nazis would have revived it, as they had revived ritual beheading.

Sentiments and emotions such as these are difficult to express to oneself unless they are illustrated by some concrete instance which stands forever as a marker, a history which clinches the matter. So it fell out for them.

One such train, full of children and adolescents – some girls – slowed to a halt upon the main line at dusk, in a light skirling snow. The doors of the wagons were open or ajar and from them flowered these pale, exhausted faces in abstract expressions of estrangement or grief. It was a bereavement just to see them and to know oneself helpless to aid them. The Red Cross truck was crossing the sidings below the main road when the lights held it up for the train to pass; the whole expressive object with its penitential cargo of suffering passed directly across the vision of Constance as she crouched beside the driver. Their own cargo consisted of medical supplies bound for Nîmes and its clinics, but it also contained a treat of one hundred whitemeal loaves for the children. The flour had been hoarded and saved with great difficulty, and every week this little offering was given to the young, either in Arles, Nîmes or Aix. It was not much, but it cost thought and time – and a certain sharp practice. As chance would have it, Nancy Quiminal was at Constance's side, for she had asked if she might be given a lift as far as the Lycée, and she shared the sombre vision with her friend. But she was quicker-witted than Constance, for as the train lingered at the level crossing she gave a sudden gasp as an idea came into her mind; and before anyone could ask what she was at she had leapt out of the car and thrown back the tarpaulin which sealed the back. "Come quick," she gasped, and before she even fully realised the intention behind the gesture Constance followed suit, bounding into the road under the dully amazed regard of the uniformed driver. They seized the two laundry baskets filled to the brim with fresh loaves of bread, and dragged them up the concrete slip to the waiting train, uttering little breathless cries to attract attention. It was like feeding seagulls; the hands floated in their anxiety above and around their upturned white faces – the wagon stood too high off the permanent way for them to hand the loaves, they must pitch them. But not one fell down, not one was missed, while here and there on the frozen faces glimmered something which approached a smile of gratitude, or perhaps something more inscrutable, like an expression of desireless fatigue and pain.

The baskets were almost empty when the expected re-action came; a whistle blew once, twice – a piercingly urgent note. In the distance, way down the long platform, a slim figure in the uniform of a Nazi lieutenant gesticulated and shook his fist to mark time with the string of imprecations he was uttering – too far away to be audible. But the action was sufficient to bring down retribution on their heads, for nearer at hand some burly civilian figures who looked like stevedores or lorry-drivers broke into a jog trot towards them, growling like mastiffs, their boots striking sparks from the concrete of the platform. One undid his belt as he ran, the other brandished as a weapon a pair of long wool-lined leather gloves, elbow length – murderously heavy. The two girls saw them advancing out of the corner of their eyes, but they kept their minds resolutely upon the task they had set themselves, and by the time the first two men reached them in a scuffle of boots and a welter of guttural oaths and snarls, their baskets were empty, down to the last loaf. Then the sky flew apart as the men – they appeared to be either Czech or Russian muleteers – waded in with their blunt weapons and crashed them down upon their poorly defended heads. They cried out in protest of course, but this only enraged their assailants and the blows redoubled in violence. They shrank down, shielding themselves as best they could with their arms, but to little avail. They were beaten to their knees, and then even lower until they were almost on the ground, gasping under this punishment.

By now the youthful officer was also upon them, his pale face contorted with a rage which hardly allowed him to speak, uttering imprecations and orders in a voice which sounded almost like that of an adolescent. Here a moment of inattention came to the rescue of the two girls crouching on the platform. The German's language was obviously foreign to the two peasants and they turned heavily round upon him in order to try and understand what he wanted of them. It was only a moment, but it sufficed for the quick-witted Nancy to cry, "Quick! Run for it!" And suiting the action to the word both girls raced along the platform, their feet barely touching it, or so it seemed: like duck upon the surface of a lake. The men turned growling and started to pursue them, but in a half-hearted surge which ended at the gate of the level crossing. Their quarry had darted sideways into the narrow streets of the town, while the driver of their car had had the wit to reverse into a nearby side street to await their return. Meanwhile they still ran frantically, in tears with rage and excitement at the humiliating beating they had received, but also aware that their escape had been providential – further down the platform they had seen soldiers running up, their rifle butts at the ready. One blow could crack a skull.

They burst at last into a small *estaminet* known to Quiminal and under the stolid and unimaginative stare of the landlord behind the bar – a man known for his Vichy sympathies – asked if they might dress their wounds in his toilet. Nancy had a lump on the back of her head, fortunately masked by her hair, and a mass of smaller contusions; Constance a black eye and a cut temple which would necessitate the wearing of dark glasses for a good week. It was mercifully limited, though both had aches and pains, bruises and sprains almost everywhere. And shock: they were still pale and trembling at their own audacity. By the time they went back to the bar the expressionless peasant behind it had set up two glasses and plenished them with yellow rum and sugar upon which he now poured hot water before pushing them forward and motioning to them with his head to drink. It was a generous gesture considering his sympathies and in view of possible consequences for himself – for already a platoon of soldiers wandered down the street checking identities, perhaps (one never knew) searching for them?

They took their drinks to the darkest corner of the establishment and drank gratefully, in this way calming themselves down before any further action. They decided to separate, Quiminal being quite near her objective; so Constance set out alone and managed to find her car and driver in a side street. Snow had begun to fall; the train had vanished into the slate-grey skies of the northern hills. Their journey was not a long one – Nîmes lay about an hour away, tucked into its dry scaly heaths called garrigues. But checkpoints were many and quite systematic, and even their quasi-official status availed them nothing. But it was at one such checkpoint near Bezouce that a familiar figure from the past floated into her presence with his arms spread to embrace. It was like some archaeological survival from a forgotten epoch – Ludovic the Honey Man, whom they had encountered in the Cevennes, and along the dusty roads of Provence so often, so very often. He was one of those unforgettable figures of the local genius who bear the full Mediterranean stamp: generous, copious, inexhaustibly rich in humour and earthy vivacity.

He walked like a bear emerging from its grotto, arms spread wide, radiating a massive benevolence. He recognised her at once – he had a peasant's eye sharpened by a lifetime of fairground practice. No country fair had been complete without the presence of this great expert, who blazed and roared and crackled like a forest fire, cajoling, teasing, provoking, inspiring his customers to invest in one of his choice honeys – "honeys from the bosom of Nature, perfumed by the Virgin herself" as he was accustomed to declare – though in prevailingly Protestant country he used other terms. "My God," said Constance, "It can't be true. . . . Ludovic!" Moreover he had with him his honeycoach as he called the great furniture removal van which he had had adapted to the needs of his exacting craft, his hives.

His horse, disshafted, cropped the grass in a nearby ditch; his capacious honeycoach with the back let down stood in a field beside the checkpoint. He had been busy selling his produce – his young son was still at it – to the German troops who manned the post in a good-natured way. Also to the passing traveller who, while his papers were being checked, strolled across to buy a pot of this "veritable nectar of the gods". It was more than an apt word spoken in jest – it was true: there was no honey on earth as delicately perfumed as the honey manufactured by Ludovic, for the simple reason that he followed the blossoms with the rotation of the seasons and took his cleverly constructed hives with him. It was work of great refinement and delicacy, like the blending of a fine wine. His great coach had been decorated by a local artist with scenes from the Fête of the Tarasque – the mythical dragon-monster of Tarascon which enjoyed a whole festival procession on its own; this gave it some of the sharp brilliance of a Sicilian country cart with painted sideboards. In this contrivance he jogged his way about, following an exacting itinerary which began in High Provence with the first chestnut blooms and linden, and gradually descended the slopes of the Cevennes towards the plains; in his mind he had a complete map of his choicest blooms and their location. And with each flavour he had recourse to one of his four "widows" as he called them, who busied herself with the bottling and labelling of his produce. He also carried in his head a clear and detailed chronological chart of the various country fairs of which he was such an ornament. But just in case of doubt he always carried with him a copy of that extraordinary great compendium of learning, *Le Lahure: les foires de France*. From these pages he could tell you the time of day, year, hour of every festival and fête, not merely in Provence but in the whole of France. It was his only reading matter, and when he had nothing to do, while "the bees were working" as he put it, he would lie under a tree reading it with massive attention; and when he tired of it he spread a red handkerchief over his face and slept massively and often convulsively. After every seventh snore his whole face contorted and he appeared to swallow a large mouse. Then, recovering, the sound would be renewed. They sat together now under a bush by the cart, to discuss matters again, after so long a time apart.

He was full of complaints; his pots of honey sold well to his new clients but the roads were getting very difficult, movement was difficult, fodder for the horse was difficult. He had become quite a scavenger for scraps in what was once a land of plenty. With his large clasp-knife he cut off a hunk of cheese for her which tasted delicious, "situated" as it was by a glass of wine. He was full of quaint expression: "*Il faut le situer avec un coup de vin.*" The meaning presumably was to wash it down with the wine. Whatever it meant the act was appropriate and the wine delicious.

"Well, what do you say now?" he asked with flamboyant gloominess. "What a pretty mess we are in – what did I tell you long ago, eh? The youth of France has gone work-shy and gun-shy – and here's the result. The country ruined and the Hun in charge." He glared malevolently at the young soldiers who were circling round his quaint coach, eyeing it with curiosity. "I shall soon be out of business. Life in the hills has become hard and dangerous."

"The Resistance?" she said, kindling, but he shook his head disdainfully and replied, "There's no such thing. Simply slave-labour on the run, dodging the draft in order not to go to Germany. The hills are full of them. But they are hungry and dangerous. The Germans must be mad."

There was nothing vastly original in the complaints of Ludovic; but it was amazing to see that he was still in business, plying his anachronistic trade despite the upsets caused by the Occupation. He had grimmer tales to tell, of course, as who had not, for he came from the poor devastated villages which had suffered reprisals for sporadic impulsive action by the odd *franc-tireur* or peasant driven mad by Nazi exactions. The smoke of burning barns and houses was still fresh in his nostrils. "And I can tell you that before the last shot is fired, I will fire one, I will take one of the swine with me, that I promise."

They talked in this strain for a while and then he said that he must get going as he hoped to reach Remoulins before curfew time to avoid trouble. "When will we meet again?" he added sadly, "now there are no more fairs, and I have to sell in towns where I am tolerated, like Carpentras and St. Gilles. Let me at least take your address." It so happened that he knew Tubain, and this cheered him up. He reharnessed his horse with a prodigious amount of purely theatrical roaring and shoving, while the little boy giggled himself witless. Then side by side they both waved to her as they clopped off down the road, while she rejoined her taciturn chauffeur and set off once more for Nîmes to despatch her business. She had been wondering what to say about the missing loaves of white bread, but when Ludovic had heard her story he at once offered to make good the loss with a dozen large pots of a choice honey, and nothing she could say would change his mind. He loaded them himself into the back of the car, expatiating on the virtues of honey for young people with big appetites and growing limbs. "Pure honey nourishes the intestinal flora," he added inconsequentially but with an air of disinterested medical gravity. Where on earth could he have picked up such a phrase, she wondered?

But after the warmth of this encounter – a voice emerging

from prehistory it seemed – she found the journey turn cold and forbidding again. The grave heathlands through which they were starting to mount looked austere and forbidding, like cruel drypoints which soon the snow would mantle and hide. Her head ached partly from the belabouring she had received at the station and partly from the strain of conversation with Ludovic who conversed in a wild and whirling manner and in a high register complete with a whole repertoire of extravagant gestures. A conversation with him was like a whole season of opera. But how well she could recall the smell of the croissants they ate at breakfast daubed with his lavender honey. Blanford made the sacrifice of cycling down to Tubain for the bread and croissants almost before first light each morning. The honey of Provence – how romantic it had seemed to them then as they sat round the breakfast table smearing it on their bread while Blanford read them the head-lines in the newspaper and commented thereon with gravity and a touch of pomposity.

So a new rhythm began and as the nights grew longer and the country a prey to the frost and the tearing mistral the journey home each night, or at the end of each professional visitation, grew more precious, more than ever desirable. Sometimes she kept the duty car for the night, sometimes she was dropped at Tu Duc at dusk. It was bliss to know that there would be a small fire in the grate, a lamp lit, an oven heating. It made her almost guilty to enjoy the mothering of the peasant girl and the warm solicitude of her husband, who had always brought off some *coup* in the matter of food for them, and sometimes even wine or a *marc* of smoky intensity.

At other times, but the occasions were rare, she managed to bring with her Nancy Quiminal for a night. Nor were there any special alarms, though once or twice at the end of the year, at the full moon, she heard steps in the road at night. But nobody stopped; as for the patrols, they made so much noise with their service cars and motor-bike combinations that it was possible to plot their journey from afar; she got used to the particular swarming noise of the Volkswagen and Mercedes engines. These coveys of armed men passed regularly, at stipulated times, and they did not seem to be seeking for any trouble in this lonely corner of the countryside. After a few weeks she could tell the time by them almost, though she was careful to avoid them if she could where her own movements were concerned. She sought no contact with the patrol station up the hill.

One day some small indisposition had made her ask for the afternoon off, and she spent the after-lunch period in turning out the upstairs rooms where, here and there, in corners and cupboards she found odd relics of their last summer stay; a bundle of newspapers, some old letters, a torn sweater belonging to Blanford. There was a little frail sunshine and she opened the window upon the garden to capture some of it. As she did so she heard, or thought she heard, the faint pure sound of a voice down by the weir – a voice pitched slightly above the steady drumming tone of the water. In fact it sounded exactly like the voice of Livia, her vanished sister, and, like her, it was intoning the *Aum* just as she used once to do at the beginning of her yoga sessions. Quite dazed with surprise Constance leaned out of the window, craning to see if there was anything which might substantiate this, for she told herself that it was a figment, a trick of memory – this low pure sound upon the cold air. Twice the voice intoned the word and then fell silent. Constance closed the window with a bang and made her way downstairs at breakneck speed. She slipped out of the verandah door and ran lightly down the avenue of planes into the dense patch of forest which bordered the weir. As she ran she parted the bushes with her hands, half afraid that at one such gesture she might reveal something so strange and frightening that she would be struck dumb with astonishment. She really did not know what to expect, so that it was a relief to discover nothing to correspond to the sound. By the old weir the frosty grass was trampled, yes, but by rabbits. There was no sign of anyone. Nonplussed, she turned and retraced her steps towards the house. And in the final alley she came nose to nose with Blaise. "You heard it?" he said, and she nodded.

"Does it sound like your sister to you?" he went on. And when she nodded he said that he had heard the sound twice before but there had never been anyone when he went to investigate. "But once my wife said she saw far away a girl on a bicycle heading down the hill for Tubain. It was too far for her to see clearly."

"My sister Livia?"

The thought echoed on in her mind, striking it with a deep amazement because of the improbability of such an eventuality. What would Livia be doing here? Strangely enough this question was soon to be answered, though for the moment she put it aside in order to apply herself completely to the work which had now become more exacting because of the season of frost and wind. For journeys now one had to count upon occasional sunny days when roads were not too frost-bound. The close friendship with Nancy Quiminal ripened day by day until they were as close as sisters – closer indeed than she had ever been with Livvie. They undertook alternate journeys, dividing up the responsibility.

Once Nancy came back from a visit to Aix and told her that she had seen all the Paris intellectuals playing at *boules*, rigged up in *berets basques* and complaining bitterly about the food shortage. "I felt such a disgust and shame that I almost wept – but then what else could the poor things have done?" Indeed. Constance was reminded of this one evening when she arrived to overhear the children of Blaise playing in the barn among the haystacks. They were exchanging caresses, making free with each other, and at the same time repeating memorable recipes of long-vanished dishes. It was one way to allaying their hunger in the prevailing dearth – she was both touched and amused. If only Sam had been there to share such things with – yet in a special sense he still was. And then from the conversations with Blaise suddenly some ancient French would rear up its head in the middle of a phrase; she was on the lookout for these cherished exceptions. As, for example: "*Quand l'arbre est vertueux taillez le en bol.*" Or else: "*Madame, je vous signale que le zinc est une matière noble!*"

Then one evening something unusual happened; the duty car dropped her at the corner of the forest path – it would return on the morrow – and she made her way on foot for the last few hundred metres, glad to breathe in the forest for a moment before closing her door upon it. It was dusk, with a fading light. Outside the garden gate stood a duty car with a soldier at the wheel. She peered in at him and with a movement of perplexity invoked an explanation of his presence there at such a time. But the chauffeur did not wind down the window. He simply pointed to the house and then turned away his gaze with an air of brutish insolence. Seeing that there was nothing to be got from him she opened the gate and entered the little garden. And peering through the lattice of the old-fashioned windows into the kitchen, now warm and rosy with firelight, ·she saw a German officer seated before the blaze, but with his chin sunk upon his chest, apparently asleep. For a moment she thought it might be the General – an irrational enough sur-mise – and then, peering more closely, she made out the profile of Smirgel. He slept on under her gaze, he seemed hardly to be breathing, with his grey eyes doubly hooded, once by the heavy vulture's eyelids which covered them, twice by the thick-lensed glass with which he covered them. He heard the snap of the latch as she entered the room and drew himself upright in the chair, sighing and rubbing his eyes apologeti-cally, shamefacedly. His greeting sounded ingratiating in its warmth and she was too startled to return it. Instead she said curtly, "What brings you here?" He looked at her for a long moment during which she discerned that his attitude towards her had changed – it was stern now and earnest. "My duty," he said sharply. "We have never really had a talk, have we? Not a really warm confidential talk, have we?"

He stood now and watched her as she went about her conventional duties, taking off her coat to hang on the hook behind the door, smoothing her hair and unpacking her shopping bag, arranging her few spare articles of kitchenware on the tall dresser. Over her shoulder she said, "I trust you know my status, if this is intended to be an official interrogation?"

"Of course I do," he said and as if to punctuate the thought gave the shadow of a heel-click. "I came to put before you some of my own problems in the hope that you may supply some answers. Your sister has been very helpful – of course you know she is here?" Her consternation both puzzled and elated him. He said, "You did not *know*? She has not made contact, then? How strange, for she spoke of you all with great affection, great affection." Constance sat down with some abruptness upon a chair before the fire. "So Livia is here after all?" she cried, almost in a fury, and the officer nodded. She is a nurse now in the Army," he said. "She is working on shock cases at Montfavet – and Quatrefages is in her ward, in her care. Why have you never asked to see him?"

"Why should I? I have only seen him once or twice; I know nothing about his activities except that he worked for Lord Galen. Livia on the contrary knew him much better. But what intrigues you about all this business? Lord Galen and the Prince were partners, hunting for the Templar treasure – mythical as it is I suppose. They thought they were on its traces. Or so I understood."

Smirgel said almost sadly, "So am I, so are we, and so far with little result. I will be frank with you. We have been able to do little with Quatrefages because of his health which has broken down under the strain of our rather harsh questioning. This is all over, now; we have placed him out of reach of the Gestapo – you know that my department belongs to the Foreign Ministry, I report direct to Ribbentrop while Fischer and his colleagues depend upon Himmler. You can imagine there is some rivalry, as in any organisation. So that much that I know is not known to Them." A very fine contempt had now entered his tone of voice upon the word "Them". But she also felt the implication that whatever she told him would be held in confidence. It was puzzling. Later, in discussing this very perturbing visit with her friend Nancy Quiminal, the latter said, "Of course you were puzzled – you were for the first time hearing the voice of the born double agent – he was taking a sounding." Constance's kettle was making a slurring noise. Without more ado she poured out two cups of sage tea and sat down opposite Smirgel, examining his face with attention as she said, "You will please now tell me what is on your mind, or ask me what you have to ask. I cannot stay up all night. I am tired after a long day."

"Of course. Of course." For a moment he was sunk in thought, coiling (so it seemed) and uncoiling his long spatulate fingers. He placed his hands about the cup as if to warm them, and spoke now in the most friendly, kindly manner, as if the act of participating in this little refreshment had brought them much closer together. "I'll tell you everything," he said, clearing his throat. "I will admit that I am under a little pressure, simply because my master is, because the Führer is himself deeply interested in this matter; not, you realise, because of the fortune involved (suppose there were) but just because other astrological predictions which have been made in the past would be confirmed by such a find. You see?"

"What a farce," she said, and he nodded as he said, "From one point of view, certainly it so seems. And yet who can say? The world is such a strange place, and we are busy refashioning

it anew . . . we must have all the facts if we can. Now, let me
carry on the story. When you were all here on holiday you
were very friendly all together, Galen, Prince Hassad, your
brother, the consul, and Quatrefages. At that time the last-
named had made advances to Livia and been refused by her, so
that he nourished a violent hatred against her. So *she* says.
There is no reason why not. You were all young and on holiday. But during this period Quatrefages gave her to understand quite clearly that he had managed to pinpoint an orchard
with a family vault or crypt in it which showed every sign of
being the site they were all looking for. To us he denied this.
Anything he might have said, he adds, would have been to
seduce her. All they did discover were Greco-Roman remains
dug up by the gypsies. We have accounted for most of these
pieces, some were sold to the Louvre, some to New York. Can
you add anything to this?"

"Nothing," she said. "Livia is the only one who might
have had such information. But had it been true either Galen or
the Prince would have blurted it out, I'm sure. There was no
secrecy about this purely financial adventure, nothing
esoteric."

"*Au contraire*," he said sharply, with a warning finger
raised. "Quatrefages is deeply steeped in the lore of the gnostics and the Templars. All this apparent rubbish had great
symbolic importance for him – he felt himself to be on the
track of the Grail, the Arthurian Grail, nothing less. The
treasure might have been a simple wooden cup or a priceless
chalice or a loving cup buried by the knights; it could have
been the cup out of which Jesus drank at the Last Supper. It was
not money or specie he thought himself hunting!" His look of
triumph matched her own look of surprise. She did not know
what to say, the whole matter was so surprisingly novel. He
now leaned forward – he had a long neck like a lizard with a
pronounced Adam's apple – and said, "This is what interests

our Führer, a lost tradition of chivalry which he wishes to re-endow and make a base for a new European model of knight-hood. But of a black order, not white."

"Chivalry!" she said contemptuously, standing up before the fire, her cheeks rosy with warmth and a vivid anger. "I suppose you have not seen the trains pulling out of the station day after day?"

He looked at her in amazement. "You surprise me," he said, "for I thought you would have grasped by now the scope of the New Order, the terrifying new order which now through German arms is trying to establish itself in the western world. You do not see beyond the fate of a few Jews and gypsies, and such riff-raff which will soon be swept away together with the whole Judeo-Christian corpus of ideas based upon gold – for in alchemical terms the Jew is the slave of gold. Spiritually we are on the gold standard of Jewish values. At last this has been recognised, at last someone has dared to break away, to break through into the historic future. You cannot belittle the enormity of the evil we have unleashed in order to outface it; we Germans are a metaphysical race *par excellence* – beyond good and evil stands the new type of man the Führer has beckoned up. But so that he perfects himself we must first go back and start from the wolf, so to speak. We must become specialists in evil until the very distinctions are effaced. Then he will come, the new man whom Nietzsche and Wagner divined. You underestimate the vast scope of the new vision. Our world will be based no more on gold, but on blood – the document of the race-might."

Constance felt the weight of this discourse fall phrase by phrase on her mind, creating an ever-growing shadow of apprehension and horror. Her flesh crept – she realised for the first time that she had, in fact, been in danger of underestimating the vast hysteria of the German belief in all this hocus pocus and Wagnerian black magic, because it did not seem that people could act upon such propositions. Here was a whole nation welded together and orientating its activities in precisely this grim sense.

"But it's a pathology," she exclaimed with a violent disgust, and to her surprise he smiled and nodded his head, as if he took it in a complimentary sense. She said to him with ever-growing dismay, "How innocent we were, how trusting! We were raised not to believe in politics but in man and his innate capacity for justice and a search for equity and happiness, and now this thing." She stared intently at him, seeing him for the first time as a new kind of species, a new kind of insect. He looked like a praying mantis, with all the cold mechanical fury of such a thing in love. After a long pause he continued in a low voice, talking as if to himself, "Nature can be both purposeful and frivolous. One must watch out. Also wasteful, a spendthrift. We are not imitating her in everything. But the minute you understand the far-reaching conception behind the New Order you cannot withstand its black violence and poetry. We are not washed in the blood of the Christian lamb, but in the blood of inferior races out of which we shall fashion the slaves which are necessary to fulfil our designs. It is not cupidity or rapacity which drives the Führer but the desire for once to let the dark side of man have his full sway, stand to his full height. Seen in this way Evil is Good, don't you see?" He raised his hand and sketched a blow upon the table. But he did not deliver it. He, too, had now a high colour, a flush as if he had been drinking. He found it difficult to support the look of the two contemptuous blue eyes which fixed themselves upon him, it was so obvious and so extreme, her feeling.

There was a long moment of silence, during which she stared fixedly at him — fixedly yet absently for she was intent upon the purport of what he had said, and indeed still shocked and surprised at so trenchant a revelation of unholy faith in this black cause. As if he followed her inner thought he said, "If I have reservations in anything it is perhaps because of our timing which has placed a great burden upon our men and materials. In my view we should have dealt with Communism first – how everyone would have welcomed that! Later the turn of the Jews would have come, more gradually. But what's done is done, and must be followed out to the end. And of course war is a game of chance as well." He suddenly took up his briefcase and hunted in it for a document which he extracted from among a number of photostated materials. "*Tiens*," he said, and the French word sounded strange on his tongue, "I thought that this might interest you – our service intercepted it. It's addressed to all heads of diplomatic missions abroad and signed by Churchill himself, as you see. At this moment to harbour illusions is rather dangerous, don't you think?"

She was curious enough to take the document and hold it to the light. It was a circular of a standard Foreign Office kind, and had been sent not in cipher but *en clair*, showing that it was not of any great secrecy. But the text had a characteristic ebullience, for it said, "By this end of this year our fortunes will seem to be at their lowest ebb, with bad news coming in from every theatre of war. Nevertheless I can with reason authorise you to feel a distinct measure of moderated optimism. A radical factor has at last emerged from the picture. The enemy has begun to think defensively for the first time; he is stockpiling in rear areas on a scale which proves that he envisages coming retreats. Maybe later historians will describe this as being the real turning-point of the war."

"Why do you show this to me?" she asked, genuinely curious, and he shook his head as he took back the document and replaced it in his briefcase. "Do you think it is a fake?" This made her angry and she said, "Please go now! You have no right to question me." He nodded sadly and said, "Very well. Then, my message is that your sister wants to see you if you can tomorrow at four at Montfavet. May I say you will come?"

"Of course I will."

His heels snapped, he saluted, and went through the door into the garden without another word. Constance sank down in her chair and tried to master her surprise at this extraordinary visit.

She heard the car doors close and the motor start as it slid away down the slope towards the town. At the same moment there came a scuffle of footsteps upon the garden path and Blaise burst into the house with a shotgun under his arm, white with apprehension. "I thought they had come to arrest you," he gasped, mixing anxiety with relief, "and I was ready to *les descendre tous les deux*". This was stupid behaviour and she cried, "For God's sake put the gun away!"

"Have they gone, then?" he said, looking wildly round as if to despatch a couple of hidden Germans lurking in the shadows of the kitchen. "Yes. Gone!" He expelled his breath in a swish of relief. Then in a typical peasant gesture he took a handful of salt from the bowl on the table and scattered it in the fire where it sparked off in blue points. "*Malédiction!*" he exclaimed – it served as an anathema on the departed Boche. "Sit down, Blaise," she said, and made him a sage tea while she told him the news – namely that Livia was indeed there and that on the morrow they would meet. It gave her a strange feeling of tremulousness as she did so. After so long, and in such a weird context. She went to bed early that night but slept badly, and was glad when day broke with its wide, wind-washed skies which presaged a day of sunny calm without wind, welcome respite after a heavy spell of mistral.

She despatched her routine duties on the next day with a perfunctory impatience, feeling that time was gnawing at her, and at last after lunch took the duty car and aimed it in the direction of Montfavet, circling the ancient walls of the town, and slowing down only for the two military checkpoints where, however, she was waved through because of the pennants on her car. The deep woods, the narrow roads came into play at once, so that within a few minutes she found herself lost in the snowy country; there was ice on some of the small saddleback bridges, and while some streams were frozen others foamed and gurgled and overleapt their narrow banks. It was like a landscape around Oxford which she remembered with a special affection because of a youthful love affair which a special kind of tenderness on the part of an undergraduate had rendered memorable. It was something one could not go back on. Now the deep woods sprang up on every side, and presently the car turned sharply and sidled into the little square planted with planes outside the little grey church, the place of rendezvous. She had switched off the engine to idle across the grass verges and come to rest at the main door of the church, which stood open. She saw nobody for the moment so that she entered the church formally dipping her fingers in the holy water stoup and signing herself. Then she saw Smirgel; he was sitting in the small side chapel on the left-hand side underneath a large, bland painting, and he was making notes in a loose-leaf folder. He looked up with a start, as if surprised to see her there. Constance looked equally at a loss. "She is outside, in the square, she is waiting for you," he added. Constance turned back and passed from the gloom of the church to the square lit by the bleak afternoon sunglow. Sure enough, standing upright in a somewhat military attitude at the far end under the planes, stood a figure in a field-grey uniform with a nurse's badge. She did not really recognise her but she advanced with a certain tremulous care, as if she were a bird, so as not to frighten her away, saying, "Livvie, dear! Is it really you?" The nurse appeared to regard her for she nodded, yet she kept her face in half-profile, turned away towards the ivy-covered wall which lined the church precincts. In a hoarse voice she answered, "Yes," and then, motioning Constance towards her, like Hamlet's ghost, as if she had something to impart, she said, "Constance, come here." And with that she sat down upon a stone seat and still keeping her face averted went on, "I could not get in touch before, partly not to compromise you – I did not know what you were doing: partly because . . ." Here a sort of hard misery took possession of her and abolished the end of the phrase. In anyone less harsh of tone it would have seemed the equivalent of a sob – an uprush of anguish. In her it just sounded unqualifiably hard, like the cinders of old emotions.

"I came here to help get the truth out of Quatrefages," she said. "But I have failed, and he has turned the tables on me."

"Livvie," said her sister, "why are you turned away like this, why don't you look at me?"

"I've lost an eye," said Livia laconically. And then continued to speak in a hollow resonant voice and with apparent indifference, asking for news of Blanford and Hilary. When she heard of Blanford's grievous wound she bowed her head briefly, but said nothing. "And Sam?" she said with a sharpened note of interrogation. Constance drew a breath and answered, "Sam is dead, killed in action." And as she said so it became for the first time a fact. Sam died now as a reality, as the figment she had been carrying around inside her like an unaborted child. "Sam dead?" said Livia in the same harsh tone. "Ha!" as if she could not quite believe it. Constance said clearly, "Sam is dead, Livvie. Sam is dead."

It was astonishing to feel a sort of relief in the depths of the statement, yet it was truly a relief suddenly to feel the ghost of Sam recede, diminish, and then all but disappear – at least to reduce itself to something of quite manageable proportions. It made her ashamed, this unexpected trick of the emotions. What a trickster life was, and how merciless to our self-respect. It was almost as if the open statement had all at once revealed a hollowness in the very calibre of her pain, had shown it up as, if not a sham, at least as something exaggerated.

"Well, that's that," cried Livia in her harsh corncrake's tone. "You will have to lump it, that's all."

But with the new sense of liberation brought by this confession Constance was also suddenly feeling the weight of her experiences here in the city. As if she had been unaware of her own fatigue. But Livia was talking now, still with the averted face, still out of the side of her mouth. "I have been up to the house once or twice, but I did not wish to embarrass you – I can imagine your job must need tact. Meanwhile I felt I must talk to you quite urgently if only to say goodbye and to tell you that Quatrefages has turned the tables on me, he has denounced us all as Jews. Smirgel is trying to keep this from the Gestapo but it can only be a matter of time before I am recalled. Perhaps suddenly in a few days."

"What rubbish," said Constance. "Surely you can tell them the truth?"

"I became a German subject, unlike you."

"But it's preposterous. I shall go and tell them that we are English, if you won't."

"I should wait until something happens before doing such a thing. Besides, you are technically Swiss, remember? They would not believe you more than me!"

"I shall ask to see the General," said Constance with an angry self righteousness. "I shall talk to him."

Livia shook her head and sighed as she said, "Things are in such a tangle that one could expect anything. I just tell you to warn you, but I ask you not to do anything rash that might compromise me further. Are you going to see Quatrefages?"

"Should I?"

"I don't know. Why, after all? He is pretending to be mad in order to avoid further interrogation, that is all."

"I won't see him," said Constance on a sudden note of resolve, "specially if he is playing us off against the Nazis."

Livia gave a world-weary shrug and sighed again, a pain-laden little sound. "Well, I'll say goodbye, Constance."

She stood up, still at the awkward half-angle to her sister, face turned away. Constance upon an impulse cried out, "Livvie, dear, do you still believe in . . ." she did not know quite how to phrase the question that was on her mind ". . . all this?" she finished rather lamely, though the comprehensive gesture of the hand was intended to encompass everything, the whole world crisis provoked by Nazism. Livia started to move off towards the trees, though she took the time to answer, "Yes. More than ever!" and there was nothing in her tone to belie her response. But she moved away towards the trees with ever-sharpening stride. Constance stopped with vexation which was at once swallowed by compassion for her sister, and she hurried after her saying, "Livia, wait! When shall we meet again?" To this however Livia had no response, and as the distance between them increased it was clear that there was not going to be one. Constance stood and watched the tall figure losing itself among the trees.

She turned back into the dark church to where Smirgel sat, absorbed in the notes he was making. He made room for her in the pew but she preferred to remain standing as she said, "Can't you do *anything* to help Livia? You know the real truth about us all, after all." He smiled his slow, obsequious smile. "The unlucky thing is that the information was confided to the Gestapo, not to my department, hence the concern. However it is too early to worry. If anything happens I will come and seek your advice, if I may."

"I thought of seeing the General," she said, for the idea still worked upon her despite all she knew about divided commands and internal rivalries among the occupying forces. Smirgel threw up his hands. "The General!" he said on a note of mocking commiseration. "He is so weighed down by his new command that he can think of nothing else. Since now the possibilities of a second front are beginning to take shape, Avignon becomes a very important strategic point to group both material and reserves. Wait and see in a few weeks." Vaguely she had followed some of the gossip about a second front, and a possible attack upon the French Riviera coast, which would cut off the German armies in both Italy and Africa. But she thought this was simply part of the propaganda war, not something serious. It was disconcerting, yet heartening, to find that the Nazis were giving credence to such ideas. "Von Esslin is in heaven," went on Smirgel. "He was pining for Russia and feeling he had been overlooked; now his command is of supreme importance and he has a whole new staff on his back. I don't believe that he would have time for you, even if he wanted to see you."

"We'll see. I must reflect."

Nor was his somewhat cynical judgement (his frankness astonished Constance) so far off the mark, for Von Esslin, after a long period of apparent neglect, during which the whole region appeared to have been earmarked simply as a back area for convalescents from the Russian fronts, suddenly found himself centre stage with a vastly increased responsibility carrying all the possibilities of professional advancement with it. The change in accent was electrifyingly sudden – fruit of some new propaganda suggestions about a Second Front – and all of a sudden he was having support troops and tank companies wished upon him in quantities too large to camouflage, too numerous to house easily in this rather barren, backward land of austere towns and empty heaths. Not only that – a whole riff-raff of pioneer regiments composed of renegade Russians and Czechs and Poles had been drafted south, designated for new, unspecified labours which had as yet not been defined. All was flux and uncertainty; and meanwhile the Allies had begun to pay some attention to the bridges over the rivers. The disposition of the rivers – it was the real nightmare of Von

Esslin. Often in his dreams the great operations board in the Castle Intelligence room floated into his vision: the Rhône, Durance and so on with their great speed and vexatious lateral cuts along the limestone outer skin of Provence. From the beginning of time they had been military hazards – preventing the Romans from reaching Britain, preventing Hannibal from reaching Rome, preventing . . . He was not sure on which side of the Rhône to keep his tanks, his precious unwieldy panzer forces, now doubled. So he kept them always in uncertain movement, crossing and withdrawing, forming and dispersing. It was wasteful in fuel. But with the new bombing patterns . . . The British had replaced the slovenly high-level bombardiers of the U.S. Air Force. They came low and were thorough, methodical; very little civilian damage seemed to follow in their path, but meanwhile the goods yards of the railways had begun to suffer, while bits began to fly off the precious bridges, the panzers' lifeline. Theories of a south European landing on the Riviera were doubtless exaggerated, yet nevertheless this new phase marked everything with a new accent of uncertainty and concern. (He had received two new decorations, which was highly pleasing. His mother was delighted of course.)

But the war had slowed, was beginning to drag a little, while this heavy stockpiling in his area was rather a perplexity. He sent out to hunt for underground caves capable of being enlarged into vast ammunition depots. Of course one thing that was quite easy in such a country of calcareous limestones was to pierce the topcrust with roadmender's tools, and seek out caverns which might suit such a purpose. But it was tedious and long, and there appeared to be no geodetic surveys of the lonely garrigues which might provide clues. Then all too easily one stumbled into underground workings of abandoned Roman mines only to find that they were full of water, possessed by some secret river, which only gave a sign of life during heavy rain, but then burst its banks, overshot its levels.

Not to speak of the Rhône itself, guzzling mud as it swept down from Geneva, increasing velocity steadily until before Avignon it developed almost twelve knots of speed. The slightest level-change in this context meant all the islands and the estuary in the centre flooded, while the water snaked its way into the cellars and granaries of the medieval central quarters of the town.

The town began to suffer sleepless nights as the bombing sharpened; from Lord Galen's best bedroom Von Esslin could hear the sirens, and hear the ambulances plying their trade after each attack. Holes in the pavements became a commonplace. But he had grouped his armour round the castle at Villeneuve, regretting its prominence as a target but insisting to himself that if the bridge was put out of action he could at least disengage in a westerly fashion; but ... this was no consolation if one thought of an enemy coming up from, say, Nice. He was teased by all this problematic strategy. Yes, things had changed, there was a new kind of urgency in the air. One day he received a personal order from the Leader telling him to turn out and witness the execution of three "conspirators" in his sector. No explanations were offered. In a cold blue dawn he watched as three young Austrian aristocrats, brown and slender as sheepdogs, entered the prison yard where they were attended by an executioner wearing a top hat and morning dress; their heads were clumsily hacked off with an axe. The General went back to his office in a quiet rage. He had not even been told their names nor why they were being executed. He did not deign to ask either the Gestapo or Smirgel – an icy formality characterised their relations. But he took pleasure in crossing them whenever he could, for he was after all, the military power while they were the civil.

The ill-omened Fischer was back once more after a refresher course in his macabre trade. He had done fatigues and courses in several of the more notable camps, and the experience had been hardly inspiriting (yes, he had been expecting something inspiring and uplifting, something also a little reassuring). He was tired like everyone else, but lately the way people looked at him without saying anything had begun to play upon his nerves. And then the camps – things were being slowed down steadily for they simply could not cope with the influx of men and women destined for the incinerators. He read a carefully reasoned Gestapo report on the matter which told him that it was no easy task to dispose of bodies – their fats and acids were hard of disposal, made poor and over-acid manures, were not suitable for soaps. It cost a fortune to gas and burn them. In spite of technical advances the rate of obliteration would have to slow down to keep pace with the machines and work task of the present system – some four hundred murder camps. He had walked dispiritedly around Buchenwald in the feathery light snow which creaked under his boots, brooding on the problem. How charming was the forest which surrounded the camp. Snow had made the slopes brindled with dark points of charcoal, stubble-like. Here in this peaceful decor had walked Goethe and Eckermann of whom he had never heard. The tall chimneys of the crematoria fumed softly on the blue icy air. Burning bodies stank like old motor tyres, he reflected, and blood hissed like rain on dead leaves. The situation was a wretched one – they had miscalculated – a humiliating state of affairs for a country with such great technical resources, such long experience, so many fine brains; but there was nothing for it, the whole process must slow down to keep pace with the available means. The latest lists of detainees would be pended and they would be allowed to return to their homes on a temporary basis. Pity. Among them was the little priest of Montfavet – it had not been difficult to convict him of having Jewish origins. It was his own fault, drawing attention to himself by absolving some of the senior officers, friends of Von Esslin. The names of the officers in question had been noted and filed for reference. But the arrest of the little priest had been a pleasant way of checkmating the General, with his superior airs!

Things at Tu Duc had changed somewhat also with the advent of heavy rainstorms followed by frosts and ice-bound forest roads. In the park another tall pine had been torn down by the mistral. It made a tremendous tearing din in the night, the owls flew whewing in all directions. The old conservatory sprang a leak and rain dripped into it, falling upon the old Freudian sofa, so that it was necessary to rescue it and drag it into the kitchen where at least Constance could lie at ease on it before the fire.

To her intense annoyance she fell ill, with high temperatures, raging migraine, toothache: indeed a whole congeries of petty troubles which all added up to an overwhelming fatigue, slowly accumulated over months. Strangely all this had tumbled in upon her like a sandcastle by the simple act of announcing Sam's death to Livia as a historic fact. With that announcement and the realisations of the stark truth she had begun to feel bereft, dispossessed. What was she doing in this bitter and beautiful country?

She must ask for leave, there was no other way of dealing with it.

Her bedroom being so cold, she spent much of her time spread out upon the old sofa in front of the fire, devouring the pamphlets and books which she had brought with her. While the wind rattled the casements she reflected that it might have been upon this very sofa that Dora or the egregious Wolf Man . . . But who the devil in this country would be interested in such things? It gave her a great sense of loneliness to be locked up here with all this information, like a bank vault, while all round her the icy country was in the grip of the monotonies that war engenders. What she needed now was a spell of calm by the lake, and to this end she contacted the

Swiss consul who came up to call on her in his old car. Yes, he was planning on a leave, and would be glad to offer her a seat in his car, but first she must really manage to shake off her ills, and scramble to her feet. The journey, though not fearfully long, was an arduous one, for as soon as the roads approached the mountains the ordinary amenities of travel – hotels, electricity, garages – failed them. But he would certainly go, and take her with him, when the time was ripe. It would anyway take a little time to get the necessary *laissez-passer* for the two of them, for Geneva must be contacted via Berlin.

Buoyed up by the thought of escape from the town and its problems she actually persuaded herself back into a state of tolerable health once more, and used her sick leave to walk in the surrounding forest which was, more often than not, snowbound, though the paths were free of access. She would come back to the kitchen grate before dusk, glad of its warmth and the secrecy with which it invested her impoverished intellectual life: a few trivial pamphlets – she gnawed on them like a dog upon a bone. But the death of Livia was completely unexpected.

As with everything concerning Livia, it seemed motiveless – or simply to belong to that category of events which history might later sum up as a sort of entropy. The sorrow, the abandon, the refusal – it was all there in the gesture: and at the same time a cry for help from the nursery of the human consciousness, for like a hunted animal she had crept back to the one burrow which had once been hers, for however short a time, in that forgotten summer. It made Constance groan in sympathy with what she imagined that profound pain must have been like to her inconstant sister; to carry the weight of it inside her like a stone. She hung there so still, some graphic illustration for a study of conceit – intellectual *hubris*, which had been her darkest driving force. Yet how had she got in and when? Later Blaise found the abandoned bicycle in the shrubbery by the pool, and one of the big Venetian shutters with weak hinges had been forced. But there were no other marks of her entry, and she had taken the stairs up to "her" room without turning aside into the habitable rooms where Constance dwelt.

That actual intimation of the fact too was curious in the manner of its advent. They had had an afternoon of blusterous tramontana, continually changing direction and force, and exploding the light snowfalls with mischievous gusts. But towards dusk it ceased abruptly and gave way to a watery sunlight and open sky, preludes to nightfall. She could not say with any accuracy that she "heard" anything, no, but at a certain moment she raised her head from her book like a gun dog who scents the presence of game. She had a feeling that something somewhere was beckoning to her, called for her attention. She stood up and stayed stock-still for a long moment before setting off to follow this enigmatic signal through the labyrinths of the intuition. Once in the hall the stairs beckoned as they always do. It was like following a note of music – perhaps only to find at the end that there was somewhere a musical tap dripping in a dry tin basin. No, but this was soundless. Up she went, and on the first floor there might have been an excuse to hover a bit, though all the rooms were shut. She threw open the doors with a definitive air, but nothing was revealed apart from traces of mice in the dust, and the obstinate tapping of fronds at the window. It was a long time since she had come up here. Next came the semi-landing with the lunette window, and here the door opened under the pressure of a single finger, and with a sigh and creak. She entered very slowly, gradually revealing to herself the hanging figure with its contrite downcast head, chapfallen now and pale from lack of blood. But all very orderly and condensed – there was no sprawling. The lost eye looked like the withered belly button of some medieval saint. With its light extinguished, the whole face, with its spectral planes, looked penitential, daunted by adversity. The pinions were quite explicitly Gestapo in their expert fit—you could pinion your own arms easily with them. The hair was sad and tired and the partings full of dandruff.

She took the pulse, though it was merely formality; the stillness told all. Then for a moment she hugged the ankles of the form, crying "Livvie! Livvie!" Then came the problem of releasing the body from its ropes—how could this be done without Blaise? Suddenly she took wing, racing down the stairs and out across the garden to the house of the couple, calling him now in urgent tones, telling him to bring his axe and follow her. Together they retraced their steps until once more they stood before Livia's body. A dull thwack of Blaise's axe and it swirled and thumped at their feet upon the floor of the little loft. Blaise crossed himself over and over again and muttered prayers of a sort. Constance sank down upon a chair.

The pain she felt now, accompanied as it was by a frustrated vexation which cast her back into the deepest depths of her childhood, was as physical as it was banal, though she could not give it a true location—what a crazy mixture of migraine, ulcer, cystitis, all coming so suddenly upon so much fever and fatigue that it seemed to lay rough hands upon her shoulders, pushing her down to the hard kitchen chair. She had put her hands over her ears and pressed them tight but this was not to hear the hoarse question of Blaise, addressed partly to her and partly to the world at large: "*Mais pourquoi?*" Indeed it was the capital question, but it had been asked of Livia since her birth, for nothing that she did or was entered into the sphere of rational explanations. That echoing "Why" had resounded already in the mind of Constance as she stood, holding the hanging body round the thighs to ease the weight on the rope and facilitate the task of the axe, weeping all the while with the tears coming from some remote and secret stronghold of infancy. The "why" extended in every direction, on all sides. Why, for example, had they not been more alike since they were brought up together by the same inadequate child-hater, deprived of the cuddling and caressing which form the self-esteem of the body so that its image can project faith and acceptance, sure of itself? This was how Constance "read" Livia when she thought of her as a case. The bitter narcissism, the jealousy, the withdrawn and melancholy character had evolved out of this background which Constance had shared with her; Hilary much less, for he had been sent away. Exasperation raged within her as she gazed down upon the face, fast setting into its mould of final secrecy. She had seen much of death professionally, but that is not the same thing.

Livia had fallen awkwardly with one leg doubled half under her, and she looked now like a dummy, a lay figure such as dressmakers use for their models. Blaise corrected the posture and then, after a moment's thought, took off his scarf and lashed the ankles together. Meanwhile her sister sat there and stared at her, though she was really staring at her own thoughts and memories. What lasted was the stinging exasperation—never to have been confided in. And now this maladroit and graceless act to round everything off; she hoped, Constance hoped, that it would not compromise her own departure to Geneva. It was a troubling thought, and as if to echo it, Blaise said: "What shall we do with her?" His own mind told him that it would be best to bury her in the garden in some secret corner and say nothing to a soul. . . . But this did not appeal to Constance who could foresee searches and questionings following upon a disappearance of that kind. "Happily Madame Nancy is coming this evening with the duty car, so we can take her down to the morgue and I can approach a doctor to certify her death. At least I hope so." The decision somehow released her frozen energy, and she went into action to prepare the body for easy transportation, pinioning the arms and covering the

features. Then they rolled Livia in a coverlet and tied the form
once round with a piece of cord. Thus she might be easily
carried out of the house. Blaise also was concerned that his wife
should not see the body – he said that he would tell her about
the matter later on, when all was in order. "Let us have a drink,"
he said, "a good drink. What an unhappy thing!" And for once
Constance did not refuse the drink in favour of tea or coffee.
Between them they placed the silent form upon the sofa, there
to wait until they could get it into the back seat of the duty car.
Constance hoped that there would be no hitch, or that
Quiminal had not forgotten her promise.

"No, no," said Blaise; "If she said she will come, she will
come. She is a Protestant, after all."

He had hardly uttered the prophetic phrase when they
heard the peculiar and characteristic seething noise of the
Volkswagen engine and the whine of its tyres on the gravel
before the gate. They stood up somewhat irresolutely and
waited for the girl, who walked down the garden path and
clicked open the latch of the kitchen door, to find herself face to
face with them. It surprised her to see Constance looking
positively ill with distress and Blaise whose sorrow for his
friend gave him a hangdog expression which would have been
hard to interpret had not the blue eyes also taken in the
wrapped and silent dummy on the sofa. She turned and put her
arms about Constance, saying simply, "Tell me! *Raconte!*" and
haltingly Constance told her the little they knew about the
motives of Livia, and also about their recent meeting at
Montfavet. Quiminal sat down on a chair and tapped the finger
of her gloved hand upon her lips. "We must avoid any trouble
if possible," she said with decision, and her firm tone re-
invigorated the resolve of her friend, who went to the sink in
the corner and washed her face and hands slowly and methodically, while they both thought of ways and means to deal with
the situation; somehow it would have to be declared – at least

to the local authorities – and indeed explained. Slowly a plan began to dawn on them.

Quiminal said, "Are you fit to come with me? Good! Then you will take her directly to the morgue, dropping me off at the office. I will join you as swiftly as I can with a doctor and with Smirgel – it would be wise to implicate him as he is likely to help rather than hinder. Do you agree? You know the morgue people already." Constance had been down once or twice to identify or advise them on civilian corpses picked up by the police. Yes, it was feasible, and this way she might avoid taking Blaise with her into town to help – it would spare him unwelcome publicity as a contact of hers. "We'll have a try," she said and jumped up with a new resolution.

Blaise was disappointed but said nothing; he went off to rejoin his wife. Together the two girls managed to carry and arrange the figure in the back of the car, somewhat awkwardly to be sure. Then they set off upon the icy road to Tubain, knowing that they must reach the town before nightfall. This bleak winter dusk with its hint of frost and snow was ideal for such an expedition. The sentries on the checkposts were half-asleep with the cold and could not bother with them – they waved them on almost with impatience. And so across the bridge and into the enceinte of the massive walls, threading their way towards the quarter where the morgue lay. Quiminal was duly dropped off by the square and scampered off like a hare to perform her part of the bargain. Constance went on alone now until she came to the ugly little building which had once been an abbatoir and now did service as a morgue. She ran up the steps and, pressing the bell, lifted the flap of the letter-box to shout through it the name of the warden: "François! *C'est Madame Constance.* Open up please. *Oui, c'est le docteur.*" With the customary sloth and groans the old man turned the key and the high doors swung open. "What do you bring?" he said, seeing nothing but an apparently empty car. "A client," she replied according to the time-honoured pleasantry among those who dealt in corpses with as much emotion as a butcher does with meat. Grumbling, he turned back and she followed him to take one end of the old and stained stretcher into whose stout frame the slender wrapped form was placed, to be carried into the building where Constance herself elected to undress it before placing it in one of the long oak drawers which covered one whole wall of the establishment. François groaned and grumbled as he assisted her, but it was largely about the difficulty of running things in the present conditions. "Don't blame me for the smell," he said with bitterness. "How do they expect me to operate on half-power? No refrigeration plant could take it. The place is beginning to smell to high heaven." He rambled on between groans as they conducted the body to the theatre where it would be placed upon a marble slab – an old-fashioned one which recalled those upon which fishmongers displayed their catch half a century before. "Careful with her – she's a friend," cried Constance in the face of his clumsy and negligent gestures, his attempts to undo the figure which was so professionally tied up by Blaise. "Let me do it."

"How old is it?" he said, and then, "A woman did you say?" But he recoiled when he saw who it was. "It's the nurse of Montfavet," he said, "I know her all right." This was an unexpected departure. He went on, "But she is in uniform, part of the army. We can't take her in here." This was one of the distinctions which Constance had foreseen and feared. She was examining those dreadful bruises upon the throat when a voice from behind her answered the objection. It was the voice of Smirgel and it said, "I will be responsible. Please do go ahead. A doctor is on his way here." He seated himself upon the only chair and seemed about to make notes or fill in forms or perform some clerical work. Meanwhile they turned on the arc lamp above the high operating table, and which at once threw up the surroundings with its light. They were in a large crypt with white tiled walls, somewhat greasy; a number of hoses depended from the ceiling, with one of which they were now able to wash the quiet body – water so hot that it contributed a distinct tint of warmth to the marble flesh. They cut off the body's dark hair which Constance put in her handbag – she would afterwards make keepsakes from it for the three survivors of the shared summer. Strangely enough while she was doing this Smirgel came to her side and stared down upon the recumbent figure for a moment before he gave a very small, a hardly audible sob, but whether of affection or contrition, or both, it was impossible to judge. Constance eyed him keenly and most curiously. "Was she anything to you?" she asked, on the spur of an impulse, but the German did not answer. He went back to his seat where he crossed his legs and closed his eyes. They went on with the preparations, drying her and cutting her nails short. Then came the cheap cotton shroud through which her shorn head peered with an expression of nervous vagueness. And now came Quiminal with a man who was apparently a doctor for he carried the forms which attested to the death of someone "from natural causes". But first he went through the parody of verifying the death by placing a stethoscope upon the pulse. (The strangulation marks were hidden by the shroud.) Then he went into the outer office and wrote industriously for a moment upon several forms which he thrust upon Quiminal before taking his leave in perfunctory fashion.

Now she was ready; but before tilting her off the table Constance asked for the traditional scalpel which the old man kept handy for such a purpose, and made a deep incision in the artery of the thigh, binding it up with a strip of tape against leakage. So she was propelled on a spider-like trolley towards the huge filing cabinet of oak which, like a gigantic chest-of-drawers, held the dead. "And the funeral?" said the keeper, who was about to start once more upon his theme concerning the current, and the difficulties of refrigeration. "She will be buried," said Smirgel unexpectedly, "with full military honours. I have seen to everything." Constance looked at him curiously. It seemed so strange that he should seem to be so moved. "Do I come?" she said, and was relieved when he shook his head. "I can't ask you, it will be in the Citadel."

Poor Livia! What an apotheosis!

They would, she supposed, fire a salute over the grave. "Natural causes" is after all the best description of such events, so refactory do they seem to human logic. A siren sounded somewhere: they had forgotten the war for a moment. The car stood in the dark street waiting for them. All of a sudden Constance felt passionately hungry, for she had eaten little or nothing all day. In the pocket of her greatcoat she found a slip of chewing gum which would have to sustain her until she got home. And Quiminal: "Do you want me to come?" she asked Constance. "Or would you prefer to be alone?" Constance nodded on the word alone, but then another thought struck her: "If I don't reappear at the office tomorrow it's because the Swiss consul has come and we've left for Geneva; you will not forget to come up and fetch the car?" It was agreed, and after a warm embrace the little car set off to carry her home across the bridge. The Rhône was ominously high; Constance's dimmed headlights did not meet with approval from a passing patrol which hooted at her. She slowed to shout "Emergency" at them, and then took the desolate and dark side-roads leading away into the hills.

The whole episode throbbed inside her, matching her fatigue which came and went in waves, stirred, it would almost seem, by the swaying and bucking of the little car. So that was the end of Livia, an end with no beginning, with no explanation. Had she been Smirgel's mistress? An idle enough thought: Livia belonged to nobody. She thought of her now, lying wrapped in her cotton *burnous* in the great sideboard —

what else could one call it? – of the morgue, a companion now
for tramps picked up in the frozen ditches, or elderly and half-
starved citizens of the town laid low by frost on their shopping
expeditions. She would lie there all night in her abstracted,
withdrawn death mood, the silence only broken by the little
withered noise of the machinery working at half-current. She
would never see her again; she repeated the words "Never
again" in order to come to grips with the idea. It was as though
someone had thrown a stone to make a sudden hole in the décor
of their lives, just as Sam's death had done; smashed reality like
a pane of glass. She realised then to what extent the dead
exercise the profession of alibi-makers for the living; she lived
in part because she was reflected in these people – they gave her
substance and being. And then another, heavier thought
visited her: what would Aubrey feel about it? Should she tell
him or wait for someone else to do so? She had a sudden picture
of his expressive face conveying sadness, and with a shock of
surprise felt a sudden wave of love for him. The beloved old
slowcoach of the almost forgotten summer. In one of the cupboards upstairs she had found a discarded and forgotten exercise book of his which still contained notes and jottings,
though now half illegible from damp. Moreover the book had
been torn across and obviously flung carelessly into the cupboard. She made no attempt to decipher any of the annotations,
feeling that in some way it would be a violation of Aubrey's
privacy – he was, like her, touchy about such things. But she
put it carefully in a folder with the intention of returning it to
him when next they met. She could not have possibly guessed
how soon this would be: the surprise must wait upon her
return to Geneva and the Head Office.

At the house, however, there was another surprise. A man
sat in front of the fireplace warming his hands, or trying to for
the fire was almost out. It was the Swiss consul. She greeted him
wonderingly. "I didn't see your car," she said, and he explained

that he had hidden it in the trees. "As I warned you, it is very sudden; we must start for Geneva tonight, as soon as you can get ready. I have had the *laissez-passer*, everything is in order. But we must hurry. I will tell you more when we get on the road." It would not take her long, for her affairs were in tolerable order, her packing almost done. "Very well," she said, between exhaustion and elation. "Very well."

She went upstairs to where the cupboard stood which housed her few clothes and rapidly completed the packing of her small suitcase; with this and a briefcase of papers and toilet gear she rejoined her companion who was now betraying every sign of anxiety, looking at his watch, and standing now upon one leg, now upon the other. Blaise appeared to lock up after her and take the keys. She explained rapidly and in low tones the chain of events which concerned the fate of Livia, reassuring him that there would be no repercussions to worry about. Then the three of them walked into the forest clearing among the tall planes to where the diplomat's car stood with its double pennants in their leather sleeves and emphatic diplomatic insignia. The consul slipped off the leather cases and released the flags – one Swiss and one with a swastika. He climbed in and started the motor. "I am ready," he said, and Constance made her goodbyes, promising to return before the end of the month. They moved off slowly down the hill and turning away from the city engaged the complicated loops and gradients of the northern road, which soon brought them down to river level. It was possible to increase speed, though in places the Rhône was exceptionally high and ran in the counter sense within a few metres of their wheels.

But the run was not all to be so calm for already at Valence they ran into a cloud of command cars buzzing about like insects to clear the main highway; they were deflected to side roads and were not sorry, for they ran through remote and beautiful villages which seemed deserted. Obviously there was a push southwards being organised, forming like a cloud upon the invisible horizon. The car was cold but the steady murmur of the powerful engine was reassuring, comforting. Apart from the grand turmoil in Valence they ran into no other traffic of consequence, but it was well after midnight when they reached the border and were halted by a military barrier. Lanterns and hurricane lamps flared everywhere inside a disused railway shed, a desolate rotting edifice full of wooden sleepers. Some human ones also.

Here they were roughly told to get out and shift their baggage on to trestles for inspection, which they did, yawning. After a methodical search through their affairs they were permitted through, though she had to walk the hundred or so yards of dark permanent way while the Swiss, being a diplomat, was allowed the privilege of driving his car along a dirt track, to emerge behind the barbed wire which marked the Swiss frontier. A man was waiting for her arrival, lurking in the shadows.

"How ill, how pale she looks," he thought as he watched her from his point of vantage in the shadow of the building. "And her hair all in rat's tails and dirty." He had half a mind to turn away and vanish, for he had not been expected and would not be missed. But his heart held him there, like a compass pointed upon Stella Polaris, yet without the courage as yet to go forward, to announce himself. She must at most have expected a duty car with a driver. He thought of that abundant blonde hair with a pang of memory. Now her head was casually done up in a coloured scarf tied under her chin. She looked like a French peasant from the occupied zone, dirty, listless and tired. He had not expected to find her in such a state of fatigue and disarray, and he did not know whether his presence might make her feel humiliated. But retire he could not, nor advance, nor decide anything whatsoever for himself.

He was revealed to her sleepy eyes by a bar of gold light

thrown from a doorway suddenly opened by a militia man. "Mr. Affad!" There was no ambiguity in her relief and enthusiasm; she went up to him in a somewhat irresolute fashion, as if about to put out her hand; but they embraced instead, and stood for a moment yoked thus, absurdly relieved and delighted by the other's presence. It was wonderful to feel his body breathing in her arms. Caresses! That is what she had been missing all this time, she realised, that is what her own body hungered for. Yet she had thought little of him, and had never as far as she could remember, dreamed of him. Now all of a sudden she was set alight by the touch of him and the firm resolution of his arms around her. She relinquished him with regret for she was obliged to introduce him to her travelling companion. To her delight she distinctly saw a frown of jealousy appear on his charming face. It was wonderful to see him feign a coldness he did not feel now, imagining heaven knows what about this portly and unimaginative figure who was all too anxious to relinquish her and head for home. She thanked him suitably, promised to keep in touch about their joint return to duty, and turned to follow Affad who already had her affairs in hand. His private car, an old American sedan, stood at the side of the road, and they piled into its warmth with gratitude. As he started the motor he said, "Look at me, Constance," and she obeyed, though it at once made her conscious of her appearance. She put her hand up to her hair and slipped off her scarf. "Why?" He smiled. "I wanted to see how you look when you are away, working."

"Grubby and crow's-footed, as you see."

He said, "Not for long. How tired are you? I have told the hotel hairdresser to stand by for breakfast-time."

"Bless you. That would be marvellous."

"But first I must tell you my real news – before you go off to sleep. Constance, we have managed to get Aubrey on to an exchange list of badly wounded prisoners of war – fifty

German against fifty English. They will come here in a week's time. Once here he can detach himself and we must see that he gets medical treatment – whatever is needed for his condition. This is where you come in. I have his whole dossier now; you will be able to study it in detail and judge. Are you listening?"

"Of course I'm listening," she said indignantly. "I am bowled over, that is all. What a miracle!"

She had planned to call back at her flat but it was not to be thus; the hour was against them. Heavy fog and a dirty white light did nothing to enhance the beauty of the lakeside town they were approaching with suitable caution. There was no traffic, fortunately, but they were obliged to hoot a warning on the curves of the hills – a sound which echoed dolefully on their ears. They were moving towards the outer suburbs now among green foothills still partly encumbered with fresh snow. She had an attack of yawns which made him smile. "Poor Constance!" he commiserated. "You could sleep for a month – and so you shall. But for today . . ." He pointed a long forefinger at the clock on the dashboard which said four o'clock. "We have fallen askew; nothing will start before six-thirty now. The best would be to come back to my suite – you know how big it is. I can give you a whole small flat to yourself, bathroom and all. Have you a change of clothes with you? Very well, then wash and have a nap. This afternoon you can go down to the hairdresser and – well, anything you feel up to. I have some mail for you, too, which is also in my room. What do you say?"

"And Aubrey? When will he get here?" The very words filled her with amazement, as if she had not fully realised the meaning they conveyed as yet. The image of Sam and Aubrey walking arm-in-arm over the bridge at Avignon came back to her like some ancient yellowed snapshot found at the bottom of a trunk. "I can't take it in," she said again and again, and then yawning fell into a deep slumber which only the sudden switching off of the motor eased into dazed wakefulness. They were at the hotel already and her companion was ringing the night bell. A sleepy hall porter opened to them and took their possessions; in the lift she leaned against Affad, almost asleep again, which gave him an excuse to put an arm about her shoulders and guide her towards his suite. Once there they explored the adjacent rooms which he had never bothered to investigate. They were sumptuous double rooms each with a bathroom which was still packed with toilet articles, soaps and scents and oils which were part of the hotel propaganda of the day. "I'll take this one," she said, relieving him of her case. "And I shall have a long bath and clean-up; then I'll come *chez vous* if you promise to be kind to me and not too violent. I need cherishing." It touched him to the heart – her disorder and grubbiness. "I understand you," he said gravely while she looked at him carefully, keenly with her fine eyes. She was actually asking herself, "What *is* it about short-sighted men that I find so attractive? And these long cervine heads . . ." But she went on sternly, as if to warn him against her inadequacy. "You see, I can't love any more; like someone with prolapse or hernia, I'm forbidden to handle heavy objects – all the mysterious symbols of attachment, heavy metaphysical baggage. I am a simple junior psychiatrist, a sorcerer's apprentice. A devil's advocate . . ." she tailed away into yet another yawn.

"I am demanding nothing of you," he said, though he knew this to be untrue. He was irritated by her attitude.

"I know," she said. "Sorry to be prosy. It's a poor return for your thoughtfulness. It's fatigue and the feeling of unreality – all that hot water and soap after my usual hip bath and a boiling kettle."

"I am going to doze a little," he said, though he knew himself to be far too excited to sleep. Constance nodded her approval. "Maybe I will too, in my bath," she said.

It was marvellous to hear the swish of the hot water into

her bath, and to finger all the toilet delicacies on the shelves. She would have liked to use everything, all at once in one terrific and wasteful splurge, but of course it would have been to no purpose; the oils and soaps cancelled each other out. Nevertheless she sank sighing down in a nest of violet bubbles, submerged completely until all she could hear was the thick drumming of the water as it rushed into the bath. She washed her hair, so badly in need of the shears, and wrapped it in a towel before falling magistrally asleep in the warmth, her head against the back of the bath. Such sleep – of the very bones it would seem – no opiate could have procured for her, and diminishing the hot flow to a steady trickle she relaxed as if for eternity.

Affad, too, was weary, for he had had no sleep while waiting at the frontier post – simply a fugitive doze in the back of the car. Now he changed into a thick winter dressing-gown and turned in, reading for a few moments by the light of his bedside lamp. For how long he did not know, but he woke with a jolt to find his bedside clock showing six, and the yellow dawn light over the lake gradually increasing in strength. There was no sign of Constance and he thought it probable that she had also taken to her bed in one of the two spare rooms of the suite. He would not have disturbed her for worlds. Then he heard the annoying and persistent sound of the over-flow running in her bathroom. He listened to it for a long moment, trying to decide what it might signify. Had she left the tap on and gone to bed? Had she gone to sleep in the bath, oblivious to the running water? Perhaps he should investigate and turn it off? He allowed curiosity and anxiety to master his disinclination and gently opened the bathroom door to see what was the matter. But unexpectedly she had crawled out of the bath and on to the wide table – the masseur's settee so to speak – after wrapping herself in the heavy white burnous of towelling provided by the hotel. White in a white decor, she slept quietly, her head still rolled up into a seashell shape. Her lips were parted on the faintest suggestion of a half-smile and she heard nothing of his stealthy approach. In all that whiteness and steam he tiptoed to close the tap, and was turning away to leave when he noticed the blood flowing down from the couch, from the half-opened gown, the half-opened legs – a red pool into which he had inadvertently trodden with his bare foot and printed the tiles. What awakened her was the sudden cessation of the noise from the bath, and dimly through half-opened eyes, and with a half-awakened mind, she saw that he was there and held out a hand to him in a gesture of sympathy which was a pure fatality, for he approached her now and pressed her, all warm and snuggly, in his arms. "O God!" she groaned. "I'm bleeding. It's too soon." But the gradual strengthening of his embrace was accompanied not only by kisses, warm and shocking in their precision, but the excited whisper: "Bleed! Thank you, Constance. Bleed!" He was overwhelmed with gratitude for he realised that it was for him, this dark menstrual flow; and turning her slightly to depress her legs and pull her downwards towards him he entered her softly, circumspectly, disregarding her faint mewing protests, which soon subsided as she quietly opened herself to him, profoundly and completely, made herself the slave of his lust in a way that had never before happened to her. Where, she wondered, had she acquired the experience to react so absolutely? It was not enough to tell herself that it was simply that she realised herself to be deeply in love with him. He stood there bending over her for a long moment, doing no more than kiss her, embrace her. He was inside her but he did not move. He waited in deliberate cunning for her to stir the first; he waited for the suspense to become intolerable. "You will get covered in blood!" she said at last to disguise the movement which took possession of her loins with a mock-attempt to rise and dis-engage. But now he had begun the fateful rhythm which joined their breaths to the universal pattern of breath. She tried to protest to herself, telling herself that this must not be; but he only drove his slender horn ever deeper into her.

Even now she felt called upon to assert some of her feminine independence, to assert a loving domination over him by her sheer physical strength. She decided that she would force him to a climax first by the sheer strength of her young animal control, the strength of her sphincters; and he felt the challenge as she seized him for it summoned up all his own strength and litheness, his defences against a premature dispersal of force. "I see you are smiling," he said between shortened breaths, while she replied "Yes," punctured with little gasps, adding, "You will give in first." He shook his head: "No." Still she smiled, and he closed his eyes in agony and put his head on one side. "Please!" Constance said boastfully, "My sphinxes are strong and in good repair. I *order* you to come." He fell forward under the discharge of her kisses, proud now at her victory and keen to share it. It was only some time later that she knew that he had given her the victory which he would have been quite capable of forcing upon her. But now she felt wildly exultant. They lay exhausted in all that blood and steam like stricken martyrs to human bliss. She had known it all along, she had known that it would be like this, that he would be like this; why had she closed her mind to it and stayed deliberately in Avignon, away from temptation? Paradoxically, to remain faithful to Sam! The thought filled her with astonishment – how old-fashioned the gesture seemed!

"I can see nothing," he said, blinded by the steam, "even your face is dim, like a wet water-colour. And I have printed the tiles all over with my bare feet – your blood, Constance." He refilled the bath once more, carefully hanging up his own wrap, and stepped into it to lie at ease, deeply thoughtful, watching the filaments of dark blood wash off his skin and hang in the warm water before dissolving. "I feel like Petronius."

But she was appalled by the mess, and had started taking measures to clean it up with damp towels, unwilling that the room service people should see it. "Come," he said. "It's their job, Constance. Come in here with me, it's not too hot for you." It was something of a jam but somehow she managed amidst much laughter to squeeze herself beside him and to shrink down sufficiently far to have the water level up to her neck. They were like eels in a jar. An enormous depression suddenly seized hold of him, and she noticed with a passionate concern which she was rather ashamed of showing and said, "O, what is it? What has happened, have I displeased you?"

He shook his head and said, "No. I have an overwhelming desire to make you pregnant – it's crazy. I have not slept with anyone for several years and I wasn't really prepared for you. I thought I was, I lived on hopes as you must feel all too clearly. But I am in disarray. You have scattered everything to the winds. I feel numb, dead, like a mummy. Can you bring me back? I doubt it."

"What happened the last time?" He smiled sadly, but did not answer. Then: "In Alexandria someone who is quite continent, apparently uninterested in sex, causes alarm and disquiet. In Arabic they say, 'He has a penis with three heads', and nobody can use it – that is the sense."

"Am I too young for you?"

"Even if you were, what difference? This thing!" He pressed his fingers upon his body in the vague region of his heart. She took them and placed them upon her own hot cheeks. "So you wished to anchor me to my loom and spoil a promising medical career?" Still troubled he was able to reply, "I could, yes."

She lay there for a long time, saying nothing, stretched beside him like a young lioness, one hand lying possessively upon his article, cupping the sinister-seeming scrotum like a nest-tumbled bird gathered up. Soft as a cloud her spirit started pouring into his and she felt, like a ship answering a shift of wind, the mast rise into the sky of his unrealised desire. But he had not finished quite for he said, "But sperm can be a poison if it is not fresh, or poorly documented, or sick like the sperm of deteriorated schizophrenics and others; undue retention can cause illness, brain fever, mind-squeeze, one can witness this in hypocritical cultures based on puritanism like yours. Sperm needs to be cultivated, it is really riches, money in its physical aspect, the girl should all the time be making more and more, manipulating the scrotum, caressing it, counting her change. She must feel it psychically coming down the urethra drop by drop, she must welcome and husband it, and let the parched womb rush at it, unleashing the ova like a pack of hungry wolves. They must both act towards each other with the highest degree of conscious effort; the more they render the orgasm conscious the deeper in phase they will be, thus the purer the child and the more harmonious the race. This takes so long to express but there is no mystery about it – real women have always known it. When a culture starts going downhill the first victim is the quality of the fucking and the defective documentation of the sperm – by documentation I mean oxygen, just lack of oxygen, which is race-knowledge, genetic nous."

Half-sleeping now in each other's arms, their desires prospering with every breath, he whispered on, telling her about the history of sex, why it had always elicited fear and an exemplary piety. It was an engine fuelled by the mind and the coarse manifold of sperm which was needed by the thirsty soil of the womb. Alone the man could do nothing, alone the woman could not resolve the dilemma of her earthly needs. And this was the base of thought and feeling – in every order of perception. The primal vision of man and woman, the primal fig leaf, the primal asterisk – they dwelt in this domain of high-tension wires whose fearful fragility was manifest every time a kiss went astray or a desiring look missed its target. "It's terrible; we can do nothing without each other. Each is the other's fatality – you with your little handbag full of Easter eggs and farthings, but attached to another, and over which you have only temporary and fleeting control: instead of having it always near, on you like a real handbag, full of powder and lipstick and French letters; and then me, a sleep-walker from the beginning of history, mesmerised by your two galactic bubs, the spring of eternal youth, which gave me my first drink on earth and comforted me from the assault of light and sound, and the agony of trying out a new stomach and lungs. Mama!"

So the sleepy commerce between them entered upon the domains of an attachment where the physical and the mental made common cause; but she realised that he had opened up something inside her mind by this conversation, had primed her, and that if they were not careful she would become im-pregnated. It was as if he had hypnotised her into this delicious satyriasis; she was dying to feel, to prosper and harvest his orgasm, but he hung back, as if reluctant – in fact to sharpen her desire for him. They lay in an agony of impatience with thoughts of loving obedience pouring out between them like some vast waterfall. "Now!" she said. "Wait!" he replied, en-grossed mentally in trying to accord their breathing, their very pulse-beat. Already he could sense the rich void of repletion they would enjoy afterwards, lying like drunks in each other's arms, driven to sleep like sheep, into a pen. He turned her lightly towards him and loosed the sails, feeling them draw breath, feeling their craft heel and strain and then gather weight with a shared ecstasy guiding it. She realised that she had never known what love was, what it could be. She was terrified to feel so much at his mercy, and at her own. To sur-render, to yield, to abdicate and receive – it made her feel dangerously vulnerable. She said sadly, "Ah, but you are joking and I am serious; you are going to be disappointed in me. I am only a scientist at heart. I believe in causality."

He raised himself on an elbow and looked closely at her, as if seeing her for the first time, as if she were some strange insect which had alighted before him on the counterpane. "Alchemically speaking, nothing can be achieved without the woman, without you; your thighs are the tuning-fork of the male intuition. You strike the spark, we light the fire in the hearth and stick you with child."

"O yes, Herr Professor," she said meekly.

They both laughed. "O no, you don't," she said in her new relaxed and confident mood. "This is a male plot to make our relationship neurotic. I'm not playing. Let us begin with ourselves, only ourselves. I'm only an old Freudian, and can't see further than my nose."

"You live in the spare parts of other people's dreams, neologisms among the nightmares which project themselves into your own daymares of violence and panic. Which *somnifère* do you take? Constance, we are full of ideas which remain obstinately homeless. I want to share, to share." There was a tap at the door and a breakfast tray appeared as it opened. With an unpremeditated gesture they both drew the sheets over their heads and lay motionless, as if in deep slumber, until the tray was placed by the bed and the maid withdrew. Then they burst out laughing, throwing off all the covers and engaging with a sudden new-found fierceness in a love bout which was deliberately pain-giving. The violence was delicious, she felt with horror and pleasure his vampire's *suçon* on her throat under her ear. It would leave a tell-tale blue mark which would need careful powdering out. Damn! But this time it was he who called the tune and she was surprised by the controlled strength of that tall, somewhat awkward body with its bony girl-like motions. At the same time it made her exultant, the inner recognition that he was completely fashioned as a male, and capable of making her groan softly with pain, to hurt her without leaving bruises or blemishes, with the sole exception of her throat—but this was a piece of pure vulgar sexual boasting and she would tell him as much. She found herself trembling under his assault, trembling at her good luck in being after all able to plunge deep into an attachment without reserve—she who had felt herself dried-up and empty of all emotion. Suddenly the thought of Livia smote her, she saw her dead face, and between pain at the memory and pleasure in the present began to cry, which made him desist. He was apologetic now; he had been thoughtless when she was so tired. Then he added an amazing thing: "And shocked too by Livia's death."

She sat up in bed, wrapping her kimono round her and said, "How on earth . . ?" but he shook his head gently to reassure her and explained, "From Smirgel, of course. He has been in our pay for a long time." It should not have surprised her, but it did. "Whose pay exactly?" she asked, and he replied, "I didn't mean the Red Cross, silly, I meant the Egyptian army, so called. It's an independent net. The British feel happier with their own old-fashioned methods and men like Quatrefages—whose field of vision is very limited. We work independently, though of course we share our labours with them when there is anything really important. But they never believe us—they don't believe in Smirgel, for example."

"Neither would I," she said. "He is a real Nazi believer, he confessed as much to me and gave me the whole gospel. I would never trust him. Really not, not an inch."

"He is a double operator, perhaps," agreed her lover equably. "But we have had a long history together. I must tell you how we've saved his head more than once from Hitler's impatience and Ribbentrop's. Head for a head, so to speak."

They rose and as they breakfasted he told her more in his quiet, smiling voice. "You see poor Smirgel in another light,

271

but in fact the wretched fellow is quite astute, quite clever; he
must be to have kept the ear of Ribbentrop. But he did not
bargain for Hitler's impatience to get to the bottom of the
Templar heresy and all the mystery surrounding it. Not only
that but the rumoured treasure which they buried somewhere
and which crackpots like Galen try to unearth. Hitler views
them as a heretical sect convicted of religious malpractice, and
he wants to found an order of black chivalry – if I may coin a
phrase – to take their place. Mad, of course, absolutely mad!
But when he has nothing better to think about he gives
Ribbentrop a shove, or his replacement, and the shove is duly
communicated to Smirgel. Recently there was some talk of
replacing Smirgel, but we managed to save his head by pro-
viding something on account, so to speak. Did you ever see the
dried Crusader head which Hassad carries about in a scarlet
hat-box container? You did? Well, we allowed Smirgel to discover this, based upon the confession of Quatrefages. Everyone
was delighted. At last something tangible! Moreover we
cooked a pedigree for it. It is supposed to be the prophesying
head of Pompey which the Crusaders believed was imprisoned
in the cannon ball which tops Pompey's Pillar in Alexandria.
Once in a while the thing is alleged to utter a prophecy, but in
one's sleep; one has to have it beside the bed. Do you know
where it is now? Beside Hitler's bed. He half-believes, is
amused and intrigued, shows it to everyone. Who can say
what a shrunken head knows?"

Who indeed? Alas, there was no way of planting ready
made speeches in its mouth to influence the ideas of the mon-
ster; but for the time being Smirgel was being left relatively
alone with his routine duties and was concentrating on the
build-up and the dumping which was going on in the new
command, herald of who knew what?

"Where can we meet at the earliest sheer possibility?
What are you going to do today?"

She was going to look in on her flat and tidy it if need be, visit the office, and then perhaps try and locate Sutcliffe, to make belated contact and let him know that she was back. Had he heard about Aubrey coming?

"Indeed he has. He groaned and said, 'It's a hard life for those of us who live vicariously.'"

She said, "Rob Sutcliffe will have to pull his weight now and stop bothering so much about her" – she expressed this opinion in rather an offhand way. "His devotion is so exaggerated that it will soon seem suspect to us, Schwarz and me."

"You must tell him."

"I will."

But despite these pious sentiments once more they fell asleep in each other's arms, and if from time to time her mind cleared and she awoke it was to a dazed abstraction which heralded something like a new life – a new attitude to her life. She felt so strange! Everything had irremediably changed.

Yes, with all this she had suddenly, dramatically assumed herself, her full femininity – something which had remained always a sort of figment, a symbol which gave off no current. To be a woman in this sense it was not necessary to be a mother, or a wife, or a nun or a whore – all these documentary forms of living were quite secondary to the central state. The doctor in her had made a discovery of the first order! To achieve some understanding of the role of the female – why, it chimed with her art, it was implicit in the craft of her job. The female was the principle of renewal and repair in the cosmic sense, it was she who made things happen, made things happen, made things grow. She was the principle of all fertility even though she might be disguised in the trappings of Mrs. Jones. (He had been brutal with her once – his joy had over-brimmed into a possessive lust, and the pain he inflicted was harsh and hard to bear; but she welcomed it, as a martyr welcomes the burning pyre.) He had split her down the centre as if with an axe.

273

"Turn again," he had cried, and she submitted and turned, quite prepared to die in his arms—but the poetic figure of speech was now the relevant one, for she "died" in the Elizabethan sense, and her own wanton cry of delight rang out on the silence, expressing many things, notably the thought: "So I can love, after all!" though up to that moment she had never once considered herself incapable of loving. It was as if she had simply not known what the animal was. His face looked so tense, so withdrawn: she recognised his male weakness, his alarming precariousness of feeling, his absolute need for the support without which no advance was possible, no creation within his own scope. This realisation made her suddenly conscious of her own strength, as if she could now use a whole set of muscles which up to now had lingered on in disuse. She glimpsed the tantric left-hand path of which he was always talking, and which so much irritated her scientific mind. He had given her much more than his love, he had given her the full maturity of her gift, her medical skill. "O thank you, thank you!" But he made a vague hopeless gesture and groaned, saying, "I don't know why the devil I am telling you all this gibberish—it will make you love me finally, and you'll find all other men insipid for about ten years after I leave you, as I have to. Damn!" But the trick was done; she possessed the secret of her own soul now, and her generous kisses and smiling eyes told him that there was nothing to regret for either of them henceforward. The imp was out of the bottle.

A bell rang somewhere and she sat up. Good God! It was late afternoon! She had slept all day, and Affad lay beside her once more. How had he come in without waking her?

He woke from his deep trance-like sleep and rubbed his eyes, saying, "That means a new drum of paper for the machine. Smirgel has become increasingly talkative, he runs on and on. It makes you think of the agony of silence spies have to endure, for keeping a secret is a real effort, like wanting to pee during a march past. He can talk to nobody. Except me. He has become like a chatterbox wife. I keep trying to shut him up but to no avail."

"I understand nothing of all this," she said, and as he rose and hunted for a wrap in the bathroom he told her to follow him and see for herself what it was all about. They tiptoed down the cool corridor to what seemed like an outside lavatory – but was a rather solid-looking room with a steel door, which bore a sign proclaiming it a power point with dangerous wires. "Do not enter," said the notice, and "do not touch".

"That is just camouflage," he said and opened the door with a small key to reveal a comfortable office-like room with a tickertape machine punctually extruding what appeared to be news items or stock reports. "It's Smirgel," said Affad with a chuckle. "He has become very alarmed and excited since the first attempt at landing. I am drowned in information." He indicated the piles of striped yellow transcription paper which littered the floor and with a grimace said, "I hardly dare to go to sleep for fear that I will find myself strangling in the coils of this infernal ticker. At any rate he works for his money, Smirgel. Look!" The machine clicked steadily on, the paper lengthened. Affad opened a hatch and replaced some paper drums with new ones, passing them into the jaws of the rotor and securing them to ensure continuity. "Where does he do this?" she asked curiously, impressed by the element of risk incurred. Affad said: "In the so-called dangerous wards at Montfavet-les-Roses, separated from the half dozen or so madmen by a bead curtain and a frail door. He is scared stiff. But it's the safest place. It was suggested by Dr. Jourdain, to whom we owe much. By the way, what sort of chap is he?"

"The doctor? Rather mannered, highly cultivated and very pro-English. He wears a college blazer – he studied at Edinburgh. Has a death-mask on his desk. I think he is secretly in love with Nancy Quiminal, though I never speak of it to her, nor has she mentioned it to me. But that is all I know!"

He sank into a chair and allowed the long paper streamer to pass through his fingers as he slowly read the progress report of the agent. "The interminable list of Jews deported – nearly forty thousand now, it's hardly to be believed," he said with sorrow. "Smirgel always sounds grimly approving – I suppose from what you say he could hardly feel otherwise."

"It is sickening."

"Yes. And doubly so, for we shall never hear the end of this calamitous blunder; the Jews will extract the last ounce of blood from our horror and repentance, they are masters of the squeeze. We will have to hang our heads in their presence for a century at least."

"You don't sound as if you like them very much."

"I am from Alexandria, I live with them and know their problem to be insoluble – so brilliant and fragile they are, so conceited and afraid and contemptuous of us. After all, Constance, the Gentiles did not invent the ghetto – it's they who wished to lock themselves up with their monomania and their pride and cosmic solipsism. The little I know about racial discrimination I learnt from them – once I had the temerity to want to marry an Orthodox Jewess in Cairo. I was offering a quite straightforward and honourable marriage. But the row it caused! Everybody, up to the Grand Rabbi, meddled in the affair, while the parents of the girl locked her away for safety in an asylum, pretending she was mentally afflicted. From which I was forced to kidnap her and force their hands, which I did. But it opened my eyes to the whole matter of race and religion – everything to do with monotheism, monolithic organisation, everything mono, which leads to this self-induced paranoia called Western Civilisation. . . . The Germans are simply following out the whole pattern in their usual gross fashion. It's heart-rending, senseless, barbaric. But even the Jews are not helping themselves! Anyway, let's hope we are in time to rescue at least half of them. Not to mention gypsies, tramps, jailbirds and 'slaves' of every persuasion. It isn't only the Jews, you know, though of course they make the most noise as a majority."

The paper was perforated at regular intervals so that one could tear off each sheet and assemble the strips in the manner of a book, giving easier readability. She helped him to do this, to assemble his dossier of information for him. It was strange to see the city from this angle of vision, to see it in depth, so to speak, and not from the blinkered viewpoint of a Red Cross employee operating in a strictly limited field. Here she could read of troop movements, of reprisals against isolated acts of sabotage, of the steady stockpiling going on under the Pont du Gard. Several thousand Czechs and Poles had been drafted in to do the work, presumably because they would be less likely to leak the information – already they had created a sizable language problem, not to mention problems of public order in the surrounding towns of Nîmes and Avignon. Their drunkenness had rendered the streets dangerous in the twilight hours before curfew – the only time when the housewife was able to shop. Happily they were only sketchily armed, the group-leaders carried pistols and pick-helves. As night fell lorries went round the town picking up the fallen and shoving them aboard in variously comatose states: and the city breathed again. But Smirgel's despatches listed two important brawls which had led to the death of two Vichy policemen and the rape of a girl of ten. There were also punitive actions against so called "terrorists" in the surrounding hills – but these were mostly work-shy youths trying to dodge the forcible deportation which had been decreed by the Germans. It was nothing to burn down a whole village, while a few exemplary hangings was argued to be a necessary deterrent to further lawlessness. But the tide had turned at last, there was no doubt: the iron jaws of the Allied war machines had begun to close on Germany slowly but inexorably. What would they do with the new world which would be born when once the guns fell silent? They did not know, for the old would be somehow buried in that fateful silence of peace. She felt consumed by restlessness at the very thought of peace, as if she could not get rid of this war-time insomnia, this persistent feeling of having her heart ravaged by the brutishness of human behaviour.

It was agony to separate, but their duty called them to do so. The next meeting was, by common consent, to be in her little flat for dinner.

So again that night the bed floated them both out to sea like some precious catafalque. Reality and dream again became coeval, time and space commingled. When sleep came it was deep as death might be.

But not entirely, for now they awoke always upon a new world both of unique privacy and of Promethean simplicity – for pain mingled with the pleasure and the reassurance of their passion. Yet in spite of this profound intimacy, this flirtation of private minds, she was still hungry to get nearer to him, to devour him woman-fashion. Almost in exasperation she cried, "O have you no other names, Affad, no Christian name? Must I invent a nickname to lay claim to you?" And to her surprise he replied, "Yes, I have, but I have never liked anyone using it after my mother died. She pronounced it in a special way."

"May I know? May I use it?"

"I am called Sebastian."

"How did she pronounce it?"

He hesitated for a long moment, staring curiously at her. Then he said, "Sebastiyanne, with the accent on the last syllable. There! I have given away my soul to the devil!"

"My love, surely not that! Surely not that, Sebast*iyanne*?"

He said nothing but lay in the stillness of his wakeful drowsing with eyes firmly shut as if he dared not open them

278

upon the rapturous face of his lover. He was debating deeply within himself, resisting an impulse to shed tears of joy and helpless fatigue. In a whisper she repeated the name, and said, "Was it like that?"

He shook his head and replied, "No. It won't do. Call me Affad like the rest of the world. Keep the other for yourself."

The revelation and the name had brought them much closer together. But lest the claims of ordinary life be neglected she permitted herself to add after a moment, "God! I am so hungry. I think I will die." He at once shook off his sleep and said, "I will make you the breakfast you deserve. Tell me where everything is and leave it to me." Which she was weak enough to do, guiding him in whispers, once more half-asleep.

"Bacon, sausages, eggs. O certainly God exists," she whispered, to which he added piously, "God bless our happy home," as he struggled into a borrowed kimono.

It was marvellous to be waited on.

"You would make a wonderful slave," she said, still mentally smoothing herself, her psyche, down as a cat might lick its own coat clean after a love-bout. He had collapsed into a state of complete submission, resembling a case of deep shock. To feel him so passive and so enslaved had aroused her to the highest pitch. Afterwards, exhausted, bathed in sweat, she said reproachfully, "You never seem to let go, damn you; you are always *there*."

He put his arms round her, as if to comfort her for her disappointment. "There is nothing to let go," he said, "I feel I am *there* the whole time, at the centre of you. I am trying to eat you alive, to swallow you like a boa. But it is not easy: you will take ages to digest." They lay breathing into each other's mouths, full of the convalescent sweetness of this transient form of death in life while their desires roved about them in packs, as yet unsatisfied, the remnant of truthful impulses perverted by lack of zeal. "In your work," he said, as if the

formulation had cost him deep thought, "you are the bondsman of the ego, but in mine I begin with the *Vor-Ich*, the pre-
self, the *pre-self*, my dearest Constance. The marvellous little
pre-self like an acorn, like an unshelled penis, like a lotus
bud . . ." He began to laugh at her exhaustion. She tried to get
up more than once, but fell back each time into his arms, sleep-
impregnated, her whole body in deep soak. At last with a groan
she turned and tore away this veil of nescience, and made her
yawning way to the lavatory, pausing only to draw hot water
for his bath. "Lie in peace," she said, "it is well earned. And let
me make you the bath you deserve!"

Later on they parted once more, but gravely, reluctantly;
he watched her set off walking along the lake reaches, the long
Corniche, towards the bankers' city, with her head bowed as if
in profound contemplation. His eyes followed the lithe,
striding figure with its impenitent head set so firmly on slender
but strong shoulders, its look tilted slightly upwards, giving
it a youthful urgency. It was as if she had forgotten all about
him – she had swallowed him like a drink, and turned her mind
back lifewards. But she was very deeply shaken, and when at
last she entered her office at the clinic it was to sit blindly before
the mountain of dossiers, staring at her own fingers. She
remembered some words uttered by the good Schwarz during
a seminar: "*Aber*, Constance, man is not a natural product of
nature – he is an excrescence like the truffle, a cancer, an illness,
it is only his high gamy flavour that makes him acceptable!" He
was smiling, of course, though the words were seriously meant.
He believed that when man had sacrificed sexual periodicity it
was the fall into a freedom he could not manage. He could not
face the freedom offered by choice, whence history.

During the afternoon she fell helplessly asleep and
dreamed archaic dreams of haunting incoherence. Somewhere
from the deepest recesses of memory there swam up upon the
white screens surrounding her bed – dream of a hospital – a

painting she had once loved, *The Parting* of Chirico, with its clinical rigour, its glacial detachment which freezes the optic nerve like anaesthetic; the palette cool, the tone-range Roman as befitted partings where grief bit too deep for expression. A mental foliage of rusty wire, barbed into drypoints of fingers or leaves or hair, bundles of twigs birds organise into the cradles and nests from which one flies into comfortless futures of thought. He had taken his ***** in quiet fingers and countered the web of tensions in her by his deep ***** and careful *****. He could hardly tell what ***** for it stirred the classical cocoon of all vice, opening and shutting her lips with his ***** while she for her part ***** and reaching into wealth behind her groaned as she *****. She concentrated on the screen memory to assuage her pain. (Paintings are to bring calm.) How deeply he hurt her now with his ***** and his violent *****, each awkward spasm lifting itself into the centre of her *****, the flower and branch of all sex. Still she clung to the lovers' goodbye, the turning away, the imprint of the primal crime, the original fall, thought catapulted into matter and fixed by Saturn into the hysteria of dust. O God! It was friends who parted in the painting, not lovers, for they can never be separated, the flesh having grown together. Such scar tissue would put them at risk. "Tell me again the *****; you know how it shames me."

Fragile as a nautilus afloat their sexes plumbed the innermost recesses of sinus, heartless as a forgotten creed, the numbing pain of the bruised bones conveyed their own amnesia. The meaning of lovecraft only grew out of parting. The breath hissed like seething milk, the whip rose and fell, but in the painting your ***** is completely ***** and you hear nothing while the imaginary figures were not designed to feel the blows. Sebastian, Sebastian, Constance, Constance. The stepping stones yield as one treads on them. The painting is complete. In the turret of the church the clock has struck two and the lovers are still there, unwilling to part with all their ***** so

fresh the ardour of genitals created to pierce and fill. Why go?
Why not stay? Soon it will be morning and all options will be
renewed.

But while you look at the ***** the couple is slowly dissolving, the acid has reached the armpits, the fair breasts, the
throat. "I am *****," she cries out in harsh triumph and he
increases the summary rhythm of his loving ***** to danger
point. Then drop by drop into ***** will go like seeds pouring
in to a drumhead. Tonight will be fatal to someone's hopes.
The whip rises and falls, the painting changes. We are lovers
who have buckled under history's pressures. Later the historians will come and set out the typology of contemporary
humours to measure us by.

The painting faded and in its place there shone out from
the heart of Avignon, lambent like the Grail, the old smoky
masterpiece of Clément, half-obliterated by grime; she saw
again so clearly its weird mixture of elements – a sort of
Paradise Regained painted, superimposed upon a *Last Supper*,
as if printed upon a gossamer veil. The painter had called it
Cockayne, and Smirgel had received a grant to clean its
blemished surface. The sleepers were asleep in their chairs, the
candles had melted and run all over the place. Strangely enough
it was outside in a grassy meadow, sheltered by a coloured
marquee. There were gold coins lying about in the grass,
handkerchieves, articles of wear. Parts took place in the
seventeenth century, Christ had the head of Spinoza. Judas
looked with a conger's gaze. The wine had been doped,
perhaps? Had they all fallen asleep at the table? Maybe the
gypsies had sneaked up and cut their throats while they slept?

She woke with a start to find Schwarz smiling at her across
the desk.

Schwarz smiled as he watched her, but his smile, as always,
contained a sort of undertow of gravity while his ugly, lined
old face contained a great sweetness of emphasis. He sighed

and said: "It's a long time since we two made love. I was thinking so today because it is Lily's birthday." Lily had been his wife. They had been together since they were students at medical school. Then they broke up, and when the Nazis came he fled from Vienna, leaving her behind. The news that she had been sent to Buchenwald finally leaked through and the full realisation of his own cowardice and callousness had caused him a severe breakdown through which, and indeed out of which, Constance both nursed and guided him. She was supposedly his student and he her controller, so the situation was paradoxical in the extreme; in order to keep their relationship private and unprofessional rather than formally medical and subject to all the boredom associated with a psychological "transfer" he had been allowed to make love to her half a dozen times until he came to his wits, and returned shamefacedly to his responsibilities. "So long ago; yes, so long that now it seems never when I think back. It has all washed away. But you are still here, my friend; we are still friends. What a lesson you gave me in sagacity – you were ahead of me in your completeness. *Ach*! It sounds clumsy. I am thinking in German." He clicked his tongue reproachfully. Indeed his English and French always had a Viennese slant.

Constance said: "You had a moment of doubt – you lost your centre of gravity. It was lucky I was there to catch you. But you'd do the same for me, would you not? Indeed you may yet have to certify me! My present behaviour . . ."

"You can't regret being in love?"

"No. Of course not, who could? But this Egyptian lover of mine is employing a strategy completely at variance with your established ideas of how the couple couples."

"You mean sexual deviances, variations?"

"No! No!" she said vehemently. "Absolutely not. Not a shadow of such oriental treats. But a reversed affect technique entirely new to me, to us, and which gives brilliant results.

And which he seems to regard as being in the very nature of things. I thought for a while that it was simply that we complemented each other perfectly, that was all. But it's more than that and it deserves our attention as psychs." She lay back in her chair for a long while, quite silently reflecting. Then she dragged herself to her feet and went to the blackboard on the far wall of the consulting room. Old Schwarz gave a chuckle. "I know," she said, "I know. I am going to sound pompous; but it is very singular what this so-called gnostic man believes about us; when the couple was created out of the original man unit, clumsily divided into male and female parts, the affective distribution did not correspond at all with the biological. The sex of the man is really the woman's property, while the breasts of the woman belong to the man. Wait! I know it sounds crazy unless Affad himself expounds it, but it seems to work, it's not a hoax. The male and female commerce centres around sperm and milk – they trade these elements in their love-making. The female's breasts first gave him life and marked him with his ineradicable thirst for creating – Tiresias! The breasts are prophecy, are vision! Her milk has made him build cities and dream up empires in order to celebrate her!"

Schwarz cried, "Wait, Connie, wait. Let us record some of this; you will want to use it. Don't waste it while it's so fresh." He quickly changed the magazine of the wire recorder and switched on the small microphone which hung by the blackboard. She had drawn two rudimentary figures, a male and a female, facing each other. She joined them with a single stroke repeated three times at the level of the eyes, the breast and the sexual organs. "Now," she said thoughtfully, "this is how we envisage the affective discharge in sexual congress – mouth attacks the mouth, breast the breast, sex the sex. But in his idea of the affect link the male sex is really the woman's handbag, it hangs at her side while her breasts belong to him with their promise of nourishment. Their souls trade sperm against milk. And of course in the practical sense the quality of his product depends in her care and manipulation of the money-bag. Exchange rather than investment! Barter!"

"But when you actually *make* love?" said the old man with some bewilderment. They both burst out laughing. She said: "He simply abandons himself, lets me have what belongs to me. The woman, according to him, should be perpetually counting her small change, manipulating the scrotum manufacturing the sort of product which will biologically enrich the race and not just impoverish it — what is happening at the moment. Indeed, hers is the complete responsibility for the erection, she can build it at will when she pleases, even if the man be tired. He is quite powerless in this sense. Poor Affad, he'd be horrified to think I was scientifically interested in his marvellous gentle love-making. That is another thing, making love with a sincere belief in this kind of reversed affect relationship leads to simultaneous orgasm — almost every time. It is built into the exchange. It sounds such rubbish doesn't it?"

"Yes."

She herself looked so overcome by these strange formulations that Schwarz could not resist the desire to tease her mildly: "What do I hear?" he said with a strong Jewish twang. "Simultaneous ejaculation every time as well as almost permanent erections in the male? Surely Christmas is coming! *Aber*, Connie, it's too good to be true." Truth to tell, she looked a trifle shamefaced herself, to be so carried away by her subject. She blushed. "You know," said the old man, "it may just be a very lucky encounter with someone who really suits — such things have been heard of, and with all the apparent miracles you mention. But for the great run of people there is no joining, no chiming, no click. They just rape each other dismally or exploit each other or become prematurely impotent, lose all their hair, go into politics. It may be unique, your love, his love."

She nodded ruefully; you could not erect a universal principle with only one example to go on. It had to work in every case, to be a rule and not an exception. Schwarz thought he had wounded her with his banter, so he came to her side and patted her shoulder. "I share your concern, my dear, who could not? We deal all day with guilt and violence and insensitivity – any solution would be marvellous to hear of. Especially as we are all hungry for an antidote to violence and what you speak of is gentle love-making."

"Yes. Gentle with a respect for the other person and a full realisation that the sexual act is a psychic one, the flesh and bone enact but the psyche directs. But the reversed affect . . ." She laughed again and threw down her chalk. The telephone rang and the old man answered it, embarking on a long conversation with a fellow doctor. She listened to him abstractedly, thinking her own thoughts which still hovered about these psychological evaluations of her love-experience. She ached to be with Affad again – and to reprove the feeling she frowned and bit her lip. But the desire persisted and she recalled how for long stretches of the night she had lain at his side, quietly building up his strength as she had been told to do, "counting her change" as he had put it irreverently, preparing with care and concern an erection which she would in her own time demolish. . . . Schwarz went on talking but as he did so pushed across his desk one from a pile of monographs and offprints.

It was a recent contribution to the medical journal of Geneva on the grim topic of sexual violence inflicted on women during congress – either by homosexuals on each other, or by particularly aggressive males upon females. The Americans had christened this fist-thrust form of sex – the pushing of the clenched fist into the vagina – as force-fucking or fist-fucking, and the surgeon who had written the paper signalled a prevalence of cases suffering from physical damage to the head of the uterus. The general belief that men should show their masculinity by being as violent as possible was causing the woman partner physical damage, he asserted. As Constance riffled through the article, Schwarz made a number of enigmatic signs to her to suggest that here was the answer to her talk about gentleness in love-making, harmony in desire, unity in building the network of powerful love-sympathies which reward the lovers with the dual orgasm. She nodded grimly. Yes, this was her answer indeed. Fist-fucking!

Schwarz put down the phone and said: "Violence to be equated with inability to ejaculate, or simply badly, or praecox or what have you! But pain is *also* exciting, Connie."

"I hope I didn't give you the impression that we have started a Sunday school; pain is part of the play, but not a cruelty-substitute for incapacity. This oriental style uses everything, but modestly – the target is the double orgasm which is the base of all dialogue – even in the genetic sense."

"Which remains to be proved in my view as being general to all men!"

"Of course," she said humbly. "I am a fool to try and attribute universal laws to what might be a solitary experience. I wonder what poor Affad would think if he could overhear us."

"That you had a rather chilling, analytic mind – it augurs ill for romantic love, if that is what it is."

"Not quite that either," she said, but she felt rather a fool for having been so youthfully enthusiastic. She switched off the recorder and eased out the cartridge which she slipped into her pocket. Yet the subject itself would not rest, and she felt impelled to pursue it while the memory of her night-long dialogues with Affad was still fresh – for where else would she find a listener and critic so apt to evaluate and recognise what her lover had had to tell her? Schwarz could scent this and was himself sufficiently curious to try to encourage her to pursue her theme. In the silence they smoked, and she walked slowly up and down, deep in thought.

"Well, you are in love," he said at last, gravely, but just as gravely she shook her head and replied, "No. The word has no context. It's a commitment far beyond that in a way, because we are sharing something. Most people just follow out their immediate desires and when they dry up they are at a loss. They don't share an experience together step by step, building it. We are much closer now, at the start, than most married people. So, it's worse than being in love, as you call it, and much surer. It's oriental or Indian in origin, I suppose, but it has its own scientific rationale."

She told him of Affad's theory about oxygen, the basis of everything, the genetic food of both sperm and ovum, without which they were, according to Affad, "poorly documented", ill-equipped to help the race struggle to maintain itself; about this element or quality which was the real nous, the genetic "document" upon which almost everything depended, including the quality of the product on both sides. "When the quality of the sperm deteriorates a whole culture can be put at risk – which is what is happening now in the whole Hegelian West! And the first sign, the first signal of alarm comes from the woman who is biologically more vulnerable and more responsible than the man for the future which they literally weave like a tissue with their kisses and caresses. The spool upon which time is woven in the ancient Greek sense – not to mention the coming child which contains, like a grenade, the elements which will unfold into a full-sized skeleton with limbs, teeth, brain, hair . . . Where should we situate human love in all this vast context? Yes, you are right, I *do* love him, but not in the way you think – but because he showed me this schema of which I had a *profound* need. At last I can rest my intellect upon something which seems solid! As he says, 'When the asterisk marries the figleaf all is well.' The rest is this marvellous amnesia of love-making where all we have to do is to bring home the harvest. It seems another world altogether where people debate 'love', where couples bring their cases against each other, and marriages wallow and founder. But it's not only that, my dear, it has a direct bearing on my poor art, my little cottage-industry psychiatry. I understand Miss Quint much better than I did!"

They both laughed; Miss Quint was one of the quaint old ladies among her patients whose fantasies and Victorian timidities had given rise to such a strange psychological state, a dream-world worthy of Lewis Carroll, a garden of puns and weird spoonerisms. "When I told Affad about Miss Quint, how she had christened her vagina after her cat, and how she claimed that it not only mewed in complaint when the milk had turned, but also followed her about and jumped on the beds of her friends, he was absolutely delighted. He said, 'Nature always supplies essential information in the form of ailments. But she is right about her pussy.' When the documentation is poor or incomplete the woman knows it at once – indeed it creates a state of alarm. The quality of loving, of coupling falls off, and the man's erections become compromised, his sterility sets in. All this not seen from the selfish point of view of a couple becoming tired of each other, but as a form of cosmic calamity threatening the race and its mental balance. Love-making this way is unaggressive and deeply logical."

Schwarz began to become a trifle plaintive. "Are we going into marriage guidance or matrimonial aids?" he asked wryly, and added sadly, "Yesterday my nice old philosopher Ginsberg committed suicide, Connie, and he had promised to confide in me the secret of the universe. But he left no message – or perhaps the act was itself the message, like love is supposed to be?"

She smiled. "You are right to shoot me down – I must seem unbearably prosy about all this. But I never heard this sort of thing before or experienced passion in such an un-requitable way – as if there were no floor to it. And it doesn't come from a man, it comes from an attitude. Why shouldn't I try to catch a hold on it and rationalise it? It might serve others like me, like I *was* before Affad arrived, bleating in the wilderness of my logical positivism?"

"Indeed! Indeed!" said the old man, touched. But to himself he said: "It smells of Vedanta! Ah, these clever Orientals, what would they do in our shoes? With every damned illness our whole culture is called into question! Damn Affad!"

Indeed! She said: "Doctors with all their phobias and philias, like statues from some Graeco-Roman museum. You begin to realise that we are cannibals in fancy dress."

"It doesn't help!" he said gloomily.

"It doesn't help!" she echoed just as sadly.

A nurse brought in a tray with coffee and cakes and for a moment their attention was deflected from these abstruse matters. "Gosh!" she said with surprise, helping herself, "I am absolutely ravenous! What a surprise!"

"I wonder why," he said drily, sipping his brew.

It was marvellous to have someone to whom she could talk, with whom she could discuss these burning topics. She kissed his forehead piously and thanked him for listening. "I should charge a consultation fee," he said.

It freed her to continue this feverish disquisition upon her new experience. "Being in love with an Oriental is eerie because we are so different. He is like a piano of perfect tone but with no sustaining pedal. I mean that we do not share the same historic pedigree, intellectual connivance. My soul, my heart is of a more recent manufacture, sixteenth- or seventeenth-century – the world where sense, sensibility, sentiment were formulated as modes of enquiry and expression, where romantic love first threw up its narcissisms, its Don Juans. His backcloth is a huge hole in space, something vast, an Egypt of utter blank indifference to actuality. I live in the contingent, he in the eternal – in prose rather than poetry. It is superior in its way, though a trifle top-heavy: I can snipe at it with my humour, which is the weapon of my insight. But I would pay for a refusal to abdicate to his maleness, and he vice versa with my femininity. It's made me see that my love for Sam was only a transaction and not a full commitment – we were eaten alive by reciprocal sentiments. I also see now that the old-style couple is simply a fortuitous composition designed by lust; the new one I envisage could be triggered by desire yet be fragile as a wine or a water-colour which are both compositions and which can achieve aesthetic value, be beautiful in a geometrical way like a bird's nest or a cradle for the future. For the first time I feel optimistic about love, do you hear? Love!"

"O God!" said Schwarz with the full weight of his Jewish pessimism compounded with a Viennese upbringing. He was thinking: man is born free, free as a nightmare. We live forever encroached on by future and past, the dead and the unborn. Both live in the full horror of a perpetual present. *Aïe*! And here she was getting enthusiastic about contrapuntal fucking or about lying all night kissbound in a honeysuckle sweat as the vulgar tavern song said! Doctors were people of limited uptake, limited intellectual outspan, faulty insight. Their function was simply to reveal what was already known but unrecognised. A monotonous and limited role, like that of the coprophagous beetle forever rolling its balls of dung. What did it matter?

"What does it matter, Connie," he cried, "if you can find some well-earned happiness? You alarm me, you are far too articulate. You will *bore* him." She nodded and said, "I know. I am in danger of becoming too bossy – I could bore him, as you say. He already says that women who think should be lapidated by psychiatrists." Schwarz said, "I wish you would stop walking about as if dragged by a huge dog or propelled by a high wind. I'm dizzy."

"I am sorry," she said, all contrition at last, and sat down at the desk with a fair semblance of composure. "But I have been thinking of ways to formulate it. Look, it's like the contrast between a cathedral and a mosque. The mosque has no altar, no centre of focus. In it the truth is everywhere, though the whole is in fact oriented only gravitationally, aiming at Mecca. The cathedral is not oriented geographically, but inside it is focused upon a special spot, the High Altar, where the critical blood-sacrifice takes place. This is, so to speak, the butcher's slab of the Christian transaction. Here the wine is diluted, the bread is cut up and consecrated. This place is also the telephone booth from which one can ring up God and try to strike a bargain with him for one's individual soul – that precious figment! All right, I know I sound rather like old Sutcliffe weighing into you about Pia, but there is the whole contrast between us – mosque and church. But this thing outweighs the difference, it's common to either. Affad in discussing it spoke of it being calculated by an 'engineer of love in terms of *puissance massique* – the mass-power of weight-ratio' I must say it sounds as elegant as it is esoteric, but I know what he means."

"Damned if I do," said the old man doggedly.

"Of course you do."

She felt as if she had been separated at last from the world against which their science was fighting – a world of attachments without resonance, adventures without depth, embraces without insight! The embrace of Affad had in some singular way acted upon her as the drop of scalding olive oil had done upon the cheek of sleeping Eros. Perhaps she had even been cured of that obstinate old dream of all women, to become indispensable to someone's happiness – the running sore of self-esteem, the old dysentery of human narcissism. . . . Or was that too much to hope?

"I'm going home," she said abruptly. "I am in no mood to work, and I have so much leave accumulated that . . ."

"I know," he said with resignation. "Go on home."

She felt she could not last another moment without seeing Affad again, so she took her leave and went back to join him at breakneck speed – but only to find an empty room and an unmade bed beside which, to her surprise, disdain and concern, from a medical point of view, lay the little hashish pipe which smelt recently used! He walked in while she was sniffing at it like a suspicious cat and she put it behind her back while they embraced. Then she wagged it at him, saying, "You didn't say you smoked."

"Must I reveal everything? I am Egyptian after all, yes, I smoke." But he added that it was neither very much nor very often.

"Does it matter?" he asked.

"Only because you do."

"It's harmless," he said. "It's ritual."

She was relieved to hear it. She took herself off to the kitchen to make some tea while he searched slowly and methodically along the bookshelves for something which might interest him. "Ah, this bogus science!" he exclaimed as he caught sight of a series of blue-backed books, a psychoanalytic series. "It doesn't go far enough." She said, "How do you know?" and he sat down slowly balancing his tea-cup as he replied, "Hear my story, then. My parents were very rich, I was brought up very carefully but all over Europe to give me languages and make me quite at ease in every society and every circumstance. But I was shy, and, being sheltered, very slow to develop. I mixed badly. I preferred to lock myself up and indulge in abstruse studies like alchemy and mathematics – Egypt is the right place for that sort of thing, indeed everything occult. An only child, I became very solitary when my parents died, locked up as I was in a vast flat in Alexandria with few friends. My gnostic studies led me to a small group of seekers among whom I found Prince Hassad, and became his man, so to speak. Apart from these people – they were of every rank and circumstance – I frequented nobody. Then by an accident a charming and ardent young woman drifted into my life and took possession of me completely. Our marriage lasted seven years, but the child we had turned out to be deficient intellectually and the shock separated us for good. My wife went to live in the monastery of the Copts at Natrun as a solitary hermit. Her old mother took charge of the boy: she lived in Geneva, that is why I come here so regularly, to see how he is getting on, and to see her and give her the news of Egypt. After that calamity I went on alone, I had lost the taste for any other close relationship, so I made do, and got to like it. Once or twice I may have had a chance encounter with a woman but I made sure that it was ephemeral – some tired cabaret artist or street walker. But this was exceptional and due to loneliness – perhaps thrice in all these years. So I am hopelessly out of practice, and can be easily put to flight if you find this situation too demanding. It was in this state of fragility that I encountered you and was attracted, heaven knows by what, for I have known greater beauties and met more massive intellects. I took my courage in both hands and with great daring tried to stake a claim to an experience which – clearly I am wrong about this – seemed to me essential if I was not to die of spleen and boredom during this senseless war!" He yawned in an outrageous way.

"I have never heard a more self-centred, a more masculine declaration of love in my whole life!" she said with a certain amusement in her voice and an unwilling tinge of admiration in her heart – for this shameless egotism was accompanied by propitiatory caresses and endearments. They were lying down now, side by side, and had kicked off their shoes.

"Don't you like omniscient men, men who are too sure

of themselves? They give such confidence, they say. When first I saw you I had a tremulous premonitory feeling which told me that I would be excused every fatuity."

"Wrongly," she said, cobwebbed herself in the drowsiness which he seemed to project with every measured breath. My goodness, she thought, soon they would be making love again, it was quite deplorable that it should seem so inexorable. Also behind the sleepy persiflage of his speech – so belied by the gentle but perfectly assured rhythm of his caresses – she felt the deep vibration of an anxiety in him, a lack of confidence in himself which made him send out these wistful probes in order to take soundings in a possibly hostile world around him. Or was it that he found the habits of solitude hard to break and the society of a woman, even a cherished woman, menacing and disquieting?

"No," he said, for all the world as if he had been reading her thoughts as they passed in her mind, "none of those things really – perhaps a little of the last might come later! My main concern was to preserve you in this world – I felt you might become suicidal in Avignon like your sister – and if possible to bring you back where I could approach you. That is why I told Smirgel to look after you very carefully, or answer for it with his head!" She was surprised. "So *that* is why he kept persecuting me with his solicitude? I thought otherwise."

"Poor man! he was doing his duty. I even came down to Avignon once myself – it was a great temptation to call on you, I don't know how I resisted, but I did. I knew your hours and movements. What heroism!" She felt a sudden pang of regret that he had not done so, yet it might have served no purpose at that time, living as she was. Affad then was hardly more than a thought in the back of her mind, without real substance, a faint beckoning thought without a tangible future. "What part did Livia play in all this?" He replied drowsily, "None. None at all. Smirgel loved her, that is all. You know he was there in Provence when you all were, working in the town gallery restoring the medieval paintings. He met Livia then. It was he who introduced her to the Nazi philosophy of the time. When she went to Germany it was to stay with him – he was an art critic in Hamburg."

"Did they live together in the accepted sense?"

"I don't know. I never asked him. They met in Avignon where he was staying. She became a party member through him and later on naturalised. He started by using her to spy on Galen, then went and fell for her."

The thought was horrible to Constance and vastly increased her sympathy and regret for her dead sister. There was a long silence now, and she feared that they might both slide away into sleep unless some new topic were introduced, so she said the first thing that came into her head without quite meaning to: or perhaps it only *appeared* to be involuntary, one could not be quite sure. At all events what she said was: "Will you marry me?" This had the desired effect – it was sufficiently unexpected to make him open his eyes. "Did you say 'would' or 'will'?" he asked cautiously. He placed his lips to her cheek and heard her answer quite distinctly, "I said 'will you'!"

"Of course not," he said at once. "At least not in fact. Whatever gave you such an idea?"

"I thought not," she said, amused. "I just wanted to make you writhe, that is all."

"Mark you, in certain undefined and relatively unimaginable contexts I would, I could, I *might*. But of course I won't."

"That was very closely argued," she said.

"Surely you follow my reasoning?"

"Only too well; supposing I were pregnant?"

"Why should I when you are not?"

"Casuist and philanderer!"

"You are like the Catholic Church, Constance. This is nothing but a hold-up." He quoted disgustedly, "Will you, won't you, can't you, might you, must you, would you ... what a catechism for a right-minded gnostic to come up against. Of course I won't!"

"Very well, then, goodbye!"

"Goodbye," he said equably (how terrible it sounded to her ears), and shut his eyes once more, adding, "Marriage may be dead as a doornail but the real couple hasn't begun to manifest as yet. At least not in the West. It will need a new psychology – or perhaps a very old one – to inaugurate the coming dispensation. O dear! It sounds terribly schematic, like cutting along the dotted line. On the other hand we can't go on as everyone is doing. The world is coming to an end faster because of the waste, the misdirection of affect. I want to begin the new thing with you."

"Truthfully," she said, "I don't give a damn about theoretical considerations. I just want to be loved by you, stop."

But she was lying and they both knew it.

Their attachment had been born into a new age of sexual friendship which would create new responsibilities and problems in the measure of its new freedoms. But somehow not for them – what he had told her made her sure of it. Yet the whole subject-matter of his thinking was still full of mysteries – perhaps even absurdities, who could say? She was still, after all, a hostage of the logicians and consequently full of scepticism. He seemed so intellectually cocksure, a bad sign in a man, and particularly an Oriental. She lay beside him and watched him sleeping so peacefully, his head turned away in half-profile from her. What, she wondered, was the meaning of the little slip of thread round his throat? Some people wore a christening chain with a cross on it, or else their names graven upon a talisman of a saint. Perhaps, like a true Mediterranean, he wore it against the evil eye – but where was the usual blue bead? Beside the bed there was a pair of nail scissors which he had been using to clean out his pipe and settle his plug of hashish. Half in a spirit of idle mischief she took them up and placed them upon the thread as if to cut it. At this moment he opened his eyes and saw what she was doing. A look of horror and supplication came over his face, and he gasped, "For goodness sake!" Constance, delighted at the alarm she had created, withdrew her scissors and said, "I knew it! The Evil Eye!" And she put the scissors back on the side table. He said, "One can't turn one's back for a moment! You were actually going to sever my lifeline, were you? And so carelessly? If I had fallen back dead upon the pillows – where would you have been then?" She could not quite make out if this were banter or not. "Explain!" she said. "What is the thread?" And slowly fingering it, he told her dreamily that it was a sign of his affiliation to the little Orphic group of which he had spoken more than once; it was the umbilical cord which united him with the buried world they were trying to bring to light with their association.

"The little thread is flax, grown on the Nile. We have imitated the Indians in that. It's the sign of the yogi, of his frugality and his mental chastity. The Templars wore it as a belt – and those idiot Inquisitors took it for some secret sexual symbol arguing a homosexual affiliation. Idiots! The double sex was quite another thing, a syzygy of the male and female affect."

"Would you have died if I had cut it?"

"Just to punish you I would have tried! But I would have regretted it, for it stands for other things. My fate, woven by Moira, the fates of Greece, my umbilical cord through which I connect with the rhythms of the earth yoga. No, not died, but been sad and regretful."

"I am sorry. It was thoughtless of me."

That night she asked her lover: "Did you know it was going to be like this?"

He looked at her and slowly nodded but said nothing; he

closed his eyes and appeared to reflect very deeply upon her question. "Did you, tell me truthfully?" She put her fingers upon the drum of his chest and felt the deep rise and fall of his breath, the archaic oxygen-pump which fed his thinking and his love-making alike.

"It isn't like a love affair at all," she said aloud, echoing a thought which had been formulated by her mind a while since. Their relationship had developed an odd kind of continuity so that it seemed to be a succession of small surprises, their endearments were like stepping stones towards . . . towards what, exactly?

"It is in fact the prototype, the original love-affair which we've tumbled into by luck: or perhaps a design we are not wise to. Today's loves are mostly debased currency, the timid investments of undischarged bankrupts with nothing to offer but undocumented sperm, trivial aggressive lusts, stuff of little richness. Sperm without oxygen, and with poor motility, will never reach the Grand Slam. All that is the domain of Unlove, Constance, it's not our concern."

"But where are we going?" she asked in a low voice full of concern. "We seem so linked now. I have changed so much in such a short time."

"It's only the beginning – that's why I hesitated so much. I did not want to go away as I must soon."

So, inchmeal, their love advanced.

And yet there was some inward check, for from time to time there would be moments of abstraction when she discerned an expression of tremendous sadness on his face; he might stand staring at the lake, or simply transfixed before the mirror in which he was knotting a tie, while this shadow of immense distress settled upon his features – it needed an effort to shake off. Then it was replaced by the look of loving wonder which he always wore when looking at her, talking to her. But she was alarmed by this sudden change and once, surprising it as she awoke (he stood by the balcony gazing down at the water) she cried out, "What *is* it that comes over you, comes between us all of a sudden? You must tell me. Is it someone else?" He laughed, and came to sit on the foot of the bed. "Yes, I must tell you because it concerns us both in the long run – it's aimed at us. Yet it's so fantastic that it is hard to realise, its novelty is so unexpected. Constance, I have been to Canada and I have seen the thing – what they call the Toy: the bomb, the new one." He fell silent for a long moment, staring at the pattern in the carpet.

He had visited the smithy of Haephaestus so to speak, the flaring forges where the huge grenades of the atomic piles roared and shivered, as if about to give birth, while the boiling steam and water rushed from the sluices and filled the air with dense acrid warmth; and outside the vast snowscapes like another inclement Russia, snow falling in the quarries with their long caterpillar-lines of linked chariots. He shivered in his soul when he remembered those shivering and sweating grenades full of a new fever.

"I had to report on this to the small group of Alexandrian searchers to which I belong and which I sometimes direct. I won't bore you with all that. But what I saw – my dear, all that is going on now, the fighting taking place, is already as out of date as the Battle of Hastings. We are fighting with bows and arrows. Compared to what has already arrived, the Toy."

"I had heard some vague talk about it from a patient who was a Viennese mathematician."

"It's not the war that's at issue. This thing is aimed at our bone marrow, and the bone marrow of the earth we live on. It confers sterility or genetic distortion – we will be born without heads and legs like illustrations to the propositions of Empedocles. Constance, nature has lost all interest in us; from now we are orphans! And how appropriate that a Jew should have triggered this murderous extract of pure matter, what a terrible revenge of the Semitic brain – a really Faustian denouement awaits us; it completely dwarfs the war, what matter who wins or loses? It is a shadow-play, for both sides are orphaned by the same stroke." He was trembling so much that she took his hands in her own strong ones and succeeded in calming him without speaking. "Not only that," he went on at last on a quieter note, "as if that were not enough – woman is compromised; in her we are destroying our nurse and muse, the earth."

They sat for a long time, as if posed for a photograph, she with her head against his shoulder, he with his arms round her shoulders. "You see what comes between our kisses?" he whispered at last, stroking her attentive and beautiful face. "When man starts to *feel* with his reason, with his intelligence, why, Monsieur is there!"

"Monsieur what? Monsieur who?" she asked.

And then, "We are being too serious," he said all of a sudden, briskly, shaking off the enormous weight of this ugly daydream, and at the same time feeling absolved because he had told her, had spoken it all aloud; at last there was someone to whom he could really talk. As she was putting on her clothes she said thoughtfully, "There must be a strategy for being happy. It's our duty to find it!" How like a woman, he thought.

"No such thing," he said.

She found some of his thinking interesting, but some downright silly. "How like a man," she said, "you are just feeling out of your depth, that is all; the new polyandry has scared you. But honey, the woman was always free, though not always allowed to say so openly. Is it a bad thing to come clean? She can now indulge her always dream of being an unpaid prostitute of pure benevolence, a public benefactor. She has become a collector – seven men to one woman seems about right – I have worked this out from what my patients have told me. Farmyard mathematics!"

"It doesn't work," he said. "Would that it did!"

"I know. But why not after all?"

"Because the poor quality of the male sperm becomes at once felt by the woman who is now the assailant. Anxiety and poor erections set in. *Ejaculatio praecox*! The poor little vagina must be likened to a little animal always eager for its nourishment. The sperm literally feeds it, it bathes the walls with their mucous membranes, it permeates the whole flesh and psyche. You can taste the odour of male sperm on the breath. The vagina starts to die of inanition, to falter from hunger; a hundred men with inferior sperm cannot feed it. In the gnostic sense a sperm which is poor in oxygen is deficient in the needed nourishment; it is poorly documented, poor in oxygen and the fruits of thought."

"Go on," she said, for it seemed a new and unusual way of looking at the sexual act, at the economy of the whole transaction. But he had turned quizzical now, as if he did not for a moment expect her to believe his theories. Smiling, however, he went on with his exposition: "The walls of the little animal – prettier often than the mouth of its owner – gives out a replete hum when the quality of the sperm is high or well-documented as we say: like a beehive or a small dynamo or a cat purring. The possibility of making a strong child with rich brain content and powerful sexuality presents itself and is eagerly welcomed by both lovers in their psyches. But with poor-quality sperm the poor little animal becomes parched and withered; sperm with no spiritual axis cannot feed the woman's ideas or her feelings. The more she performs the more diminished she feels. Genetically she is being starved, her ideas become poor and exhausted, the joy of living deserts her. And then comes the last stage." He put on a story-book voice and wagged a cautionary finger at her as he said, with great assurance. "Guess what? *Nymphomania!*" She clapped her hands at this revelation. "The girls begin to scratch themselves to death; the men find that they cannot achieve a climax easily—even younger men. Their hair recedes. They go into politics . . ."

"Or come to the analyst. I have restored the hair to two tired men, and have heard of analysis unblocking the sex drive. But you must know that. Where did you pick up your psychological knowledge?"

"Here and there. But I went to a woman and she could not resist my honesty—she fell in love with me."

"And?"

"And!"

He took her hand and put it to his cheek. "Your life is full of hazards because as yet your science is inexact. She went mad and was locked up: she writes to me, long, long letters of self-reproach for having loved me. Yet there was nothing between us of a personal sort—it all went on in her head!"

"Love! It's all done by mirrors!"

"Exactly. But I don't care. I invest! I love you!"

"Prove it."

He shook his head. "We are living out the death of the couple, the basic brick of all culture."

"You are out of date and out of focus," she said.

"Out of date and out of fashion, rather," he admitted.

She said: "It's all going too fast; you understand too much; I shall use you up too soon. I had imagined this relationship being slow, full of hesitations and nuances and unwitting naivetés. I wanted to build it slowly, match by match, like a ship in a publican's bottle."

He: "I thought you were too beautiful to be really clever."

"You are not against me because I am a Freudian and a doctor? I was scared to death that it might make a sort of shadow between us—that I knew too much to be sufficiently feminine to appease you, to get my hooks into you: but it's been so easy sliding downhill, *en pente douce*. I have forgotten how to brake."

"It's a sign of our intellectual abjectness that psychology with its miserly physical categories and positivist bias should prove liberating and enriching as it does; it proves that the psyche is seriously ankylosed by the rigour of our *moeurs*. The real seed of the neurosis is the belief in the discrete ego; as fast as you cure 'em the contemporary metaphysic which is Judeo-Christianity manufactures more I's to become sick Me's. On my word as a Professor!"

"O Lord! you *are* anti-Freudian after all."

"No. I revere him, I even revere the purity of his un-shakeable belief in scientific reason. His discovery was as important as the microscope, or the petrol engine, a sudden enlarging of our field of vision. How *could* one not admire it?"

"Okay. I forgive you. But there is one thing most aggravating about you – I'd better tell you now, right at the beginning, instead of waiting until we are divorced . . ."

"Well?"

"You talk as if you had some privileged information which is not accessible to me. It's typically masculine and it makes one inclined to sympathise with the heavy brigade – as we call the clitoris club in the clinic."

"It's a serious charge."

"Have you?"

"No."

TEN

The General

THE MISADVENTURE WHICH VIRTUALLY COST VON ESSLIN his sight was also, by a paradox, instrumental in saving his life, for it supervened at about the time when the tide had turned and hostilities in and around his Provençal stronghold were sharpening to a climax. It resulted in his being incarcerated in an eye clinic near Nîmes, there to lie in sombre darkness with a pad over his eyes, drowned in self-reproaches and self-questionings. Whatever his body decreed, his soldier's mind was still on the active list, and the little radio by the bed brought him no consoling news, though the bulletins were under heavy censorship. Heaven knew how much was left unsaid. But truth to tell, his own decline had been going on for some time, for a year or more; this sudden flurry of a build-up involving so many new officers and material had only emphasised a fatigue which had slowly been gaining on him since the Avignon command had first become his. Though not unduly introspective he found himself often wondering about the cause. It was not only the calamitous withdrawal from Russia which could hardly be disguised any longer, nor the failure in Egypt and Italy, no. It was the inability to speak openly about them, and thus to devise ways and means to stem the tide until they could re-form their ranks. He did not believe the war lost, but still under debate, while there was plenty of life in the old German war dog yet to redress the failures of the past and assure future victory. But in other times the subject would have been discussed and ventilated, there would have been great conferences of strategists, self-criticism, truthful, intelligent assessments of the situation. But in this case one could not voice a single criticism that did not touch the question of the Leader's good faith, good judgement; what was at stake was quite literally the divinity of the Führer – who dared to gainsay that?

And then . . . Von Esslin had aged, he felt the gradually lengthening shadows of a change of life start spreading before him; his reactions were slower. The younger officers grew impatient with the timidity of his troops' dispositions and felt that the three lateral rivers had begun to obsess him. In the fortress, standing in front of the great European chart with its interlapping sections, he still held forth, terminating his discourse with the old, once dramatic gesture of placing his thumb upon Avignon and spreading his fingers to turn them in a slow arc to show the extent of their strategic coverage – the gateway to Italy and the Côte d'Azur were both comprised in this expository gesture. The thought of a landing further north was a novelty which he did not take into account: others would deal with such an eventuality. But the numbers needed close supervision, things had become very crowded, not only because of the wounded from the Russian front but also because of the hordes of slave-workers or volunteer Fascists of all nationalities, even Russian, who were tunnelling the vast underground corridors of the new dumps under the Pont du Gard. He had vague thoughts about his retirement in a few years, of what he would do with himself; but here a thrill of incertitude swept his mind. What sort of world would he retire into? In order to call himself to order and replenish his morale he commenced a close study of the Protocols of Zion and the Imperial Testament of Peter, the documents he carried with him always in their little plastic envelope. It calmed and even invigorated his mind, this regular study every evening. But he felt rather cut off and a trifle moribund as he contemplated the impatient energy of the younger officers, and so often read on their faces expressions of a smiling condescension when he was talking. He was annoyed to discover that he had been accorded the nickname of "Grandfather" by the command. It only emphasised the gulf which was spreading between two generations, two historic attitudes. He began to drink rather heavily.

It was at this moment that he was informed that he could release his servant for regular soldiering and replace him with a slave-prisoner if he so wished; at first he was regretful, for his batman had been with him quite a time, but his regrets were short-lived once Krov appeared upon the scene, saluting smartly with that captivating smile, at once so knowledgeable and so self-deprecating. He was handsome and slender and he turned his youthful agility in the direction of making himself indispensable. In a world full of surly mastiffs he was something quite new, a ray of sunshine. What was there he could not do? Sometimes Von Esslin enumerated his skills with amazement – and he said that his family background was rich bourgeois; his father had been a doctor. Cook, sweep, maintain, polish, set to rights . . . Banquo's old house had never shown to better advantage; gardener, handyman, mason, electrician . . . every new problem showed Krov's versatility accompanied by charm and good nature. His German was imperfect and he made delightful mistakes which sometimes turned into puns of great felicity. Von Esslin recounted these to his mess and earned hearty laughter for his new slave. Krov exercised a charm over his master which was positively Mephistophelean. He tended and brushed his clothes with passion and frequently made some small adjustment of dress, brushing off a crumb or cigar ash from Von Esslin's tunic before letting him depart for the office. The old man was bemused by his good luck – never had an establishment been run so efficiently and with such warm good-feeling. "Ah, Krov," he would say, "how did you never marry? You would make a very fine husband. Or perhaps a wife, eh? Ha! Ha!"

"I did, I was. I have two children."

"Where?"

"I don't know where they are," said Krov quite seriously but without undue emotion. "Somewhere they must be." Von Esslin felt a wave of sympathy heavy as lead around his heart. "Well, I must be going, I shall be late," he said and stumped off. Poland!

Sometimes when he came back for lunch he might find Krov sitting on the front steps of the villa in the sun polishing his boots and shoes; he would spring up and salute with his warm smile of greeting, so obviously glad to see his master back that Von Esslin's heart was warmed and he became almost human, almost talkative, despite the official warning that there must be no fraternising with slave-labourers. Or else he might find him on top of a ladder arranging the grape trellis on the garden balcony. It was difficult when one received such superlative and willing service not to fall a victim to it, to become a little slack and dependent. You had only to say "Bring me a clean handkerchief, Krov," and the youth would dart away like a deer to find the article. Sometimes when he lay awake in bed the General's thoughts turned homewards and sometimes he accorded the Polish servant a sad passing thought. Krov's country villa had been in roughly the same region – bought against his father's retirement, he explained. His master grunted, but did not ask him for any more details about Poland before the war. But in a fit of elephantine playfulness intended in some profounder way to show his awkward gratitude, he learnt a few words of Polish from the little phrase book which the servant carried and both pleased and surprised him by saying "Good morning" in that language; but only when they were alone, of course. And when Von Esslin fell ill of a 'flu Krov nursed him tenderly, even feeding him with a spoon when he had a high fever, as one would a child. The old man was touched and grateful, though he refrained from thanking him openly, for after all he was only doing his duty in the official sense.

It proved a welcome change. Krov afforded him company and interest at a time when he was withdrawing from the coarse jovialities and philistine high spirits of the mess with its new faces.

He tried in unobtrusive ways to lighten the burden of the younger man's slavery, but it was difficult to go against field instructions which insisted that his slave was "expendable" and should be "used up in hard labour". He feared that Krov must present himself to the world as rather too well off, too well fed. He felt reckless, however, and even got him some cast-off clothes with boots and a tattered green mess jacket in which he served meals, which he did with professional aplomb. His cooking also was something special. Von Esslin was so charged with intellectual infatuation about the slave that he wrote and described some of his virtues to his mother who replied by saying, "It's as if you speak of your son." The observation struck him quite forcibly. One day when he cut his hand opening the car door he found a sympathetic Krov rushing to bandage it up, first dressing it with ether – he knew where everything was. His speed, tact and sympathy made the elder man say to himself, "But he really *seems* like a son to me," a sentimental idea which was so novel that he all but felt tears start to his eyes. "There!" said Krov at last, satisfied with his skilful bandage. "That will hold firm until tonight when we'll change it. Would you be in need of any anti-tetanus injection?" The General snorted with scorn. "For that little scratch? No." Krov said, "Anyway, the trigger finger is all right, so you can still shoot, sir, without any difficulty."

"Yes." Von Esslin smiled.

The weather had been so variable that one did not any longer know what to make of it; snow was followed by rain and warm winds, then frost, then sunshine again. The mean temperatures rose and fell like the waves of the sea. Now, during his convalescence, they had entered a sunny passage which was almost like summer; he could spend the afternoons out of doors, among the vines at the edge of the copse, reading or writing letters while Krov scurried about his tasks in the house, all the while humming or singing under his breath songs in his own unfamiliar tongue – songs which pleased the old man as much as the fine tenor of the singer. But of course he could say nothing to compliment him. The evenings too had become more supportable since Krov had shown him how to play solitaire. How strange life was! He often wondered nevertheless how Krov could maintain such a continuous amiability – for a man with his country over-run, his family dispersed and lost, his people sold into slavery, it was astonishing. There must be times when he felt the tug of sadness when he thought about these things? It was better not to let his thoughts take this direction, however, for it was the sort of situation which would never be redressed under the New Order.

Krov had placed an old fashioned rocking-chair which he had found in an attic at the end of the garden and it was here that the General sat in the evening to read or write; if the weather was at all chilly Krov put an old military cloak round his shoulders with great solicitude. It was from this habit that the shooting developed, for during the handing in of the guns as dictated by the Army a number of rather fine ones naturally figured among the general run of cheap farmers' twelves and sixteens. These were naturally regarded as "on loan" to the occupier, and when there was a shoot they were distributed to all senior officers. In this way Von Esslin "inherited" two fine hammerless twelves which he used once or twice for duck on the Camargue. But now, from his rocking chair, he found that on days of mistral his little hillock where the house stood was in the direct line for the evening flight of turtle doves and partridge. The turtle doves could hardly make headway against the wind and certainly not gain height; pressed down earthwards by its violence they flew in little gasps, little bursts, digging their way into the wind, and at each stroke falling back towards the earth once more with a lost momentum. They presented a very easy target even for such a moderate shot as Von Esslin, and on flight evenings he usually disposed of a dozen for dinner with rapidity and ease.

Krov went out of his way to encourage such activity, for he knew how to pluck and dress the birds which fell to his master's guns; sometimes when the flights were big and he had nothing to do he might take on the role of loader, thus increasing the speed of Von Esslin's firepower. On the evening of the accident the wind had come up but the day had proved so very exceptional that one felt one was in the month of August; only the clipped and raked vineyards belied the thought, for as yet the first green pilot leaves had not appeared on the black crucifixes. But birds there were in plenty, and the General popped away at them while his slave loaded the smoking guns for him. A certain wilful confusion hangs over the incident which now took place – some believing it an accident due to the General's thoughtlessness. What actually happened was as follows. Beside the chair of the General was an extremely damp mud parapet which was still soaked with the heavy rain of the preceding days. Inadvertently – he was to claim that the action was inadvertent, though nobody believed him – Krov in exchanging guns lightly stuck the barrels in the muddy bank, thus stopping the ends with heavy pellets of soil. He wiped the end of the gun before handing it to Von Esslin and busied himself with the second weapon. Now came the accident. The old man had got into the habit of discharging both barrels of his sparrow-shot together, aiming just in front of the dover-flights so that the birds dived into the sprayed pattern of lead. But this time when the hammers struck the gun blew back, the barrels exploded and the stock flew off; he received the blow-back of the charge full in the face. Enough to kill one outright, as they said later when dressing his complicated criss-cross wounds.

He turned in horror and perplexity, his features runnelled in trickles of blood, powder-markings and mud, as if to invoke the help of Krov; then in a flash he saw that his servant must have been expecting the accident for he had prudently stepped behind the old olive tree, and had his hands half-raised to his ears, as if anticipating an explosion. Von Esslin roared like a bull and stood up shaking all over with shock and pain; but in the roar also was another note, a note of pain and sadness and affliction at the betrayal of his affections by the Polish slave. He stood trembling, looking at him, with his smashed-looking face, and then slowly sank to his knees, grabbing the chair and overturning it as he fell face downwards in the grass.

Unfortunately there was a witness to the scene in the form of the A.D.C. to the General; this young staff officer had been looking for him in order to deliver a service message of some urgency; the house being empty he went out into the garden, and just as he located his chief he saw the whole thing take place; he also saw the incriminating move of the servant as he hid behind the tree. There was no doubt that Krov knew it was going to happen, and was therefore responsible. Consternation seized the young soldier as he saw the General fall, heard him roar with pain and anger. The sparrow shot whizzed in the bushes. The whole thing was so sudden that he stood stock-still before having the presence of mind to race to the General's aid, at the same time blowing his whistle to alert the duty picket, which now came thumping and panting out on to the balcony with a clatter of useless rifles. Krov was already beside his master, down on one knee, when the officer arrived, so that together they managed to take up the still writhing form and carry it towards the balcony; here someone with presence of mind had produced a stretcher, and the General, who was still swearing and groaning, was piled on to it. The heavy duty wagon had a capacious end with fold-down seats, and this obviated calling an ambulance. The thing was to get him to the general hospital in the Citadel as quickly as possible. They hoisted the wounded man in. Then the officer drew his Luger. To Krov he said, "You are coming with me."

Krov did not show any particular emotion, but he asked if he might go to the lavatory. The officer said he might, but with the door open and with himself posted outside, his weapon at the ready. They drove in silence to the Fortress where he turned out the guard and asked the officer of the watch to convene a provisional court martial for that afternoon. Then he announced what had happened to the duty officers and confided to the operational telex the news that the Senior Commander had had a serious accident and that a bulletin about it might be expected from the medical staff that same evening. Nor was this long delayed, for they washed the blood and powder and mud from the face of Von Esslin and pronounced with relief that all the wounds were superficial but that the explosion had only compromised his sight. He was almost completely blind and likely to remain so, if not forever, at least for the foreseeable future. A command was out of the question in such a case, and it would not be long before a replacement arrived to take over. It was of course catastrophic in one sense for the *amour-propre* of an active man to be plunged in the dark like this, with the prospect of hospitalisation and retirement to look forward to as a future. Apart from the shock and the pain, the stitches in his cheek and chin, he was beset by a fearful sense of despondency and utter helplessness. An oculist came and tried various kinds of light upon the eye, but was non-committal about the future. The eyes must be given time to settle down, he said, for they too were in a shocked state from the accident.

Accident? That evening a drum head court martial heard the evidence of the A.D.C. concerning the guilt of the Polish servant in grim silence; it was not thought necessary to ask the wounded man whether he would concur to this statement or not – the thing was so conclusive. Krov was sentenced to death by firing squad the following morning. It was not the only execution, for a couple of *franc-tireurs* were also going to be executed. The General sat in a chair by the window. His face had been repaired and dressed. He sat there patiently under the full weight of his near sightlessness – how unfamiliar it was! Yet he recognised the voice of the A.D.C., who came to tell him about the verdict on Krov, hoping no doubt to please him by this summary revenge. But the old man said nothing. Finally the A.D.C. took his leave, closing the door softly behind him. When the nurse came in to the room she found her charge still sitting by the window, but his chin had sunk on his breast and he was breathing rather more rapidly than usual, which indicated nervous stress; it was most necessary to make some bright conversation to infuse a bit of optimism into the General. She was right. He was soon chatting away in his kindly fashion, thanking her warmly for all that they were doing for him. When the question of his convalescence came up the oculist invited him to the eye clinic in Nîmes where his progress could be checked. It was only a question of clearing up – and there was no Krov to undertake such an operation. Finally a couple of clumsy orderlies assembled his few possessions and helped him into the duty car. In this way he cleared the decks for his successor.

All this, in much abbreviated form, was retailed by Smirgel in his secret bulletins to Geneva, and he was even able to supply the name of the new Commander. It was Von Ritter, a stern disciplinarian and party man, as ugly as he was un-principled. The news of his appointment caused a ripple of interest, for he was fresh from some spectacular civilian

314

reprisals in Russia. His arrival was celebrated by a mass hanging of twenty "partisans" in Nîmes: they were actually youths who, to dodge the labour conscription, had taken to the hills where they lived like the shepherds. They were unarmed, but what matter? It would teach everyone a good lesson.

So the news of the new dispensation filtered through the opaque medium of the gossiping Intelligence agencies, and the name of Von Esslin was gradually obliterated from the reports. In Geneva as in Avignon the cold set in again with high wind and heavy snowfalls.

ELEVEN

Confrontations

AROUND THE COMPANIONABLE GREEN BAIZE OF THE billiard table moved the two figures of Affad and Toby, each with half his mind on his ball and the other on the subject in hand, namely, did Ritter's appointment prefigure a policy change; or was it a ruse? For Toby "it smelt ratty". The accident was an excuse merely to replace an old-fashioned regular with old-fashioned notions by an active, fire-eating young general who would ginger things up. Affad shook his head: "You over-elaborate the obvious. I believe Smirgel." Toby sighed with resignation and said, "As always. But you just wait. That man is going to fail you."

"I have asked for an independent medical check on the matter, so we'll see who is right." Then, in order to rub a little salt into the open wound of British Intelligence he went on, "By the way, I did not ask you people for the dates of the Second Front landings, I got them from Cairo. I did not want to embarrass you. But here on this visiting card I have jotted down the false dates which I have passed to Smirgel. You will find quite a response to them already – a whole lot of armour has been shunted north to contain this hypothetical landing – but I am sure you know that."

Toby swore silently for as a matter of fact he did not know, though it would not have done to say so; he looked vexed, however, and Affad smiled, for he liked teasing him. The result was that Toby missed his shot and vented his spleen with an audible oath which did service for both groups of sentiment.

The Secret Service was really no fun at all. One was always being upstaged by some other agency and one was forced to accept old-fashioned histrionic methods of work, some of them elaborated at the turn of the century. It was the influence of bad fiction like the Sherlock Holmes series (which he adored); the Foreign Office believed that every spy should carry a big magnifying glass with him night and day in case of footprints. And here this blinking Gyppo Prince went about openly tapping telephones ... "Nobody tells us anything," he said plaintively, and by a lucky shot broke even.

Constance who watched them thoughtfully from the corner where she was answering letters in her swift shorthand said, "I find it galling to hear you two talk – you know more than I do about Avignon, and yet I live and work there, and my job takes me everywhere. Poor old General; how sad to lose your sight!"

But the new General had wasted no time; he had sacked subordinates right and left, signalling for new staff appointees whom he could personally trust to be "firm", and had spread terror into all departments including those which dabbled in counter-espionage. "Smirgel himself is scared and wants to shut down his transmitter for a week or so to let the simmering settle down. I must say when I see these whopping reverses and withdrawals in Russia I can't help feeling that that little embalmed head we supplied is giving Hitler pretty destructive guidance."

"Let me tell you the most important news of all – for the first time I see a faint hope that we might just win the war. Lord Galen has been *sacked*." Both men burst out clapping with delight. "O not that we don't love him," explained Sutcliffe. "But really we want to win, don't we?" They explained that Lord Galen, in order as he said "to show up the other side for the rotters they were" persuaded the War Cabinet to announce that no monuments of historic or aesthetic value in Europe would be subjected to bombardment. Moreover he had this piously announced over the radio. The result was not hard to foresee for at once the Nazis took advantage of this knowledge and turned it to account in their ammunition stockpiling. Toby said, "For example that mysterious dump they have coded as W.X. in Avignon is being burrowed out slap under the Pont du Gard – you must have noticed a vast increase of activity around the Remoulins area. Huge teams of foreign workers are being housed in makeshift huts all round about in the garrigue. It's quite an operation. But finally somebody has tumbled to Lord Galen's role as a hot potato, and he has been invited to abstract himself from the task of Information. May God be with him in his new post in the colonies."

"No colonies for him. He is too clever for them. He will suddenly emerge as an admiral."

"But tell us your news," said Toby, turning to Constance apologetically. "How have things been?"

"It sticks in my throat," she said. "It's an unheroic story of discomfort and sadness, with sporadic little outbursts of danger or outrage, shootings and disappearances. Bread from maize full of straw and other sweepings. Coffee made of mud. Hungry children. Queues for medical attention. I feel ashamed to live where I do, eat what I eat, thanks to Blaise and the office and the black market in everything."

"And Livia, is she really dead?"

"Yes." And she told them how and when.

"And no clue to why?"

"I could think of none, save that such a stark gesture was in her character, and that it may have been somehow connected with the failure of her central beliefs – though she said not. But who could see the face of Nazism from close up and not want to retch? She was not a fool. But I am aware all the time that you probably know more than I do about everything. Perhaps you have answers to all these questions."

"No," said Sutcliffe. "Perhaps Affad has, though; we don't use the same source of supply as he does."

"Smirgel?"

"Yes."

"But Quatrefages is surely just as likely to be untrust-worthy; remember all his romancing about Galen's child and the Templars? He would tell you anything."

"He is not alone, there are others."

They rose to play and she returned to her correspondence, pencil in hand, making draft notes for the replies to letters which would later be typed. Toby opened the game with a magistral flourish. "It's all very well for you to jabber about the Jews, MacSutcliffe, but I find it sometimes most irritating the way they go on; why, the last bunch of intels were extra-ordinary. They were not only reporting each other in Paris, but some had actually joined the Milice. As if it were not enough to be more industrious and more conceited than everyone else!"

"Whatever you may think of Jews," she said, "you would not stand by and see those trains pull out and hear Smirgel's snigger."

"Speaking as a historian," said Toby, "if the whole thing weren't tragic it would be risible. Do you realise what the Germans want? They want to be the Chosen People – they have announced the fact. They want to do away with the Jews so that they can take their place. It is quite unbelievable – if you told me I would not believe you. The Chosen Race! Whose blood is thicker than whose? Washed in the blood of whose lamb if I may ask? This is where Luther's great worm bag has led them. It's like children snatching at each other's coloured balloons. But to descend to the total abolition of Jews – it would take a really serious metaphysical nation to do that!"

"According to Affad it has a metaphysical base: it is an involuntary organic reaction, like the rejection by the stomach of something disagreeable, against Judeo-Christianity as exemplified by our present world philosophy which as you know is dominated by brilliant Jewish thinkers."

"Illustrate, please," said Toby, trying an awkward shot which lost him the match. "Damn!"

"The triad of great Jews who have dominated thought – Marx, Freud, Einstein. Great adventurers in the realm of matter. Marx equated human happiness with money – matter; Freud found that the notion of value came from faeces, and for him love was called investment; Einstein, the most Luciferian, is releasing the forces sleeping in matter to make a toy which . . ."

"O God," she said in dismay, "don't tell me you are half-hearted about Nazism? I've just come from a country which can't make up its mind. So many French seem indifferent to this purge which Laval calls a 'prophylaxis', if you please."

"I don't think the Russians are any better," said Sutcliffe. "We have a number of distasteful choices – the world as a kibbutz, with obligatory psychoanalysis lasting a lifetime and replacing Catholicism . . . and then atomic robotisation I suppose. It makes me feel all old-fashioned; I don't know what to say."

"*Honi soit qui Malebranche*," said Toby.

"And it's all very well you being pious, but all this started with the French, the Republic having no need of *savants*. And Jews like that foul painter David presiding on committees to cut off the head of Chénier. Tumbrilitis has slopped over and reached the whole world now. To think that the first statue which was erected by the revolutionaries was one to the Goddess of Reason!"

"It still goes on; I used to wait for her outside the ivy-covered building in Raspail which houses part of the University, against which wall I taught her how to hold her chopsticks. Love was never the same again, in the light drizzle falling on our faces, sticking our kisses like postage stamps upon each other's lips. Above us, written on the wall, nay, engraved in it were the fatal words: '*Université. Evolution des*

Etres Organisés. Ville de Paris.' It was the equivalent of 'Abandon hope, all ye who enter here', though we did not know it at the time . . . and now Schwarz has her in dark keeping which harmeth not. Or so you say."

"I can't follow," she said.

"Wait till Aubrey comes. He will tell you all about Hitler and his ideas."

"It will be your first meeting? No?"

Sutcliffe looked at her in a curious fashion but said nothing. At that moment a familiar voice said, "They arrive next Monday by air from Cairo." Affad stood at the door cleaning his glasses with a pocket handkerchief. Her heart turned over involuntarily, which surprised her: she did not as yet know how to behave in the presence of other people. But he came lightly across the room, avoiding the two players, and after kissing her sat down, putting his arm in hers. "All this confusion and talk about Hitler and Jews comes from one factor – the refusal to see that the Jewish faith is not a confession but that the Jews are really a *nation* bereft of a homeland and forced to become the world's cuckoo. This is where we have permitted ourselves to work against the British and further the claims of Palestine. Of course the British are scared about their Arab oil, but nevertheless it is of world importance that the Jews be housed nationally. Then it does not much matter what form their Judaism takes, monotheism or whatever. But we persist in treating them as simply a confession."

"Well, as a convinced Freudian analyst I feel a bit compromised; perhaps I am Jewish from this point of view."

Sutcliffe said, "You know what Aubrey would say – he would say that you are simply running what the Americans would call a massage-parlour of the soul. You cannot analyse Psyche without coming upon Cupid."

"But that is exactly what Freud says."

"Does he?"

"Of course."

"But Cupid is simply an investor, not a god."

"That's another matter."

"A Luciferian remark if I know you."

"I did not mean it as such."

"How about Libido?"

She sighed a long sigh and decided not to deliver the heated exposé which seethed inside her. She rose.

"Let's go, I'm hungry."

Delighted, Affad sprang to his feet at once. "I was just about to say the same. Where shall we go?"

Sutcliffe said, "Somewhere where we can join you for coffee, before the office opens."

"The Old Barge" – everyone echoed the name of a familiar haunt, a boat converted into a restaurant and anchored against the quay, hard by the elegant and well-tended gardens. It was central to the town, not too smart or expensive, and very close to the Embassy. They took their leave of the billiardaires, as Toby called himself and Sutcliffe, and drove to the appointed place. They were suddenly, unaccountably, shy with each other. It was difficult to understand. "I know," he said at last. "It's because you seem so different all of a sudden, sort of sophisticated and well turned out, and far too beautiful for safety."

"Whose safety?"

"Mine! Everyone's!"

"I suddenly felt I needed to get away from you, to stand off from you in order to see you more clearly; I am going to desert you after lunch and visit my old clinic to see how they are getting on with my old patients."

"And tonight?"

"I must sleep in my flat, alone."

He used a lot of bad language under his breath, swearing in French, Arabic, Greek and English, but what the target of these objurgations was he could not say – it had nothing to do with her, and everything to do with this strange love-predicament. Just when he most wanted to seem a man of the world, sincere but experienced. "What are you mumbling?" she asked suspiciously, but he only shook his head and said, "I was swearing at my own lack of subtlety. I should have got tickets for a concert. It would have been one way of being together without chewing each other with our eyes."

It was hardly surprising that they lacked appetite as well, though she found an excuse in the fact that she had only just arrived from a starving country and was not used to all this abundance. But she drank a couple of stiff whiskies – a fact which he noted with disapproval. They were joined fairly soon by their two billiardaire companions who were indulging in their usual desultory wrangling. "Just because our old friend Blanford is about to manifest, Robin here has set up as a new Einstein, just to *épater* him. On the bathroom mirror he has in lipstick $E = mc^2$ with the legend ERECTION EQUALS MEDITATION PLUS CONNIVANCE SQUARED. As if that were not enough he had added on the mirror in the hall, MEDITATION OVER FORNICATION LIKE MASS OVER FORCE YIELDS REINCARNATION. I do not think either Blanford or Einstein would approve, but there it is."

"It's the fruit of my inmost supposings," said Sutcliffe, a trifle coyly. "It's such a bore just going on being a cricketer." He was referring to his famous namesake, now in honourable retirement. "Can't one change hearses in mainstream? Why not Jack the Stripper or someone more colourful? I shall ask Aubrey when he comes if it's all the same to him."

"Will you come to meet him?" she asked curiously, and he said, "Of course I will, if you will drive." But she did not believe him. Somehow she thought he would avoid the meeting. On an impulse she decided to go home to bed, but once she walked into her flat a terrible desolation seized her by the hair. She telephoned Affad and he came to her, as swift as magic.

They looked at one another for a long moment; and then, no word said, they went outside and got into the car. He felt as if he was hardly breathing, he was pale. Once they reached the hotel they rang for the lift, and still silent went up to his room where he at once drew the curtain to shut out the daylight, while she was naked in a flash and in his arms. She was so excited that she wanted to live out a sort of expiation, and through clenched teeth she whispered, *"Fais-moi mal, chéri. Déchirez-moi."* To hurt her, to drive his nails into that firm body – yes, but he wanted to bide his time as yet for their breathing was not in synchro. They would scatter the precious orgasm, mercury all over the place like a smashed thermometer. "Ah, you are holding back!" she cried in anguish, and scratched. "I'm not, Constance." She began to laugh at their precipitation, and their disarray, and then the laughter turned to tears and she buried her face in his shoulders and planted a dejected blue bruise on the fine brown skin. Two arms, two legs, two eyes . . . an apparatus both for surfeit and for bliss. *Tristia!* What a tremendous novitiate loving was – no, she was taking it too seriously. It was just beauty and pleasure. He was saying to himself, "It is like drinking a whole honeycomb slowly. O Divine Entropy – even God dissolves and melts away. Ah, my poor dream of a committed love which is no longer possible because of the direction women have taken."

Suddenly he gave her a tremendous slap across the face, and almost before she could react with surprise and pain he was on her, had taken her by the shoulders and penetrated her; and to still her cries of rage and injured pride he sealed his mouth upon hers. There was no doubt who led, for now he mastered her and inflicted orgasm upon orgasm upon her like welcome punishments. And suddenly, after a struggle, she accepted the fact, she played the role of slave, knowing that her perfect submission would tire him sooner and bring him down to her feet once more. The charm of that inner compliance excited him beyond endurance almost; later he told her it was like being covered in honey and tied down to an ant-hill, to be devoured slowly kiss by kiss, ant-mouthful by ant-mouthful. So the time ran on until the two exhausted creatures fell asleep.

"I knew this would happen," she said much later, combing out her hair in the mirror. "I simply knew that I could be something to you." Then added, "Bloody fool that I am!" Almost every day now they dined at her flat, which enabled her to show off a culinary aptitude which was fair to good for a bachelor girl, and which he appraised as well as praised with discrimination; then he helped her stack the washing up for the servant and played a little on the sweet, small upright piano which was her solace in times of melancholy, and on which the ponderous Sutcliffe amidst sighs swathed himself in the moods of Chopin. Affad did not play as well as she did – good!

He stood up and said, "Were you happy as a child? I think I must have been because I never asked myself the question. I stood between my father and mother, each held a hand, as if between a great king and queen, two gods. It would have been unthinkable to regret or doubt. I lived in a dream, and it is still going on in the depths of things, for me. Yes, still going on." And he softly repeated the word which he did not like others to use: "Sebastiyanne."

They lay down side by side on the couch, fully dressed and thoughtful. He said, "You know, this war is coming to an end, slowly but surely. Italy has been turned inside out like the sleeve of a coat. I have been checking the reports of all posts. We have a date now for a landing in Europe in full force. It is all coming together, becoming coherent, and the Germans know it. They will turn very nasty now before they are finally convinced. How right Tacitus was about their national character. How marvellous the British have been to hold on, how can we ever thank them?"

"What do you see beyond – what sort of world?"

"A smashed Europe like an old clock; it will take about six or seven years to get it working again, unless the Russians decide to prevent it ever working. They will emerge from this thing strong, while we shall be exhausted."

"I shall stay here," she said, "and operate from here if I can. We shall see. But meanwhile, for the present, we mustn't forget that Aubrey arrives tomorrow at dawn. Sutcliffe has panicked and retired to bed with a heavy cold. He dare not look upon the face of his Maker, it would seem."

He slept quietly where he lay, and she in her turn also did so, though she first made herself more comfortable in a silk dressing-gown, and combed out her unruly hair in the bathroom; the little radio was on but turned quite low. She heard Chevalier singing "Louise" and for some reason she felt moved, tears came into her eyes and threatened her make-up which she was too lazy to remove. She restored her looks and her composure with the help of a tissue and told her reflection, "All this will end in a fine neurasthenia, you see."

She unlaced his suedes and drew them softly from his feet, while he hardly stirred; what had he been doing to get so tired? Then she arranged a rug over their feet and crawled under it, nestling beside him, trying to remain quite still, almost breathless like a bird, so as not to disturb him. In the middle of the night she woke to find him staring at her with his eyes wide open, so intently that for a moment she wondered if he were still asleep. But no. "How marvellous!" he whispered and in a flash was asleep once more. She felt proud and contented, as if she had suckled him. Her own sleep was troubled lightly by questions about the future – intellectual nest-building which she reproved. It seemed hardly an hour before the little alarm clock squealed and they woke reluctantly upon the darkness, to envisage the distant airfield in its remote valley under the snows. The car was sluggish, too, but at last they got it going and crawled across the sleeping town towards the lakeside where there was much more light, with a distinct promise of a clear dawn coming up apace.

"Can I smoke?"

"No. Or I shall too."

"Very well."

They drove on in sleepy silence, until he asked: "Have you precise plans for Aubrey Blanford's treatment? You said you had seen a detailed dossier."

"Yes I have; there may be one fairly big operation and two minor ones to do, but the picture is not without hope. I have invoked the aid of Kessley and his clinic – he is by far the cleverest surgeon for the job. Aubrey is young still and in quite good physical shape. There is no need for a gloomy prognosis in his case, as in some of the others. I have made all the arrangements – a pleasant lakeside room, and of course the hot water spa right at his elbow. Let's see what he says."

The airport was hardly awake, and the bar provided them with deplorably weak coffee and a croissant. But they were glad of the shelter and the warmth, for outside on the field a chill wind was blowing. In a while they heard the distant droning of the three Ensigns which were bringing the chosen fifty to safety and medical aid. They circled the field once or twice before making their run in one after the other. They came to rest and taxied up to within hailing distance of the terminal before releasing their occupants – a cluster of uniformed nurses and orderlies, followed by a mass of stretchers and wheelchairs. They waited patiently, trying to sort out the throng with their eyes. "There!" Affad said at last; as a matter of fact it was not Blanford he had recognised, for he was huddled in his wheelchair, covered in a rug, and deeply asleep. It was the snake-headed valet, Cade, who wheeled him out of the plane and towards them. He wore a kind of desert uniform with a bush-jacket, and his service cap sported a cock feather. "Good morning!" he cried cheerfully as he saw Affad. "Here he is all safe and sound. But sound asleep," and as if to explain, Cade groped at the feet under the rug and produced an empty whisky bottle. He frowned and said, "Too much of this for my liking, but what can I do? I have to obey orders." He gave a brief canine smile, full of yellowish teeth. The sick man stirred.

He seemed to Constance to be very much thinner than she remembered, and indeed more youthful in a strained sort of way, but surprisingly brown, which gave the tone of fitness to the general impression he made, lying there asleep.

Presently he woke, due perhaps to a slight jolt of his wheelchair or some unaccustomed change of silence or sound or temperature – a cold wind blew across the airfield and the air was full of cries and greetings. Yet he woke smiling a trifle shyly, to give each a hand, saying, "I'm sorry to be in this disarray; it was a long twelve-hour flight and my backache drove me to gag the pain with whisky, which annoyed Cade." She told him with genuine delight that he had not changed – yes, he had allowed a small moustache to grow, that was all. Nor had she, he said, and blushed with a sort of delighted confusion, with emotion at meeting, so to speak, with a survivor of that last Provençal summer. Yet both made the same disclaimer: "Ah, but inside!" she said, and he agreed that the change was there, though invisible. They felt aged in the heart of their experience. He held on to her hand as they talked, as if to draw from it warmth and support; and Affad, feeling that a third party would increase the dilemma of constraint and shyness, said a brief fond word and took his leave, on the understanding that she would ride in the ambulance with Aubrey, and that he himself would send a duty car to the clinic for her.

Some provision had to be made for Cade and the wheel-chair, and this she arranged with the driver of the ambulance, squeezing in beside him so that she could keep Aubrey's hand in hers while they drove in companionable silence to their destination. "It's quite unbelievable!" he said once, and that was all; but she noticed that he was feverish and a little hysterical, no doubt due to fatigue and the claustrophobia of the journey in an old-fashioned plane. At any rate he berated Cade for trivial lapses or oversights with an unusual violence and outspokenness. The hireling did not reply, but simply drew his lips back to expose his teeth with an expression of pain, or as if he were a dog about to snap. His resentment he showed by breathing hard through his nose. Aubrey saw that she remarked this departure with curiosity and coloured as he said, trying to laugh the matter off, "One becomes a bit of an old maid, as you see. We quarrel like an old married couple – Cade is the wife." Disgusted, the valet pretended not to hear. He looked out of the window with his dogged expression, impatient of their arrival at Dr. Kessley's clinic. It did not take very long before they turned into a well-tended property full of green grass and firs, and dotted about with elegant chalets. At one of these they disembarked and found their way to his quarters which delighted him by their seclusion and the beauty of the view. "I was hoping for snow," he said. "I wanted to see snow again." Dr. Kessley made his appearance and created a most favourable impression on the patient by his modesty and by the fact that he was fully abreast of the case. Constance he called by her first name, which increased the sense of intimacy, of being among friends. "We want you for a few days to do nothing but take hot water massage in the spa waterfall and sleep a great deal; we want you completely at ease and relaxed before we go any further. You have received excellent attention in Cairo for the first stage – there is no work to be undone. We can continue from the present state of affairs with some confidence. I suppose you know about your condition." He said that he did; Dr. Drexel in Cairo had given him a thorough brief as to the general shape of things. "Good," said the surgeon and took his leave.

They busied themselves in getting him washed and put to rights before tucking him up in his bed. While the valet was out of the room she said, "You know you will have expert nursing here; you could get rid of Cade for good if you wished."

He shook his head. "Not yet."

There was a silence during which she was wondering whether her suggestion had upset him in any way; Cade re-entered the room and went about his tasks in silence. His presence imposed a constraint upon them, so they smiled at each other and said nothing. Then the valet left the room again on some pretext and Blanford was able to say, "I can't sack him yet. He is my only link with my mother. Every day he tells me some little thing, some little incident about her which enables me to see a bit further into why I hated her so much and so unjustly; I *must* have, to find myself in this situation – I don't believe in chance accidents. It's a situation which might keep me childless."

"But that's *Freud* on women," she said with some surprise.

"Everything he says about women is true of men," said Aubrey Blanford with a sudden return to the old curate's tone for which they used to tease him so remorselessly in the past. It was so delightful, the serious way he said it, that she clapped her hands and laughed as childishly as she would have done had they both been at Tu Duc. She could not refrain from kissing him warmly, which made him blush with pleasure. "O childless one!" she said, adopting for a moment the mock-papal tone of Sam. "Will you let Cade psychoanalyse you?" And he made an impatient gesture.

The duty nurse came in to be presented to her patient and it was time to take her leave, so Constance felt, for her car had already been signalled as waiting in the drive. She would leave him to acclimatise and return on the morrow, she said, and he acquiesced. Kissing him again almost rapturously she said, "Thank God you haven't changed – still the old sobersides Aubrey Blanford Esq. I am so happy about that." He was less so: "I have changed profoundly," he said gravely but with twinkling eyes, "but for the worse; I have become a cynic. I want you to take a message of disdain to Robin, for his cowardice in not daring to face me; I know he has retired to a flat with a lift too narrow to accommodate my wheelchair. There he is throwing a fit of influenza as an excuse. Tell him that he will be punished by the visit of a dark woman of unexpected force and glory with whom he will be forced to couple." But she decided that she would leave him to deal with Sutcliffe on his own, without her interference. She bade him goodbye without precisely saying so. "Don't be too annoyed with Robin, he really is under the weather." Yet Blanford answered darkly, "I am annoyed because my power is not absolute over him – he is after all my creation; but he can sometimes break loose and show traces of free will. My domination is incomplete, damn him. I told him to come to the airport. He mutinied. He must be punished!"

Leaving him, Constance drove back to her old clinic to find Schwarz, who was delighted to see her, as always. Pia and Trash who were passing through a relatively tranquil period, were working together on an ambitious tapestry. The subject was Clément's celebrated painting from Avignon, *The Land of Plenty: Cockayne*, which had been commercialised by Gobelin among other masterpieces. The quiet work, the skeins of colour, absorbed them both and they sat before the white window, quiet as nuns. Constance had to wait awhile for Schwarz to finish with a young ardent American analyst who was working with him, and who was submitting to his "control discussion" concerning some patients who were giving him trouble; they were apostates from the Rudolf Steiner groups so numerous in Geneva, and their astral theology was unfamiliar to the young man. His voice carried plangently and plaintively through the door of Schwarz's office: "So I gave him the suppository you prescribed, but in his present state he can't keep anything down."

"*Down?*"

"Sorry, up."

"I see."

Apparently, though apostate, the patient still had fragments of theosophical belief clinging to his thinking. "What do you propose?" said Schwarz.

"He's the most religious of the two; he's been deep into what he calls Astral Communication – so deep he had an attack of Poetic Apprehension – that's what he calls it. After that his wife refused to sleep with him. She said his breath smelt of embalming fluid. Boy, that Apprehension was certainly a bitch. I've locked him up with a sedation mixture."

"What else can we do?" said the old man; it was a question he always uttered with a strongly flavoured Yiddish accent; and he repeated it now to Constance. "*Aber*, Constance, what can we do?" He had half a mind to try an insulin shock convulsion-therapy on Pia but Constance had pleaded so earnestly against it that he had abandoned the idea. "You'd blow out what little brain is left," said Constance. "After all there's a whole situation attached to the matter of her illness, and it concerns several people." Since the discovery of Affad and the vertiginous glories of their affair she had become much more sympathetic to people in love – had even begun to see the elephantine love of Sutcliffe as moving rather than grotesque and preposterous; while the manoeuvres of the innocent and warm-hearted negress added both charm and despair to the whole business. Pia whined and whimpered like the sick child she had become, while Trash answered her with force and energy, saying stupid things with great conviction in that sweet dark voice, heavy as a bass viol. "I wanted us to sleep in one great bed," she told Schwarz once. "There'd be room for everyone, for Robin and Pia, and even their friends could come for a fix when they felt that way. My mother always said Never Refuse; and the preacher at the church said Give It All You Got. But Robin won't and Pia won't. Would it help if I went away?"

"No. You've tried that; Pia is still too fragile for anything drastic. She would withdraw again. We want to keep her in the field of vision still."

It was an unearthly waste of time and talent and medicine. Doctors nowadays are supposed to cure everything, even soul-complaints. But what could a priest have done anyway?

TWELVE

A Visit from Trash

THE AFFLICTION WHICH LAID ROB SUTCLIFFE LOW WAS of his own making, compounded for the most part of sheer alcohol and *tabac gris* in immoderate quantities, irregular meals and unusually large doses of medicines like aspirins and vitamins plus a geriatric invention of the Swiss called Nix which was supposed to make you younger. Now he lay, feverish and snorting like a billygoat in a rumpled bed, smarting under the sallies of his co-sharer and workmate who resented having to play nurse to a man who would not see the Embassy doctor because he was called Bruce Hardbane. "I am superstitious about names," he explained. Nor would he see a Swiss because that would mean his having to pay for a consultation; the Foreign Office provided free medical supervision. Toby was already late for the office but he stayed to mix his colleague a grog to take with his aspirin, and then swept into his threadbare overcoat and smartly disappeared from the flat. Sutcliffe sighed; another long day to spend supine with too much of a headache to read, and no company to divert him from gloomy and aggressive thoughts about Bloshford who lay also supine with a hole in his back, but in incomparably prettier surroundings, looking out upon the lake. He would have rung Aubrey up to insult him but the telephone was out of order for the nonce. There he lay like the Brothers Grimm, like the Brothers Karamazov, like the whole tribe of guttering Goncourts, steeped in sadness.

He was surprised to hear the lift start to mount in its cage, and even more so to hear it stop at their landing while its occupant vacated it and sent it down again before advancing up to the door of the flat and giving a little tattoo of the fingernails upon it before pushing it open – for it was always ajar. He was delighted to think it was a surprise visit from Constance and called her name aloud triumphantly, but who should walk in with dramatic slowness but the negress Trash? "The ogre!" he cried aloud, swearing a little. "How did you find me?" She looked utterly beautiful, like a black pearl – as a matter of fact she wore large pearl earrings which looked divine on that black satin headpiece. Then the most magnificent furs in which she was sweating lightly, giving off incensuous musk of gorgeous body odour. Robin raised himself and snuffed her like an equatorial balsam wafted from the still vexed Bermoothes of his heart. He knew that she did a little mannequin work for Polak's, and that they let her borrow furs sometimes – so this sombre plumage worthy of the helm of the Black Prince must be on loan. "I jest had to see you Robin, honey," she said, advancing to sit on his bed, and at the same time laying a large hand, graceful as a coffee table, upon his forehead. "You're quite a mite feverish," she told him, and he lay back, putting on his haughty and disagreeable expression. "What brings you here?" he said, trying to "rasp" as one would if one wrote it in a novel. For a while there was no answer to his rasp. He watched rather uncharitably while she took a swig at his grog, burning her cherry-red mouth. "Is there anything wrong with Pia?" She shook that black mausoleum of hair in a negative sense. "She is being sedate until two," she said. "But we've been talking and I told her I was coming to see you and tell you what we think." She opened her red maw like some great sea-whore in search of some plankton; modelling furs had brought out the seal in her. She said confidingly, "You ain't ill, Robin, you jest ain't strivin' enough; you gotta latch on to the affirmative, man, like the song says, and eliminate the negative. You gotta *be* it Bing's way! I guess you are jest sad cause you ain't got a good girl to plough, Robin. Them Embassy dames are mighty cold turkey, isn't that it?"

He thought, "I could not love thee dear so much loved I not killing more." But really she was right, this ebony glistening pillow consultant. What he needed was pillow music or even a pillow fight with an untrussed nun. The terrible thing was that she seemed half in love with him herself, even a little jealous of his cold turkey, for she slipped her warm hand inside his pyjama jacket as she talked and scrumped softly at his chest hair and Tiresian tits. "Listen," he said, "I'm ill, Trash." She shook her head playfully and said, "Not really, Robin." He was just not striving, she repeated, but clearly her ploy was to soften up his resolve before producing her revelation, whatever that might be. But she smelt wonderful, like a whole coconut grove, and as her hand went slowly lower the most delicious ripples of sensuous reaction spread in slow curdles over the stagnant pond of his unused body. She began to hum softly now in her deeply melodious contralto, some sort of wanton spiritual to mine his defences – never very strong. It was a cradle song calculated to disperse influenza and restore health together with an unswerving and invincible erection. Rob groaned with pleasure, and as he did so her fur fell open and he discovered that she was naked under it save for stockings and shoes. "You can't do this, Trash," he croaked, but already she had guided his costive fingers towards the moist scarlet slit, her second mouth, where they found their tender purchase in the one place which made her lift her head with pleasure and snuff the air like a tigress, moving slightly to feel his finger caressing her vital trigger. When she was ready she threw off her fur and mounted him with delight, like a child with its first rocking-horse. He was angry with her and it put him on heat, so that he turned in an excellent dogmatic performance which had her groggy. They melted at last into the supreme fiction of joining with a sable orgasm of deep lust and pith. She was made for love, this nymph! Kiss, kiss, the taxonomy of virtuous compliancy with nothing grim, nothing furtive, just the cryptic vision of wholeness. It was Eros versus Agape. And here he was, condemned to spend his life shooting his brains through his fist because this nymph refused her jumps. He lay there in a tousle feeling that he must smell of babies' milk stools and antiseptic soap while she panted beside him, her breasts as fresh as dewponds. "God, Trash!" he said with a sadness the size of a cauliflower. She had begun to recite the 16th Psalm in a whisper. "*Don't*," he said in an agony and Trash replied, "She said if I did you would say yes, you would agree." He grew angry and said, "Come on now. Out with it! What do you want?" But she was rousing him again, her skilful hands were trying to rebuilding the sandcastle of his erection which the tide of their passion had demolished. "Give me that hangin' fruit, Buster," she muttered as she grabbed and manipulated his choicest possession. But now he revolted against her and refused to get an erection until she answered his question. He did this by closing his eyes and thinking of ice cream. She was dismayed by this unusual display of independence and took herself off to make water which she did with enough noise for four thoroughbreds. Then she came back and standing by the bed said, simply, pregnantly, "We have decided we want to go round the world. Will you let us?"

The question was so astonishing that for a moment he was nonplussed. "What world?" he asked at last. "The war is nearly over. Pretty soon we shall be able to get going. You see, she wants to give me all the culture you gave her, Robin." "What on *earth*?" he said, genuinely puzzled. She must have heard of the Allied landings and the latest triumphant battles which had all but driven the Germans out of Europe and back to the fatherland.

"The war is far from over," he said, and she said, obstinately, "Yes it is, soon will be, now the U.S. Marines have landed. You don't know the U.S. Marines, Robin. I know the

337

U.S. Marines. They got the biggest pricks in Christendom."
He did not know what to say. "Do you mean they *are* the
biggest pricks?" but she shook her head determinedly and said,
"No. GOT the biggest I said."

"The Lord be your shepherd," he said, praying to
heaven for sweet reason to supervene. "Sit down, Trash, and
let me explain about the war." He took a deep breath, and
assuming the sort of tone and accent of the B.B.C. producer of
"Tiny Tots' Hour" he explained to Trash that even if by some
miracle everything stopped tomorrow and peace was declared,
it would mean years before conditions returned to normal:
certainly all travel as private individuals would not be possible
for years as yet, unless one managed to represent some
organisation civil or military. She sat listening to this logical
exposition with bright and attentive eyes, nodding from time
to time, and moistening her lips as if about to speak. But on he
went, listing all the ugly calamities of the past and the present,
and trying to draw a portrait of a future which would be heavily
compromised for ages yet; to demobilise, to repair cities, to
revive shattered economies, to rebuild civic habits . . . it would
take an age! And here they were talking about travelling round
the world like tourists.

"Don't you see, Trash?" he said, with something like
agony, for now it looked as if she had been thinking of
something else all the time he had been exposing his case to
her.

"You could come with us, Rob. She told me to tell you.
So long as you don't get mad at us. She only wants to give me
the culture you gave her." He snorted wildly. He had inherited
a sum of money from an old aunt which carried with it a condition: that he spend it in travel. Nothing more desirable, what
with the war coming on – at least everyone seemed to feel it
was. So he took Pia on a lightning-rod tour of the basic
antiquities of the world, first Europe, then as much of the

Orient as was within the reach of railways and flying-boats. They came back dazed and confused, but with all the money gone, and a library of prospectuses and travel brochures. Pia went through it all with speechless gratitude – God only knew how much she had taken in, but the journey marked her. And it was invaluable to him, of course, as a guide to places he knew he did not want to see again. To do India, cockroach by cockroach, for example, was beyond all imagining; the original *cafard* must have dwelt there in the plains. But the Himalayas now, there one could stay forever. He found Pia lacking in all serious instruction, almost analphabetic, yet they met a Nepalese lady nun who said that she was spiritually very advanced – higher up than he was. "You do not have to be clever to be wise," said this pleasant woman who had been educated at an English school and spoke Druid fluently. He loved Pia more than ever after that, he smothered her with instruction and kisses thicker than flying fish in the Indian Ocean. But she turned up her nose at the *Kama Sutra* and said it was "unhealthy". She thought the Taj Mahal would have looked nicer in brick. Now she wished to impart all this wisdom to Trash, darling Trash, who sat with her hands in her lap – her coat lay open like her thighs. She looked a bit crestfallen, as if her mission had failed. "When would you go?" She shrugged and said, "Whenever it's possible. We only want you to say YES, because she won't do nothing without your okay; you know that, Robin. But if you jest say yes we can start collecting the guide books and planning. It will save her mentation, honey, just to be told 'Go Ahead'." His face cleared. "So *that* was all you wanted? Just my okay?" She nodded. "Of course you can," he cried robustly. "Of course you can go. You *shall* go!" Whereupon she threw off her skin and did a soft shoe routine crying, "*Wow and Superwow!*" over and over again. And then a short eloquent verse which went:

"When I wanta
I've simply gotta
When I have ter
I simply Must!
Babe, have I got a Wanderlust!"

It was clear that she was already on the journey. "What a gift-horse you turned out to be," he said, and made as if to re-open sextilities, but she had to rush off and tell Pia. In a flash she was gone, forgetting her earrings.

Sutcliffe tried them on and found that they rather suited him; he put them carefully aside. One day he would walk into the Consulate wearing them. It would create, he hoped, quite an effect. But now the telephone thrilled and he took it up to hear the central exchange assure him that the line had been re-established. His heart sank a little for there was no longer any excuse not to ring Aubrey, the Blanford-Bloshford who presided over his life. He took up at last his battered address book in which Constance had jotted down the clinic number. He asked in an agitated falsetto if he might speak to Mrs. Benzedrine Papadopoulos, but of course Aubrey recognised his voice. "Speaking," he said, and Sutcliffe groaned aloud. His mentor said, "Why are you groaning like a Heathcliff in labour when you are only a common Sutcliffe in disfavour; what have you been tri- turating, you common fellow, while my back has been turned?"

"I have been ill," said Sutcliffe with a deeply dramatic expression, "and now I am ringing to tell you that I have been raped by Trash – very enjoyably but against my will. Pure rape!"

"It is not possible; you are fictions."

"Have we no future, then?"

"You have contexts, but no future and no past."

He laughed and then recited:

> "Tell me, how do fictions fuck?
> All our swains commend their pluck!"

Sutcliffe improvised in return:

> "Like shucking grain, expressing pain,
> Emptying opiates to a drain."

But he was listening with close attention to the timbre of Blanford's voice. He knew that very often his emotions under stress were masked by a deliberate and perverse flippancy – he retreated into his private despair like a crab under a stone, and was not to be dislodged. Fundamentally there was a lack of passion in him, a power-cut now so markedly symbolised by the physical disability under which he laboured. He grunted, and Blanford who had been following his thoughts said, "Everything you say is true."

"I said nothing," said Sutcliffe. "I merely thought a lot. It's as if we were versions of one another set upon differing time-tracks. Reality is very fatiguing."

"Exactly," said Aubrey. "Be ye members of one another – the good book invokes you."

B. "Which book? Yours or mine?"

S. "Mine. It's a better title, I think."

Blanford sighed and said, "Mine is still unfinished, but I have an ant-hill of notes which should help me complete it. When did you finish yours?"

"When I heard you were coming."

"What is it called?"

"*The Prince of Darkness*."

"Hum."

Sutcliffe could not forbear to quote his Shakespeare: "The Prince of Darkness is a gentleman."

"You must manifest at last," said Blanford in a changed,

sharper tone; his bondsman recognised the grim note and
agreed with surprising meekness. "I knew we must meet one
day in order to exchange versions – it's in the order of
things. Maybe we can help each other solve a few problems –
some of yours, for example, are not easy. What about the
lovers?"

Blanford replied with irritation, "Since you like Shakespeare so much you'll know that journeys end in lovers'
partings."

"Ah, the pity of it!" said Sutcliffe ironically. "How are
you going to make a job of that? My own version corresponds
to the reality. She will be hurt by his going but unbroken. In
my version he offers to take her with him and she refuses."

"Dead true!" cried Blanford with pleasure and surprise.
"How the devil did you know?"

"You know how I knew!"

Blanford paused and then said, "You must come now, the
sooner the better. Come to tea at four, and don't forget to bring
your version since it's complete. It will help me, as I am in a bit
of a muddle. Yesterday she spent the afternoon with me and I
started to read her bits of my book; but in the middle dozed
off, and I fear with without permission she did a brief riffle of
the rest, while I slept. I am vexed, she was supposed not to
know until he went back to Egypt."

"Unconscious sabotage?"

"Of course. I'm jealous!"

"You are no artist, then."

"Let's leave that open. I am waiting for you this afternoon
at four. I shall recognise you at once. I will cry, 'Doctor
Liebfraumilch I presume', removing my topee."

He put down the phone and reflected for a long moment;
a sudden world weariness afflicted him. What would he not
have given to tip the whole damned bundle of manuscript into
the lake. The incident of yesterday afflicted him, nagging like

a toothache. Constance had come to spend an hour with him, unfortunately towards siesta time. He had read her a passage from his book, but sleep had overcome him. He turned back to it now and re-read it, recalling the scene between them. It went:

"Akkad in his stained brown *abba*, looking so fragile, so weightless, as he sat upon the sand went on: 'From the cosmic point of view, to have opinions or preferences at *all* is to be ill; for by harbouring them one dams up the flow of the ineluctable force which, like a river, bears us down to the ocean of everything's unknowing. Reality is a running noose, one is brought up short with a jerk by death. It would have been wiser to co-operate with the inevitable and learn to profit by this unhappy state of things – by realising and accommodating death! But we don't, we allow the ego to foul its own nest. Therefore we have insecurity, stress, the midnight-fruit of insomnia, with a whole culture crying itself to sleep. How to repair this state of affairs except through art, through gifts which render to us language manumitted by emotion, poetry twisted into the service of direct insight?"

"Art?" she cried, angrily. "Rubbish, Aubrey!"

"Art!" he echoed firmly.

"Out!" Constance, wearied and exasperated beyond reason by this wilfully mendacious reasoning, put out her hand thumbs down and stared sighing out upon the calm lake. Suddenly he broke out, as if to refute her thoughts, "You see? He is not joking, the fraternity is quite decided to pre-empt death by voluntary suicide – you might call it that, though actually the blow is struck invisibly, by someone or something else, an instrument of their collective fate, so to speak. O God, can't you see?" He could read the expression of angry disdain upon her face.

"Well, it's one way of saying goodbye," she said coldly. Truly, Affad might have spared her all that had grown up between them, luxuriant as some tropical jungle, since he had

known from the beginning that it must all come to nothing –
that sooner or later they must come up against the blank wall of
his voluntary disappearance – despatched by an unknown hand
selected by an invisible committee in conclave back there in the
deserts of Egypt? The whole of her training, her science, her
practice was dedicated to working against this cowardly
principle of suicide and abdication. And they spoke about art
as if it were some sort of vitamin. "Art!" she said aloud with
disgust. She was dumbfounded by the pusillanimity of men!
The psychologist in her recalled all she knew about aberrant
states like autism or catatonia, with their stark suggestion of a
narcissism overwhelmed by reality. She thought of the diffident
and troubled gaze of her lover's sea-green eyes with compassion mixed with hatred. So he was a weakling really, and
not a man. And this playing about with abstruse gnostic states
was surely dangerous for him, for his equilibrium? She told
herself, "It's when the mind strays out of touch with its own
caresses – its own catlicks upon the body-image of itself – then
it loses the power to cherish and restore itself through self-
esteem. The actual tunic of the flesh dries up, man becomes an
articulated skeleton, that is to say, a machine."

Art! Who cared about that? Inwardly she laughed
sardonically; outwardly she looked cold, white, numb and
a prey to a thousand indecisions. "I think I shall leave the Red
Cross and get back to my job if it is still possible," she said,
and he gazed at her in puzzlement. "I know," she said, staring
back, "it's running away, and I don't approve of it. But I need
time to think." But escape in the direction of Avignon was, she
knew already, no more possible; and anyway surely her excess
of feeling was itself misplaced, for surely they were all under
sentence of death, the whole world? All Europe was a suicide
club, was it not?

These notions increased her vexation. Why did she feel
such a keen sense of reproach towards him simply because he

was a card-holding member, so to speak, of this absurd suicide confraternity with its cowardly refusal to face the world as it was? It's because (she thought) Eros demands a false reassurance, a promise of immortality, in order to flourish – and "flourish" simply meant to bear a child. That was it! In the depths of herself she had planned to love by extension into the future, to share a child with him. This abrupt reminder of his possible disappearance at any moment, it was unnerving. The feeling that it compromised the continuity of love – the purest illusion – made her draw back. And now she became furious, not only with him but with herself as well. She had been cheating at cards, so to speak. The sleepy Blanford watched the play of thought and emotion on her angry face with curiosity.

They were silent for a long moment; then he took up the manuscript once more, saying, "It's only a novel, the bare bones of a draft of a story based on true findings. I was led to it by a lot of sporadic and scattered reading first of all: by the mystery of the Templars' abject surrender and their obvious guilt. It was Affad who told me they were simply gnostics dedicated to cross swords with Monsieur instead of putting up with his rule. Then I took up the threads right there in Alexandria. They are not joking you know! The cult of the human head is with us even today. In the novel the death-map of Piers was an attempt to assess his chances – he had put the names of his friends on it, under the names of the Templar knights. He suddenly realised that his number was up – but who was going to strike the blow? I haven't finished the book yet but in the final version it could be Sabine." He paused before going on in a slower tone: "Suicide was forbidden to them, so it *had* to be some sort of death-preempting ritual murder. But of course it is only the inner circle of the confraternity who take this vow; as their ranks thin others are elected. Affad had to wait years he tells me. And of course there is no way of knowing when he will get the message – the short straws gummed to a piece of rice paper with his name on it. The letter with the Egyptian stamp."

There was a pause. "Schoolboys!" she cried in accents of distress.

"Affad is leaving the day after tomorrow. He rang me and asked where you were. He thinks you are going to be bitter and reproach him for what you once called his 'pre-lapsarian twaddle'." She smiled a trifle wistfully. "Perhaps I shall, when next we meet."

She had sent the car away, and now set off to walk back around the lake shore; at their old meeting-place opposite the promontory near the town approaches she saw the car of Affad standing, its engine uncovered, apparently in difficulties. Its owner was trying to execute some inexpert repairs, or remedy some defect in a fashion that seemed almost laughably inept and despairing. He was no good with machines, as he always said, and the machines knew it. He saw her coming and for a moment did not know quite what line of action to take – it seemed so ignominious to be stranded there with an expensive car. So he did nothing, simply stood still and smiled sadly at her in all his humiliating dishevelment. When she was still a little way off he said, "Have you heard? I've been recalled at last." She said nothing but went on walking towards him, looking at him with such hungry intensity that one would imagine her to be storing up memories of this moment against his fatal departure. "You have come to reproach me," he said, and she shook her head. She had suddenly seen him as he really was, she had seen his *eidolon* in all its gentle passivity and feminine warmth. There he stood, covered in oil and with his hair standing on end, pained beyond measure and quite humiliated by his defaulting motor car. She felt a tremendous shock of sympathy, a warmth about the heart, and with her eyes full of happy tears, put her arms round him, as if to comfort him in his defeat. A new pang had shaken her, and with it a new and quite unexpected magnanimity. "Yes, I came to reproach you, damn you." But the malediction was not really meant as such – it was an endearment. He looked at her with his sad, protesting, sea-grey eyes. She said, "I really came to thank you for giving me the key to myself – teaching me to live and create without a man. I owe you that." They kissed exultantly. She added, "I know you are ready to take me back with you, but I am staying here where I belong; perhaps you will come back, perhaps not. We shall see." His look was a whole discourse of rapture and deep gratitude. "With so much death in the world surely we have a right to a little love?" she said. "Let's not spoil this, diminish it by pettiness or play-acting."

She got into the car and pressed the self-starter. By some miracle it worked. They drove off along the lake. Never had friendship and love joined forces in this way for her. It was as if henceforward she understood everything, no more turning back. It was the right way to part even if it was not forever.

"What will you do with yourself?" he said, putting his arm round her shoulders, for she had elected to drive. "We may have years ahead of us."

"I shall pursue my obstinate theology course – building the Taj Mahal on an icefloe, as you call it."

"Deciding how many psychoanalysts can dance on the point of a pin!"

"Of Jews an infinite number, I feel sure."

There was a long silence as they watched the blue lake unrolling beside them, and then he said, "What made me so suddenly and acutely aware that perhaps I wasn't being fair to you was a conversation I had with the Prince; for the first time on a somewhat acrimonious note. He said that in the present state of my engagements – about which you now know I don't doubt – I was not free to love you. In the most literal sense. I could not prejudice my commitments towards the committee –

it would be like breaking the chain of belief which binds us. Like breaking a letter chain. In fact, that I was loving you under false pretences and he, the Prince, was jolly well not going to have it!" He could not help grinning affectionately as he mimicked the tone of the Prince's voice. Constance smiled also, "Good for him," she said, "at least somebody loves me."

Affad said, "I am duty bound to go back and consult the brotherhood as to my chances of freeing myself from them. If I could achieve that I would be free to return to you – it would change everything. One could envisage another sort of life based on this experience. Would you encourage such an idea?"

"You would never do it," she said after a long pause. "It's your whole life. You would be wrong to try. I'm sure when you reflect – when it comes to the point – you will feel bound to them, to the organisation, and not to me. Outwardly I will still be there, of course, and nothing forbids us to continue to meet. But the inward landscape has changed, and that may well be for good, forever."

"For love it's the acid test," he admitted. "But I refuse to pre-empt the future. In my present mood I feel sure that I am going to free myself and join you while there is still time. Constance, look at me." She turned her bright eyes on him for a second and then bent them back upon the road. He said, "Can I leave you a hostage of a kind – a hostage of a strange sort? I have been meaning to ask you if you would study and pronounce upon the illness of my little son. I hesitated; but now I feel it is right to ask you if you will see him while I am away. Will you?"

She said nothing, but her eyes filled slowly with tears, though she did not shed them. An appalling thought had come into her mind, shocking in its baseness, namely: "He wants me to cure his child in order to recover the love of his wife." How could she think anything so foul and so untrue? In order to expurgate the fearful supposition she leaned towards him and kissed him quickly on the mouth. "Of course I will, my darling," she said, "of course." And he thanked her, saying, "Lily suggested it long ago. She will be glad. And the thought will link us while I'm away."

They drew up at the office of the Red Cross and left the car in the courtyard. It was an appropriate place to say goodbye – even a provisional goodbye. She kissed him and walked away towards the billiard bar, leaving him to look after her with his gentle and hesitant regard which somehow held finality in it. She seemed as she walked to overhear the voice of Sutcliffe say, "There are no more great loves, my lad, just Snakes and Ladders instead."

Soon there would only be reminiscence left, going backwards into time as one unwinds, undoes an old sweater, on and on towards the dropped stitch, the original sin. Most love just lapses from satiety and indifference, but he had given her a version of the old text which one could continue to follow out, like a salient dialogue which went on even in absence. The rendering conscious of the orgasm as a gradually shared experience, it was like something new to science! Later the thought of him would perhaps ache on like a poisoned arrow, but for the moment she felt only her exultation, her solidarity with him.

This love was a separate culture. The world like some great express switches points without asking anyone's permission, passing from tobacco smoke to wine, from steam to sail, satyr to faun, from one calculus to another: we live under the thrall of its symbolism. One simple default, a switch thrown too late, and the giant can be sent howling and hurtling from the rails out into the night, into the sky, among the stars. It was hard to try and see things clearly. Twixt *vérismo* and *trompe l'oeil* they were doomed to try to live and love. That night, watching dusk fall over the impassive lake which reflected a heartless city, she seemed to see death and love like a single centaur joined at the waist walking through the ice-blue waters to reach her.

THIRTEEN

Counterpoint

SUTCLIFFE, DESPITE HIS DISPOSITION TO WAGGISHNESS and frivolity, was nevertheless a most obedient slave. Obsessions usually are. He materialised on the chair beside the bed just as Blanford woke from a somewhat unrefreshing sleep, opiate-imposed. "Well," he said robustly, "at last we meet. Dr. Dyingstone, I presume." Sutcliffe nodded gravely, and said, "At your service!"

They both burst out laughing as they eyed each other. "I imagined you as much fatter," said one, and the other replied, "And I much thinner." Well, they would have to make do with reality – it was all they had to work on; it's boring, this question of there being several different versions of a self, so to speak, no? Sutcliffe had actually combed his hair and donned a respectable suit – it might have been described as *tenue de ville*, his get-up. With him he carried the battered scarlet minute-box with the monogram of the Royal Arms on the lid; it contained his novel – the "other" one. "What are you calling it?" asked Aubrey curiously, and nodded when he heard the title, to show that he found it suitable: *Monsieur*. His own version was not quite finished, and he hoped during this convalescence to complete it, taking his cue from Sutcliffe. His visitor held up the red box and said, "It's all here!"

"The whole quinx of the matter. Your quinx?"

"No. Your quinx, rather. My cunx."

Aubrey gazed admiringly at his friend and chuckled as he said, "By the five wives of Gampopa, you keep up a pretty recondite style. Quinx to Cunx, eh?"

"A dialogue twixt Gog and Magog."

"Between Mr. Quiquenparle and Mr. Quiquengrogne."

"Ban! Ban! Ban! Caliban!"

"That's the spirit!"

It was marvellous to see eye-to-eye like this. Sutcliffe had already spotted the whisky decanter in the corner with the tray full of glasses and soda syphons. "May I?" he asked politely, inclining his throat and trembling wattles in its direction. Without waiting for an answer he crossed the room and primed a glass. Then he stood and admired the lake view while Aubrey watched him with an affectionate if somewhat disembodied air. "My vision, like yours, is not absolutely panoramic yet. it's selective: so there is always the blind spot." Sutcliffe nodded, frowning, and said, "It's the point where Monsieur intrudes on the cosmic scheme. The Counterfeit Demon in the pages of Zosimos. Or in more modern terms the demon figuring among the electrical properties of Faraday."

"I was delighted to find that he was reborn to the R.A.F. Command as 'the gremlin' and is still with us. His uncles – the joker in the pack of cards and the Hanged Man of the old Tarot – are proud of him."

"And no wonder. He lives a very full life."

"And now that the war is ending, Robin, what is going to become of us? With our sad bifocal vision and the awful sense of *déjà vu?*"

"We will go slowly out of date like real life."

"I doubt that; much remains to be done."

"Where?"

"In the city! We return there!"

"All of us? To the dead city?"

"As many as remain. The survivors of love."

They reflected on the probability with doubt, almost with distaste. Aubrey said, "In the Templar legends there is one crediting the Last Supper with having taken place in Avignon. *If five sat down to dine which was Judas?* So runs a riddle without an answer."

"Will Constance come?"

"Of course! Constance is a key."

That seemed a slightly less bleak vision of the future. At any rate to Aubrey it seemed still a way ahead – the other side of his convalescence. Here he must lie for months as yet, woozy from drugs, with reality dissolving like a tablet in spittle.

"In my version," he said, "I return to Provence with the *ogres* after a war something like this, having retired from the world to a chateau called Verfeuille. It's unsatisfactory; something about their ill-starred love wasn't right – you will help me there, I hope. The reality we had lived was more engrossing than the fiction, which was unpardonable. Now we are going back at a different angle, and with a different crew, so to speak."

"Can't I opt out, go away, right away?" cried Sutcliffe in exasperation. "To India, say, or China?"

"You want to go back into life and you can't," said Blanford with his bitter smile. "Nor can I – it's back on to the drawing-board, back to the blueprint stage. Back to Avignon! There are only two ways out of Avignon, the way up and the way down, and they are both the same. The two roses belong to the same family and grow on the same stalk – Sade and Laura, the point where extremes meet. Passion sobered by pain, an *amor fati* frozen by the flesh. The old love-triangle on which Plato based the Nuptial Number taken from Pythagoras, a triangle the value of whose hypotenuse is 5."

"Quack! Quack!" said Sutcliffe irreverently. "You will not distract me in my search for the perfect she, the mistress of the sexual tangent, *les éléments limitrophes*. I demand as my right love-in-idleness, a Laura unconscious of her fate, *femme fatale, féotale, féodale*."

"Instead you will find only the 'five-stranded' Tibetan breath, the 'mount' or 'steed' of white light, and a titanic silence with no geography. A tall tree with the sap arrested in its veins."

"But where?"

"In Avignon, rose of all the world."

FOURTEEN

By the Lake

THE DAY DAWNED SO UNUSUALLY WARM OVER THE LAKE that Blanford grew impatient to be lying thus, gazing across the green lawns to the still blue water. Why not a sortie? His first operation was in two days' time. "Cade," he said, "today is my birthday. I want to get a breath of air. I want to go for a push along the lake. I want to celebrate the birth of my mother's death. Get a chair and a rug, and bring your Bible. You will read to me as you used to do to her." To his surprise the valet looked almost elated as he bobbed his assent to the idea. "Very good, sir." Tucked down in rugs, elongated in the rubber cradle, Blanford hardly felt the rubber tyres on the paved Corniche. But he was still drowsy and also light-headed from calming drugs, and his thoughts evolved in pericopes without a sequential pattern.

"Cade, we shall never see Greek drama as the Greeks themselves saw it."

"No, sir."

"For them it was an expiation."

"Yes, sir. Shall I read? And where from? D'you want 'In the beginning was the Word'?"

"No. 'The Lord is My Shepherd', rather."

"Very good, sir."

The words reached deep inside him and he felt his bowels moved, his entrails plucked by their ravenous splendour of language – an English which was no more. And paradoxically while he listened he thought of other things, of Nietzsche's missing essay on Empedocles, of madness, of evolution, of the emergence of man from the belly of the time-bound woman, and with him all nature. Slime and warmth and water-lulling plants and infusoria and larval fish. The Creator thrusts his hand into the glove, up to his arm, as into a sausage skin, and then withdraws it while a collection of wet organs rushes in to develop into man. A weird assemblage of arms, legs, eyes, teeth, gradually sorting themselves into completeness: a ditto of mental attributes flowed out like electricity playing – sensation, ideation, perception, cognition: the whole held together by the centrifugal forces of the spinning turntable of a world. *Whee*! Then each in its category rose – plant into tree into fish into man, whose mind's eye would lead him into the mischief of paint, words, music and above all buildings to exteriorise, celebrate, and even house his body – living, as a temple, dead, as a tomb. Hubris came somewhere after this and with it dread. The antlers of the god grew on his temples, he went mad, dared to *see*!

He discovered fire, wine, weapons and tools, but also the stone-fulcrum for building, the enigmatic formula of Pythagoras, the arm of gold. (Every man his own true pyramid.) He could not detach himself enough from the maternal shadow to understand Death and come to terms with it, even to harness it as he harnessed rivers. (The Druids had a way perhaps?)

The voice of Cade ran on like gravel in the stream of the language; his coarse diction gave the words a robust music of their own. The vowels swelled like sails. Meanwhile Blanford's mind played hopscotch among the pericopes of fond ideas which might one day inform his prose. "The crisis came when early man first lost sexual periodicity, for then he risked running out of desire. The race was imperilled by his indifference. So the anxious divinity, Nature, invented the specious beautiful crutch of Beauty to spur him on. What could be more unnatural, more delightfully perverse? Looking through each other's eyes the lovers saw more than the memory of each other, they saw 'it', and were at once humbled and captivated.

The body knelt to enter the mother-image like a cathedral and to die, so that the fruitful larval worm could hatch its butterfly, the nextborn soul, a child."

"In the midst of life we are in death," said Cade.

But, Blanford thought on obstinately, the Greek ideal of Beauty was a wonderful invention, for its value was transferable to other things, projected like a ray from man's own precious body. Artisan and his artifact improved into art pure. Beauty can reside, like the smell of musk, even in functional machines: substitute-bodies enjoying proportion and bias (callipygous women with haunches rich in *galbe*). Mental orgasm can be approached, abstract as paper-money or music or rain. The poet droops, suffers and invites his Muse – a one-man intensive care unit for the romantic invalid! You cannot look upon Eve future with impunity, for she carries within her the seeds of the idea of Death!

Yet within hours of death bodies begin to unravel like old sweaters, dissipating into random chaos again, mulch, mud, *merde* mind. Hail-hungry ghosts! Shades of the Luteran worm-loaf of the world-view drawn from big intestines with their slimy code. The great dams of consciousness admit only trickles of reality through them – thirst is rife, the waters of life ever-lasting. On the great treadmill of consciousness what outlook can he have, the poor neuro-Christian twisted out of his original innocence? Cade was silent now, walking with lowered head staring at the ground below his feet. "What are you thinking, Cade? You never say." But the servant only shook his head in a determined way and showed yellow teeth in a nervous smile.

Sweet as geometry to the troubled heart, Method was born and the magician's footrule. Mental faculties separated into kinds. Ah, maniacs, so rubicond and exophthalmic! Ah, melancholics, so dark and shaggy and pale from excess of black bile! Love became mania. "Then I saw her ther, my lyttel

357

quene." Hebephrenia set in like a tide, the helpless laughter of schizoid niggers. Fordolked, my masters, fordolked! *Morfondu*! Knocked for six!

Cade said, "At times she was not herself, sir. She said to me: 'Cade, I have gone beyond love, now I hate everyone, even my own son.' I was afraid for her reason."

Blanford listens, head on one side, and hears his own heart quietly beating under the rug. It was these small unexpected insights which were valuable. One thinks one knows better always; then comes the truth like a thunderbolt. He told himself that love overcomes magic by its very powerlessness. Both Merlin and Prospero gave in, surrendered their weapons at last, repletion was all.

> The meaning of meaninglessness is the code of
> the Grail
> As Merlin divined it, it never can fail.

Once replete with this knowledge he could retire to Esplumior, his island home, to play cards forever with his friend Prospero by the hushing sea. The old game of Fortune, played with a Tarot pack without a Hanged Man! Esplumior!

He heard the voice of Sutcliffe admonishing him: "More work for the Institute of Hallucination and Coitus! You want to combine ratiocinations in a Pelagsian fuck and it won't work. Even Trash knows that. She told me yesterday: 'Sperm washes off, honey, but love don't wash out. It's with you to the end. You have to wear it out like an old shoe.'" When they met now they would greet each other simultaneously with the words: "*Salut! Bon Viveur et Mort Future! Salut!*"

He had carried with him the clinic cat which purred quietly on his lap under the rug, like a small motor. What a peculiar kind of concentration it is that leads to the artistic product, he thought. One exudes a kind of emblaming fluid, an agonising ectoplasmic exudation, memory. The way a cat coats a mouse with its saliva before swallowing it – anointing it with a slimy coat to make the passage of the gullet easier. Was this the way to invoke shy Psyche, the love-child asleep on his mother's wedding cake or his father's coffin?

> The bazaars of silence where she dwells
> In double childhood, eyes in all the wells.

The end of death is the beginning of sex and vice versa. Children are abstract toys, representations of love, models of time, a resource against nothingness.

Suppose one wrote a book in which all the characters were omniscient, were God? What then? One would have to compose it in a death-mood, as if dawn would bring with it the firing-squad. But this is what the artist *does*! Does poor Constance really grasp what Affad is saying – namely that in trying to render the orgasm conscious he is trying to extend the human understanding of what, up to now, has been regarded as apparently involuntary and unpremeditated? This is real love!

> The couple was dead
> Ere we were wed
> All under the greenwood tree!

Maybe, however, she thinks him simply disinterestedly interested in human virtue but unable to regard it, as so many do, as a guarantee against The Thing – cruel fate which is indifferent to theological distinctions. Stupidity and hypocrisy, the indispensable elements for illness and consequently for religion! O thieve me some happiness, Constance, I am tired of steeplechasing with this tired out old cab horse! My soul camps in the ruins of India while my mind is gathering dolphins' eggs! *Le double je de Rimbaud*! The double game!

The whole strength of the woman comes from a studied self-abasement, an Archimedean fulcrum; and young girls taken warm from under their mothers' wings, stolen from a warm nest still need mothering awhile. In this pleasant morning drowse he saw them come, hip-swinging, callipygous nautch-dancers, *sécheresses, vengeresses, castratrices de choix,* and he knew that the guillotine was invented by a homosexual French-woman. "Cade!" he said sharply, "Amend thy trousers, for the flies have fled!" She was beautiful with her swarthy rose-black skin and the apricot-fashioned mouth sticky as a fresh hymen – the silkworm's tacky passage across a mulberry leaf. Kisses that clung and cloyed. What was the name of her father, the old banker who made love to his dog and wintered in Portugal – a caninophile, gone in the tooth, gone in the wind? As Sutcliffe remembered her she wore the white nightdress like a uniform, a carnival disguise, archly, coyly. More appropriate would have been a butcher's smock with fresh bloodstains from the abattoir! There they sit, while we lie alone and suffer, sticking ripe plums up their arses, as happy as a sackful of rats! Memory is like having a dog on your back gnawing at your eyeballs. Venereal fevers shake the heart's dark tree. The Happy Few – *ceux qui ont le foutre loyal*!

Realising that all truths are equally false he becomes a posthumous person, makes his shadow melt away. All shadowless men are perfected in their *ghost*! The cinema in the head has fallen silent.

In science the exact is by consent the beautiful and seems new, pristine. In language beauty lies in the explicitness, in the nakedness of thought clothed in a sound. He saw Constance coming towards them across the gardens, waving. Her strange lithe walk was full of an endearing eagerness, an unspoiled freshness of approach as if some new discovery awaited her when she reached you. It was like someone walking a rainbow. She took his hands softly in hers and he said, "You are the only one who realises how frightened I am. Thank you." She was in love, she was glowing with the experience – one can never disguise it. It seemed so strange, for here they were alive and in their own skins, while round them for miles stretched the dead, the countless dead. Yet, he thought, Constance and I are really equidistant from the darkness on the circle of probability. Tomorrow perhaps an absence, a hole in the darkness which rapidly heals up, closes over. "I know you are," she said, "and in a way it's good as a reaction." The walk with all its fevered ratiocination had tired him and he felt a little tearful. He dabbed his eyes with a tissue while Cade with a sudden surprising tenderness patted his shoulder. "I say to myself all the time, 'Why die? Why go? It's so nice here!' " There was no short way to counter this mood of depression, so she said nothing, but helped the valet set him up once more in his mountain of pillows. All of a sudden he felt much better; he was used to such mercuric swings of mood. "The torn notebook you brought back," he said, "did you look in it?" She had not. "It's got some of Sam's jottings in it, among them poems like

> Because he was a decent chap
> He wore the fairies gave him clap
> But Mrs. Gilchrist took the rap
> Because he was a decent chap."

There were other trifles which amused them for a while but then she had to leave to keep an appointment and he took his sleeping draughts and composed his mind to sleep, sipping the while a green tea which she had left him and which Cade prepared. He fell once more to dreaming in slogans and pictograms, trying to visualise the words as he thought them. "Secret Practices – lovers sharpened by slavery. A committee of dolls ruling everything. *Terrain giboyeux à vendre pour roman à clef.* He who once vaccinates the novel with heraldic doubt, must poke to let the sawdust out!"

On this note he fell asleep at last and was only woken by

the silver chiming of his little travelling clock. He was surprised to find Constance sitting at his bedside, watching him sleep, deeply thinking. It was reassuring in a way to renew his hold on life again through her – for the effect of pain and drugs and fatigue had begun to make him live in a sort of twilight state, between realities, as it were. Constance was real, she rang out like a note in music. But profoundly sad. "He's gone!" she said in a half-whisper. "O Aubrey, what a dilemma!"

There was a tap at the door and Cade entered the room with a silver salver upon which there lay a letter. He smiled in his sly conniving way as he said, "There's a letter for Mr. Affad, sir." They looked at each other in total indecision. "But he's gone," she said at last, and Blanford put out his hand to take up the envelope and examine it. The postmark of origin, the Egyptian stamp . . . He said sharply, "Very well, Cade. I'll take charge of it. You may leave." As the door closed behind the manservant he said to her, "I am going to confide it to your care and discretion. Wait until you can give it to him personally. Let the present issue resolve itself first. Don't hurry, don't tempt providence. Wait!"

"Alternatively to open it myself, to see what it contains, to be sure . . . what a temptation!"

"That is for you to decide of course. The temptation of Eve in a new form. Darling, do what you feel you must."

The girl rose and took the letter. "Or else just to tear it up and throw it on the fire! Why not?"

"Why not?" he echoed. She stood for a while looking down at the letter in her hand. Then she said, "I must think about the matter. I must really think, Aubrey."

He watched her slow and perplexed retreat across the green lawns of the clinic towards the car park where her car awaited her. What would she do? It was a pregnant decision to take. He could not for the life of him predict.

FIFTEEN

The City's Fall

FOR THE HISTORIAN EVERYTHING BECOMES HISTORY, there are no surprises, for it repeats itself eternally, of that he is sure. In the history books it will always be a Friday the thirteenth. It is not surprising, for human folly is persistently repetitive and the issues always similar. The moralist can say what he pleases. History triumphantly describes the victory of divine entropy over the aspirations of the majority – the hope for a quiet life this side of the grave. For Avignon, as for Rome, it would not be the first time; before the city of the Popes existed its inhabitants had seen the swarthy troops of Hannibal swimming over their thirty elephants, animals whose odour and fearful trumpeting struck terror into the Roman legionaries as well as their cavalry. Today it was a depleted 11th Panzer division, that was the only difference; much armour had been drawn off for the impending collisions of the war in the north. But the preoccupations were the same: the transverse lines of the swift precarious rivers and their vulnerable bridges.

The pressure had increased, just as the tension in the news bulletins had sharpened; all of a sudden the sky filled up with giant bombers which flowed steadily down the railway lines at dawn and dusk dropping high explosive upon the culverts and rails, or spending a whole night at work on the marshalling yards of Nîmes from which in spouting red plumes of flame one might see whole wagons thrown into the air like toys, and human figures like ants shaken from them. Of course some went astray. In some market garden or down some country road full of flowering Judas one might come upon houses which had become very tired, been forced to kneel down, even to fall: some old medieval *bergerie* turned inside out with live-stock and the farmer's clothes blown into nearby trees. The weight of the silence when the bombardment ended – that was insupportable, for the shattered fragments of reality re-assembled themselves and then one could estimate the result. Say that one had fallen in the middle of a Sunday School picnic among olive groves. You only heard the screaming then. The children blown down among the crockery, some without heads, and one leaning sideways against a tree with a straw boater dangling from her neck. The old black priest held on to his stomach as if it were a runaway horse. He was of an exceptional pallor, he was leaning on a wall, which itself was leaning on an empty space upheld by pure gravity. It was no use calling for stretchers and doctors, for yet another roar was approaching them, more bombers moving against the sunset and picking at the bridge this time; but they passed so low that one could see the expressionless eye of the rear gunners as they sprayed their surroundings with lead. The guns on the fortress responded, but the small calibre made them sound as if they were yapping like bandogs while the bombers bayed and gave tongue like hounds in cry.

Away over the green meadows at Montfavet the noise was simply a distant blur, but the flight-path of the aircraft brought them over the village at roof level so that the trees were pollarded by the rippling machine guns and showers of green plane leaves fell everywhere like a benediction from on high. The lunatics in the central courtyard gathered up all the branches they could and waved their thanks to the planes. They did not notice if here or there one of their number sat on a park bench completely immobile, or lay in a flowerbed dozing. They were used to variations in behaviour. In the case of Quatre-fages it was neither one thing nor the other, for he had managed to achieve a kind of heightened consciousness which allowed him to see everything as a purely historical manifestation.

He slept in a monkish cell in the most ancient part of the building, and the light of passing cars flared briefly upon the whitewashed wall, bringing him pictures from his past, the projections of troubled memory, once full of armoured knights riding down infidels in a gorgeous array of plumes and helms – like great fowls on horseback; now the same space peopled with the dark-robed exemplars of the new Inquisition, thirsty for booty, not for knowledge. He laughed aloud, for with all the cars and tanks passing the wall went on and off in cinematic fashion, and each time it was a new picture. A feeling of continuity resided only in the fact that the one that repeated was the old Crucifixion of Clément – the land of Cockayne. It was amazing that – it had not been carried off like so much else in the town, for it was quite a celebrated work of art; so much so that Smirgel had managed to get a half-size colour print of it which he pinned to the wall of the nearby cell in the Danger Ward where he composed his despatches. Quatrefages could hear the tapping of his little cipher machine, insistent as a woodpecker. Smirgel had changed into civilian clothes of dull, pewter-coloured stuff which suggested an out-of-work clergyman; he walked now, no longer strutted. He seemed, unlike the rest of the German garrison, to have become weighed down with the gravity of things, whereas for the others a new anxiety was mirrored in their sharp squeaky commands and the restless running to and fro at speeds which suggested the movements of an undercranked ciné film. The armour had moved off, and they felt bereft, uncovered; reports now spoke of landings on the Côte d'Azur in the area of Nice. The three squadrons of spotter aircraft upon whom they relied for firm intelligence had been bombed into immobility and silence. Nor was it possible to interest the high command in their plight, for all eyes were turned on Normandy where the battles were absolutely critical not only for their own future but also for armies further south – not to mention the Italians!

From the personal point of view, however, what Quatrefages most deplored was that the noise had silenced the amours
of the frogs in the lily ponds, for he loved their deep thrilling
bassoons, loved watching them in the love act, their throats
swollen out with lyrics, like human tenors at the music
festivals of Marseilles. He had been taught that their love
clamour could be scripted, after Aristophanes, with the phrase
"Brek ek kek kek Koax-Koax" a pretty enough transcription
of the sound. But after a few days of this he thought that the
sound became *"Bouc Bouc Bouc-Emissaire"*. Yes, that was it!
And how much more appropriate it was. He used to lie for
hours by the pond, flat on his face, with his chin on the side, to
watch them as they struggled amorously, sometimes in chains,
tacked on to each other by simple imitation – three frogs, let us
say, with a dead female at the end of the line, still penetrated
by her mate who could neither disengage himself nor rid himself of the younger ones which had clambered on his back.
Quatrefages was at heart a kindly youth and he spent some
time with a long metal spatula which he had stolen from the
kitchens trying to disengage the dead from the living. The
little animals were so much on heat that they made no further
distinction. The younger and less experienced, driven mad
with the delicious copula of their lust, clambered anything that
presented itself, alive or dead, male or female. This complete
abandonment to ruthless passion was wholly admirable. Sometimes to send himself to sleep he drowsily imitated their plaint,
laughing and hugging himself with waggish delight. With the
disappearance of his reason, in the formal sense, he had been
filled with a wonderful notion of freedom. And now great
changes were in the air. The hated Milice had suddenly disbanded and thrown away their uniforms, though some had
kept their small arms before heading for the hills where
ambushes organised by the Resistance awaited them.

He heard Dr. Jourdain call out this choice information to

Smirgel as he locked or unlocked one of the doors in the ward; the information had come from a casual visitor on a bicycle. How empty the town must feel! He began to wonder if he might not return there for a while and make a mental inventory of everything which had changed. He had never seen a siege but he had read of many and could predict much of the present reality, like the bands of famished dogs which roamed about, driven mad by the noise and the lack of food; they set upon the heaps of uncollected garbage and the piled dustbins with a will. Meanwhile odd bands of leaderless men, not very numerous but distraught – Poles? Russians? It was not quite clear – roamed about armed with sticks. They manned the ferries which buzzed back and forth but lacked passengers.

But it was far from the end, you would have thought, to see Ritter and his staff, pale but determined as they went about their tasks in the fortress and ensured their control of the roads and bridges by frequent patrols, lightly emphasised by the appearance of an occasional heavy tank which fired a few rounds across the river, or into the surrounding hills from which came from time to time sporadic ripples of gunfire, one presumed from partisans or infiltrators, or even runagates from among the forced labour groups hidden in the forests. Only the pile of cigarettes beside him – the butts thereof – suggested that Smirgel himself was under strain, for the rate of his bird-like pecking remained slow and calm. He worked from shorthand notes on the back of service messages or grey envelopes, building these into the messages that Affad received by the lake of Geneva and, as like as not, transmitted to Toby in his cellar. He gave a succinct and sharply focussed picture of the new command at work, recounting their high morale under this determined party general whose perpetual toothache made him seem to be grinning always. A rictus of pain served as a permanent facial expression. Small, slightly round-shouldered, he had the long ape-like arms most suitable for declamatory gestures before a map; he took over from Von Esslin's old-fashioned rhetoric and produced a new version, with up-to-date oaths and outlandish jokes which made him strike his thigh with imaginary amusement, though the grin of pain did not change. To him they owed a new idea of some consequence. The plum target for the bombers had always been, would always be, the railway bridge over the Rhône. Since he had been told that when the time came he would have to retreat upon Toulouse it came to him that an ammunition train halted on the bridge might, if hit by the Allies, blow up and inflict a marvellous, undreamt-of wound to the town which he had come to hate so profoundly. Alternatively, if the Allies knew about the train they might spare the bridge. With this in view he had commanded an empty train to be backed into a siding at Remoulins and quietly loaded with the more powerful and effective explosives from the great underground ammunition dump in the hills near Vers. This would be his parting gesture to Avignon! The train arrived in the darkness of a moonless night and was shunted up on to the bridge before being deprived of its engine and abandoned. Meanwhile the town was also abandoned in all but seeming, for it was most effectively covered from the new base in Villeneuve across the river, and within a protective shoulder of medieval wall which, in the event of the train being blown up, would protect the Germans adequately from blast. They were within days of leaving now and they knew it, but it was necessary to keep up a show of force to make a withdrawal across country more safe. They had "leaked" the train as well so that after some days, bombing switched to other targets and other bridges, thus avoiding catastrophe for the town. It was only when with-drawal became a fact that Ritter elaborated his ideas, and decided that it would be pleasant to make sure of the explosion after all; why should the train not blow up within moments of their retreat?

He would, he thought, give orders for time fuses to be set along the whole length of the train, and these they could light as they departed. He imagined himself, some miles off in the hills towards Nîmes, suddenly hearing the dull, ground-rocking boom of the explosive and seeing the sky behind him grow white suddenly, as if drained of blood, and then red, deep red! How he hated this town – and more so now when everything was shut and bolted with not so much as a cat on the streets. Half the population lived in the cellars underneath the cathedral, secure from bombs but with no sanitary facilities. Moreover they seemed unable to organise themselves in any fashion whatsoever. What filth, what misery!

But the fuses would entail special knowledge, and the only sappers left in the command were a small Austrian unit whose job would be to sink the ferries and dynamite the eastern approaches to the town. He decided that he would call upon them to prime the train. But when they were driven down to the bridge and learned what was expected of them they suddenly mutinied and flatly refused to be a party to such an act which might inflict incalculable damage on the town. This severe blow illustrated how low morale had fallen in the occupying force and it could only be met in one way, according to Ritter's military code. The sappers were piniored and set against a wall in the inner fortress which had already – to judge by the traces of bullet marks along it – served as a point of execution. So as the long column tapered away into the night, crossing the river and taking the road to Nîmes, it left behind fifteen more dead and the silent train. The grateful townsfolk later buried them in consecrated ground and covered their graves in roses.

In the town nothing stirred; most people had either gone underground or taken to their heels with whatever provisions they could lay hands on. All the doors and gates of the fortress hung open. The departing troops had expressed themselves in a manner which had become for them conventional in war. Everywhere there was excrement, on tables, on chairs, in doorways, on stairs. And of course notices warning of booby traps, another speciality of the German army. Smirgel had spent his last few uniformed days in an unconspicuous manner, though it was clear that he, like all the other agencies around him, was winding up his affairs and preparing to move off with the regrouping. He had allowed his cipher clerk to pack up the impedimenta of his modest office, burn all standing instructions and late messages, and load whatever remained into the army lorry which was at his disposal. He himself would come on later in the little staff Volkswagen which was his. Instead, however, he found his way to Montfavet, and burying the car in the deepest recesses of a convenient grange changed into the anonymity of civilian clothes and resumed his despatches with all the calm of a provincial recorder reporting upon his home town. Avignon had practically become that for him after so many adventures. He had been up to the mess to pick up his small kit, plus the precious volume of *Faust* which he always anchored beside his bed – a verse or two at night secured a good sleep, he was wont to say with a chuckle. Everyone had gone. The last orderly was putting the finishing touches to the baggage. He was a bullet-headed Swabian corporal with a sense of humour. He saluted and said, "Shall I show you something funny, sir officer?" and when Smirgel agreed led him into the garden and opened the door of the earth closet. Surprisingly there was someone sitting on the roost and it was Landsdorf. At first you did not realise that he stayed upright because he was leaning back against the wall. His chin was raised like a chicken drinking. He was dead. He had shot himself through the soft palate with his service Luger. The corporal burst out laughing, and Smirgel nervously followed suit though his laughter ended in a croak and a sigh. He had liked old Landsdorf.

But the German was not the only one. Up in Tu Duc there had been little enough movement, except at night by small groups; the main troop movements had been along the great highways, the bombing mostly across the river. Blaise could, if he wished, watch everything without taking part, simply by climbing the hillock in the wood and overlooking the town from the open glades at the summit. At night he went to ground like a fox, locking everything up very carefully and extinguishing every gleam of light. How then could he have not heard the fusillade which cut short the life of the honey man Ludo? The ambush into which he had strayed with his one-horse caravan was barely three hundred yards away up the forest road. Blaise heard nothing, and would have known nothing had not a passing woodcutter whom he knew come stealing out of the wood to borrow a light for his cigarette butt and told him that he had just passed, higher up the road, a mutual friend of theirs, done to death by the Resistance – a presumption based on the fact that the overturned caravan which lay half in the ditch was liberally daubed with red paint proclaiming the victim to have been an informer. The woodcutter told his tale with angry emotion. Such an error seemed almost inconceivable. It always does. Yet in war as in peace it is like that – one is hurt by one's own side.

Like good Provençaux they knew they must bury their friend, and with a heavy heart Blaise called his wife and marshalled spades for the three of them. "Take some sacks," said the woodcutter, "for he is all in pieces." They walked in grim silence up the road until they came to the site of the calamity: the caravan half on its side in the ditch, the dead horse and the pool of honey mixed with blood. The man was just ahead – he had fallen with outspread arms, as if he had tried to protect his horse, to explain, to plead. His body appeared to smoke, but it was just the carpet of sleepy bees which covered his bloodstained frame in its tattered shirt and scarf which

371

stirred from time to time, giving a fictitious life to the still form. The machine-gun had traversed the whole interior, quite riddling the hives. It had cut its target into several separate pieces. The woodcutter was right, the old olive-crop sacks were useful. In them they assembled the fragments of their friend and the head of his horse and carried them a little way into the forest until they found a suitable place for the long slow dig. The caravan they dragged off the road and hid in the bushes, also the body of the horse. The bees did not sting, they drowsed on in the bloody honey, as if shocked. Nor was there any trace of the little boy, the son of Ludovic of whom he had been so inordinately proud. Happily? Yes, perhaps he had escaped. In affairs of this sort there is always a missing child. In this way history manages to perpetuate itself.

It was going to be a long dig. The earth in this forest glade was not too soft. But the wife of Blaise had had the fore-thought to bring a supply of bread and cheese, two cigarettes, and a small bottle of fiery *marc*. They rolled up their sleeves, and marked out the grave of Ludo. But before beginning to dig the wife of Blaise put her arms round her husband and kissed him on the mouth with all her determination – something she had never done before.

With method, slowly, they worked late into the night, while always to the left came the shock of distant explosions and stabs of white light waxing and waning as the bombers came swishing in like great winnowing fans to release their loads.

The crisis was ripening like some ugly fistula. At the asylum Jourdain woke one morning to find that the kitchen staff had vanished, leaving no stocks of food for his lunatics. It was critical, something would have to be done, but what? The telephone had gone dead. There was nobody to appeal to. In order to calm himself he sat for a moment cross-legged before the full length mirror in his flat and performed a couple of yoga postures with the appropriate breathing. Then, in order not to waste the last of the hot water, he took a long and leisurely shower and shampoo. He donned his college blazer and dressed in formal fashion with a dark shirt and a college tie. Beside his bed lay the proofs of his new book on schizophrenia, at which he gazed lovingly. It had taken ages to formulate these scattered observations drawn from his flock and to translate them into theory. He read a passage to himself in a whisper, frowning with critical pleasure: "My proposition is, then, that the state of schizophrenia is not one of mental disorder, but one in which a different sort of order rules. When you shout 'Go away' to a fly, are you presuming upon its knowledge of French? And if it goes away dare one suppose that it in fact has understood? For the schizophrene . . ."

He sat down on the bed and reflected on his plight with bitterness; here he was, with a hundred and fifty mental patients to feed and wash, and with no staff to help him perform this miracle, and no food in the kitchen. "*Merde!*" he cried aloud after a moment, solacing himself with an echo from the exasperated soul of Cambronne. "*Triple merde!*" But he realised that this would not get him very far. Then he heard steps in the corridor and the insect-like pecking of the spy's machine. The main generator still held for a while, but for how long? Its charge would soon expend itself – three hours was the most! Then even the spy's little apparatus would be silenced. He listened grimly for a moment. Then he took his last whisky bottle from its hiding place and selected the two glasses from the bathroom before making his way to join Smirgel.

At this moment the stick of bombs fell on the house and the gardens with a mind-swamping roaring that abused all consciousness. A vast pall of dust rose now – he saw himself standing there with a bottle, and with his clothes apparently smoking, as if he were on fire. An invisible hand pinned him for ten full seconds to the nearby wall and then released him so that he fell like an unjointed doll first to his knees, and then flat, with a scream that he himself hardly recognised. It took an age for the dust to settle and for him to verify that he was physically unhurt, and that the precious bottle remained unbroken. As for the howling and drumming of his charges, the screams and laughter, he was used to these sudden waves of feeling, often provoked by nothing tangible. Here at least there was a good excuse; half the building was peppered with holes, holes which seemed like new magical doors through which one could get "outside" – the symbol of prime reality to a prisoner of any category. He joined Smirgel and without another word they drank down a life-giving draught of alcohol, listening gloomily the while to the noise of falling rafters and crumbling masonry. The distant cannonade of the town had diminished now; it was they who were in the centre of the stage. Yet apart from that one fortuitous stick of bombs nothing more fell upon the asylum. Nor was there any need, for the one salvo was destined to change their whole lives, the pattern of their behaviour. It had blown holes in every ward wall, and it had shaken every door off its hinges. How open the world seemed to Quatrefages, who had also been blown to the wall of his cell and had cracked his skull on the iron bedrail. But from the window now he saw them all emerge, walking with circumspection, on tiptoe, gazing about with wonder at "outside" from their "inside", being born again. The square was slowly filling up with them, each with his personal vocabulary, the triumph of his destiny over reason! The Crusaders of the new reality!

The main gates still stood, but only just, for the hinges had been blown to pieces. How slowly the inhabitants emerged into the quiet square under the trees, some of which had fallen! The silence was brand-new after the thunderclap. The two men, Smirgel and Jourdain, watched from an upper window, glass in hand but forgetting to drink, so preoccupying was the scene. The whole staircase leading to the Dangerous Ward had gone, leaving a theatrical looking arch through which the hungry inmates were now making a surprised entry upon the life which they had abused and rejected. Smirgel's flesh crept, he was terrified of lunatics like all deceitful people; it was as if these criminal ones with their pious and deceptive air were poisonous snakes set suddenly free in a bathroom. "My God!" he said. "Your Dangerous Ward!" But the doctor's professional interest had been awakened and he leaned forward eagerly to watch, as a supporter watches the home team, full of sympathy. "It will be most interesting to see what they do," he said, and the German stared at him as if he were mad. Now everything suddenly fell into place, reality reasserted itself for them thanks to the bombing.

The asylum, set in green land, abutted upon two farms, and often the inmates were encouraged to help the farmers with the agricultural work, while the series of vast cellars and stables were rented out to the farms. The doors of these caves had been stoved in, and they revealed the four animals, two horses and two cows which shared their labours. They shyly ducked and snuffled in the gloom, dimly aware that something unusual was afoot for it was late for ordinary work, and the clients seemed unduly numerous. A vague indecision hovered in the crowd, their purpose in seeking the light had not been yet revealed. It was Quatrefages who condensed everything, who now endowed them with a purpose and a coherence. Raising his arms he gave a few imploring cries and beckoned them to follow him into the stables whence they dragged the four long carts, old-fashioned hay-wains which so often had brought in the harvest with their sincere aid. "*Allons, mes enfants!*" he cried with such fervour that everyone was galvanised, everyone rushed to join him with chirps and moans of happiness. They felt the beauty of function, the beauty of belonging to method. The doctor at the window watched them carefully, jealously;

the dangerous and the harmless together, what did it matter?
But the dangerous were his special possession, he treasured
them. "Baudoin!" he shouted suddenly. It was Baudoin de
St.-Just, the notorious murderer who looked so quietly pious –
all those years he went to confession and never once mentioned
the fact! The man looked up and waved merrily like a schoolboy. "The harness is on the wall inside!" the doctor told him,
and the man turned away obediently into the darkness to find
it. Out came the cattle in a sort of foam of agitation. They
smoothed and patted them, some curried them with leaves;
and under the leadership of Quatrefages they harnessed them
to the wains with shouts of indifference. Then there was a
scramble to get aboard, though no fighting as with normal
people, just a few in tears and one with stomach-ache. "Are
they all there?" said Jourdain with keen interest. "I don't see
Tortville the butcher nor Jean Taillefer. O yes! There he is.
Where did he get that knife I wonder? What people! He will
be troublesome tonight." Smirgel: "But not to us I hope."
Raynier de Larchant was preaching a sermon – he was never
dangerous when allowed to play on a piano. Moreover you
knew where he was. His mother confided as much before he ...
Molay, Pairaud were looking dazed and sullen which was not
so good. The wains were harnessed. With one single push the
great courtyard gates tumbled over and quivered in the dust.
A shout went up from every throat. The wains were chock-a-
block. Vaguely the crowd sensed the similarity of the situation
to half-forgotten harvests and fairings, to village fêtes and
dancings on the famous old bridge. Quatrefages mounted a
horse and started to lead them. He looked around him, joyfully, childishly, and brandished a pick-helve like a broad-
sword. "We will find food and water in the town," he informed
his forces, and they set up a ragged cheer. He caught sight of
Jourdain on the balcony and swept him a mock bow as he cried
again, "To the town!" But to the doctor he shouted, "I will

lead them to Rome!" and curiously enough the occupants of
the wains and those who tagged along overheard and took up
the cry. "To Rome!" they shouted, growled and piped.
"Onwards to Rome!"

Jourdain sighed. "Science is wonderful!" he remarked
apropos of nothing in particular. They watched the motley
throng form up behind the wains as if for a harvest or a funeral
or a fairing. "This is the way revolutions start, by accident,"
he went on, for he could hear that somewhere in the crowd
someone had given tongue with the *Marseillaise*, and as the
distance lengthened they heard the marvellous verses begin to
take shape. "If anything can make one march on an empty
stomach, that song can," said Smirgel, shaking his head. But
now they noticed that the bombing seemed to have stopped.
The doctor held out his hand as if to feel whether it was raining
or not. Indeed a light shower had started. But the silence which
flowed in was absolute, and one could hear the rain purring
like a cat. Smirgel asked if he might have another drink. "Well,
the Swiss Army has closed the border. The Allies are moving
up on us from Nice. I have enough petrol in my little car to take
us somewhere where we might find some scraps to eat, north
or east, I leave it to you."

"Did you notice how once they united in a purpose music
was necessary to mark time, to mark step?" In fact two of the
"dangerous ones" had found tambourines and a trumpet,
relics of some village band, and beat out an admirable rhythm
with them, while the trumpet choked and squeaked. The doctor
sighed again as he heard the diminishing chant and thought of
Cock Lorel's Boate and the *Bateau Ivre*. "Have you ever heard
of The Ship of Fools?" he asked his companion but Smirgel
shook his head. It would take too long to explain the medieval
notion of treatment for lunatics, specially to a German, so
the doctor dropped the subject. "There is one person I didn't
see," he said, "and that was our great stationmaster Imhof, by

the way he is English. I wonder where he has got to." But
Imhof had slept through it all, comforted by the model train
which he kept under his pillow; he hardly stirred when his
pulse was taken.

The two men made their way down to the old cowshed
where the German's car lay hidden; they were still undecided
about which direction to take. Only one thing seemed certain:
there would be no point in following the procession of lunatics
towards the town. That way lay trouble – or that is what they
surmised. They would sneak across country to the Fontaine de
Vaucluse and then turn north. Who knows?

Now that the bombers had gone away the little procession
was filled with renewed confidence, and made good time on the
road to Avignon, the tambourines keeping them in a good
humour when they were exhausted with singing the anthem.
Quatrefages was transfigured, like an actor now, turned into a
medieval knight bearing high his standard. From time to time
he thought of the great wall in the hotel with "his" Templars
and their dates recorded on it – the solemn procession of
forgotten knights. No, not forgotten, so long as one person
could remember them! History was like that – a negative of
which one was the print, the positive. He thought: "People
are not separate individuals as they think, they are variations
on themes outside themselves. Think: Galen's daughter pro-
gressed could be Sylvie who was only imagined, who could be
Sabine child of Banquo. The lost remain the lost, the found the
found. Oranges and Lemons!"

The trumpet blared.

On they went boldly, extravagant in their fine optimism,
the mad leading the blind, the blind leading the sane. "Variations on themes," he repeated aloud, "Just as a diamond is a
variation on carbon, or a caterpillar on a butterfly."

They approached the mother city with confident tread,
sure of their welcome, sure of food and drink. For its own part

Avignon had begun to stir from its forced sleep. The silence and the emptiness had at last evoked some response; a few faint news bulletins had managed to penetrate the overwhelming sense of desolation and hopelessness in which they had existed for so long, tortured both by the enemy and by their own fascist kind, the Milice. As soon as the mayor of the town found the incredible thought of an empty city begin to dawn in his mind, he opened his front door cautiously and surveyed the deserted streets with suspicion mingled with mounting elation. No noise but the rain, the soft thistle-sifting rain of the Vaucluse. *"Ils sont partis,"* someone said above his head, someone behind a shuttered window. It was as if they were trying out the phrase, so long rehearsed in the mind: though as yet it had no real substance and they did not dare to fling back the shutters. The mayor gave a small sob and groped for his old bicycle. Very slowly and circumspectly he set out on a tour of the walls, bastion by bastion, feeling the rain on his neck like a benediction. Yes, they had gone; once more they were master of their fate as he was master of his town. He returned to the Mairie and unlocked the doors, throwing them wide. Now people were emerging from holes and corners, from cellars and stables and garrets, saluting each other in hushed voices and gazing about them. The mayor, filled with a sudden vertiginous ecstasy, raced up the stairs to his office and went out on to the balcony. He was going to do something he had not done for years, namely call his friend Hippolyte, the *pompier de service,* who lived opposite the Mairie on the square. Cupping his mouth he roared, *"Hippolyte-e-e-e-e!"* After the third bellow he saw his friend trotting towards him across the square waving his arms. *"Ils sont partis, partis, partis, partis!"* the words were taken up and repeated, rattled like peas on a drum. The first act was to announce the fact to the town in time-honoured fashion through the town-crier, and Hippolyte, already in uniform, had already started to assume his official responsibilities. He had belted on the sour kettle-drum and fixed the rubber hooter to his bicycle handle. At the four quarters of the town he would now announce after a preliminary klaxoning, followed by a long ripple on the kettle-drum, "*Oyez! Oyez! Oyez! Official announcement by the Mairie. The Germans have gone. The curfew is lifted until further notice.*" At each repetition he was mobbed. More and more people came forth from the ruins, many in tears, some with great difficulty because of age or wounds or for other reasons. Hippolyte was kissed and embraced almost senseless. And slowly the crowd began to wend its away towards the cathedral and the main square over the river. To celebrate, to give thanks, to express their overwhelming relief—that was the first instinctive reaction to the news. Perhaps M. le Maire would speak? But when they got to the square they found him at the head of a dense crowd ready to lead them to the cathedral for a service of thanksgiving.

Within the echoing precincts (there was only candle-light, the electricity had cut out) the atmosphere echoed with an extraordinary fervour, with tears and groans, with sobs and cries—for everybody had something or someone to mourn and few had recovered enough to manage to rejoice with any wholeheartedness. And so many were hungry!

The service was long and though improvised upon the occasion elaborate and memorable. Who would wish to relive those years again? Down in the town, however, new crowds had begun to form of a dissimilar caste and colour. They were composed of a heterogeneous collection of men and women of the lower layers of society, workmen, sempstresses, night watchmen, farm-hands, mechanics and railway-workers—a laic image in sharp contrast to the bourgeois image produced in the cathedral. A dozen such groups milled about with conflicting or parallel intentions centred vaguely about a civic celebration. Their activity was only co-ordinated by mood, for they had not decided whether to give the proceedings a political colour (there were many Communists, as usual well organised) or simply a national and patriotic flavour. Gypsies had come forward now, crawling like snakes out of nowhere, also Arabs in their indolent and lustreless fashion, waiting to start picking pockets; then an amorphous band of "slaves" composed of Czechs, Russians and heaven alone knows what other breeds swept down south by the tides of war. Worst of all, though perhaps most suitable to the scene, was the appearance of some great casks of red wine which were at once made available in the square by the Monument des Morts with its frieze of debased lions and flying heroines, vaguely evoking both Marianne and Mistral's dearer Mireille. All the cafés now opened and did what they could to promote festivities. Some had bricked up their cellars at the beginning of the war and now were content to release stocks of drink which had ripened in the darkness for those who drank harder stuff – *marc, calva, fine.* . . .

The procession from Montfavet finally joined forces with the forming surging crowd at the Magnagnon Gate where they were wildly applauded as being – so people vaguely imagined – a body of country people who had done something gallant to resist the Germans, perhaps even killed a few, to judge by the histrionic attitudes of Quatrefages. He was on the one hand acting out his role, shouting the word "Citizens!" over and over again as if he were about to make a speech; and at the same time inside himself he was quite serious and was talking to himself in his mother's voice, encouraging himself, soothing himself. He had bad stage fright. Moreover he feared that someone, perhaps a member of the Milice, might take a pot at him from a balcony. But they advanced with a will, driving their carts into the centre of the melée and letting the crowd surge approvingly round them. By now, to compensate for the lack of light, fires had been lit everywhere, as if it were the

Eve of St. John; at almost every street corner there was a blaze throwing sparks up into the drizzle which was soon to part dramatically upon a gaunt moon. With the leaping light and the capering shadows, the cries and the crack of wood, the whole scene resembled some wild *kermesse* taking place in the appropriate decor of the medieval walls of the second Rome.

But if Quatrefages was shouting the word "Citizens", his echo, the mad preacher from Anduze, Raynier de Larchant, was producing a headier slogan, which had the power to ignite souls. With his shock of white hair and his deep-set eyes he was an impressive figure – a generation of Protestant worshippers had been swayed by his delivery. He threw back his head and roared like a lion the words "Vengeance!" and "Justice!" This roar punctuated their progress like a ripple of kettle-drum music. Though mad, he knew how to carry the crowd, for everyone has something to expatiate and everyone seeks retribution. In this wild, colourful way they advanced towards the central square of the town. Some bread had appeared from somewhere, but there was precious little food, so that the floods of coarse wine and spirits kindled and warmed the hearts of the demonstrators with speed. Here and there people reeled. Incidents exploded on the screen of light – a man fell into a fire and was rescued by children. There were no police to interfere with the folly of so many fires. They were all hiding in civilian clothes from the vengeance of the Milice. *Their* central propaganda office with its pictures of Pétain had been stormed and set on fire.

Here and there in a completely arbitrary and unorganised fashion dancers had appeared: each music had its little circle, like eddies in the vast crowd. In one corner the celebrated wooden-legged Jaco set up shop with his wheezy accordion. Where *had* he been? everyone asked. All through the occupation there had not been a sign of him, and suddenly here he was again, quaffing the *pinard* and playing *Sous les toits de Paris* and *Madelon* as if the whole world had become a *guingette* and all the people revellers. In another corner fragments of the town band tried hard to assemble a *farandole,* for this type of folklore seemed appropriate to a nationalist and patriotic celebration. A tribune had been erected, at one end and suitably covered by flags and decorative emblems. One vaguely thought that here the mayor, backed by the town band, would make an excessively long peroration and end by burning the Nazi flag before the approving eyes of the people.

It did indeed start like this, in a confused sort of way. The band was reduced to three instruments, it was true, and lacked drive, for the soloist played a violin. But they played the national anthem creditably as an introduction and then the mayor in his sash started to orate, though he could hardly make himself heard above the buzz and roar of the crowd. Moreover the crowd was restive, they were after other game; vaguely they would have liked to execute some Nazi criminals on the spot to express their feelings of frustration and pain – for of course many had lost friends and relatives in the carnage of the years of war. The long tally of savageries, deportations, tortures and murders still lingered in the consciousness, their memory hung like a miasma over the music and the dancing, the relief and the joy.

The mad preacher's roars, calling for justice and retribution, could not have come at a more apposite moment, for just as they burst into the square with the firelight dappling their cows and horses, there emerged from the old quarter of the Balances another procession, of women this time, marching in a bedraggled column with lowered heads, and guided by a guard of youths and prostitutes and old women, some with lighted torches. At first one thought them penitents, perhaps come to offer thanks or some signal sacrifice to the forces of liberation. But no, they were those who had collaborated in whatever degree with the occupying forces. Some had been the concubines of soldiers, some had fraternised, unaware that they were being noted down by that group of festering moralists who plague the decency of every town by their puritanical fervours. Many had done nothing at all, they had simply been pretty enough to earn the jealousy of old maids who had "reported" them to the Vichy police, or sent in their names anonymously as "fraternisers". They must pay for it now. A roar went up from the crowd – they were not after all going to be deprived of a summary vengeance on someone or something. "The scissors!" they cried. "Where are the scissors?"

A corridor of fires the whole length of the square was cleared and organised by the crowd, while the victims were mobilised at one end in a group, looking pathetically like a group of schoolgirls about to participate in a race. They were in fact about to be forced to run the gauntlet, launched by a committee of old hags who brandished several large pairs of scissors such as dressmakers use to cut up lengths of cloth for their creations. Each was first shorn of her hair, had her face smacked soundly and her dress torn or pulled down over her shoulder; then with a sound push she was launched upon her course down the gauntlet where the public waited to take a smack at her with a belt or a switch. Conspicuous were the old women who in this way compensated for loveless lives, calamitous disappointments, or simple childlessness. They whipped away as if they were invoking fertility on the young bodies of virgins – they say that in Roman Italy statues were whipped to provoke fertility. The victims, for their part, though they cried tears of shame and indignation at the cries of "Prostitute!" were glad enough to escape with their lives, for the mood was ugly and the crowd under the influence of the drink had become temperamental and capricious. Already a fight or two had broken out among the spectators, and there were several disputes among armed onlookers somewhat the worse for red wine. But the best was yet to come.

It was rather like a Roman triumph, in which the best and most lucrative hostages, or those whose rank carried prestige beyond the common crew, were displayed at the end of the procession. So it now proved, for with a crackle of drum beats a smaller group emerged from the shadows guarding a single prisoner, *pièce de résistance*, it would seem of the evening's pieties. She, for it was a woman, walked with a deathly pale composure inside a square of guards who looked vaguely like beadles, though they carried the short trident of the Camargue cowboys as part of their fancy dress. They guarded her preciously though she did not seem to need guarding. She walked quietly with apparent composure and lowered head but her pallor betrayed her mortal fear—her skin glowed almost nacrous in the warm rose of the *flambeaux*. Her hands were tied behind her back. "*There! There!*" cried the crones as the little group advanced. "There she is at last!" It was clear that they spoke of the Evil One herself. The woman as she advanced overheard the tumult and slowly raised her head. Her wonderful head of blonde hair rippled upon her shoulders, her blue eyes were wide and cold. Her nervousness gave her the air of almost smiling. It was as if she had stage fright, she hung back in the wings, so to speak, for she had never acted this part before. "*Up! Up! Up with you!*" cried the crowd, indicating the rostrum upon which at last they mounted her, attaching her wrists to a column of wood. A pandemonium of rage broke out. The women with the scissors scuttled up on to the dais and waving to the crowd histrionically made as if to chop off her tresses, pulling them to full length so that they gleamed like the fruit of the silkworm's agony. "Justice!" shouted the madman down below and the crowd echoed him. "Vengeance! Justice! Prostitute! Traitor!" The scissors began their work and the blonde tresses were shorn and thrown into the crowd as one throws meat to a pack of dogs. They were torn to bits. Meanwhile the phalanx of kettle-drums—for new musical reinforcements had arrived – kept up a heart-shaking tattoo, such as might accompany the last and most dangerous act of a trapezist. They tore down her dress until she stood there clad only in her shift; the more they tried to debase her the greater her beauty was. Her little ears were pointed, like those of a tiny deer. And now they poured water on her head and shaved her with a cut-throat razor until she was as bald as an egg. "Shame on you!" they cried hoarsely, for she did not seem to be repentant at all, she did not weep. The truth was that she was too afraid. Everything had become a blur. She felt her wrists tugging at the post. They held her upright, for she felt on the point of fainting.

Then came something which, though quite unpremeditated, might easily have been expected, given the context of such an evening. She was pelted with refuse from the dustbins. God knows, there were enough of these. A pile of refuse built up around her feet. Eggs were not plentiful. Then a young man, extremely drunk, mounted the stage and rather unsteadily produced a heavy revolver. The crowd roared. He took up several menacing postures as he flourished the weapon and pointed it at her, so as to show the crowd what her deserts should really have been had they not been true patriots and civilised people. That is, at any rate, what the majority of the crowd thought.

As for the young man, so far-gone in wine, he was bursting with civic pride and a deep-seated sense of misgivings about his own inconspicuous role in the war and the Resistance. He longed to affirm by some dramatic act that he was an adult and a warrior of principle. Lurching about on the rostrum in front of the victim he took the roars of the crowd for approval. At first he had had in mind to fire a few shots as an alarm, or a *feu de joie* or . . . to tell the truth the devil only knew what. But this was the hated concubine of the Gestapo chief, after all. The cries which exhorted justice and vengeance had gradually worked on his fuddled adolescence until, almost without thinking, he placed the cold barrel of the pistol against the brows of the tethered woman, right between the eyes, and pulled the trigger.

As always in such instances there are people who say they did not mean it, that it was all a mistake, that they were misinformed; and it is true that a moan of surprise and shock was heard from the crowd but it was rapidly drowned in the roars of approval and the music of the kettle-drum. Nevertheless a silence fell, or a lessening of noise, and the crowd wept, for people felt that they had gone too far. And then pushing into the crowd came a small group of nuns who quietly but firmly forced their way up on to the stage to take possession of the mortal remains of Nancy Quiminal.

Then as if to finally wash away and quite expunge every trace of these ignoble proceedings a thunder broke loose and it began to rain as it can only rain in the City of the Popes. Gutters brimmed and overflowed, leaves were broomed from the trees, the fires hissed and spat but went out. And the crowd began to slink away, at first hiding under eaves and in doorways, and then disappearing for good. The curfew habit was still deeply engrained. By midnight the rain had veered off and a candid moon shone in the sky. There was no sign of either enemy or friend. Even the lunatics had disbanded. Each had gone about his former task as if he had returned from a holiday. De Larchant had found his way to the cathedral where a terrified sacristan who recognised him surrendered the key of the organ loft. The grave strains of Bach suddenly swelled like a dark sail in that lightless cavern. Taillefer had gone back to the railway station to resume his job. Baudoin de St.-Just sat at a table in the rain outside the café playing a hand of solitaire with a pack of cards he had appropriated.

It was towards morning when the night watchman of the morgue heard horses' hooves followed by the sour buzz of the night bell. He had only just turned in after a full evening of work without light and his temper was ruffled. "What now?" he growled aloud as he opened, expecting some emergency delivery from the town. But it was only a pale tall man with two girls, his daughters. He had a letter from the mayor authorising him to see his wife's mortal remains. It was the husband of Nancy Quiminal, a man never as yet seen for he was bed-bound by illness. Once he had been a musician and had played in the town orchestra. He was pale and thin and ravaged by illness, and so weak that his two daughters held him by the elbows. The night watchman touched his forelock to him awkwardly in a gesture of sympathy. The nuns had dressed and composed the body and tucked it into its white winding cloth. They awaited only a *pasteur* now to arrange for the funeral. And then the medical certificate, what of that? Was it murder or judicial murder or what? Finally it would prove to figure as an unlucky accident. The family was in no position to contest the official view.

He hoisted a white blind and wound up a long handle so that the long chest-of-drawers swung towards them. Then he drew out a drawer to reveal the quiet form of the murdered woman. She looked like a little wakeful gnome in her snood, she was bald as a baby but with alert little ears like crocuses. Yet what affected them most was the sweet panoramic regard of the wide open eyes, the blue French eyes which held just a gleam of satirical humour in them. There were no powder-markings, just the blue hole neatly drilled between the eyes. The children were on the verge of tears and it was time to go. Her husband put out his hand to touch her pale cheek, left it for a moment and then withdrew it. He said he would come back in the morning and attend to the details with the authorities. But he never did. It remained for her two daughters to accompany their mother to a pauper's grave – the *fosse communale*.

A day or so later French troops relieved the town and at long last the bells of Avignon recovered their fearful tintinabulation which once, long ago, had driven Rabelais wild with annoyance. For the city the war had ended.

Appendix

LAST WILL AND TESTAMENT OF
PETER THE GREAT

IN THE NAME OF THE MOST HOLY AND INDIVISIBLE TRINITY, We, Peter the First, address all our successors to the throne and to the governors of the Russian Nation!

Almighty God, to whom we owe our life and our crown, has endowed us with his light and supported us with his might, and He has made us come to see the Russians as a people called to dominate all Europe in the future.

I base my thoughts upon the observation that most of the European nations are in a state of old age bordering on decrepitude towards which they are hastening with big strides. In consequence it is easy and certain that they will be conquered by a new and young people when it has reached the apogee of its growth, its maximum expansion. I consider therefore that the invasion of the Occident and the Orient by the northern peoples is a periodic mission decreed by providence – which by analogy in the past regenerated the Romans by barbarian invasions.

The emigration of the peoples of the Polar regions are like the overflowings of the Nile which, at certain fixed times, enrich with their rich silt the impoverished lands of southern Egypt. I found Russia like a small rivulet and I leave to my successors a great river; they in turn will make it into a vast sea destined to fertilise an impoverished Europe; its waves will overflow everything in spite of the dykes which faltering hands may dig to restrain them; waves which my successors will know how to direct. With this objective in view I leave them the following instruction which I commend to their unwavering attention and constant observation.

(1) To keep the Russian nation in a constant state of warlike readiness, keeping the Russian soldier forever at war, and only letting him have a respite if there be need to ameliorate the State's finances; reform the army and choose the most opportune moments for launching it into the attack. Turn things in such a way that peace can serve the needs of war, and war those of peace, all in the interests of the greatness and growing prosperity of Russia.

(2) Address ourselves to the people of cultivation in Europe, reaching them by any possible means – the officers in wartime and the scholars in peace, in order to let the Russian nation profit from the advantages of other nations without losing her own.

(3) Take part whenever we have the chance in popular affairs and legal disputes in Europe – above all in those which touch Germany, which interest us more deeply as being nearer to us than the rest.

(4) Divide Poland by fomenting internal dissensions and jealousies on a permanent basis; seduce the powers that be with gold, influence the Diets and corrupt them so that they favour the election of a king; seek out dissenters and protect them; send in Russian troops to foreign nations and keep them there until there is a suitable occasion to leave them there for good. If neighbouring states make difficulties, appease them temporarily by splitting up the place until such time as one can secure what one needs to hold permanently.

(5) Provoke Sweden as much as possible until she is forced to attack us, giving us a pretext for conquering her. With this objective in view it is essential that Sweden be separated from Denmark and Denmark from Sweden – by carefully encouraging their rivalries.

(6) Always to give German princesses in marriage to Russian princes in order to increase the number of family

alliances; thus to bring the interests of both countries closer together and win Germany to our cause, asserting thus our influence.

(7) For our trade orient ourselves in preference towards England, a power which has great need of us for its fleet and could be useful to the development of our own naval power; offering in exchange for gold our wood and other products, establishing firm links between their sailors and traders and our own, so that we can increase the scope of our own trade and a naval power.

(8) Advance our power without a halt northwards along the Baltic coast and southward around the Black Sea.

(9) To get as close as possible to Constantinople and India, for whoever rules over these regions will be the real ruler of the world. In consequence we must provoke unceasingly troubles between Turks and Persians. We must establish shipyards along the Black Sea, gradually extending our domination over it and over the Baltic – two land masses necessary to us if we envisage the success of the plan. Accelerate the decadence of Persia; penetrate as far as the Persian Gulf; re-establish if possible through Syria the ancient trade routes to advance to India, the entrepôts of the whole world. Once arrived there we will no longer need the gold of England.

(10) Seek out and maintain with care the Austrian alliance; appear to support its growing ideas of domination over Germany, but at the same time secretly fomenting the jealousy of princes against Austria. Operate so that both states ask for Russian aid and allow us to exercise over them a protective role which will prepare our future domination.

(11) Interest the Royal House of Austria in the plan for clearing the Turks out of Europe and neutralise its jealousies over the conquest of Constantinople either by

provoking a war with the older European states, or by sharing a part of the conquered territory with her; this we could take back later.

(12) Unite all the Orthodox Greeks who are divided or who support schisms throughout Hungary and Poland; gather them together and support them so that they constitute in a group a sort of predominant and sacerdotally important body; thus we will have many friends amongst many of our enemies.

(13) Sweden partitioned. Persia conquered. Poland subjugated. Turkey defeated. Our armies reunited. The Black Sea and the Baltic guarded by our sailing ships. For the moment we should propose, separately and in absolute secrecy, first to the Court of Versailles, then to that of Vienna, to share with them our world empire. Should one of them accept – inevitable if we know how to flatter their self esteem – we must turn one against the other and wage against them a battle whose issue is in no doubt, seeing that Russia will already hold all the Orient and a great part of Europe.

(14) If by chance both refuse the Russian offer – a highly improbable issue – we must set alight conflicts which will ruin them both; then can Russia at a decisive moment launch an attack on Germany with her forces concentrated.

(15) At the same time two vast fleets will set sail, one from the sea of Azov and the other from Archangel, full of Asiatic troops to join forces with the Black Sea and the Baltic fleets. Our army and navy will advance and cross the Mediterranean and Indian Oceans, on the one hand invading France, on the other Germany. Once these two regions are conquered the rest of Europe will pass easily and without much effort under our control.

That is how Europe could and must be subdued.